Ephemeral and Fleeting

PATRICIA REDING

PRAISE FOR THE MULTI-AWARD WINNING *OATHTAKER*

The Oathtaker Series, Volume One
A Literary Classics International Gold Medal Winner
A Readers' Favorite International Book Award Winner
A Beverly Hills International Book Award Finalist

Oathtaker, the first book in a series by Patricia Reding, is [a] refreshingly unique novel . . . of epic proportions in which ancient prophecies are revealed and good wages war upon evil. This highly engaging book boasts a robust plot paired with a healthy share of life and death struggles and a delightful love story woven throughout. In this adventure-filled tale, Reding incorporates devious characters and charming heroes . . . Each . . . is distinctive, believable and well developed. We loved the story, the flow, the excitement, and can't wait for the next book in what promises to be a great series.
   —Literary Classics

Reding has created a wonderful tale of love, devotion and desperation . . . With tremendous depth and creativity, *Oathtaker* becomes real and the emotions and trials of the characters are felt stronger and deeper as the story proceeds . . A story of courage worthy of the designation of a classic.
   —Melinda Hills for Readers' Favorite

An excellent book holds you captive . . . it is impossible to lay . . . down. It draws you in . . . until you become one with the main character. *Oathtaker* is such a book. From the first page, *Oathtaker* . . . promises to take the reader on an epic journey that [she] will long remember . . . [Reding] writes with the talent of a seasoned author . . . yet her plot is refreshing in a world of stale ideas. In the words of Oliver Twist: "More please!"
   —Anne Boling for Readers' Favorite

Oathtaker is a complex and thrilling story that will mesmerize readers and stir the imagination with untold depths of intrigue, loyalty, excitement and resolve. Teens and adults will be spellbound by the lovable and evil characters and they will want to jump right into the pages . . .
   —Karen Pirnot for Readers' Favorite

The author follows her own admonition to "always aim high."
   —Jean Hall for Readers' Favorite

Oathtaker . . . is a book about courage, loss, decisions, friendship, love, and adventure . . . It's the kind of book that draws you in and makes you care about the characters and the world they are living in.
   —Kim Anisi for Readers' Favorite

Oathtaker . . . draws you in from the beginning and, while there's tons of action, Reding doesn't let that get in the way of character growth . . . A great read for anyone looking for good, clean fantasy.

—*Kayti Nika Raet for Readers' Favorite*

Oathtaker is an impeccable read. The prose is flawless with a well-thought plot . . . I intend to follow this exciting series . . .

—*Lit Amri for Readers' Favorite*

Reding does not seem like a fantasy writer immersed in the legend and lore of all the books . . . that came before her. Rather, she seems to be using the possibilities of fantasy as a metaphor for the deepest quest of all: a human being in search of herself . . . Reding unfolds a world full of mystery, majesty, yet simple humanity . . . [She] parts the mists and introduces us to a flesh and blood human being . . . who anyone could immediately identify with . . . [Reding's] prime concern is to tell a gripping human story . . .

—*Joshua Grasso, Associate Professor of English Literature*

From the very beginning I was pulled into this story. The author writes with clarity and creativity. She successfully created characters with such great depth that the issues of commitment, honor and integrity were skillfully woven throughout the story. I loved the fantasy world I found myself immersed in, and the thrilling ride that the characters took me on. This was a great read! I will definitely look for more books from this author.

—*Lori Stevic-Rust, a Goodreads author*

When you pick up this book be prepared to fall in love with Mara as she battles her way through the maze of evil and magic . . . This story contains adventure, intrigue, battles to the death and, of course, love . . . Reding is truly a gifted storyteller. This is not a book to miss. I am anxiously waiting . . . *Select* the next book in this series.

—*Mary A. Adair, a Readers' Favorite 5-star author*

This is a wonderful adventure filled with believable characters, plenty of twists, and an enthralling storyline. This is a fantastic book for a new author and I would read more in this series. Highly recommended to fans of fantasy fiction.

—*E.B. Brown, a Goodreads author*

Reding has skillfully woven the many and varied threads of this fantasy . . . into a very satisfying epic adventure . . . The characters are extremely well-drawn and memorable . . . *Oathtaker* is fab!

—*Kate Larkinson, a Literary Classics award-winning author*

I . . . discovered a wordsmith of impeccable talent, and I invite other readers to make the same discovery . . . Read *Oathtaker*. I heartily recommend it . . .

—*Steven Wilson, a Literary Classics award-winning author*

I have never been able to get into a fantasy book before BUT . . . Reding opened by eyes to a brand new world! I found myself falling in love with the characters . . . I spent so many late nights reading because I couldn't put my Kindle down . . . I am looking forward to reading more from this author in the future. To me it goes on my top 10 books of the year!

—*Anne*

Oathtaker is a beautiful and fantastic epic adventure filled with all the things I love most— a captivating storyline, edge-of-your-seat suspense, thought-provoking characters, and never-ending twists and turns . . . Reding has created a wonderfully enjoyable story filled with a spectacular array of characters that are so rich and vivid that you will wonder if you can still hear them talking to you even after you have finished reading this book . . . Reding is a marvelous new author that you simply have to discover for yourself!

—*Amber*

What an awesome story. Best fantasy I've read in ages . . . It's a masterful work . . . There is a world created . . . that makes me want more . . . This book makes me want to read the next one, and the one after that, and so on and so on . . . I wanted a saga, a story I could sink into and read for hours and not put down. I got exactly that. The plot was superbly executed, very detailed and an adventure at every page turn. Be prepared to put down every other book you own when you pick this one up.

—*Naomi*

Fantasy is not a genre that I usually read, but I think *Oathtaker* may have changed that . . . Also, I just wanted to say, Mara and Dixon are adorable. I cried at some points . . . I've decided to call them Mixon.

—*Kenna*

An Epic book deserves an Epic review! . . . Reding weaves this story that just sucks you in. Two thumbs up . . . two very big thumbs up!

—*Kel*

Oathtaker kept me busy at nights under my blankets with a light, in the car, and pretty much everywhere else I could smuggle a book. I would definitely recommend this book . . . and I can't wait until *Select* comes out . . . I almost cried when the story came to an end . . .

—*Kerrisa*

Oathtaker . . . immediately grabbed my attention and pulled me into its alternate world. I became intrigued by the characters, their history and the land they inhabited . . . I felt personally invested in the story . . . Battles between good and evil, the struggle to meet a challenge you never imagined you could face, not backing away from an oath no matter what the sacrifice — being there, side-by-side with the characters in *Oathtaker*, I came away feeling challenged and emboldened in my own life.

    —Sharon

A beautifully crafted epic fantasy adventure . . . masterfully written prose . . . I would definitely recommend this one . . .

    —Kerry

It's time for me to lose the notion that I don't care for fantasy novels . . . I recently tore through . . . Reding's *Oathtaker*. It is a perfectly paced story . . . I thought about the characters when I wasn't reading and couldn't wait to get back to them . . . The plot kept me reading longer and later at night than I normally can stay awake for . . . The best thing about *Oathtaker* is that there's more! It's the first in a series . . . I look forward to the next book . . . I guess I really am a reader of fantasy.

    —Tammy

A satisfying glow accompanies the final chapter of *Oathtaker* and leaves me begging for more with the same excitement that comes with receiving a . . . present. A new kind of magic laces this book, not with typical wands and wizards, but a . . . magic that is as unique as the characters that sit in the pages. My heart aches that they are not sitting at my kitchen table sharing stories . . . Reding truly earns herself her first Readers' Favorite Award with *Oathtaker* . . . impossible to put down . . . I give *Oathtaker* five stars and beg for sequels, prequels and spin offs!

    —Annie

I couldn't stand it anymore and had to read the last 120 pages in one night. I laughed, cried, and even yelled . . . a few times. I'd call *Oathtaker* a magnificent adventure story that lures you in from the very beginning . . . I loved this book so much I gave it to . . . teachers, friends, and family members . . .

    —Deanna

I am in awe of the author's descriptive, clever and imaginative writing . . .

    —Charlene

What an awesome storyline! This novel can be enjoyed by a broad range of readers, including the younger . . . This . . . is definitely a "5 star." I am anxiously awaiting [*Select*] . . .

    —Jean

This book is fantastic and beautifully written! I love everything about it . . .
   –*Brianna*

I felt like I was transported to another realm. I . . . am looking forward to reading her next book as well. I would definitely recommend this . . . to others . . .
   –*Deb*

I loved this book . . . I . . . enjoy it when an author puts her heart and soul into a story that compels you to turn the page . . . I can't wait for the next . . .
   –*Raymond*

I highly recommend [*Oathtaker*] and am looking forward to reading the next books in the series!!!
   –*Linda Ellison*

I highly recommend this book to anyone looking to stay up all night, as it's difficult to put down.
   –*Tammy H.*

I found *Oathtaker* to be refreshing. From the very beginning it had me holding my breath and anxious to read what would happen next. The spiritual analogies are sometimes subtle, but powerful.
   –*Julie Pruett*

This book is for all ages . . . I am sure mine will be passed on in the very near future.
   –*Barb Donohue*

Oathtaker is a riveting, wonderful fantasy . . . that sucks you in from the very first chapter. There are many things that contribute to this book being extraordinary. The characters . . . the plot, the setting, and the way it is written. You know you are reading a wonderfully written novel when you can visually picture yourself in the world that is being written about . . .
   –*Lindsey Potter*

PRAISE FOR THE MULTI-AWARD WINNING *SELECT*

The Oathtaker Series, Volume Two
A Literary Classics International Silver Medal Winner
A Readers' Favorite International Finalist Award Winner

Author Patricia Reding thrills and delights readers with elements of excitement and adventure in a world where magic abounds . . . In a tale that flows effortlessly, this delightful story is a most enjoyable read, which spurs the imagination and makes one's heart race with anticipation . . . What an astounding read! The first book was terrific, the second is marvelous; we wait with great anticipation for the next offering in this dynamic series.

    —Literary Classics

I so, so enjoyed *Select* . . . Reding has done an absolutely breathtaking job in creating a world that is both fantastic and somehow realistic . . . Reding's character development skills are simply second to none. Her readers will be able to connect with, relate to, and care about these characters, and will think about them long after the last page has been read. I am so glad that this book is one of a series because I can't wait to read more from this world . . . Any reader who loves a great work of fantasy, young adult or not, would enjoy this book . . .

    —Tracy A. Fischer for Readers' Favorite

Reding's *Select* is a quest to find what you are made of. It is not just a journey of one, but the pursuit of many . . . Reding's character development is brilliant. Mara's amnesia . . . was a stroke of genius . . . The story ends . . . leaving you in awe of what will happen next . . .

    —Cheryl E. Rodriguez for Readers' Favorite

Not having read book one, I found the summary [of it at the back of the book] superbly useful . . . I was able to jump right in with the adventure and immerse myself in the phenomenally detailed world that . . . Reding has created. I found all of the characters deep and well-developed . . . [By] its end I did not want to leave the world I was in . . . Overall, I'd highly recommend this novel to serious readers of the fantasy genre.

    —K.C. Finn for Readers' Favorite

Reding has done it again . . . Though *Select* is set . . . years after the first, it loses none of the intrigue . . . Reding shines in her world-building and her interesting and dynamic characters . . . *Select* . . . is a great sequel and I'm looking forward to more from this author.

    —Kayti Nika Raet for Readers' Favorite

An excellent story . . . well worth reading. Another winner! I love it and can't wait for more!

    —Melinda Hills for Readers' Favorite

Select . . . was just as well written as the first book in the series and I enjoyed every single page. Once more, the characters immediately grab you . . . and the world pulls you in . . . The flow of the plot is close to perfect and the settings and scenes are beautifully described in a language that uses neither too little nor too much of anything.

    —Kim Anisi for Readers' Favorite

Having met the . . . characters in *Oathtaker*, I couldn't resist finding out what happens to them . . . I was suitably rewarded with a gripping tale that masterfully expands on the storylines and characters of the first book, while introducing new characters and storylines that fit superbly with those I had already encountered. There is also a very helpful synopsis of *Oathtaker* [Volume One] provided for anyone who might want to refresh [his] memory. I am now looking forward to the third book . . .

    —K. Larkinson, a Literary Classics and Readers' Favorite Award-winning Author

Select is a masterful continuation of a truly breathtaking and inspiring journey into a magnificent world that blends mystery and magic with undeniable truth and unfailing love . . . This is an epic adventure that you will not want to miss . . . Reding has proven without a doubt that she has been gifted an absolutely extraordinary talent . . . Her words will instantly transport you to a world beyond your imagination that will challenge your senses, your mind, and above all, your heart . . . This is a story that needs to be declared from the rooftops and the highest mountains . . .

    —Amber

This book has everything I was looking for . . . fantasy, mystery, love. I recommend this book, and if I could give it more than 5 stars, I would!

    —Anne Gooch

After reading the first book in the fantasy series, *Oathtaker*, I could not wait for her second book . . . Somehow, book two was just as [much] of a pageturner for me. [Reding] has the gift of making the reader feel the emotions of each character. I found myself unable to put the book down because I NEEDED to know what was going to happen next.

    —Tammy H.

I couldn't wait to read the sequel to *Oathtaker*, and *Select* did not disappoint! Both books grab you and pull you into a world that you don't want to leave . . . Reding has created characters with traits, strengths and weaknesses, who are real . . . [T]hey can't help but become a part of your life. *Select* is beautifully written, creative, engaging, and although easy to read, contains a depth . . . that is surprising, pleasing, and intellectually challenging.
  —*Sharon Poland*

This is the number one book and series to read for the year! . . . The many characters keep the story alive with anticipation of what actions and decisions they will make next . . . The author has created a world that feels real . . . The underlying themes of love and faith add dimension . . . as evil is battled . . . I have recommended and shared this book with others and everyone rates it 5-stars.
  —*Judy Adams*

Once again, I was taken on an exciting journey . . . It's not like you have to read the first book to enjoy this one, but I . . . read *Oathtaker* and swiftly moved on to *Select* . . . I normally do not read fantasy books, always figured it would be like reading a fairytale. This, however, is nothing like a fairytale . . . [Reding] has great imagination . . .
  —*Barb*

I read the first in the series and I was hooked . . . The writing style, as in the first book, is . . . detailed and colorful. You feel like you are in the world . . . It s like you stepped into the movie and became one of the characters . . . Great story . . . [W]aiting with baited breath for the next one.
  —*Raymond Vinzant*

Reding has done it again. She has written an epic tale that will leave you satisfied and imploring her for more at the same time. Without a doubt, she is an extraordinarily gifted author . . . Her words instantly take you to another world . . . Reding develops . . . characters so well you feel like you have known them from the beginning . . . This is by far my new favorite book. At least until part three is released.
  —*Deanna Lancow*

I read it as a stand alone book. I found the synopsis of the first nove . . . . very helpful. It was easy to understand the characters . . . I look for the [next] book in the series . . . Excellent read.
  —*Linda Klages*

Award winning author Patricia Reding once again returns readers to her fantasy world in *Select*, the sequel to *Oathtaker* . . . Reding amazes me. She has conjured up a fantasy world and brought it to life. It is a world filled with enchantment and mystery. She breathed life into her characters . . . In this magical land, we find certainty and abiding love. We discover truths . . . secreted and evident. Truths that you can enact in your everyday life . . . There is a deep message in this book . . .

    —Annie

Ephemeral and Fleeting

The Oathtaker Series: Volume Three

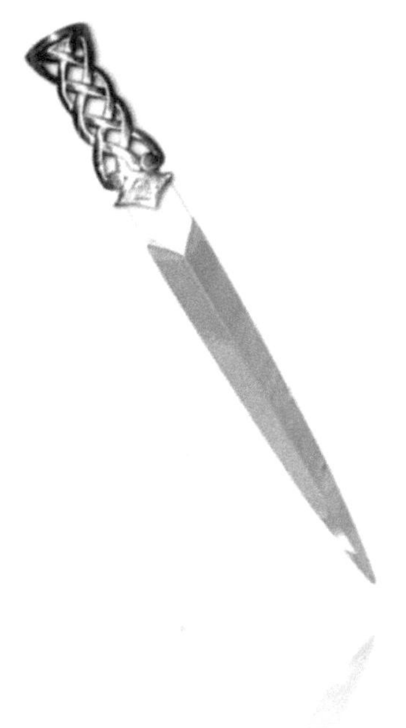

PATRICIA REDING

Scripta Manent Publishing
WRITTEN WORDS REMAIN

BOOKS BY PATRICIA REDING

The Oathtaker Series
Oathtaker
Select
Ephemeral and Fleeting

DEDICATION

Ephemeral and Fleeting: The Oathtaker Series, Volume Three, is dedicated to all my new author friends around the world. You inspire me. Keep on writing!

A Note About the Multi-Award-Winning Volumes One and Two of *The Oathtaker Series*

As is often the case with a fantasy series, new portions follow along after the passage of some time. Thus, for your convenience, included at the back of this, *Ephemeral and Fleeting: The Oathtaker Series, Volume Three*, is a full synopsis of *Oathtaker: The Oathtaker Series, Volume One*, and another of *Select: The Oathtaker Series, Volume Two*. Each covers the high points of the tales, in the order in which they were told, and thus, should help to refresh your memory. Enjoy the journey!

Chapter One

It almost tickled, the way it ran down from behind her ear and across her neck before dripping from her hair, its crimson warmth collecting in a puddle before her. The pain nearly unbearable, and unable to move, as a weight pinned her to the floor, she watched the glistening ruby pool grow. How ironic that with all her efforts over the past years to protect Ehyeh's chosen, her days would end as the result of an accident entirely of her own making.

She knew her time ran short, as the Good One had revealed things to her some time ago. But this was not at all what she'd expected. Her mind racing, she revisited images from her past. Two, in particular, troubled her. She'd not been mindful of discussing some things with others who had a need to know. The thought made her wince. Also, she'd failed to understand, failed to allow that there were those who might know as well—or even better—than she, failed to appreciate the difficulties they faced.

If only Ehyeh would grant me the opportunity to set things right and to make amends . . .

No longer able to watch the puddle of her life force grow larger, she closed her eyes, even as a wisp of air passed over her face.

"Gracious!" someone gasped.

Then came the lightest touch at her cheek like the wings of a lightfly.

With what seemed to be the last of her strength, she opened her eyes again.

"Hold on," Ephemeral—generally known as Effie—the queen of the flits, urged, as she flitted at her shoulder. "Help is coming."

"They're almost here," her husband, Fleet, short for Fleeting, added.

A long quiet minute passed. Only the whisper of the flits' wings, and a faint rustling from the woman's labored, shallow breathing, sounded out.

Then with a resounding crash, the door burst open. Chaos in the form of over a half dozen Oathtakers, Mara at the lead, entered. A single member of the Select, Basha's charge, Therese, accompanied them.

"Hold on, Lucy," Mara urged as she rushed to her side, "hold on." Then, "Dixon, Jerrett," she called over her shoulder, "get this thing off of her!"

"Lend us a hand here," Dixon said to his cohorts, Marshall, Kayson, and Raman.

"I'll help with my attendant magic," Basha offered. Drawing on her power, she concentrated on moving the beam that pinned Lucy to the floor.

As she, along with the men, saw to the task, Mara placed her hands on Lucy's shoulders. She reached inside for her magic power—power that granted her the ability to heal—and then let it loose.

As the beam dropped back to the floor with a thud, Basha rushed to Mara's side. "Great Good One, she doesn't look good!" she exclaimed.

Velia knelt and, like her fellow Oathtaker, placed her hands on the woman. Then, "Ahhhhh," she cried out, the sound so intense, it made the hair on Mara's arms rise. "Uhhhhhh," she then moaned, gasping for another breath.

The men approached.

"What is it?" Jerrett asked, his hand on his wife, Velia's, shoulder.

"Ohhhh, the . . ."

"If it's too much, you shouldn't do it. Just because your magic allows you to take on the pain of another, doesn't mean that you should."

"Ahhh, I just . . . Ohhh . . . Mara, I—" She gulped. "I think she's . . . broken her back. I feel intense pain, but nothing from her waist down."

"I can't see to that now, I've got to stop the bleeding from this cut here and check for internal injuries."

"Hurry. It's . . . excruciating." Velia cried out again, then gasped as she sucked another breath in through her teeth.

Shaking her head, signifying she required quiet, Mara released more magic into Lucy. She knew the woman still lived—she could feel the flicker of life within her. She followed her power, as it raced to the source of Lucy's most serious injury.

"Gracious Ehyeh, she's ruptured her spleen," she whispered. "She's bled internally so, so badly."

"Can you heal her?" Therese asked.

"Shhh." Mara concentrated more acutely, filling Lucy with her magic. Mere seconds later, nearly spent, she dropped her head and shuddered.

"That's enough," Dixon said. "You have to stop now."

"I just need a little . . ."

He tore her hands away. "Please, stop. That's enough. We don't want to lose Lucy, but neither can we lose you."

"But, Dixon—"

"No, that's enough now."

"I can't stop. Not yet! Dixon—"

"Please, Mara, no."

"Maybe you should try," Velia called over her shoulder to Kayson, another of the Oathtakers.

Mara touched Lucy again. "Hold on. I think she's passed out," she said.

"You're right," Velia muttered, "I don't feel her pain any longer—and thank goodness for that."

At that precise moment, Lucy gurgled, then went utterly still. The earlier sporadic, yet shallow rise and fall of her chest, halted.

Mara touched her once more. "Wait." She gasped. Her hands shook. "She's . . ." She grabbed the woman's wrist and felt for a pulse. There was nothing. Then she thought she saw a shimmer of light form and radiate over her before it, just as quickly, dissipated.

"I can't feel anything!" she cried. "Please, no. No!" She turned tear-filled eyes Dixon's way.

Basha held her hand to her mouth. "No."

"Great Good One," Velia said, "is she—"

"Dead?" Mara whispered. She closed her eyes and nodded.

Fleet hovered at her shoulder. "We came the minute it happened. We found you as quickly as—"

Mara held out her hand so that the flits could land in her palm.

"I'm so sorry," Effie said.

"It's not your fault." Mara shook her head. "I should have done more myself."

"No," Dixon assured her, "you did all you could."

Once again, she looked his way. A single tear rolled down her cheek. "I did try. Truly, I never meant for—"

"No, of course you didn't." He reached for her hand. Then, as Effie and Fleet flew into the air, he crouched down at her side. He wrapped his arms around her. "We all know that you did everything you could."

Silence ensued. Only the scratching of a branch outside, brushing against the window, interrupted it. Seconds later came a howl from Jerrett's nearly constant companion—the wolf, Bane—sitting just outside the door.

Jerrett stepped nearer. "We'll take her body to the infirmary to prepare it for burial."

Velia, at his side, leaned toward him, then buried her face in his chest. "This is awful," she said.

"What'll we do without her?" Therese asked no one in particular. "I just . . . can't believe this. It can't be true. She wasn't supposed to . . . die."

Marshall sighed. "But of course, as we all know, the gift of 'continued youth' that Ehyeh granted to her as an Oathtaker, was just that. It was not immortality."

Basha patted her charge's back. "Therese, I know how you feel, but . . ." She sucked in a deep breath and stood to her full height. "Listen, everyone, we all have to be strong now, and we have to stick together. We can't let this loss cause any division amongst us, or create any difficulties with the others."

She glanced at each of her companions in turn. "Now I know this may seem premature to you, but we have to face facts. For starters, we'd best determine right here and right now who will be our administrative lead going forward." She hesitated. "Of course, the natural person would be Mara," she added as her eyes rested on her friend.

"Oh, no! Not me! I've enough to do without—"

Just then, the door burst open again. Mara's charges, the twins—and the current ranking members of the first family of the Select, Reigna and Eden—entered.

"Felicity had a spell," Reigna cried. "She rambled something that made Trumble think that someone was hurt." She hurried to Mara's side. "What happened?"

With tears welled in her eyes, Mara looked her way, then at Eden. "I'm so sorry, girls. It's Lucy. I'm afraid she's . . ." She swallowed hard, unable to say the word.

"No!" Reigna dropped to her knees. She grabbed Lucy's hand and squeezed it. "No, Ehyeh! No! Please, return her to us. Please, please, don't take her!" She wept. "Oh, why couldn't it be someone else? We need her! No, no, no. This can't be! Please," she pleaded.

Mara crouched down and put her arm around her. "I'm sorry, Reigna. I tried. Truly . . ."

Reigna brushed her hand away. "No, Mara. Lucy may be difficult—but we need her!" Still weeping, she hung her head, muttering, praying.

Eden knelt at her sister's side. She leaned in and brushed the back of her hand against Lucy's cheek. "Reigna, that's enough now. There's nothing more you can do."

"We have to save her!"

"It's too late," Mara said. "I'm so sorry . . ."

At that very moment, Lucy sucked in a deep breath.

⚔

Eden pulled back, her eyes wide. "But . . . she was dead!"

Shaking her head, Mara looked from Dixon, to each of her Oathtaker friends in turn, to Therese, and finally, back to Lucy. "This isn't possible," she said. "She was dead. I felt—I saw—the life leave her, myself."

Groaning, Lucy opened her eyes and looked about.

"Are you all right?" Eden asked her.

She stared at her. "I . . . should be dead." She glanced Reigna's way. "You shouldn't have done that."

"Done what?"

"Here, help me sit up."

Mara gave her a hand. "You need to be careful. We thought we'd lost you."

"You did."

"But that's not . . . possible."

Lucy exhaled audibly. "You shouldn't have done that, Reigna," she repeated. "It was . . . my time."

"What are you talking about?" she asked.

Lucy dropped her head into her hands. "I'd hoped to have time to explain this all to you before I—" She glanced back up. "Well, I guess you've discovered for yourself that . . ." Her voice trailed off to nothing. Then, "I need to speak with you, Reigna and Eden," she said, "and with you, Mara. I see I should have done this earlier."

"What's this all about, Lucy?" Dixon asked. "What just happened here?"

She took to her knees. "As to what happened here, it was foolish, really. I was moving those things," she pointed to some crates at the back of the room, "when I looked out the window. I thought I saw someone I knew." She closed her eyes tightly.

"Who did you think you saw?" Mara asked. "The prospect seems to trouble you."

"Oh, never mind. It wasn't . . . possible. He's probably . . ." Her brow furrowed.

She stood, approached the window, and then looked out searchingly through the autumn leaves falling, floating, on the cool breeze.

"Anyway," she said upon returning, "the beam fell and I didn't move fast enough."

"Who did you think you saw, Lucy?" Mara persisted.

She waved her hand. "Never mind. Listen, why don't you all get comfortable? I've some things to share. I thought it could wait, but . . . Well, I suppose I should have realized that life can change drastically in an unplanned moment, so I'd best fill you in now, before something happens that keeps me from being able to do so later."

Dixon patted a rhythm on his thigh. "All right, Lucy, let's hear it."

"Please, Dixon," she motioned with her hand, "have a seat. Everyone, have a seat. There are things you all should know."

Amidst the sounds of shuffling and of weapons clanging, they sat on the floor, as they'd previously removed all the furniture from the building.

Lucy pulled her shoulders back. "Let me begin with a heartfelt . . . apology." She glanced Mara and Dixon's way. "I owe the two of you . . . Well, the truth is that I owe you more than I could ever repay. You've been instrumental in so many things, and I'm sorry to say that I . . ."

"What is it, Lucy?" Mara asked.

She turned to Basha and Therese, sitting side-by-side. "You two tried to tell me some time back, that I shouldn't be so quick to find fault—that I should recognize that I, too, could make a mistake—that I should join you 'lowly mortals in the land of the living.'" She sighed. "You were right." She looked back at Dixon. "I was wrong, Dixon. I know I said it before, but I'm not sure that I truly appreciated what I'd done."

"What are you talking about?"

"You know. When I had you taken captive. When I planned to have you tried for treason. It was . . . wrong of me. Very, very wrong." She motioned toward where she'd fallen, earlier. "When that beam fell on me, I thought I was dead. While pinned beneath it, I discovered that one of the things I most regretted—and believe me, I've been around long enough to have many regrets—was that I'd not made proper amends to you." She turned Mara's way. "Nor to you, she added. "I suppose the truth is . . ." She fell silent, holding her mouth firmly shut.

"Yes?" Mara asked.

Sighing, Lucy twisted her fingers together. "I suppose the truth is that I behaved so badly because I'm . . ."

"You're what, Lucy?"

"I'm . . . envious . . . that you two were able to follow your hearts. The same has never been true for any Oathtaker before you while his charge still lived. There are those who've . . ." Once more, she weaved her fingers together. "Well, who've loved and lost."

Mara took Dixon's hand in her own. "I'm sorry," she said.

"You've nothing to be sorry about. Once I swore oaths for the protection of my charges, I never expected that the rules would be any different for me than for any other Oathtaker." She held Mara's gaze for a moment, then looked down. "Still, I suppose somewhere in the deepest part of me, I felt I might have lost something and . . ." She swallowed hard. "In any case, like I said, I deeply regret how I treated you."

"It's forgiven, Lucy—just like we told you earlier."

"Yes, well, I mean to show you that I understand how wrong I was. I knew my time was running short, yet it seems Ehyeh has now granted me this second opportunity. I can promise you that I won't allow it to pass by without taking full advantage of it." She faced Dixon. "I'm especially sorry for what I did to you, my dear friend. I know you've long been faithful to our cause—to Ehyeh's cause—of life and freedom. Rowena was eternally grateful to you. She trusted you completely—and for good reason. I'm sorry, truly and deeply sorry, for how I behaved."

He shrugged. "Mara's right—and the twins were right when they said that we need to stick together. All is forgiven."

Lucy smiled, wanly. "Thank you both for being bigger and better people than I showed myself to be." She sighed. "Well now, as I said, there are some things you should know. However, what I'm about to tell you can never leave this room. Have I got your agreement?" She looked at each of her comrades, in turn. "If you don't think you can live up to this requirement, then please, leave now."

No one moved.

She stood and paced, her hands fidgeting. Then she turned back again. "Reigna and Eden," she said, "when you arrived back to the City of Light after you were tested in The Tearless and found Ehyeh's favor, everything was in chaos. We all headed here, back to the compound, to pack our things for returning to the palace. In all the turmoil, I didn't bother to take the time to discuss the most important facts with you." She bit her lip, then paced again.

"Some time ago," she continued, "Ehyeh shared information with me. I had awaited the new seventh seventh and her Oathtaker for decades. There were things I didn't understand about the Good One's revelations to me, but they made more sense when I discovered that there were *two* of you born to Rowena, and not just the one intended—or expected, that is."

She returned to the group, then sat. "You see, the Good One revealed to me the powers of the rightful next seventh seventh. Like I said, they didn't make much sense then. But in light of what just happened here, I suspect you've already figured out some things for yourselves."

"I don't know what you're talking about, Lucy," Reigna said.

"Nor I," Eden added.

"As the rightful ranking members of the Select, you've been endowed with certain magic powers," Lucy said. "Have you wondered at all what they might be?"

Reigna shrugged. "No. I figured when the time came, they'd make themselves known."

"And indeed they have. Or, at least they have in part."

Eden shuffled in her seat. "I don't understand. I haven't noticed any magic."

"No, but your sister has."

"What?" Reigna asked. "What are you talking about?"

Lucy bit her lip. "You, Reigna, possess a single power—an incredible, unique, and extraordinary, power. You exercised it today."

She pulled back. "Again I ask, 'what are you talking about?'"

"You have the power to bring someone back to life."

"What?" Mara cried, her eyes wide.

"At your word and on your touch," Lucy added, her gaze never leaving the young woman.

Reigna sat, her mouth open, struggling for words. Finally, she asked, "Are you sure?"

"I'm . . . quite certain."

Tears sprang to her eyes. "But—I don't want it!"

"Nevertheless, it is yours. And that leads me to believe that you, Eden," Lucy said, turning her way, "will possess an equally unique and extraordinary power. It will be the . . . opposite of your sister's." She cocked her head.

"I don't understand."

"I believe that you possess the power to bring death to someone upon your spoken word and touch."

"No!" she gasped. "I agree with Reigna. I don't want a power like that."

"Yet, if I've understood correctly what Ehyeh revealed to me, you have it."

Eden held her hand up, palm out. Her eyes narrowed. "Wait. First of all, this sounds . . ." She shook her head. "Listen . . . Reigna is the warrior. I'm a peacemaker. These powers, if indeed you are right, seem . . . wrong . . . backward. Shouldn't they be the other way around?"

"Leave it to the Good One, with His sense of humor, to do precisely what He did," Lucy said with a sad smile. "You see, each of you needs the ability to do that which is the most unnatural to you. For Reigna, a warrior, bringing someone back to life is an ability she will likely exercise . . . sparingly. Likewise, if you, Eden, as a peacemaker, are able to make someone die on your demand that they do so, I suspect that you will use your power only on extremely rare occasions. And this is important, as I'm sure you'll appreciate."

The twins stared at one another.

Dixon frowned at Lucy. "Are you sure about this?"

"I'm pretty sure. I was dead and . . . now I'm not. I know it may have been only seconds here, but you can believe me when I say that I felt my spirit depart."

"I saw it," Mara muttered, as though to herself.

Lucy nodded. "I'm afraid there's not a great deal more that I can tell you about all of this," she said to the twins.

"Where did you say you got such an idea?" Mara asked.

"From Ehyeh himself. But I learned something more about the girls' powers from a resource that Basha and Therese," she gestured their direction, "found the last time they were at the palace."

"What was that?" Basha asked.

"You brought back a book entitled, *When the Two May Overcome*. Do you remember?"

"Yes, that's right."

Lucy turned back to the twins. "From that book I read something you girls must understand and never, ever, forget—or take lightly. And that is this: there will be a price to be paid every time you exercise your power."

As the twins glanced at one another yet again, an expression of confusion on the face of each, the door burst open once more.

"Lucy!" the newcomer, an Oathtaker, Dalton, cried. "You have to come!"

She jumped to her feet. "What is it?"

"That woman you brought with you here from the city to help you with all of the books and to pack up—"

"Saga?" she asked.

"Yes! She's— She's dead! She was fine just a few minutes ago. She asked me to have Adele make her some parsnip root tea. I returned with it and gave it to her and then, minutes later, she doubled over in pain. The next thing I knew, she seemed to have a . . . a seizure of some kind. And then she couldn't breathe! And now, she's— She's dead! I don't know what could have happened."

Lucy dropped her head in her hands, shook it, and then looked back up at Dalton. "I'll be right with you," she said. "Would you kindly wait outside for a minute?"

He stepped out.

She turned back to the twins. "The price has been exacted."

Eden's brow furrowed.

Reigna shook her head. "I don't understand. What price?"

Crouching down before her, Lucy whispered, "Whenever you use your power, Reigna, to bring someone back from the dead, an innocent person will die. It may be someone you'd least expect, or can least afford to lose. It may or may not appear to be due to natural circumstances. I don't know. All I know for sure is that the person will be in your general vicinity."

"But—" Reigna pulled back, in thought. "Anyone? Any time? You mean I could bring back . . ." She paused, thinking. "Could I bring back our mother?"

"No, I'm sorry, that you cannot do. You must be able to touch the person's body, and you would have to act to bring the person back to life before sunset on the third day following his—or her—death." Lucy patted her shoulder, then turned to Eden. "As I said, if you do indeed possess the power that I believe you have, you should know that anytime you use your power, someone will . . . return to life."

The twins both stared at her.

"How is that possible?" Eden asked.

"With Ehyeh, *all* things are possible. So, remember that the person who comes back may not be someone you'd want back. And you should know that neither you nor your sister will be able to undo what the other, with her magic, has done."

Eden shook her head in disbelief. "You mean they'll crawl out of their grave somehow and—"

"Actually, Eden, I believe it will be more a matter of their deceased spirit taking over the life of another."

"So . . . I'd be responsible for the loss of that life, as well?"

Lucy nodded, wincing.

Mara grasped Lucy's arm. "Are you sure about this? It sounds . . . preposterous, to say the least."

"As sure as I can be without asking them to test their powers." She turned back to the others. "Now listen, everyone, this information must stay within this group. Imagine the requests—the demands—others might impose on the girls if they knew." She turned back to the twins. "For your part, do you know how Dixon has always said that 'doing a good thing is not the same as doing the *right* thing?'"

"Yes," they answered, in unison.

"Well, keep that in mind when you're tempted to use your abilities. I know you did so innocently today, Reigna, but because you brought me back to life, Saga is dead."

Chapter Two

Lucy had asked Saga to accompany her from the City of Light to the compound—the place where she and a number of other Oathtakers had kept Reigna and Eden safe for about two decades—hoping to draw on her expertise. The woman, an old friend of Leala and Fidel's, was considered the preeminent expert on the oldest tomes in Oosa. With her assistance, Lucy had intended to go through all of the compound resources so as to separate the wheat from the chaff, since there simply wouldn't be room to take everything along to the palace of the first family of the Select, located in Shimeron. That would be folly; it would only delay things. Now, with Saga's untimely death, Lucy would have a great deal more work to complete before she'd be ready to leave.

She and Mara followed Dalton to the cabin where Saga had stayed. Once there, they examined her body. They found no signs of injury. Indeed, but for a bit of froth at her mouth, she appeared unchanged.

"She was pretty much a loner," Lucy said as she wiped the foamy spittle away, "and to the best of my knowledge, she had no family."

"So there's no one we should notify?" Dalton asked.

"I suppose we could let someone at sanctuary in the City of Light know of her passing. She'd lived there for some time after all, so they might appreciate our informing them." She paused. "Oh, goodness, but Leala and Fidel will be heartbroken," she added in a whisper.

"What do you suppose happened to her? What are we to tell them?" he asked.

She glanced briefly Mara's way. "I . . ." She paused, then said, "I don't know. Just tell them we found her dead, and that's all we know."

His brow furrowed. "All right," he agreed.

"Why don't you get some help to get her body prepared for burial, Dalton?" Mara suggested. "We'll hold a service for her this evening."

"Certainly. I'll take care of it."

Lucy walked out and started down the pathway that led to Adele's kitchens and just beyond, to her own cabin.

Mara rushed up from behind. "Lucy, what is it?"

"What?"

"Something's troubling you."

She stopped short, then wiped her curly locks away from her brow. "I just . . . Oh, it's nothing, really." She stepped out again, pulling her shawl more tightly closed. Then she made her way around a group of Oathtakers packing one of the wagons for their journey to Shimeron.

"Wait, Lucy." Mara, still following, grabbed her arm, then hurried up to keep pace with her. "I can feel it. Something's bothering you. I'd like to help."

"There's nothing to be done."

Mara pulled her to a stop.

Pursing her lips, Lucy shook her head. "I just feel . . . responsible, is all."

"There was no way you could have known that Reigna would do what she did. Even if what you say about her power is true, you're not to blame."

"No, I mean, I feel . . ." She sighed, deeply.

"What? You feel what?"

Lucy held her gaze. "I said I thought I saw someone I knew." She glanced across the yard. "If I hadn't been distracted, I'd never have had that accident. And if that hadn't happened, then Reigna wouldn't—"

"You know better," Mara interrupted. "You didn't intend any of this, and you could hardly have anticipated it."

Again, Lucy wiped her hand across her brow. "Still, it was all so foolish of me."

Grasping her arm again, Mara urged her on. "Let's go to my place. I'll get you some tea."

"I'm fine. Really, I—"

"Come on," she said, guiding her around a corner, "I brought a good peppermint and lemon balm mix back with me from the city. It's a pleasant change from our usual fare around here. It'll lift your spirits."

A minute later, upon entering her cabin, Mara directed Lucy to a chair. Then she retrieved a pot of water kept hot over the hearth, and set it on the table. She filled two tea balls with herbal leaves, dropped one into each of two mugs, and then poured scalding water over them. Instantly, a fresh, sweet, citrusy smell rose up into the air.

"Here, drink this," Mara said, placing a cup before her long-time friend.

She grabbed the chain of the infuser in her own, and pulled it up, then dropped it back down. After a quiet minute repeating the procedure, all the while watching Lucy closely, she removed the tea ball and set it on a saucer. Then she picked up her cup to drink and looked out, over its edge.

"So, who is it you think you saw?" she finally asked.

"I'm sure I was mistaken."

"Who?"

Lucy ran her finger around the edge of her mug. "Ahhh . . . Well, I'm sure this will come as something of a surprise to you, but . . ." She removed her tea ball with a sigh, then took a teaspoon of sugar and added it to her drink. She stirred it in. "Sometimes I think everyone believes I've no heart."

Raising her brow, Mara chuckled. "No, Lucy. We just think you keep it . . . well concealed."

Glancing up, Lucy caught Mara's eye, and grinned. Then her smile turned down. "You're not the first to tell me that."

"Oh?"

"Remember earlier, when I told you that other Oathtakers before you have loved and . . . lost?"

Mara set her drink down. "Yes. I take it that you are one of those 'other Oathtakers?'"

Pursing her lips, Lucy sighed. "Yes, although I'm sure that's difficult for you to believe."

"No, it's not." Mara tapped on the table. "So, who did you love and lose?"

Lucy opened her mouth as though to speak, then closed it again, tightly.

"Does this have something to do with who you thought you saw earlier? Before your accident today?"

Lucy stood. "I should be going. Thank you for the tea, Mara."

"Come on, now, sit down. Tell me."

Pausing, Lucy wrung her hands, then sat again. "You and Dixon are sure to have a good laugh at my expense when you tell him all about this later . . ."

"That's not true."

"No, of course not. You've never been cruel. I'm sorry."

"Who was it, Lucy?"

She sighed. Then, "His name was Petrus Feoras," she said. "He . . . Well, I guess I . . . loved him."

"How long ago was this?"

She stood, then paced. "Oh . . . a while back."

Mara warmed her tea. "But you've been free from a life with a living charge for some time. You could have followed your heart. So . . . what happened?"

Approaching a nearby window, Lucy looked out. She seemed momentarily mesmerized by falling leaves dancing in the air in an array of gold and bronze.

"I said I loved him and . . . I did," she said, looking back. "I suppose maybe I just didn't love him . . . enough."

"What does that mean?"

She cocked head. "I was on a mission. I refused to be turned from it. He . . . distracted me."

"So you let him go?"

"I did. But you see, there was something even more important."

"What was that?"

Lucy sat again. "Mara, do you remember the hearing you had with the Council after Lilith's death, when the twins were just infants?" She waved her hand. "Oh, never mind, of course you do. Anyway, you'd made a decision . . . about Dixon."

Mara bit her lip. "Yes."

"Believing there was no way for the two of you to be together—to love one another and commit to one another—you decided that you would send Dixon away."

"Yes, that's right."

Lucy looked at her, searchingly. "Did you ever think it was because . . ." She pulled back, sat up straighter. "Oh, never mind."

"What? Was I going to send him away because I didn't 'love him enough,' as you say?"

"Well . . . yes."

"No. The very thought left me cold. But—" Tears sprang to Mara's eyes. "I couldn't break my oath, Lucy. I couldn't bear the thought of losing the girls. At the time, that idea was even worse to me than the idea of losing Dixon. They were so helpless. They depended on me."

She looked out the window at her side. "I couldn't break my vow, and Dixon would never have asked me to. It's like I told Nina all those years ago: if I'd turned from my oath, Dixon would forever after have wondered when I'd turn from him."

"Yes, I understand."

"What does this have to do with Petrus?" She took her friend's hand in her own.

Lucy closed her eyes, as though viewing her memories in her mind's eye. "He had a charge of his own," she finally said. "I told him that if he broke his vow, I'd not have him. He was . . . not pleased. He said he didn't believe me—that he thought I was incapable of loving—or at least of showing it." She straightened her shoulders. "Maybe he was right. I don't know. In any case, I never saw him again after that. I went on my way to follow my first love—Ehyeh and the Select—and I suppose he did the same."

"Is this who you thought you saw today?"

"Yes." She pulled her hand free and sighed. "But of course, it wasn't possible. Still, for a moment, I . . ."

Once more, Mara tapped on the table. Then, "You know," she said, "now that the twins have found their way, maybe you want to be free from all of this. You could still make a life for yourself, you know."

Lucy shook her head.

"But suppose Petrus is free from his oath now. Perhaps his charge is deceased."

Lucy held Mara's gaze. "No." She sighed. "I've had a lot of time to think this all through. Why would I do that? Allow someone into my life like that? A man I can't even grow old with? No, Mara, I say I let him go, but I suppose in truth, there were more things than just my mission—and his charge—that kept us apart. You see, I knew that eventually, he would grow old and that, therefore, one day he would . . . die. This 'gift' we Oathtakers to seventh-born members of the Select enjoy is, in some respects, a curse. Sure, it seems a blessing never to physically age, never to grow old and weak, but . . ."

Looking down, Lucy wrung her hands once more. "Well, when it comes to dealing with others, it can prove difficult—especially for those like us." She glanced back up. "It's not like he's the only one who ever showed an interest. I mean— Well, had I never had a charge who was a seventh, I too, would have aged after losing mine. Perhaps the idea of starting over then wouldn't have seemed so . . . daunting, but . . ."

She leaned back. "Well, you know, you and Dixon are the only ones who could have found a happy ending together given that you'd both had a seventh-born of the Select for a charge. For me, the differences between Petrus and I seemed—no, they were—insurmountable. It was easier for me to call an end to it all back then, than it was for me to face the possibility that I might lose him later."

"I see. So, you went your separate ways."

"We did." Lucy sipped at her tea. "I haven't thought about him in . . . years. But today, when I thought I saw him, it so surprised me that I was careless." She shook her head. "He didn't appear to have aged all that much—if any . . . and his charge was quite young when we first met," she muttered, looking off as though seeking answers in the air. "Assuming his charge lived a normal lifespan . . . Well," she sighed, "I'm sure I was simply mistaken."

She put her cup down. It clinked when it hit the saucer. "I don't know why this is so hard for me to talk about—except, of course, that I fear people will find it all rather . . . amusing."

Mara put her hand over Lucy's. "There is nothing humorous about losing someone we love," she said.

"No." Lucy smiled for a brief second, then turned somber. "I suppose you're right. But I do feel very foolish. And to think that because of it, Saga died. It's just . . . shaken me, I guess."

Mara squeezed her hand. "I understand. So, let's just keep this between the two of us then, shall we?"

Holding her gaze, Lucy nodded.

Having recently learned of the existence and location of the compound, he'd arrived there just before its residents who'd gone to the City of Light for a time, returned. But for days now, it had bustled with activity.

Hidden behind a tree, the remaining fall foliage that surrounded him concealed his lean form.

He peeked out. His black eyes narrowed. Things had grown quiet.

That had been a close call earlier. He was sure he'd been seen—by none other than Lucy Haven. When all those people rushed into the building that he'd seen her enter earlier, he'd feared they'd come looking for him. But then, no one did.

So . . . perhaps he was mistaken.

He pulled up the hood of his woolen robe. He'd best return to the cave in which he'd been staying.

He made his way through the woods striving to avoid stepping on dry, fallen leaves that might tattle on his presence. Fortunately, they were mostly damp now from a recent rain.

When he arrived at his camp, he settled in, and then retrieved some dried food from his pack. He'd need to return home soon. He hadn't expected to be away for so long. He'd just longed to see her again . . . It had been some time since she'd gone into hiding.

After several hours of sitting silently, the first of the moons rose, and with it, the cold descended. He was grateful he was alone. He enjoyed his own company far more than that of anyone else. It gave him time to think.

She's as beautiful as ever.

He cringed at the thought.

Oh, how I love her.

And hate her.

She should pay. They all should pay. Who were they anyway, endeavoring to determine his future?

He'd best them all.

Chapter Three

"I'm staying," Nina cried. Her sobs shook her shoulders.

"But—" Mara started.

Jules pulled her to the side. "I've tried, Mara, but she won't hear of leaving."

"We need you with us at the palace to oversee security there," she told him. "But then there wouldn't be anyone here to see to her safety."

"And the children are staying with me," Nina added.

Mara's eyes pleaded with Jules. "Let me talk to her. Please."

He shrugged. "If you like."

She approached Nina, then knelt at her side. She took one of her hands in her own. "Nina, listen—"

"I am not going!" She pulled free, took to her feet, stepped away, and then wiped her eyes. "I can't believe any of you would even ask this of me. My child is in the hands of that monster!" She breathed in heavy gasps. "Haven't I lost enough to him already? Three of my own children, all those years ago? And then I almost lost Calandra when his men invaded the compound. When does it stop? Huh? How much is enough?" Shaking her head, she moaned. "Oh, why would Ehyeh do this—"

"Ehyeh did not do this," Mara whispered.

"Right," Nina snapped. "As you are so fond of saying: 'He has but allowed it.'" She turned away. "How could you understand anyway? You've never had one of your own." She glanced back, her eyes glaring. "You have no idea what I'm suffering."

Mara bowed her head and looked at the floor. Nina had hit on a subject that had caused her some pain of late. She'd spent her entire adult life raising the children of another, never to have had her own. Fortunately, her attendant magic provided for her continued youth, so she certainly could have a child . . . But, no. She couldn't allow for that. The risks were too great. So, with Lucy's assistance— and a daily cup of barrenseed tea—she'd remained childless all these years. Sure, there were times she wished she could see her own—Dixon's own—child in her arms, but she felt that would inhibit her ability to honor her oath for the twins' safety. In the end, it was better to leave well enough alone.

Tears welled in her eyes. She tried to hold them back as she rose to her feet. She approached her long-time friend and cohort. "You're right, Nina," she said, reaching for her.

Nina pulled away.

Mara followed. She took Nina's hands in her own. "You're right. I don't know what you're feeling. But I do know this: we can't afford to lose Jules. We need his expertise. And I know that you don't want harm to come to the twins any more than I do. You love them like your own. I know you do. And you know that we can't afford to leave you here with Caden and Calandra without protection. Most of all, though, I don't want to see your family divided."

"So what's good for you others, is good for me. Is that what you're trying to tell me?"

Mara looked down. "No, Nina, it's not." She looked back up. "I can't even begin to understand the pain you're going through." She bit her lip. "Listen, I know it's no consolation, but you thought you'd lost her. Now you know—"

"Don't you dare!" Nina seethed. "Don't you dare try to tell me that 'all is well' since she still lives. She is in Chiran. She is a slave. Can't you understand what I'm saying? If she manages to break free, she'll come here looking for us—looking for me! I have to be here." She glanced her husband's way and scowled. "And Jules belongs here. With me. With his children."

Wincing, he approached.

Mara turned to him. "Please, may I have just one more minute with her . . . alone?"

Sighing, he turned away and then stepped outside.

"I need to talk to you, Nina."

"Just go, Mara. Haven't I done enough for you over the years?"

Her words stabbed at Mara's heart. She cringed at the sound of them and then, swallowing hard, directed her friend toward two nearby chairs.

"Nina—"

"Don't even try, Mara."

"Please, hear me out." She clasped her hand. "Let me set out my plan, and then you can respond."

Clenching her jaw, Nina sat, glaring.

Mara looked down at their hands, once again, interwoven. She looked back up, "Our lives have been . . . connected for many years," she said.

After pulling her hand free, Nina folded her arms. She looked away, said nothing.

"I know of your sacrifices, although as you are so right in saying, I've never had to experience them for myself. I want to make it right for you, but I also want to do what's right for all of us—"

Nina glanced back and opened her mouth to speak.

"And for all of *you*," Mara quickly added. "So, I've a proposal. We'll leave a couple Oathtakers who are without charges here, at the compound, in the event Carlie makes her way back here. Then we'll send a couple more back into Chiran to see if they can find out where the Chiranians are keeping her, and hopefully, to bring her back to you."

"But, of course, you wouldn't dream of going yourself," Nina spat, shaking her head. "No, that would be too much to ask," she muttered.

Mara grimaced. "I would go myself, but it's no place for a woman. I know that thought doesn't make any of this any easier for you. You are right to worry for Carlie and to insist that we do what we can for her—and we will."

Nina closed her eyes.

"Please, Nina, for all of us. We need you and Jules—and he needs you and your children. And I know that you're angry and hurt—and you've every right to be—but the twins need you, too. Don't you see?"

"Hah!"

Nina sat quietly for a minute. Finally, she asked, "So, who would you send?"

Mara shrugged. "I don't know. Truthfully, I wish Marshall and Jerrett could return, as they already know how things work there. But I don't want to divide Jerrett's family again, particularly so soon after he's just returned. And as for Marshall . . . Well, he would be in considerable danger there." She paused, in thought. "In any case, we'll figure it out. I'll bring it up at the meeting tonight after the ceremony for Saga."

Nina stood and paced. Finally, she sighed deeply, and turned back. "I liked her," she said. "Saga, I mean. What happened to her?"

Mara's shoulders slumped. "Ahhh . . . magic. Magic happened to her."

Nina's eyes narrowed. "Magic?"

"Yes. I'm sorry, that's all I can say. But we've been together too long for me to keep this truth from you. It was a terrible, terrible accident. So, I'd appreciate it if you kept this to yourself."

A knock came at the door. Mara turned as Dixon entered. He held her gaze for a long moment.

Finally, she turned back Nina's way. "What do you say, then? Are we in agreement?"

"Very well."

The compound residents all gathered in the sanctuary they'd build years back, to offer their "farewells" to Saga. Not a few eyes shed great tears. Although she'd only been with the group for a short period, she'd made fast friends with a number of them. Still, it was the old-timers, Leala and Fidel, who clearly suffered the greatest loss with her death.

When the ceremony was over, they all made their way to the burial grounds. Fortunately, they'd not had occasion to see many of their own off over the past two decades, so only a few headstones dotted the earth. Sadly, today, they would add another.

Dalton and his charge, Declan, along with Farrell and his charge, Ellian, lowered her body into the ground.

Reigna, tears running down her face, stood in the back with Eden. When she turned toward Lucy, who, standing nearby, held her arms out to her, she stepped up to accept the woman's embrace.

"I feel so responsible," she muttered.

Lucy squeezed her tightly, then loosened her hold. She held Reigna's gaze as she shook her head. "No, child," she said, "it's me who should be sorry. I failed to share critical details with you before it was too late."

"I don't want this power, Lucy," she whispered.

"I know. For what it's worth, those things that are the greatest blessings to us, can also sometimes be the greatest curses. You know, I was just telling Mara that earlier today."

Eden, listening in, neared. "What curses are you talking about?"

Lucy smiled at her, wanly. "Mmmm . . . nothing, in particular. Just know that I appreciate the difficulties your powers are likely to impose on you two."

Reigna embraced her once more. "You know, Lucy, you've . . . changed," she said.

She pulled back. "Have I?"

"Yes. Since we returned here, you seem . . . I don't know . . . more—"

"Introspective?" she offered.

"Yes, that's right."

"Perhaps I am. Which just goes to show you that one is never too old to learn— and for the record, you two played no small part in reminding me of that. Thank you." She released Reigna. "Then again, it is equally true that you've changed since your journey and your testing in The Tearless."

"Have I?"

"You both have. You've . . . grown up." She squeezed Reigna's hand. After releasing her, she directed the residents to the dining hall. There, she told them, they'd hold their last meeting at the compound while enjoying one of Adele's famous meals.

They made their way to the hall. Inside, it smelled of herbs and spices, fresh bread, and chicken grilled on an open fire.

Reigna and Eden sat at a table with Mara and Dixon, along with Jarrett and Velia, Jules and Nina, and Lucy. Before long, they'd all nearly eaten their fill. Even so, they expected Adele would arrive shortly with assorted sweets to finish off the refection.

Mara took another bite of her food. "You know," she said, "one of the best things that happened to us all those years ago when we sought a place of safety for you girls," she nodded at the twins, "was when Adele got caught up in my magic and accidentally ended up traveling with me and joining our little company." She chuckled.

Jerrett grinned at her. "What brought that up?"

"Well, honestly, I mean— Where does she come up with these ideas?" She gestured with her fork at her plate.

"What have you got there?" Dixon asked her.

"Some kind of . . . I don't know. Adele topped this crunchy bread with a mixture of a soft, creamy, almost fruity cheese, chopped basil and scallions, sun-dried tomatoes, salty olives, and garlic. Then she grilled it." She took another bite. "And if I had to guess," she added, her mouth still full, "I'd say there's a bit of lemon zest in it." She moaned. "Gracious Ehyeh, I think I've died myself and moved on."

Eden laughed. "I love her cooking. Trust me, Mara, when I say that Reigna and I greatly appreciated that venison you brought to us when we were in The Tearless, but honestly, I'll take Adele's home cooking any day!"

Her sister nudged her. "You'll get no argument here."

Lucy pushed her chair back. "Well, we'd best get things started," she said. Then she made her way to the front of the room as she called out, "May I have your attention everyone?"

Slowly, the din died down.

"Of course, I expect Reigna and Eden will be handling matters going forward, but I wanted to take a minute to thank you all for the great work you've done in preparing things here so quickly in anticipation of our trip to Shimeron. Your attention to detail is most appreciated. At this time, there's not much left to do, although I understand that Adele could use some assistance in packing up the rest of the kitchen this evening."

She glanced about. "For now, given Saga's death," she said, her eyes flickering in Reigna's direction, "all I've got left, is to finish going through some books. One way or another though, I'll finish that up tonight so that we can be on our way first thing in the morning. If any of you would like to assist me, I won't turn you away." Again, she looked to the twins. "Would you two like to take it from here?" she asked them.

The sisters rose. Then, with Mara between them, they made their way to the front of the room.

Reigna spoke first. "Actually, Eden and I don't have anything for now, but Mara has a request she'd like to make," she said.

"Yes, thank you." She faced the crowd. "There are a couple of things that have come up, with which we need your help. First, we've decided to leave a small group behind—here at the compound—in the event that Carlie escapes from Chiran and finds her way back. Are there any volunteers?"

A few Oathtakers raised their hands.

"Very well, Georgana, thank you. I'll feel better knowing there's a healer here. And thank you too, Macall," she added turning to the other volunteer before glancing back at Nina "Will that be acceptable to you?"

As she nodded, Jules reached for her hand.

"Second," Mara said, once again addressing the crowd, "I'd like to send a couple Oathtakers into Chiran again."

"What's this about?" Lucy asked, sitting up straighter.

"Suffice it to say, it's necessary."

"Honestly," Jerrett spoke up, "I don't recommend it."

"Nor do I," Marshall added.

Chaya, to his right, whispered something to him. When he nodded, she raised her hand.

"Yes?" Eden responded.

"May I speak?"

"Certainly. This is an open forum."

She cleared her throat. "Then I must say that I highly recommend against that plan."

"Excuse me?" Nina said as she got to her feet. "You've no—"

"Hold on, Nina," Mara said, "let's hear her out."

Nina glared at her, then turned back to Chaya. "Fine, then. What is it?"

"It's just that they're such . . . barbarians," Chaya said. "Honestly, I don't think—"

"You think I don't know that?" Nina cried. "I've been a victim of their savagery—their brutality. And now they have our daughter!"

"I understand, but—"

"No. Someone needs to go for her, or . . . or I'll go in search of her myself!" As Nina spoke, she glared at Mara, as though defying her to rise to the challenge of taking a trip to Chiran.

Jules, now standing at her side, encouraged her to take back to her seat.

Chaya bit her lip. "I understand," she said. "I'm sorry for interrupting."

"That's quite all right," Mara said. "You should always feel free to share your thoughts in these meetings. We don't all agree on everything, every time, but we value one another's opinions." She looked the group over. "Are there any volunteers then?"

Marshall raised his hand.

Chaya shook her head at him and whispered, "You can't go back there. You know what it would mean. Besides, I can't do this without you. I need you."

He turned her way, his brow furrowed.

"She's right, my friend, you can't go," Jerrett said to him. "If you're caught there and they discover you're responsible for Cark's death . . ." He glanced back at Mara. "I suppose I could go," he said.

"No," Jules said to him, "you've done your turn there."

Nina scowled at her husband.

"It's all right," he told her. "We'll find someone."

"We'll go," said someone sitting in the back of the room.

Mara looked up. "Thank you, Liam. And you too, Rafal. I suggest you meet with Marshall and Jerrett to learn what you can before you set out." She paused, tapping her fingertips together. "Now, as you all know, once the twins gained Ehyeh's favor, a few things changed—not the least of which is that any current or former Oathtaker to a seventh of the Select now has the same attendant magic power to travel that I have—although with only a single additional person at a time. So, tomorrow morning, the twins and I will oversee things here while Lucy and Dixon take Liam and Rafal to see Ezra."

She turned to the volunteers. "It won't take you long to get to Chiran from there." Then, glancing at Nina, she asked, "Will that be acceptable to you?"

Her lips pursed, her arms folded, Nina tipped her head, signifying her agreement.

Lucy stood. "Liam," she said, nodding his direction, and then "Rafal," she added, turning to his companion, "I've been working on a trinket you can use to communicate with us."

She approached them, then handed Liam a case. Similar in appearance to the compact that she'd created years ago, and that any Oathtaker to a seventh of the Select could use to send messages back and forth, it was a small, silver thing.

"A compact," Liam said, grinning. "Won't this be rather odd for two men to carry?"

"Open it," Lucy said.

He did. "Ahhh, a compass," he said.

"Yes, but it works the same as the compact—except of course, that you won't be able to see the person with whom you communicate. As with the compact, you just open it and voice your message. Then I'll retrieve it from my compact when I can." She frowned. "I'm sorry. I know the flits can get word back and forth between us, but as they require travel time, their communications are not quite as 'instant' as I'd like. So this, I'm afraid, is the best I can do considering that neither of you ever had a seventh for your charge."

"It'll work," Rafal said.

"Very well then," Mara said, once again addressing the crowd, "this meeting is adjourned. Now, let's all plan to get an early start come morning. Fall is already well upon us, and our goal is to reach the palace before winter sets in with a fury."

As Bane howled in the distance, Mara, standing on the porch of the cabin she shared with Dixon and the twins, watched the second moon rise. Its light emphasized the cloud cover moving into the area. Likely, it would rain overnight.

Dixon approached from behind, then wrapped his arms around her.

Melting in his embrace, she breathed in his scent of cedar and leather

"It's good to be home," he said, his mouth to her ear.

"Yes." She turned to face him. "Just in time to leave again."

He kissed her, slowly, sweetly. Then, "What was all that with Nina?" he asked.

Mara explained the conditions Nina set before she'd leave the compound. "She said I didn't understand—that I couldn't understand—because I've never had one of my own." Tears sprang to her eyes.

Releasing his hold, then taking her hand, Dixon guided her to a chair. Sitting next to her, he patted out a rhythm on his thigh. "We're in uncharted territory here, you know," he said. "The rules provided a way for us to be together. They never said anything about children. You know that's what I want."

Nodding, she met his gaze, then said, "Shortly after the Council hearing, Lucy caught up with me." When a tear rolled down her cheek, she brushed it away brusquely.

"Oh? Was there something she said that's troubling you?"

Shrugging, she frowned. "She handed me a packet of barrenseed tea, telling me that she thought I might be needing it. And more recently, she reminded me that I can't go on using it forever. Soon, its effects will be . . . irreversible." She choked back a cry.

He got on his knees before her. "Mara, you know I want a child, too." He took her hands. "I say we should do it."

She sighed. "Dixon, it's not the right time. I mean—"

"It will never be the right time. Let's face it, there's always—"

"No, I mean with Zarek about to invade . . . I think we have to beat back this threat first."

He sat back down, then resumed patting out a rhythm. "I understand."

She reached for his hand. "I know it's what you want, Dixon—and I do too. But these are very dangerous times. It's one thing to think of protecting the twins now that they're grown, but quite another to think of protecting an infant. I'm . . ." She looked in his eyes.

"Afraid?"

"Yes." She stood and then, still facing him, leaned against the deck railing. "But I'm equally afraid that soon, I'll have no—" Looking down, she paused. "Well, it's one thing to choose not to have a child for a time, it's quite another to have no say in the matter." A shiver ran through her.

Dixon approached. He took his cape and draped it over her shoulders, then took her hand. "I wish I could take on that burden, but to date, Lucy's found nothing that would work." He sighed. "Aren't there any other options for us?"

"Lucy says the others would be even more dangerous to my health—with the possible exception of using a cassus tincture, but . . ." Pausing, she pulled the cape more tightly around her shoulders.

"But what? Maybe we should try that for a time."

She bit her lip and shook her head. "I'm sorry. I just . . . can't bring myself to do it."

"Why?"

She wrung her hands. "Because Lucy says she doesn't know if it prevents pregnancy, or if it actually acts as an abortifacient." She held his gaze. "I— I can't do that."

With his thumb, Dixon wiped away a tear slipping down her cheek. Then he gathered her in his arms and kissed the top of her head. "I'm sorry," he said. "I understand. Truly, I do."

He pulled back, then tipped her chin up, forcing her to look at him. "The truth is that I have all I've ever needed. I'd love for us to have a child, but if it's not to be, then at least I'll get to spend my days knowing that I got the one thing that was the most important to me." Drawing her closer again, he said, "I got *you*." Again, he kissed the top of her head.

"You know, when I thought I couldn't be with you all those years ago, when you nearly sent me away—I thought my heart would break. Then, when you were injured and didn't even know who I was, I thought I'd lost you all over again."

Once again, he pulled back to look at her.

Her eyes met his.

"Truly, Mara, all I need is *you*."

⁂

She sat up with a start, ramrod straight. Her breath caught in her throat. Her hand to her chest, she breathed in and out in short, quick gasps.

Dixon stirred at her side. He opened his eyes and then, with the bedding rustling beneath him, reached for her. He rubbed her arm. "Are you all right?"

She covered her face with her hands, and took in a deep breath. "Y—yes."

He sat up. "What is it?"

"Just a nightmare."

"Want to talk about it?"

"I—"

"You're shaking. Come on now, tell me. It'll take away its power."

"Right." She inhaled deeply and then exhaled slowly. "Well, it was strange. It was like I was dreaming that I was someone else."

"Who?"

"Rowena."

He pulled back. "Oh? What happened?"

She bit her lip. Then, "It was . . . odd," she said, "but so real. It was almost like it happened and I was re-living it."

He took her hand.

"I dreamed that I was carrying the twins and that some grut chased us. I was so afraid I'd lose them and—" She fought back a sob.

"Mara, it was just a nightmare. Rowena died when they were born. You know that. She never carried the twins and ran from the grut. They didn't show up until she was already in the wayfarers' hut where I left her. And besides—"

"No, when I said I was 'carrying' them, I mean that I was— You know." She patted her abdomen. "Carrying them. I was pregnant with them."

"Ahhh, I see." There was a smile in his voice.

"What?"

"We were talking of children earlier. It seems your dreams took that into account."

"But I was so afraid I'd lose them."

He rubbed her back. "What happened?"

"The grut chased me. I ran through the forest. Branches reached out and snagged at me, as though trying to hold me back. Then I saw a place of refuge—like the wayfarers' hut where Rowena birthed the twins." She shook her head and closed her eyes, struggling to recollect further details.

"Then what?"

"Then, I—" She turned to him with tear-filled eyes that sparkled in the scant moonlight coming in through the window. "I had these pains—these contractions, I guess they were. The next thing, I saw blood—lots and lots of it. It was what happened to Rowena, you know. Anyway, that's when I awakened."

"Shhhh . . . Shhhh, now." He put his arms around her. "You're fine. You're safe. The twins are safe."

"All that blood, Dixon," she said, shuddering.

"You're all safe," he repeated.

"I don't think I ever really considered things from Rowena's perspective. How awful for her."

"Yes," he agreed. As he rubbed her back again, her breathing slowly returned to normal.

"Come on now," he said, patting her pillow.

When she was comfortable, he stroked her hair and kissed her forehead. "Get some sleep now," he said as he snuggled around her and held her closely.

Chapter Four

Before dawn broke, painting the eastern horizon in glorious pink strokes, Dixon and Lucy whisked Liam and Rafal off to find Ezra at The Clandest Inn in the City of Light. Then, immediately upon their return to the compound, the caravan set out.

Jerrett and Velia were amongst those in the lead. Nina's sister, Erin, rode in the wagon designated for their family, to watch their four boys, Aden, Drew, Jedrek, and Carlow. The eldest was eight years of age, the youngest, just under a year.

Marshall rode at Jerrett's other side. "Where's Bane?" he asked.

Jerrett laughed. "I was going to have him ride with Erin and the little ones, but he'd have none of it. He's roaming around somewhere."

"You sure that's safe?"

"Ahhh, I'm not concerned with Bane. He's a good one."

"For a wolf," Velia offered, chuckling. She looked at Jerrett, shaking her head. "I still can't believe you thought he was a dog."

"Well," he responded, in mock surprise, "how was I to know?"

"You might have looked at him a bit more closely," she teased.

Just then, Chaya approached. "Good morning, all."

"Good morning," Velia said.

Jerrett tipped his head her way in greeting.

Silent, Marshall watched the landscape ahead. After a long minute, he turned to her. "I was thinking, Chaya," he said, "that you might want to find things that interest you here—things you could assist with."

"But I want to be with you."

"I know, for example," he said as though he hadn't heard her, "that Adele needs help keeping us all fed."

She glanced his way, her eyes narrowed. "Sure, Marshall. I'd like to do whatever I can. If you want me to help Adele, then—"

"No, I didn't say I *wanted* you to help her, I only suggested it. There are other options. You could . . ."

"That's fine, Marshall, I'll check with her." She turned her horse back.

Velia, watching the exchange, bit her lip. Then, "Is there something wrong, Marshall?" she asked.

"Wrong? No. Why do you ask?"

She shrugged. "I just— Well, it seems Chaya would like to stay as near you as possible. You rescued her from a terrible situation in Chiran, and I know how you feel about her. I can see it. So it seems odd that you'd be so short with her—that you'd send her away."

Glancing her way, his brow dropped. "I didn't send her away."

"Very well then." She turned to Jerrett. "You two got in late last night," she said. "I take it that you filled Liam and Rafal in on what they're likely to find in Chiran?"

Jerrett patted the neck of the gelding he rode. "Yes, it was a long night. I hope I didn't wake you when I got back."

"No." She smiled at him. "But I wouldn't have minded if you had," she added in a whisper.

He grinned at her. Then, "We suggested they start with the camp near Darth, Chiran," he said, "as that's where Zarek was when Marshall and I left there."

"That sounds good." She stole another peek Marshall's way. "Listen, since you two have things covered here, I'm going to check in with Mara. I've seen so little of her since she left the compound all those months ago."

"Sure, love, we've got this," Jerrett said.

Velia turned her horse around, then headed back to the middle of the pack where Mara and Dixon rode near the twins. When she drew near, she patted Mara's arm. "Would you ride with me for a minute?"

"Certainly." She followed Velia off a distance. Then, "What is it?" she asked.

Velia's brow rose. "I hesitate saying anything, but . . . Well, I noticed this morning that it seems something is bothering you. I thought you might like to talk, and— Well, the truth is that I missed you terribly while you were away. I'm so glad you're back. I just wish I'd known what had happened. Maybe I could have helped."

Mara offered her a half-hearted smile. "I appreciate it," she said, "but I'm fine— just not feeling all that well. I'm still so tired from all the former traveling—and now, here I am, doing it again after such a short stay at the compound. Anyway, I'm sure there was nothing you could have done when I was injured." She glanced her friend's way. "Really, all is well, Velia. It's just hard saying 'good-bye' to the place I've known as 'home,' for longer than any other of my life. Especially after having just returned there from so long a journey."

Velia made her way around a puddle of rainwater left behind from the night before, then returned to Mara's side. "Are you sure there isn't anything more?"

"I'm sure."

"All right then. So . . . what do you make of these new powers the girls have?"

"Uggh. I'm sure glad I didn't get saddled with them. The power of life and death? At a word and touch? No, thank you!" Mara grimaced.

"I agree."

At that moment, Basha rode up. "Mind if I intrude on your conversation?" she asked.

"Not at all." Mara glanced her way, then back at Velia. "Honestly, I missed the two of you so much. When my memory returned, and after Dixon finally showed up at the Council meeting, one of the things I thought about most, was how I missed our 'girl time.'"

Her friends chuckled.

"Me, too," Basha said. She glanced over her shoulder, then turned back. "What do you say the two of you leave your men behind for a bit this evening and join me for a little nip?" Grinning, she pulled a flask out from her saddlebag. "I brought a little something along for us to share."

"Consider it done," Velia said.

"Count me in!" Mara exclaimed.

Standing at the back of Velia's tent, Mara called out her presence.

Velia opened the flap and greeted her. "Step in while I say 'good night' to the boys," she said. Then she turned to them. "Hush now, Aden," she reprimanded the eldest. "Stop teasing your brother. I told you, it's time for sleeping."

"But Drew is just a baby," he whined.

"Yet it's *you* who's trying to keep me here," she said, grinning.

Drew punched his brother in the arm. "I am not a baby!" he cried. "I'm almost five winters old!" He pointed at the nearly one-year-old, Carlow, in his mother's arms. "Carlow's the baby."

Aden frowned, then turned back to his mother. "Why do you have to go?"

Smiling at him, her brow raised, she shook her head. "Come on now, it's past your bedtime."

"Where's Dad?" Jedrek, a robust three-year-old who hadn't yet dropped all of his baby-like plumpness asked as he bounced up and down before getting into his bedroll.

She pulled a blanket up to his chin, then leaned over and kissed his cheek. "He'll be here to say 'good night' to you boys soon. Then he's off to meet with Dixon."

"But who's going to be here?" Aden asked.

She chuckled. "I told you. Erin will keep an eye on you boys until one or both of us get back."

Just then, Jerrett stepped in. "What's this I hear?" he asked as he made his way to the boys' bedside. "Oh, hello, Mara," he added upon sight of her.

She greeted him with a smile.

"Is someone here causing trouble?" he asked the boys. Then he reached out and tickled one, then another, then another of them, ending with Carlow.

In a fit of giggles, Aden grabbed Jerrett's hand. He pulled his thumb back, growling.

Jerrett, feigning that he was in pain, pulled free, then grabbed both of the boy's wrists and held them firmly. "Oh, so you're a tough guy, huh?" Laughing now, he made a claw with his free hand. "I'm going to get you," he threatened, drawing closer and closer.

"Oh, Jerrett, please don't get them all riled up," Velia said, chuckling. "Erin won't appreciate it, I'm sure."

He released Aden's wrists, then tickled each of the little ones once again. "Yes, you're right. So, boys, that's enough now," he said to the sounds of their giggling. "Time for sleeping."

"Ahhh, Dad," Drew whined.

"Good night!" he said. Then he turned to Velia and kissed her. "I won't be late."

"Ewwww!" Aden exclaimed. "You kissed a girl, Dad!"

"Don't be ridicul— ridi— ri-di-cli-ous. She's not a girl," Drew said. "She's just a mom."

"You mean ridi-*cu*-lous, not ridi-*cli*-ous," Velia corrected him.

"Hello!" Erin called from outside.

Velia fluffed up Drew's hair. Then she grinned at Jerrett as she handed Carlow off to him. "Let's go," she said.

After they and Mara stepped out, Erin took Carlow from Jerrett. "I've got him," she said.

"See you later then," he called out as he jogged away.

With that, Mara and Velia set out to join Basha who waited for them on a brush-covered hillside not far from the main camp. A modest bonfire sat before her.

For a time, the three Oathtakers communed in silence. Chattering fox and hooting owls sounded out around them. Amidst that strangely synchronized musical background, Bane howled at the moon from afar, while an occasional hare scurried about in the surrounding brush.

Finally, grinning, Basha pulled out her flask and offered it to Mara.

"No, thanks," she said, waving her hand. "I've been having trouble sleeping and, truth to tell, that wouldn't help."

"Anything in particular wrong?"

"No. Just . . . nightmares."

"I'm sorry. Care to share?"

"No—but thanks. And don't be. Sorry, I mean." Mara shrugged. "I'm fine so long as Dixon's there."

"After saying 'good night' to my five boys, I could certainly use some," Velia said.

"Five!" Basha exclaimed. "But you only have four boys."

Velia chuckled. "Ahhh . . . Have you met my husband? Jerrett? Big guy? Lots of muscle? And body art?"

The three friends laughed.

Basha handed the flask over.

Velia took a swallow. "Good thinking with this," she said, raising the vessel in the air, "although in truth, it'll take us a few weeks to get to the palace, and this won't even last the evening!"

"Oh, there's more where that came from," Basha replied.

Once again, they all laughed.

"Tell us about your trip," Mara said to her. "I've heard so little."

"There's not much to tell, really. We found as many Oathtakers and Select as we could, and then sent them to the City of Light. You know the rest."

Mara cast a sideways glance her way. "I like Felicity. She's a lovely young thing. Rather . . . *spritely*, wouldn't you say?"

Basha nodded. "She is. For a while there, out of concern for her, I didn't think Trumble would join us. But when he realized that at least some of the visions Felicity had been having seemed to have something to do with the twins, he relented."

"I like him, too. Trumble, I mean. He's a good man."

Biting her lip, Basha nodded. "Yes, he is," she said. "Now, tell us about your venture."

Noting how quickly she sought to change the subject, Mara tucked her hair behind her ear, then proceeded to tell her friends all about her travels with Dixon after she'd lost her memory and insisted on returning to her childhood home.

"The strangest times were when some trinket seemed to propel me to travel magically to the twins," she said. "First it was a grut tooth, then the oracle—"

"The oracle?" Basha asked. "Really?"

"Yes, it just said 'Go,' the same as it always has. At least I now know why that was."

"Oh? What do you mean?" Velia asked.

"Well, Effie and Fleet explained it all to me. You see, when I first took the oracle from the cave all those years ago, the flits were released. But they couldn't communicate directly with us until the twins found Ehyeh's favor. In the meantime, they could get Ehyeh's intended messages to us only through their use of the oracle."

Basha reached for the flask from Velia, and then took a drink. "How did they do that?"

"From what I've gathered—although truthfully, they didn't say much—it literally took their blood. That is, one of them was sacrificed each time, just to get the message to us."

"That's awful!" Velia cried.

"I agree. But it seems they believed the messages were sufficiently important, such that the sacrifices they made were worth it. In any case, had I not correctly deciphered what it was that I was to 'go' for each time, or had I not taken heed of the messages with sufficient haste, the flits' sacrifices would have been in vain. And, you know, that almost happened . . ."

Pausing, she shook her head. "When the twins were infants, after I'd sent you, Basha," she nodded her way, "and some of the others of our group ahead to the compound with the great scepter, the oracle had been telling me to 'go.' I knew it meant that I was to leave the City of Light. But I thought that Dixon and I should first meet with Edmond at sanctuary there. So I waited. As it turned out, Edmond was the one who betrayed us to Lilith. And because of my stalling, she managed to get to the twins."

"Hmmm." Basha gestured with the flask toward Velia.

She took it. "So during the time that you didn't know who you were, how many times did you travel to the twins then? Just those two?"

"No. Each time it occurred when the girls were most in need. I brought them water after finding the grut tooth, then food after finding the oracle. But it seems the most important thing I brought them—as they tell it—was courage." She grinned. "That was my third trip."

"What sent you to them that time?"

"I found some crystals in Dixon's pocket and they triggered my reaction.'

"But it was your blade that brought everything back to you and that sent you to them that last time, right?" Velia asked.

"Yes—that was my fourth and last trip. When I saw Spira, I just . . . knew the blade was mine. Then, when I touched it, everything came back."

"And when you went to the girls that last time—that's when Lucy had Dixon taken captive."

"That's right."

The three sat quietly for a minute.

"You know," Mara finally said, "after Lucy's comments the day of her accident—when she apologized to Dixon and me again, I spent some time with her. We talked about . . . Well, about those who've 'loved and lost.'"

Basha's head jerked her way. "What?"

Not noticing her reaction, Mara continued. "I can't reveal any details, of course, as I've sworn myself to secrecy, but you know, there's more to Lucy than sometimes meets the eye."

Basha visibly relaxed. "Lucy? Loved and lost? Huh. Well, she's been around for centuries. I guess with that much time to fill, anything is possible."

Velia laughed outright, then took a swallow before passing the flask back to Basha. "You want to know a real strange love-twist?" she then asked.

Basha's eyes darted her way. "What's that?"

"Marshall."

Grinning, Mara nudged her. "Who would have thought it! Still, he seems entirely smitten with Chaya."

"Yes, but he's acting so strangely about it."

"Oh? What do you mean?" Basha asked.

Velia repositioned herself, then added more wood to the fire. "Well, I rode at the front today, from time to time, with him and Jerrett. It seemed that whenever Chaya approached, Marshall went . . . cold."

Mara's brow dropped. "Why do you suppose that was?"

"I don't know. He suggested she might help Adele with the cooking and all. You probably saw her doing that earlier tonight."

"I thought maybe she just liked that sort of thing."

"It's possible. Anyway, I've tried to encourage her to get to know Nina and Erin. I would think they'd make fast friends, given that they are all Chiranian born, and all share something of the same history—having been enslaved there."

"That was good thinking," Mara said, "but don't count on Nina's warming up to her any time soon." She waved away the flask when Basha offered it to her again. "Did you see the way she glared at Chaya during the meeting when she cautioned anyone against traveling to Chiran?"

Basha looked up at the sound of an owl hooting. "Yes," she said, "but then Nina must be sick with worry about Carlie."

"She is," Mara agreed. "Actually, she's a bit difficult to reason with just now."

"Oh?"

She shrugged.

"I don't understand why they treat women the way they do," Velia said, reaching once again, for the flask from Basha. "It's . . . disgusting. Jerrett says he and Marshall didn't see a single free one while there."

Just then, a long shrill scream rent the air.

The three Oathtakers all jumped to their feet.

"Let's get back!" Basha cried as she sprinted toward the main camp, her friends at her heels. "That sounded like Felicity!"

Turmoil had erupted in the midst of camp. When the three Oathtaker friends neared, they followed several others headed toward the wagon that Trumble shared with his charge, Felicity, and his friend, Raiden.

Basha pushed her way to the middle of a gathered crowd, just as Trumble arrived from the other side. "What is it?" she asked him, her eyes wide.

"It's— I don't know! I just got here. I—"

Mara reached them. "What's happened?"

The back flap of the tent opened with a loud crinkling sound, and Felicity peeked out. With Trumble's assistance, she made her way down, trembling all the while.

"I'm sorry I frightened everyone," she said, pulling a blanket over her shoulders.

"There's no need to be sorry," Mara said. "What happened?"

Felicity put her arms around Trumble's waist. "They're coming for them," she said before burying her face in his chest.

He held her tightly. "For who, Felicity?"

"For the girls."

"The twins? Reigna and Eden?"

"Well . . . yes . . . but for others, as well."

He pulled back, then with a finger beneath her chin, tilted her head up. "I don't understand," he said. "What girls?"

Still shaking, she closed her eyes. "All of them. All they can . . . get."

"Do you know who's doing this?"

"The men in black." Then she buried her face again in his chest. "They hurt girls. They trap them."

"Shhhh . . . shhhh now," he said, wrapping his arms more tightly around her.

Standing nearby, stroking the young woman's arm, Basha held Trumble's gaze.

"Visitors!" a deep voice called out.

Dixon, Marshall, and Jerrett, with Bane following, joined the mix. Each of the men held his blade. Collectively, they surrounded four young women, one of whom stepped to the fore.

"You can't hold us," she said.

Mara neared her. "No, of course not." She motioned for the men to step back.

Bane drew closer, sniffed at the girls' heels, and then, with his hackles raised, growled.

When they jumped at the sound, Mara caught Jerrett's eye. "Call him off, will you?" she asked him before turning back. "All right now, what are your names?"

"I'm Birdie," the first of them said, "and this is Sugar," she pointed to one of her friends, "and Echo, and Trixie," she identified her remaining companions with a nod toward each of them.

Despite the seriousness of the situation, Mara's brow rose, even as she choked back a laugh. "Seriously? Those are your real names?"

Birdie made a face at her. "What do you want with us?"

"I want to know what you're doing out here."

She sneered. "It's none of your concern."

"What are you? All of . . . fourteen years old?" Mara asked. "Fifteen, maybe? What are you doing out here by yourselves? Where are your parents?"

"Like I said, that's 'none of your concern.'"

Mara looked Dixon's way. "What happened?"

He stepped to her side. "I saw them in the distance," he whispered in her ear, "with my attendant magic. Bane, approaching them at the time, informed Jerrett who was with me, via his magic link to him, of their presence. The girls were headed this way—and we didn't know what to expect. So we got Marshall, and then the three of us brought them in so that we could question them. Honestly, we had no idea they were so young."

Felicity dropped her hold on Trumble and then stepped toward the newcomers. "Please, please don't do this," she said, a cry in her voice.

Birdie glared at her. "What's it to you where we go or what we do?"

"It's a trick. They hurt people." Tears ran down Felicity's face.

Tapping the toe of her boot, Birdie turned to her friends. "Come on girls, let's go. They can't hold us here." She started off.

Once again, Felicity cried out. Then she dropped to the ground in convulsions.

The crowd turned her way.

Before Trumble reached her side, Velia did. Grabbing her hand, she fell back with a scream.

"What is it?" Jerrett asked.

"It seems she's experiencing some pain that someone is suffering and—Ohhhh! Ahhhh!"

"What?" He pulled her hand free.

With tears pooled in her eyes, Velia pulled back to her knees and then turned to address Birdie. "If you choose to do this, know that the pain you'll encounter, both physically and emotionally, is more than you'll ever be able to bear." As she stood, she reached for her hand. "Don't do this. Don't go. Convince your friends to stay. Please. Please, listen to me." Then she addressed Echo and Sugar, "Don't go. I beg you." Her voiced sounded as though her heart was breaking. Finally, "Trixie, don't do it," she added, catching the eye of the last of the girls.

Trumble, who had crouched down near Felicity, helped her to rise.

At that moment, Chaya stepped up. "You said something about 'men in black,' is that right, Felicity?"

As she nodded, the crowd turned Chaya's way.

She addressed Mara. "I believe I know who she's talking about. There's an offshoot of the Chiranian guard. Its members wear nothing but black. They even cover their faces so that they can't be identified—and they carry black flags marked with skulls with snakes crawling out from their eye sockets. They call themselves 'succedunt' soldiers."

"So?" Echo asked.

She turned her way. "So, trust me. You don't want to be in their presence."

Birdie stepped up. "We don't know anything about the succedunt you mentioned. We're going to Chiran to become brides to the 'descendants.'"

"Yes, that's another name the succedunt use," Chaya said. "But . . . become their brides?" She grimaced. "Have you lost your minds?"

"Who are these people, Chaya?" Mara asked.

She turned her way. "You think Zarek's regular guard is filled with evil men? They are nothing compared to the succedunt. They, like Zarek, are descendants—successors—of a line of Chiranians known as the Hazarik. I suppose that's where Zarek got his name," she added as though in afterthought. "In any case, they, along with their supporters, have grown significantly in number over the past few years—and you should know this: the succedunt will stop at nothing."

"What could they possibly do that's worse than Zarek's regular guard?" Jerrett asked.

"Huh!" Chaya scoffed. "Zarek's regular guards may kill indiscriminately and without remorse, but succedunt soldiers make a . . . a sport of it."

"Oh?"

"They burn people alive. They cage them and drown them. They . . . cut off body parts, rendering their victims helpless. They . . ." She shuddered. "The things they do are too awful to imagine. Even then, it might be fair to say that those who die at their hands are the lucky ones. What they do to their women, you don't even want to know."

Mara turned to their visitors. "I'd listen to her if I were you," she said. "Chaya is a former Chiranian. She knows of what she speaks."

Birdie stared at her. Then, "Come on, girls," she said, waving for her friends to join her.

"Wait," Mara said. "Where did you hear about these Chiranians who are looking for brides? What gave you such an idea to join up with them?"

Birdie made a face at her, expressing her disdain. "There's a lot of information that the town criers and fliers don't make readily available."

"Meaning?"

"Meaning that those who seek to learn of more than what is commonly distributed, can do so." With that, she walked away, her friends at her heels. Only Trixie stole a quick look back.

Jerrett stepped up, Bane at his side. "Well, I guess it's like I always say, it seems everyone carries within him, the seeds of his own destruction. And in the end, you can't save someone from himself—or *herself*—as the case may be."

As the crowd started dispersing, Bane shot out into the darkness. Moments later he returned with one of the young woman at his side.

Approaching her, Mara recognized Trixie. "You've decided not to go, then?" she asked.

Not able to meet the Oathtaker's eye, the girl nodded. "I just want to go home."

"Where is that?"

Pulling her cloak closed more tightly, Trixie shuffled her feet. Then, shrugging, she pointed in the direction from whence she'd come.

"Well, why don't you stay with us for tonight then? We'll see you back home safely in the morning."

Chapter Five

Two weeks into their journey, and as dusk set in once again, the travelers headed toward the dinner wagon. Marshall and Jerrett stood off to the side as others filled their plates.

"Marshall, you're back!" Chaya exclaimed, approaching. She held a bowl of steaming food, its savory scent filling the air.

He pulled in a deep breath. "Chaya," he responded, with a nod.

"I prepared a place where we can eat together." She tipped her head toward it. "I just have to set this out," she continued, glancing at the bowl she held, "and then we can—"

"Why don't you go on without me? I've got things I need to attend to."

Looking down, she bit her lip. "Very well." She turned away, set the dish down, and then walked off.

Jerrett smirked.

"What's funny?" Marshall asked.

"Nothing's funny. Actually, it's a bit sad."

"What?"

"The way you're treating Chaya. Why such a cold shoulder, anyway?" He shook his head. "Goodness, but you've a lot to learn about women."

Marshall stood tall and squared his shoulders. "I'm just trying to do what's right by her—trying to make certain she gets to know us all."

"Oh, I see. You don't want to monopolize her time. Is that it?" Jerrett asked as Velia approached.

"Well . . . yes."

"You might tell her that, my friend."

"I couldn't agree more," Velia said, having overheard the exchange, as she approached with baby Carlow in her arms, and her and Jerrett's three other boys in tow.

"She's fine. What are you two talking about?"

Just then Mara arrived with Dixon, the twins, and Lucy. She suggested they all get their dinners, then congregate at a place she designated where Basha and Therese already sat.

A nearby campfire crackled. Sparks few into the air. At its side, Jules and Nina supervised Caden and Calandra as the children piled more sticks on top. When Calandra drew too close, Nina jumped ahead to caution her. Then she pulled her back a safe distance.

After filling their plates, Mara and her companions joined Basha and Therese. In short order, Jules joined them.

"Thank you for riding ahead, Marshall, to check on things," Mara said. "So, tell us, what did you find?" She crouched down, then sat on the ground next to Dixon, a woolen blanket spread out beneath them.

"I made good time to Ethanward. It's actually quite close, but will likely take our caravan here more than a full day to reach. In any case, I found the place overrun with children who appear homeless."

"Oh?"

"It's odd. They range in age from— Oh, I'd say, likely four, or so . . . to early teens. They appear to have no supervision. They're dirty, hungry—"

"Where are they from?"

"I've no idea. But it may explain some of those we've seen passing by our caravan of late. I tried to talk to a few of them, but they just gave me the cold shoulder."

"Not the only one doing that," Jerrett muttered near Velia's ear.

Grinning, she nudged him.

"They live on the streets?" Mara asked.

"Appears so," Marshall said. "But there's a criminal element amongst them, as well. I saw several of them picking pockets in the crowds."

"Hmmm. What of those in positions of authority?"

"Truthfully, I didn't see anyone. I did, however, notice some folks agitating the crowds in the town square—and I overheard several teens discuss their interest in going to join the ranks of the succedunt."

"Oh? They used that name?"

"No, they called them the 'descendants' just like those young women we met earlier. The young men say they want to join their fighting forces. The women seem . . . mesmerized, I suppose you'd say, over the idea of engaging with them."

When Bane howled in the distance, Jerrett jumped to his feet.

"What is it?" Velia asked.

He turned toward the sound. "I'm not sure, but he's calling me. I'll be right back." He pulled out his blade, Fortitudo.

"I wanna come too," Aden said to his father.

"No, you stay here—safe—with your mother," he said as he sprinted away.

"I'll go," Dixon offered, taking off behind his friend.

As they disappeared into the darkness, several of the other travelers finished up their meals and then headed back to their wagons and tents for the night.

Adele approached. "Would you like anything more?" she asked. "If not, we'll start packing up for morning."

"You do that," Mara said.

"Say, Adele," Marshall caught her attention, "how is Chaya working out with you?"

She shrugged and raised her brow. "She's fine. Why?"

"No reason."

Just then, Jerrett and Dixon returned with Bane at their side. The men wore scowls.

Bane sat. Then, turning his nose to the sky, he howled.

Mara got to her feet. "What is it?" she asked.

Dixon glanced Jerrett's way, then back at her. "Ahhh . . . Bane happened upon a few corpses." Grimacing, he whispered, "They were just . . . children."

She pulled back. "Fresh corpses?"

"I'd say they hadn't been there for more than a day."

"Do you know what happened to them?"

He leaned in. "Honestly, I don't know if they died of exposure, or something more sinister. We thought it best we not hang around to find out." He shrugged. "In any case, I suggest we get what we came here for, and then be on our way as quickly as possible."

"I agree," Lucy said. "Tomorrow we'll continue straight toward Ethanward and Vida's. I'll let everyone know that we need to get an early start and make good time."

<hr>

Late the next afternoon, numerous carts packed near to overflowing passed by the traveling entourage, along with the occasional party on horseback. Interspersed amongst them came a few children, dirty and disheveled, and not adequately dressed for the decidedly cool weather.

Riding at the front with Dixon, Marshall, Jerrett, and her charges, Mara brought the caravan to a halt.

"I believe that's it," she said, pointing toward a valley village in the distance. Her breath fogged in the air.

"Yes, that's Ethanward," Marshall agreed.

"It's still quite a way off, so I suggest we camp here for the night."

"Sounds good to me," Dixon said before speaking with a couple nearby Oathtaker guards, asking them to inform the other travelers of their plans.

"Oh, Reigna, can you believe it? We're almost there!" Eden exclaimed.

The twins glanced at one another, both smiling broadly.

"Soon enough, you two," Mara teased them. "Still, I can appreciate how excited you must be."

"It seems we've waited forever to meet our sisters. Finally, one of them is about to join us!" Eden said.

"There's a great deal of traffic going through this area," Mara commented, just as Chaya rode up. "Was it like this when you came this way earlier?" she asked Marshall.

He shook his head.

"Well, perhaps we should send someone ahead to determine the cause."

"I'll go," he offered.

"May I come along?" Chaya asked.

He glanced her way. "Ahhh . . . Well, it would be better for you to wait until after I've confirmed that all is safe."

Mara's eyes narrowed as she watched the exchange. Then she turned to the young woman. "Actually, I agree with Marshall. Since we're unsure of what's ahead, I think we should send a few of the trained Oathtakers in first."

Biting her lip, Chaya nodded. "Fine," she said.

"We sure could use your help getting camp set up, though."

"Yes, I've been helping Adele, at Marshall's suggestion." Her eyes darted his direction.

He cocked his head. "My suggestion? Chaya, if you'd prefer to do something else, I'm sure we can find other areas where your assistance would be appreciated. Perhaps you could help with the horses, or—"

"Never mind." She turned her mount around and headed back.

"What was that all about?" Mara asked Marshall, watching her retreat.

His eyes narrowed. "What?"

"Are you trying to avoid her or something? You've spent almost no time with her since we set out."

"Ahhh . . . no."

"Is something wrong Marshall? Is there something about Chaya that you're not telling us? Something we should know?"

"No, of course not."

She watched him closely, her eyes narrowed and her lips pursed. "Very well then," she said. "Now, please, take someone along with you. We'll expect you back by the time Adele has dinner ready."

As he rode off, Dixon and the twins approached. "What's going on?"

"That's what I'd like to know," Mara said. "He was so cold to Chaya."

"Should I ask him about it?"

She shook her head. "No, we'll just see what happens. I do wonder how she's doing, though. She looked . . . heartbroken. And really, we're all as good as strangers to her."

"I feel badly for her," Eden said. "Marshall seems so callous."

"It's very unlike him," Reigna agreed. "When the two of them first arrived in the City of Light, you never saw one of them without the other nearby. Now it's as though he avoids her."

The sound of crunching gravel sounded out, as Lucy rode up to their side. She smiled at the twins. "Well, we're almost there," she commented.

"Yes," Reigna said, "we're so excited! It's high time we met our sisters. So," she glanced out, "Vida, the eldest, is nearby. I can hardly wait to meet her!"

"Yes, but don't you wish," Eden said, "that Asmeret, Diella, Pina, Tirona and Adamina could also join us right away?"

"I sure do!"

"Don't get your hopes up too high, now," Lucy cautioned them. "Vida may not agree to join us—and we won't be passing by where any of the others live on our journey to the palace."

"She might not want to join us? I never thought of that," Reigna said. "Why wouldn't she?"

Lucy shrugged. "There's no telling. She's about ten years your senior, don't forget. She may already have a family here. Truthfully, it's some time since I last saw her."

Reigna, astride a dapple-grey mare, patted the equine's neck. "There, Breeze, that's a good girl," she said, calming it before turning Mara's way. Then, "I can hardly wait to meet her!" she exclaimed.

Mara laughed. "Let's set up camp. Tomorrow will be here soon enough."

They joined the others, raising tents, grooming horses, and preparing meals. Before long, the smell of grilling venison hung in the air.

The twins approached the meal wagon.

"Hey, Adele, dinner smells great!" Reigna said.

She blushed at the compliment. "One of your favorites tonight. I hope you enjoy it."

"Oh, we're sure to."

Eden noticed Chaya setting up a table. She approached. "Hey," she said, "I wanted to thank you for all your help."

"Certainly." She bit her lip. Clearly, she held back tears.

"Are you all right?"

"I'm fine." She refused to look Eden in the eye. "Why do you ask?"

"No reason. I just . . . You know . . . I'm glad you're with us."

Chaya uncovered a pot of mixed potatoes and vegetables that had been cooked over a campfire. "Well, that makes one of you anyway," she muttered as she turned away.

"Wait!"

She turned back.

"I'm sure Marshall doesn't mean anything . . ."

Chaya looked up and into the distance shaking her head, and then, scowling, stepped away. "Excuse me," she said.

Reigna stood at her sister's side. "Do you suppose they argued over something?"

"I've no idea."

"Oh, look! Here he comes now."

Marshall rode up on a fine mahogany gelding, its heaving breath billowing in the cold air. He got down, then turned to the girls. "Just in time for dinner, I see," he said. Then, upon looking about, noticing Chaya nearby, he started off in the opposite direction.

"Marshall, wait!" Eden called. She ran to his side and then, clutching his arm, asked, "Are you all right?"

"Sure. Why wouldn't I be?"

She shuffled her feet as she glanced Chaya's way. "Nothing. Never mind."

Just then, Mara approached. "Oh, Marshall, good. I'm glad you're back. Did you find anything particularly concerning?"

"Nothing more than what I reported the other day."

"Good." She turned to the twins. "It'll soon be dark. We should all eat and then get down early so that we can get another good start tomorrow morning."

Graced with a clear morning and what promised to be a more tepid late autumn day than the past few had been, the caravan set off early, with Marshall, Jerrett, and Velia, in the lead. The twins, Mara, Dixon, and Lucy, followed immediately behind.

They skirted the edges of a swamp. Tall grasses waved in the breeze, and cattails showed off their furry brown cylindrical heads from which seed tuffs billowed out. Mara, enjoying the beauty of the place, imagined the classic *conk-la-ree* ending in a musical trill that its seasonal resident red-winged blackbirds would make there. In her mind, she could hear the scolding *chak chak chak* of the females of the species alarming their kind, along with the interspersed rattling of a flock of sandhill crane. Unfortunately, both varieties had already made their way south for warmer climates.

Beyond the swamp, they traveled in silence for some time. The twins seemed to have turned introspective, as each looked forward to meeting, for the first time, the eldest of their six other sisters.

Soon they passed through the town gates and came to a stop at a house just inside of them. Built of logs, its sturdy presence suggested that someone cared well for it. Herb gardens sidled up near the front entrance. The stalks and leaves of some of the plants had already turned brown. Still, the dusty scent of sage, and the savory aroma of thyme, filled the air. When the first freezing nights came, they too, would die away, then await a spring rebirth.

From around the side of the residence, children came running, laughing, and chasing one another, before disappearing once again behind the building.

A low cloud cover seemed to swirl in the air. The phenomenon cast an ethereal look and feel to the place.

Lucy turned to the twins. "Are you ready?"

In quiet anticipation, they nodded.

Then Lucy addressed Mara. "I suggest that you and Dixon, the girls, and I, go ahead."

"Agreed."

The five dismounted.

Reigna brushed bits of hay from her clothing, while Eden tucked a few unruly sprigs of her light auburn hair behind her ear. Then they set out behind Lucy, to the front door.

Once there, she stood silent, glancing at the twins and nodding, before taking in a deep breath and then knocking.

Voices from inside came faintly, then gradually increased in volume. In short order, someone peeked out of the window situated just to the side. Then the door opened to reveal a woman with a handful of children about her.

Smiling, Lucy put her arms out. "Clarimonde, it has been too, too long."

The woman embraced her with enthusiasm. Bright eyed, and with a pert and winsome smile, she wore her curled red tresses tied up with a leather band. Pulling back, she patted her hair.

"Oh, Lucy, I am so happy to see you!" She embraced her old friend once again. "You are so right. It has been some years since you last visited."

"Upwards of a decade, I'd say."

Clarimonde glanced at the twins at Lucy's side. She drew her hand to her mouth. "Oh, gracious! It's them, isn't it?" she asked, her dark brown eyes sparkling. "The twins. Why, they look just like Rowena!"

Lucy chuckled. "Yes, these are Rowena's twins." She motioned for the girls to step up and then introduced them.

"Oh, my," Clarimonde gasped, "Oh my! It seems like I've waited forever to meet you two! And that says nothing of how your sister, Vida, has been feeling." She turned to the youngsters gathered around her, and then addressed one of them. "Wade, please, run get Vida."

The boy raced off, clearly anxious to do her bidding.

Mara stepped up and introduced herself.

Finally, Dixon approached.

"Dixon!" Clarimonde exclaimed. "Oh, Dixon!" She threw her arms around him. "It's so good to see you!"

"Clarimonde, I've missed you," he said with a smile as he returned her embrace. "We all have. Ever since you left with Vida, it's been as though one of the most important of our ranks has been missing."

She blushed. "Oh, please, do come in," she said. Then, glancing out, she noticed the caravan. She turned questioning eyes to Lucy.

"We're all moving back to the palace," she offered.

"Oh, I see." Clarimonde bit her lip.

"We're intending, of course, that you and Vida will join us," Reigna said.

Her brow rose. "Well, now, that might prove difficult."

"Oh?"

"Come in. Come in," she urged them all forward. "We'll explain everything."

At that moment, a woman entered. Taller than average, she gasped upon sight of the twins.

"Vida," Clarimonde urged her forward with a wave of her hand, "we have visitors. This is Lucy—who you might remember," she said, tipping her head in her direction, "although it has been some time since you've seen her."

"Yes, of course, I remember Lucy." As Vida approached, filling the air with her unique scent of the Select—an energetic combination of smells reminiscent of grapefruit, blood orange, jasmine, cedar, and iris—she nodded at her visitors.

"And this is Mara, and Dixon," Clarimonde added, gesturing toward each of them, in turn. "Dixon and I have known each other since we were children." She laughed as she glanced his way, as though silently sharing comical memories. "And at long last, your sisters, Reigna and Eden," she added, tipping her head in their direction, "to whom Mara is Oathtaker."

The twins stepped up. Somewhat awkwardly, Reigna approached her sister, and then embraced her.

Vida accepted the greeting, visibly taking in her sister's scent, and then pulled back. Smiling, her eyes brimmed with tears.

"Goodness, I don't remember Mother all that well—but I know this," she said, her gaze skipping from Reigna to Eden, "you two are her spitting image."

"They are," Dixon said, "but for their hair color, which is a bit lighter than Rowena's was—and of course, the color of their eyes."

"You remember Mother?" Eden asked.

Vida hugged, then released, her. "I do. Just barely, but I do." She grinned. "In truth, your scents remind me a bit of her—and as you no doubt know, smell is a powerful memory trigger."

The twins turned to Lucy, each with a question in her eyes.

"A couple of the oldest were with Rowena for a short time," she explained. "As the firstborn, Vida, of course, spent the most time with your mother, and is the most likely to remember anything of her. When she was about . . . What do you think, Vida? About four?"

"Yes, that's right."

"By the time she was about four," Lucy continued, "things had become terribly dangerous for the Select in Oosa. That's when Rowena decided to send all the children then living at the palace, away. Her sister, Eve, had one child, and Dianna had two." She paused momentarily, in thought. "And, as I recall, in addition to

Vida, your sisters, Asmeret and Diella, had been born by then. An Oathtaker had sworn to the safety of each of them upon birth, so that matter was resolved.

"The Oathtakers then took their charges away to predetermined places for their safety. Later, when your mother bore each of your other sisters, and after an Oathtaker had sworn to that newborn's safety, your mother arranged for that child to be taken away, as well."

"You've never really told us where they all are, Lucy," Eden said.

"There is one residing in all but one of Ocsa's seven provinces, although their specific whereabouts are kept secret. Your mother's plan—her hope all along—was that, whatever else happened, at least one of you would survive and come to power one day." She smiled at the twins. "And now, you two have."

Clarimonde stepped away. "Please, everyone, let me put the tea on."

Soon, they were all gathered around a heavy oak kitchen table. Lucy tapped on its surface as Clarimonde set down a tray of tea and fixings. "This is different from the one you used to have," she commented.

"Yes, we needed a larger table for all of the children."

"We saw some of them outside in the yard Who are they?"

Glancing at her charge, Clarimonde asked her, "Would you like to explain?"

Vida grinned. "You might say that they are my charges."

Her eyes narrowed, Lucy reached for the pot of tea, filled her cup, and then passed it to Mara who sat to her left. "A member of the Select with charges? Ahhh . . . I don't understand."

"Well, over the past few years, Ethanward has been flooded with orphaned children. I grew weary of seeing them hungry and ill kept. So Clarimonde and I turned this place into a refuge for them."

"I see."

"But, Vida," Reigna interrupted, "we're hoping you'll come to the palace with us. What will become of them then?"

Vida's brow rose. "I'm not leaving the children."

The twins glanced at Mara and Dixon, and then turned Lucy's way.

"But she has to come," Eden said.

"She is free to do as she chooses, girls. I told you not to get your hopes up," Lucy said.

Reigna addressed Vida. "Can't someone else care for them so that you can join us?"

"I'm sorry, I'm—well, that is, Clarimonde and I—are all they've got."

"But—"

"I'm sorry," Vida repeated.

Mara sat up straighter. She put her teacup down. "Clarimonde, we found the bodies of some dead children on our way here. What might you know of that?"

She rose to her feet. "Dead? Oh, goodness, such a tragedy." Slowly, she sat back down.

"Yes. Have you any idea what might have happened? What's going on around these parts?"

Vida sighed. "I wish I'd known about those you found. Perhaps we could have . . . Well, all I can tell you is that we've seen to the needs of many young ones over the past few years. I guess word has spread that they'll be safe here. Often they arrive nearly on death's door."

"So, do you think those we found may have been on their way here?"

She shrugged. "It's possible. Or, to be more accurate, it's likely."

"Is that a good idea, do you think?" Dixon interrupted. "To encourage the children to come this way? The dangers out there—"

"What else can we do?" Vida asked. "At least they've some chance of survival if they make their way here."

"I see," Mara said, looking down. She bit her lip, then glanced up again. "Well, if it weren't for the children, Vida, would you agree to go to Shimeron with us?"

"Sure. I mean, I suppose."

"Then I think I've got the solution."

The twins turned Mara's way.

"What's that?" Eden asked.

"I suggest we take them all with us," she said.

"But . . . what would we do with them all?" Lucy asked.

Reigna sat up straighter. "They'll stay with us at the palace," she said.

"I agree," Eden added.

"Girls," Lucy cautioned, "we've not the resources to care for orphans."

"But we'd have Vida and Clarimonde—and they've already been caring for them. What else do we need?"

"Wait," Vida interrupted, "there are more than thirty with us now, and new ones arrive regularly. If we leave, there'd be no one left for them here."

Mara stood and walked to a window overlooking the yard. Several children ran and chased one another. The eldest appeared not more than ten years old, the youngest, likely about four. One of the older girls stood off to the side helping a little one, brushing dirt from her scraped knee.

She turned back to the group. "I suggest we leave a couple Oathtakers here in the event more show up," she said. She paused, cocking her head. "Vida, where are they all coming from? The children, I mean? And what drives them here?"

"Most are from this province, a few from farther out. Some are children whose parents have abandoned them. Then, of course, there are those who've made their way here from Chiran."

"Oh?"

"They are refugees."

"I see." Mara turned Dixon's way. "Perhaps Chaya, a Chiranian herself, would like to help with the children when we get to the palace." Then she addressed Vida again. "Would you be willing to go if we took the children with us and left someone here for those who might arrive later? They could get them to the palace, or to some other place of safety."

"Please," Reigna urged.

Grinning at her sister, Vida nodded her agreement.

Chapter Six

After Lucy and Dixon had traveled to, and had then dropped Liam and Rafal off with Ezra at, The Clandest Inn in the City of Light, the men had met with Adli, a former Chiranian who'd turned to Ehyeh years back. Now he assisted others in their efforts against Zarek. From him, the Oathtakers got themselves two sets of forged documents. The first provided that they'd been sent into Oosa on a special mission for Zarek. The second assigned them positions as messengers who would travel regularly between the city of Fallique, where the emperor's palace sat, and Darth, the town to which Marshall and Jerrett had traveled earlier.

Now, having arrived at the border, Liam dismounted. He swept back his shoulder-length dark hair and tied it up with a leather cord. Then he fastened the reins of the gelding he rode next to Rafal's horse before joining his comrade who hid in a tangle of shrubbery encircling an oak grove.

The smell of damp and rotting leaves filled the air.

"Guards?" he asked.

Rafal nodded. "Yes. Zarek's army must be vast to have such numbers available to do nothing but watch the border."

When a crow's scolding caw sounded out, Liam jumped. "Blasted birds," he commented. He motioned that he intended to move closer, but before he did, his cohort caught his arm and with a roll of his eyes, pointed out more men.

"Why are there so many here, do you suppose?" Liam whispered. "Do they actually fear others will try to enter Chiran?"

Rafal pondered. "Perhaps they simply fear that more of their own will try to leave," he said.

Just above them, a crow landed. Staring at the Oathtakers, it flapped its wings and cackled menacingly—maniacally, even.

Suppressing a shudder, Liam grabbed Rafal's wrist. "Our papers should get us in without fuss. Let's go."

As they turned back toward their mounts, a band of four regular Chiranian guards, recognizable by their disheveled appearance and varied weapons, met them. Two more men, outfitted entirely in black, flanked them. These men had wrapped their heads in black cloths, leaving only narrow openings for their eyes.

One carried a black flag upon which was the semblance of a human skull with snakes crawling through its eye sockets.

Liam sucked in a deep breath.

"What are you doing here?" one of the men in black demanded to know as he neared.

"We just noticed the commotion and wondered what was going on," Liam said. "This is the border between Chiran and Oosa, is it not?"

"It is." The man held a knife with an ugly serrated blade. "You've got one chance to turn back, or you'll become prisoners of Zarek."

Rafal raised his hands. "Wait. We have our orders. Here—"

"No sudden moves."

The Oathtaker reached into a pocket of his tunic and drew out a document that Adli had forged for him.

Liam followed suit.

With a tip of his head, the man in black ordered them to approach.

They did, and then handed over their papers.

"What are you doing slinking around here?"

"The troops surprised us, is all. The border wasn't so closely guarded when we left on our mission."

The man perused their documents. Once done, he returned them.

"Get on your way then," he ordered.

Slowly, Liam and Rafal turned away.

They both mounted. Then, side-by-side, they rode over the border and into Chiran.

After riding for days through the barren countryside, Liam and Rafal finally arrived at Darth. They knew a bit about the camp from Marshall and Jerrett. Still, they could tell things had changed since their cohorts' departure, likely as a result of the death of Cark, its former leader.

They entered the grounds amidst a flurry of activity. Men in training rushed about, shouting. Horses neighing, fires crackling, and the sounds of metal-on-metal as soldiers trained, filled the air. Guards, all dressed in black, like some of those the Oathtakers had seen at the border, kept a close eye on events. Soon, the Oathtakers learned that they were known as "succedunt" soldiers.

Approaching a building someone had pointed out to them earlier as the check-in point, Liam and Rafal watched on as several young men ushered a group of crying and hysterical young women to a building. Liam estimated they ranged in age from their mid-teens, to their early thirties. Nearby soldiers stared as they passed by. Some hooted. Others called out threats their way.

When a boy rushed toward the Oathtakers, a knife in hand, they halted.

The child stopped, just feet away, and made a face at them. "Who are you?" he growled.

Liam waved his hand at him. "Go about your business, little one."

"Little one!" He ducked his head and charged, weapon first.

Rafal grabbed the youngster's tunic before he could make contact with his companion and whipped him about. Then he clutched the boy's wrist and twisted.

"Hold it there. What's this all about?" he asked as the child's knife dropped to the ground.

"There, ya see?" came the gruff voice of a man approaching. "Go on, now," he ordered the young one.

The boy grimaced on sight of the newcomer, then reached down for his weapon. When Rafal stepped on its blade, he looked up at the Oathtaker and growled again.

"Ha ha ha!" the man who neared them all, laughed. "Well, I'll give ya points for yer efforts, Odin. Now, git 'long wi' cha."

When Rafal refused to let the child's weapon loose, he huffed, then shuffled away.

The man watched him retreat, a smile on his face, then turned back to the Oathtakers. "He's a good 'un. Jus' too anxious tuh be a warrior."

"He's nothing but a child," Liam said.

The man's eyes narrowed. "Where ya from?"

"We've just returned from a mission into Oosa," Rafal said. "We came here because our next stop was to bring messages to Zarek. We heard he was here."

The man watched him closely, as though measuring his words. "Huh. Well, he was here. He came tuh o'rsee the openin' of the new quarters for the slave wimmen, but he left some weeks back."

"I see."

"He has us trainin' the boys."

"Oh?"

"Zarek says we can't start 'em too young. But, Odin . . ." He looked back in the direction in which the child had gone. "Like I said, he's a bit too anxious." He turned back. "Now, are ya off 'gain right away then? Or will ya be stayin' here for a time?"

Liam and Rafal shared a glance.

"We heard Zarek visited here with an entire entourage. Did they all head back to Fallique with him?" Liam asked.

"Most of 'em . . . though Brother Pestifere set off 'fore 'im on some journey of 'is own. I don't recall that he said where he 'as headed."

"And Zarek's son? We heard he accompanied the emperor, as well."

"Yeah, he 'as 'ere."

"What was he like?" Rafal asked.

The man shrugged. "Can't rightly say. Didn't see much of 'im m'self."

"I see." Liam shuffled his foot in the sand. "Well," he said to his cohort, "I guess we'd best continue on our way to Fallique, then. We've a report to make."

"Agreed."

With that, he and Rafal set off.

Chapter Seven

A single candle burned, its light flickering, creating dancing shadows on the walls. The room was bathed in quiet, but for some sniffling sounds. Around a table sat Broden on one side, with the woman he called "Mouse" to his left. The man he'd chosen as his tutor upon arriving in Chiran, Striver, sat at his other side. Broden's other slave women stood nearby.

The tutor opened his mouth as though to speak, but then closed it again. He sighed.

"There's nothing I can do," Broden said, holding his gaze.

"But, master, Ghazala is my sister!" Farida, one of the slave women present, cried.

"What would you have me do?" Broden held his hands out, palms up.

"Save her! I would have that you save her!"

Yasmin, the other slave woman, put her arm around Farida as she, once again, burst into tears. She stared at Broden all the while.

"Oh, I don't know why you would expect him to do anything to help," she said. "After all, they're all alike, you know."

Broden ground his teeth. "No, Yasmin, that's not so."

"Then do something," she snarled at him.

Mouse grabbed Broden's arm. "Surely, there's something . . ."

He sighed. "You're the only one over whom Zarek has given me full authority, Mouse. If I try to help Ghazala, I may put Yasmin and Farida in danger."

"But things have improved for you since Brother Pestifere set off on his journey, haven't they?"

Tapping his fingers on the table, Broden nodded. "I suppose, somewhat," he conceded.

"Then use that to your advantage—before he returns," Mouse urged.

Standing, Broden rubbed the back of his neck, a gesture common to him when he was confused or frustrated. Then he glanced up at the ceiling as though seeking inspiration. Sighing, he once again looked Striver's way.

"You think that's possible?" he asked him.

"Perhaps you could ask your father to put you to use," Striver suggested. "What if you told him that you're weary of studying and want to . . . I don't know . . . prove yourself. Be of service to him."

"But he doesn't trust me yet."

"Still, you could try."

"You mean, suggest that I work with the slave traders or something?"

"Maybe. Or . . . What if you asked him to put you in charge of those endeavors?"

"Of the slave women? You mean, as they're brought in?"

"Why not? Offer to prepare them for further shipment."

Broden sat back down, folded his hands, and then rested them on the table. "I may have an idea," he said. "Still . . ."

"I want you to save my sister before she's sent away with the other slaves. Please, master!" Farida cried, sensing a weakness in his resolve. "Please, at least try."

Mouse patted his hand. "Surely, there would be no harm in trying," she suggested.

He nodded. "I guess." He turned to Yasmin and Farida. "But you must understand that if I do this, and if anything goes wrong, Zarek may take the two of you from me. I've already managed to make an enemy of Pestifere—"

"*Brother* Pestifere," Striver corrected him.

"Yes, *Brother* Pestifere," he repeated. "In any case, if anything goes wrong—"

"That's a risk I'm willing to take," Farida said, holding his gaze.

"I understand that. But you need to consider that the price for the risk you're willing to take, may be the safety or security of someone else." Then he addressed Yasmin. "And what about you?"

She grimaced. "I guess. I mean . . ." She looked at her friend. "I'd want someone to do the same for me and for mine."

"Very well then," Broden said. "I'll try."

He marched down the corridor toward his father's quarters, wringing his clammy hands even while reminding himself to stay calm. His heels *click-clacked* on the hardwood floor, seemingly keeping rhythm to his wildly beating heart.

Guards stood stationed every few feet along the hallway. As he passed them, endeavoring to portray a sense of confidence, he held his head high and his shoulders back. His arms swung freely at his sides.

Just before reaching the door that he sought, a succedunt soldier seemed to appear from out of nowhere. He held a thick chain. Attached at its other end, was what was unmistakably an underworld beast—a grut. Smoky black hair covered the creature, which sported a spiky spine and a razor sharp tail. Greasy black mucus oozed from its bulging red eyes, and its rank smell—the smell of death and decay—filled the air.

The sight shocked Broden, who'd never seen one before. Still, he recognized it for what it was, on sight. Stopping in his tracks, he took note of the spiked, heavy metal collar around its neck.

In that same instant, the beast lunged, displaying its three rows of teeth, curved slightly inward.

Broden jumped back—almost too late. Looking down, he found a tear in his pants on his inner thigh, just inches from his privates. Shocked, he looked back at the guard as he pulled on the grut's chain, causing the spikes on the beast's collar to bite into its hide. Drops of thick black blood seeped from punctures they made, ran down the grut's coarse, steel bristle brush-like hair, and then dribbled to the floor, where they steamed.

The beast's eyes seemed to pierce into Broden as it stood, prepared to attack again, and stared, its hackles up.

Broden took another step back. Then he crossed his arms and pulled himself to his full height. Fortunately, he was able to look down at the man with the grut, who was shorter than he. This one, like all the men in black who'd recently descended upon Zarek's palace, unnerved him, but the beast was of even greater concern. A single drop of its blood or saliva on his skin would mean certain death.

He vowed he'd show no fear. "Let me pass," he ordered.

The man's full expression could not be seen through the black wrapping around his head. Only his eyes were visible. They sparkled. "Oh? Where are you headed?" he asked, a taunting smile in his voice.

"To see my father—Zarek."

"He's not expecting you."

"No, he's not."

The man seemed to take his measure. "Wait here."

He turned away and entered the room.

Broden bit his lip. He didn't want to invite trouble, but more than that, he didn't want Zarek's men, succedunt or not, to think they could order him about. So, with a deep breath, he grabbed the door handle, flung it open, and then boldly marched inside.

Immediately, the grut, growling, lurched. Coming within feet of him, it pulled on its chain. Its claws scratched on the floor.

Meanwhile, a guard grabbed Broden from behind and then wrapped an arm around his neck in a vise-like grip while holding, in his other hand, a knife at his throat. Its blade glittered in the lamplight.

His eyes wide, Broden struggled to release his captor's hold.

The knife came closer, grazing his skin. A trickle of blood dribbled down his neck.

"That's enough," someone ordered.

Broden's eyes flashed up to find Zarek sitting, a grin on his face.

"Ha ha ha!" The gold and silver chains that the emperor wore jingled as he guffawed. "Oh, but I do appreciate your spirit."

When the man in black loosened his grip, Broden pushed him off. Then he shook himself. Grabbing the sides of his vest and straightening up, he turned to the guard with the grut and glared at him.

"Take the beast away," Zarek ordered the man.

Grinding his teeth, Broden turned to face his father. "Why the grut?" he asked.

"Just extra precautions that I've put into place here at the palace."

"Precautions? Against what?"

He grinned, but said nothing.

"Huh. Well, you've been hard to connect with since our return from Darth. I decided I'd wait no longer."

"Oh?" Zarek chuckled.

"There's a matter of importance I'd like to discuss with you."

The emperor sat back and slouched, nonchalantly. "And what matter is that?" His melodious baritone voice seemed to reverberate off the walls.

Once again, Broden glared at the man who'd attacked him before his eyes flickered back toward his father.

"I'd prefer to discuss it with you in private," he said.

With a grin and a shake of his head, Zarek waved his hand toward those in attendance, four regular guards, and two succedunt soldiers. One by one, they turned away and exited through a back door.

"What's on your mind then?" he asked.

Biting the inside of his cheek, Broden approached. Then, recollecting that he didn't want to portray any weakness, he clamped his jaw tight, squared his shoulders, and looked his father in the eye.

"I'm tired of wasting time, of studying and being of no use to anyone," he said. "I'd like an assignment, and I've got just the one in mind."

"Brother Pestifere said I was not to trust you."

"Brother Pestifere!" Broden scoffed. "Because I question him, because I insist on answers to my queries, he belittles me." His eyes held his father's gaze. "But you are different. You can appreciate that I cannot make firm decisions without first possessing all the pertinent information."

"Oh? You know me so well then?"

"I know what I see."

"And what is that?"

"I see a man of power. I see a man who doesn't accept things for what they seem, but for what they are. To do that, you must satisfy yourself that you have the necessary information before acting in any given situation. You don't take things at face value. You— You prod at them," Broden said, gesturing as though plunging a knife.

"Your flattery is—"

"I'm not flattering you," he interrupted. "I'm stating facts. Just because a statement is complimentary, doesn't mean it's insincere."

Zarek's brow rose. He appeared to be stifling a grin. "Are you ready to make your decision then? To swear your allegiance to Daeva and the lords of the underworld?"

Broden rubbed the back of his neck, hesitating. "No, I am not," he said. "As I mentioned, I've still got questions."

"Yet you think you might be of service to me. Well, I think not." Zarek rose.

"Let me show you. Perhaps, in working for you, I might happen upon—"

"I need to be able to trust those who surround me," his father interrupted. "That's why I require that you study *Serving Daeva*. From it, you will learn all you need to be of service to me."

Broden took another step forward. "I am studying. Now, let me show you how I can be of service."

Zarek stared at his son. "What have you in mind?"

Sensing an opening in the man's resolve, Broden nearly grinned. "I want to be put in charge of the slave program."

Zarek pulled back. His eyes narrowed. "Of the women?"

"Yes."

He scoffed. "Why would I trust you with them? I don't even trust my regular guards with them. That's one of the reasons the succedunt—"

"Excuse me," Broden interrupted, "but who are these men in black anyway? These 'succedunt' guards? Where did they come from?"

"Perhaps if you studied a bit more, you'd learn the answers to your questions on your own." Zarek stepped away. "They are an elite guard. They are—like me—descendants of the Hazarik."

"Ahhh, yes . . . Brother Pestifere did mention them once. So, will I learn more of them from *Serving Daeva*?"

Zarek chuckled. "No, but you will learn of their origins."

"I see."

"Brother Pestifere will teach you the remainder of what you need to know of the succedunt, in due time."

"Very well." Broden shuffled his feet. "Is there some reason there are so many of them here now? I didn't see any of them before we left for our journey. But since our return, they're everywhere."

"They're overseeing massive changes for me here, in Chiran." Zarek resumed his seat. "So, about this position you seek . . ."

"Yes?"

"I say we should try it out. The succedunt soldiers will oversee you. They'll report to me anything you might try that is out of the ordinary."

"Excellent. Now, about changes I'll need to make—"

"Yes?" Zarek asked, grinning. Then, "Oh, never mind," he said, waving his hand. "You go about your business any way you see fit, and I'll get my reports as and when necessary."

"I will need the services of some of the women to do my job."

"Like I said, 'you go about your business any way you see fit.'"

Broden fought to hold back his grin. "Very well," he said.

Just then, the door opened.

Looking up, Broden immediately cautioned himself against showing any reaction—as there stood Brother Pestifere, himself.

As usual, Pestifere was clad in a robe with a belt of braided hemp about his waist. Also, as usual, his feet, dirty and with long yellow nails, were bare. His staff clacked on the floor as he entered.

Broden could smell the man, as he reeked of burned incense, old sweat, and dried blood, resulting from his self-flagellations. His heart pounded at the thought of having to bear the priest's presence once again. He'd known respite since Pestifere had left the group, back when Zarek returned from Darth with the entourage that had traveled there to oversee the opening of a women's brothel of slaves for the soldier's benefit. But now, it seemed, Broden's nightmares would return.

Still, if I could make peace . . .

He tipped his head at the priest in acknowledgement.

Pestifere scowled. Then he bowed toward Zarek. "I have returned."

The emperor smiled broadly. "Ahhhh, yes, so I see. And none too soon." He approached his chief advisor.

"Oh?" Pestifere responded.

"Well, it seems that my son," Zarek motioned with an uplifted hand in his direction, "seeks to be of service."

The priest's eyes flickered from him, to Broden, and then back again. "Oh?" he repeated.

Broden stepped forward. "Welcome back, Brother Pestifere."

He growled in response.

"Yes, he thinks I ought to put him to use." Zarek said.

He looped his arm through Pestifere's and guided him toward a table. After pulling a chair out for him, he sat to his side.

"I've decided to give it a try. As a matter of fact, we were just discussing plans when you arrived."

"I advise against—"

"How was your journey?" Broden asked as he approached, cutting him off.

Scowling, the priest ignored him. "As I was saying before being so rudely interrupted, I advise against that." He held the emperor's gaze.

Zarek laughed. "I've taken your thoughts into consideration, Brother Pestifere, but it seems that Broden has made a compelling case on his own behalf."

The priest's brow rose. His lips pursed.

"Brother Pestifere, as you know, I have questions," Broden said. When the man appeared about to interrupt, he continued. "I know that fact troubles you. But as I've explained to my father, I need all the relevant facts before—"

"You need nothing!" Pestifere seethed between clenched teeth as he jumped to his feet. Unsteady, he grabbed the edge of the table and turned back to Zarek. "You know my position on this."

"Yes . . . Yes, I do. But as I said, Broden has made a case for himself."

A young servant woman entered the room. Lightly clad, she carried a tray upon which sat a carafe, one brass drinking vessel, two of stoneware, and a small wooden mug. Behind her came a boy, not more than ten years old. She poured some wine from the carafe into the wooden mug and handed it to the child.

Broden watched closely, then looked at his father. "You have children testing your drinks now?"

Zarek scowled. "It's one way to put the little ruffians to use."

"But—"

"Perhaps Brother Pestifere is right after all," he said, leaning back. "You ask too many questions. Maybe . . ."

Broden's jaw dropped. He held up a hand. "I just . . . was surprised, that's all."

"The succedunt have rightly reminded me that there is a service that may be performed by even the least amongst the masses," Zarek said. "Can you think of anything else that these vagabond, orphaned children might do to be of assistance?" When no response came, he shook his head. "I thought not. In truth, I've grown weary of their begging at the palace gates."

Recognizing that this was not a battle he would likely win, Broden conceded it without further argument.

Inhaling deeply, Zarek turned back to the priest. "Broden will be in charge of the slave program," he said.

"I see."

"He's explained to me his desire for understanding. In truth, I can appreciate his position. Let's not forget that I had years of instruction and guidance before I swore to Daeva and later, came to power."

Pestifere glared at Broden.

"So, effective immediately, he'll oversee the program," Zarek said, "and the succedunt will oversee him."

The priest broke into a slow, malicious smile. "Perhaps you are right after all."

Broden trudged back to his quarters. Upon arrival, he pushed the attending guard aside without a word. Then he entered.

"Master!" Farida jumped up to meet him.

"It's done," he said.

"Oh, Master Broden!" She dropped to her knees before him, grabbed his hands, and smothered them with kisses.

He pulled free of her. "Don't thank me. I've done nothing yet. I'm to oversee the women, but the succedunt will oversee me." He paused, rubbing the back of his neck. "But Zarek did give me authority to see to my mission without interference, so I'm on my way shortly to get Ghazala released from the group that was prepared for shipment."

Yasmin approached, her head bowed. "Master, I should not have lashed out earlier. I had no right. You should punish me."

He looked at her, his eyes wide. "Really, Yasmin? Is that what I should do?"

"Yes, Master Broden."

"Have you ever known me to do that?"

She opened her mouth as though to speak, then clamped it shut.

"Forget it. Now, go! The both of you."

She and Farida shared a glance, then looked toward Striver and Mouse before heading to their room.

"Pestifere is back," Broden said to no one in particular.

"Broth—"

"Never mind!" he scolded his tutor. "I know his name: *Brother* Pestifere!" He seethed. "In any case, he's back." Then, looking back at Yasmin and Farida, still present, he gestured toward their room. "Go!" he repeated his order.

When they'd retreated to the room they shared with Mouse and closed the door behind, he turned back.

Mouse approached. She put her arms around him. "You did right, Broden. Maybe you can help."

"I need to get you out of here, Carlie."

"Come on, Broden, let's go for a walk," Striver said. "Some brisk cool air will clear your mind."

He shook his head. "Perhaps later. For now, I need to speak with the two of you and we can't risk being overheard." He growled. "Oh, I cannot tolerate that man! He makes my head ache and my skin crawl." He shuddered.

"Broden—" Striver started.

"I know. I know!" He took in a deep breath and let it out slowly. He ran his hand over the top of his head and down to the back of his neck. "I just— I don't understand why he didn't seek me out, why he didn't take Carlie—err, 'Mouse,' that is—along with him."

"You mean your friend from Oosa?"

"Maybe it wasn't him you saw," Carlie said. "Surely, Jerrett wouldn't have left you behind in Darth if he knew . . ."

He hung his head. "No, it was him. We've been over this. I walked out for a breath of fresh air and I saw Jerrett in the distance. I know it was him. I'd recognize his outline, his dress, his gait, anywhere. Like I told you before, I chased behind, but . . ." He growled again.

"Pestifere had been watching me, and he'd followed me. Shortly before arriving at Cark's home, he caught up with me. I know that's where Jerrett was headed because the next day, we learned of the two dead guards found there, and a short while later, of that tunnel from Cark's home that someone had blown up. It had to have been Jerrett that did it—and I'm sure he used a crystal to destroy the place."

"But if he knew you were there, why would he leave you behind?" Striver asked. "It doesn't make sense."

Broden closed his eyes. "I fear he may have seen enough to have jumped to the wrong conclusion."

"He wouldn't have," Carlie said. "He knows you."

"I would have thought he'd believe in me." Broden shook his head. Then he glanced her way. "Still, you have to admit, it didn't look good with me being here. He must have known that I'd brought the great sword along. Zarek wielded it when we first arrived in Darth, when he addressed the crowd. Remember? What's more, Jerrett wasn't at the compound when I was taken, so . . . what else could he conclude?"

He turned to Striver. "And from everything you told me about the man who came to check things out—the man who called himself 'Jabari'— Well, what you told him may well have convinced him that I was loyal to Zarek. Moreover, he had to know it was Carlie who was with me. I'd always called her 'Mouse.'"

She embraced him yet again. "But he wouldn't have left *me* here, Broden."

"No? Even if he thought we might have planned something together?"

She pulled back. Tears sprang to her eyes. "No!" she cried, covering her mouth with her hand.

"No, you're right. He'd never doubt you." Once again, he ran his hand over the top of his head.

Weeping now, she buried her head in his shoulder.

"It's going to be all right, Mouse," he said, pulling her back into his embrace. I'm going to get you out of here, whatever it takes. But for now, I'm off to do what I can about Farida's sister, Ghazala."

Chapter Eight

After having left behind a handful of Oathtakers in the event that more orphaned children showed up at Vida and Clarimonde's home in Ethanward, the traveling entourage of Oathtakers and Select finally arrived in Shimeron. Bernard, a longtime doorman at the palace, and the only person who'd resided there for some years, was delighted with their arrival.

It was fortunate that Basha and Therese had visited the palace fairly recently and that they'd cleaned much of it, preparing for the day the twins might eventually move there. Even so, it took days to unpack and to rearrange things so as to accommodate some of the former compound residents.

In the end, they found room in the palace for all of the members of the Select who had made the trip, and their Oathtakers, as well as for Vida, Clarimonde, and their children. With the exception of some household staff, the remaining people who'd traveled with them to Shimeron—for the most part, Oathtakers without living charges—set up camp on the palace grounds. There they'd remain until they could construct more buildings, or make other plans.

The youngsters' rough and tumble shenanigans, both inside the palace and without, had kept everyone's spirits high over the past days. On her way to the kitchens, Lucy marched past a number of them who were on their way out to the grounds to play. Nearby, Bane sat, panting, with his tail thumping on the floor, and with his tongue hanging out.

A minute later, she stood before the larder, scanning its contents.

"May I help you?" Adele asked, approaching from behind.

"I'm looking for the peppermint tea. Erin was sick all last night," she said, referring to Nina's sister who generally watched her and Jules's children, and sometimes, Velia and Jerrett's boys. "And Mara's not feeling herself, either."

"Oh, no! Is it anything serious, do you think?"

"Not really. But I thought I might bring each of Erin and Mara something to settle her stomach. What's more, a number of the children have been unwell." She glanced at Adele. "When not assisting Erin, I helped Clarimonde and Vida with them most of last night after designating one of the rooms next to their suite for use as an infirmary." She frowned. "Who knows what diseases those children have introduced us all to? Gracious Ehyeh!"

"What are their symptoms?"

"Just coughs and low fevers for some, and nausea, for others."

"Can't someone just . . . you know—heal them?"

Lucy chuckled. "I suppose it's possible, Adele, but there are so many of them, and frankly, we need the energies of the Oathtakers elsewhere just now." She paused, cocking her head. "Also, I've found that people who're allowed some sickness when they are young seem better able to resist illnesses as they grow older. And considering that a healer is not always present, I prefer to err on the side of letting nature take its course."

"That's interesting."

"Yes. In any case, I've told Erin not to watch Nina or Velia's children until she's well again. I'd hate to see them catch something—not to mention the twins. Imagine having gone through all we have, only to end up with the two of them sick—or worse—and at a time like this when we've need of them performing at their peak. Still, taking the children along meant that Vida would join us."

She stopped suddenly, her lips pursed, thinking. Then, "Adele," she said, "why don't you make up a large batch of catswort tea? Perhaps we can nip this illness in the bud."

She turned and walked to a window overlooking the back yard, motioning with a wave of her hand for Adele to follow.

"I saw some old sage plants and rosemary bushes just . . . there," she said, pointing. "Fortunately, the temperature hasn't dropped low enough here to freeze them out just yet. So we should prepare some for smudging in each of the rooms." She glanced back at Adele. "Do you know how to do that?"

"Sure. I'll just tie up together, sprigs of them, put a bundle in a bowl in each room, and then light them all."

"Perfect." Lucy returned to the cupboard and rummaged through the items again. "Goodness, but this all needs some organizing," she muttered.

"Yes," Adele agreed.

"Oh," she said, grabbing a bag of tea tied closed with a leather strand, "here it is." She opened it and sniffed at it, then looked at Adele, scowling, her brow lowered. "This isn't peppermint."

"It's not?"

"No, it's— She smelled it again. "It's spearmint."

"Oh?" Adele reached for it.

Lucy handed it to her, then searched for another bag. "Who's been in charge of all the herbs?" she asked.

Adele smelled the dried tealeaves. "While we were at the compound, Barbara Jo supervised them," she said.

"Hmmm." Then upon finding the one marked "spearmint," Lucy opened it and took a whiff. "Yes, this is it," she said. She pulled the ties closed again and handed the bag to Adele. "Make sure these get marked correctly. They serve different purposes, after all."

"I will. My apologies. Truthfully, things were out of order before we left the compound." She paused, thinking. "Actually, they've been amiss since the night of the raid there—you know, shortly after the twins left on their journey? When Broden was captured? In any case, we had to move everything into bags—to make the traveling easier—and we've yet to return all the herbs to labeled jars."

She turned away and dropped the package of tea on a nearby counter. "I'll make some up right away and get it to Mara and Erin, and then," she gestured toward the larder, "I'll get Barbara Jo after that mess."

"Do that."

"And I'll get the catswort tea brewing."

"Thank you. Serve it to everyone at mealtimes."

Lucy started walking away. Then she stopped suddenly. "Adele," she said over her shoulder before turning back, "now that Chaya is assisting with the children, and given our increased numbers, I imagine you'll be needing more help in the kitchens here. I'll make arrangements for that straight away."

"I'd appreciate that, Lucy." She bobbed her head. "Thank you."

"Well, we've received word from Liam and Rafal, so I'm off to a meeting to go over their findings to date."

Making her way through the vestibule, Lucy found amongst the children now there, Aden, Velia and Jerrett's eldest, tussling with Bane on the floor. The wolf bared his teeth and growled.

Nearby, Jerrett stood watching the two of them. Along with his second son, Drew, he cheered them on. Then, suddenly, "Ah, ah, ah, no riding him, Aden!" he cautioned.

"But, Dad—"

"No. Horses are for riding. Not dogs."

"Or wolves, as the case may be," Lucy muttered.

Jerrett glanced her way, laughed, and then turned back to his boys. "You two get along now. Go out and play."

"But, Dad—" Aden whined.

"Go on!" he said. "Take Drew with you. I'll come find you boys when we're through. We'll do some training with Bane then."

"Come on, Drew!" Aden cried, clearly excited by the prospect. "Let's go!"

With Jerrett now at her side, Lucy headed down the hall to the office that Rowena, and later, Lilith, had used. Upon entering, they marched down the new brown rug that Lucy had set out to replace the red one that Lilith had put there years back, to a table and a dozen chairs the Oathtakers had set up earlier, at her request.

She was pleased to find all of the others whom she'd asked to meet with her, with the exception of Mara, already waiting there. The group consisted only of those Oathtakers and Select who knew of the twins' powers, along with the twins themselves, and the flits, Effie and Fleet. Collectively Lucy referred to them as "the inner circle."

As she and Jerrett took their seats, Bernard entered in his slow old way, and bowed.

Approaching, he gestured at the coffee, tea, and scones on the table, their sweet smell filling the air. "Is there anything more you'll require at this time?" he asked.

"No, thank you," Lucy said, her eyes on the paperwork before her. Then looking up, she added, "You know, Bernard, we can have others take over your former duties here. I—"

"Excuse me?" he asked, a hand to his ear.

She stood. "I said," she raised her voice to accommodate his lack of hearing, "others can take over your duties. You've earned your respite. I can find a replacement for you."

"Thank you, ma'am, but it's my pleasure to assist." With that, and a smile, he shuffled his way out.

"Very well then, I'm just about ready here." Taking her seat once again, she addressed Dixon. "Adele is bringing some peppermint tea to Mara."

"Thank you."

She glanced back at the others. On sight of Jerrett, she paused and frowned. "You know, about Bane . . ."

"What about him?"

She frowned. "Are you sure he's safe with the children? It makes me nervous watching them tussle about with him. Someone could get hurt."

"They're fine, Lucy. He won't harm them."

Sighing, she shook her head. "Very well. I can't stop you from allowing Aden, Drew, and Jedrek, to wrestle with him, but I won't have him running free with the rest of the children. It's not enough to merely hold you responsible should any of them get hurt—it's a matter of protecting them against the possibility. Now, to business."

She removed a compact from her pocket and placed it on the table. "We can start with Liam and Rafal's message." With that, she opened it.

<hr>

"We've arrived in Darth," came Liam's voice from the trinket, "but discovered that Zarek had already returned to his palace in Fallique. So we're headed there now. You should know that the border is crawling with a special guard. We learned that they're called 'succedunt' soldiers. They wear all black, even over their faces, leaving only their eyes uncovered. It's difficult to get past them without their noticing, and from things we've seen, and from stories we've heard, they are vicious. Also, we saw numerous refugees from Chiran in Oosa on our way here, so we suspect that Zarek ordered the succedunt to guard the border only recently."

"Yes, we've learned something of the succedunt. Steer clear of them and keep us informed," Lucy said into the compact before snapping it closed. Liam and Rafal would retrieve her response when able.

She turned back to the other attendees. "Well, no news of any significance there, I guess."

Dixon sat up straighter and patted a rhythm out on his thigh. "But, based on that message, it sounds as though we'd best get at training our army—post haste."

"I agree."

Reigna leaned in. "As you know," she said, "we left, in the City of Light, most of the Oathtakers and Select who went there—to the gathering you all called for while Eden and I were in The Tearless. We asked around about who might be the best person to leave in charge of the training there. The name we kept hearing was 'Galen Dax'—although I understand he prefers to be called simply 'Dax.' Anyway, Eden and I spoke to Lucy about him, and we all agreed that he should be in charge there. Fortunately, he agreed to the plan." She lowered her brow. "Oh yes, and his first assistant is . . ." She glanced down at her notes. "Aliza . . . Kensey."

"Aliza? Oh, that was a great choice," Velia said.

"You know her?"

"We did our Oathtaker training together."

"Who was her charge?" Lucy asked.

"Ahhhh, let me think." Velia tapped her finger to her chin. "Oh, yes!" Her eyes lit up. "Kimber . . . ahhh . . ." Her brow dropped. "Colder? No, that's not right. Kimber . . . Calder. Yes, that's it!"

"Rowena's cousin—of sorts."

"Oh, is that right?"

"She was one of her grandmother's oldest sister's children." Lucy paused, frowning. Then she reached for the tea and filled her cup. "But Aliza couldn't have been Kimber's first Oathtaker." She passed the teapot to Jerrett at her left.

"Yes, that's right," Velia agreed. "Aliza was Kimber's second Oathtaker after her first died while in her service. Aliza swore to Kimber's safety shortly after we completed our training, and then served her until she died."

"Kimber was a fifth-born, I believe," Lucy said.

"That's right."

"Any idea of Aliza's powers?" Lucy asked Reigna. "I suppose I should have thought to ask her myself," she added apologetically.

"No," Reigna said, "I don't know."

Velia tapped on the table. "She's able to take on different forms," she said.

"Goodness! You mean, like the form of an animal? Something like that?" Eden asked.

"No, not animals—people." Velia grinned. "It really is quite amazing. She can take on the persona of man or woman." She looked Lucy in the eye. "She can make herself look like someone else. Honestly, you wouldn't recognize her when she does so. The resemblances she's able to re-create are . . . uncanny."

"What of her clothing? Her voice?"

"That's just it. Everything about her changes—even her clothing. Well, in truth, as she tells it, she doesn't actually change anything about *herself*. Rather, she's able to make others see and hear her as she wants them to see and hear her."

"Hmmm," Dixon said, "that's interesting. It's a power I don't recall ever having heard of before."

"Yes, it's quite unusual," Lucy agreed.

"What of Dax?" Reigna asked. "What are his powers?"

Lucy chuckled.

"What? What's funny?"

"Actually," she said, still grinning, "he is unique among Oathtakers."

"What do you mean?"

"Well, once in a great while, an Oathtaker like Galen Dax comes along. He has no powers whatsoever—except of course, for the power of his blade which, like any Oathtaker's blade, will never miss its mark."

The attendees all looked at Lucy, clearly surprised by her news.

"None?" Eden said. "But then, what qualifies him to lead the guard?"

"Did I say 'none?'" Lucy laughed again. "I guess to be more accurate, I should say that he possesses a single power."

"And that is?"

"He is completely immune to magic imposed upon his person. Even the name of his blade—*Immunis*—reflects that fact."

Velia grabbed a tray of scones sitting before her, then stood and brought it to the other end of the table where Basha and Therese sat.

"Surely, he can be banded," she said as she returned to her seat.

"Band him all you like, but it will not work. He can exercise no other magic, and no magic of any kind—good or evil—will work directly against him."

"I wasn't aware," Reigna said.

"In any case," Lucy said, her attention now turned back to her and Eden, "Dax and Aliza will handle the training of the Oathtakers in the City of Light. Now . . . what about the couple thousand troops here with us?"

"Well, for starters," Reigna said, "I've ordered them to clear the former gardens for a training ground."

"The gardens!"

"Yes. We haven't time to beautify the palace grounds anyway. So they'll be razed. Just this morning, I ordered some of the Oathtakers to get started on that. It shouldn't take them long. Then training can begin."

"I suppose you're right."

"Eden and I will start working with them later today. We'll organize them into companies of approximately a couple hundred each, and choose a captain for each group."

"Have you determined who else will work with them?" Jerrett asked. "Besides you two, I mean."

"For starters, I'm hoping you and Velia will," Reigna said, glancing at the two of them, "and you, Marshall," she continued, looking his way, "and Raman," she added, acknowledging his presence. "Also . . . Kayson," she turned his way, "we should have a healer available at all times when we train. What do you say?"

"Sure. I'll do that."

"Good. And you should put together your own company of any Oathtakers with the attendant magic power to heal." She turned to Therese. "Have you any objection with Basha also assisting with the training?"

"None whatsoever."

"Thank you. Are you up to it then, Basha?" Reigna asked, glancing her way.

"Certainly."

"Excellent." She glanced down at her notes again. "Finally, I thought I'd speak to Jules," she said, turning to Lucy.

"Let's leave him to palace security," she suggested. "Perhaps Samuel could assist you, though."

"Samuel the Silent?" Reigna teased with a grin, using her secret childhood moniker for him.

Eden nudged her. "I think he's the perfect choice. He doesn't say much, but at least that way, you can be certain he'll waste no time with unnecessary words."

"True," her sister acknowledged, smiling at her. Then she addressed the others again. "As you know, we've not the numbers to defend ourselves against Zarek's army in the traditional sense. We'll have to use more . . . stealth methods. So, perhaps Samuel's silence will come in handy." Once again, she grinned.

"What do you mean?" Lucy asked.

"I've been thinking. There are too many of them—and too few of us. So I believe we'll have to use unconventional methods. For example, we could identify where their food comes from and how it's delivered, and then destroy it before it makes its way to them. Likewise, with their weapons."

"Excellent ideas," Marshall said. "But how do you suggest we determine those things?"

Just then, the door opened and in walked Mara, carrying a cup of tea. Upon reaching Dixon's side, she reached for the empty chair situated between him and Lucy.

He jumped to his feet and pulled it out for her. "Here, you go," he said.

"Thank you."

"Are you feeling better?"

"A bit, I guess." She turned to Lucy and raised her cup. "Thanks for the tea."

"Certainly." She paused. "Actually, before I forget to mention it, you all should know that I've set up an infirmary in the room next to Vida's suite. Those children of theirs have introduced the grippe to us. I've also made some arrangements with Adele."

She explained to the others about the catswort tea and how it could help to fend off illness, and of the herbal bundles they'd soon find burning in the palace suites.

"You really all should start drinking the tea right away. In the meantime, I ask that you be on the watch for anything out of the ordinary. We can't risk having an epidemic of anything truly serious break out."

"You think that's possible?" Velia asked, clearly concerned.

"Not likely, but . . . possible."

Jerrett patted Velia's arm. "The boys'll be fine."

"I agree," Lucy said. "So far, it doesn't appear that the illness will have the children down for more than a couple days, as I've seen nothing particularly serious."

She held her finger up. "Oh, and by the way, I've asked Clarimonde if she and Vida would allow your children," she nodded at Velia and Jerrett, "to spend their days with theirs while the two of you are busy. Actually, that will apply to all of the children from the compound. Clarimonde agreed they could do so. In fact, her plan is to run a school here for them all. Since we've no current need for the former carriage house, she'll set things up there."

"That's an excellent idea," Velia said, "although I think we'll wait until Vida's children are all healthy again before we send our boys." She paused, taking a drink of her tea. Then, "Will Nina and Erin teach with her as well?" she asked. "Like they did when we were at the compound?"

"I see no reason why not," Lucy said. "All right, then," she turned to Reigna, "how will we gain our intelligence?"

Chapter Nine

The twins helped clear the formal gardens in the afternoon and then, when the weather turned sour, headed in for dinner. Later, they joined Mara and Dixon for a palace tour, along with Vida and Clarimonde.

They started on the top floor. In the past, mostly servants had inhabited it. Even so, Dixon and Clarimonde shared stories of some of the interesting palace visitors of days gone by who'd spent time there.

Eventually they made their way to the second floor. Dixon did most of the talking and explaining, as Mara had only visited the place once in the past, under Basha's direction. He highlighted the architectural details, and identified when he could, those people who'd been responsible for particular design and decorative elements. He also shared stories about the personalities who'd lived in the past, within some of the rooms they toured, and of their relationship to the twins' mother, and therefore, to them. From time to time, Clarimonde added stories she recalled from old, to his comments.

Its majesty astonishing them, the three sisters stopped repeatedly to examine the finest of details. The most obscure trinkets, works of art, fine silver pieces, porcelain tea sets, tapestries, and figurines, captured their attention. Occasionally Vida purported to recollect a particular item from her childhood—before she'd been whisked away for safety—if only vaguely. All the while, the three sisters begged for stories of the palace's various prior inhabitants.

When they entered Lilith's former quarters—the only rooms that had not been cleaned to date—Reigna shuddered on sight of the blood-red colored walls, curtains, and of the bed's canopy. She sauntered about, Eden following.

Clarimonde and Vida stood aside as Mara, to the occasional flash of lightning coming in through the shades, told them the story of her last visit there—two decades prior. Then, the lord of the underworld, Daeva, had appeared before her in Lilith's looking glass. When Mara threw a crystal at him in response to his heckling Basha, the mirror had exploded into millions of tiny glass fragments before disappearing.

"It sounded almost . . . musical—when the glass shards fell," Mara said, "which was odd considering . . ."

"Why haven't these rooms been cleaned yet?" Eden asked.

Dixon shrugged. "Mara and I talked about it. We thought you two should take a look here first—that it might give you an idea of the person Lilith was." He turned to Vida. "And you, Vida, do you recall anything of your Aunt Lilith?"

"A bit."

"She was . . . disorganized," Reigna offered, "flighty."

"Vain," Eden added, "and self-centered."

"Yes . . . but quite bright," Vida offered. "And beautiful, too. I do remember that much."

"Yes, that's all true," Dixon said to the sisters. Yet," he added, picking up a silk scarf from the floor and draping it over the bed, "she hadn't always been so lacking in focus and so . . . sloppy. I believe that as thoughts of her coming to power one day grew, she paid less and less attention to anything else."

"About when did she start changing, do you think?" Eden asked.

Dixon pondered for a moment. "I'm not sure. But remember, I wasn't your mother's first Oathtaker. By the time I first met Lilith, she was already quite difficult to manage. Rowena was always very careful around her."

Mara sat down as the others continued their survey.

"Are you feeling all right?" he asked her.

She waved her hand. "I'm fine. Just tired. The grippe has weakened me."

"Perhaps you should go lie down."

"Yes, Mara," Clarimonde agreed.

"No, I'm fine—really. Now, if you're ready to move on," she said, glancing at each of the three sisters in turn, "you might like to take a look at the portraits of some of your ancestors. A number of them line the hallway near here."

Eden took her Oathtaker's hand. "I'll make arrangements to have this all cleaned up first thing tomorrow. There's no sense in wasting this space. And I'll go through Lilith's old belongings here for anything of interest. When I'm through, we can have what remains, burned."

"Good idea. I'll give you a hand."

Mara stepped out and down the hall with the twins and Dixon at her side. Clarimonde and Vida followed.

Shortly, she stopped before some paintings. "This is your mother's mother— your grandmother—Mae," she said gesturing at one of them. "And here," she motioned toward the one next to it, "is your grandfather, Max."

Reigna neared the painting of Mae. With her eyes narrowed, she examined it closely. Then her gaze flickered toward Eden. "You look like her," she said.

Her twin burst into laughter. "*I* look like her! Ha ha ha ha ha! *We* look like her!"

Chuckling with them, Mara took an arm of each. "Dixon needs to go meet with Jules about palace security, but there are some things I'd like to show the two of you, and Vida. They're in our room."

"All right," Reigna said.

"You go along," Clarimonde said to her charge. "I'm off to check on the children. I'll see you when you're through."

Thunder rumbled as they sat on Mara's bed, Reigna at one side, her legs hanging over the edge, Eden semi-reclined, leaning on one elbow, and Vida at the end, wiping her hand against the smooth softness of the cotton bedding.

Holding a rosewood box that boasted intricately carved scrolls and whirls on its cover, Mara opened it, then retrieved something from within.

"This belonged to your mother," she said, holding it up.

Reigna took the trinket, a hairpin of gold, studded in multi-colored crystals that shone in the candlelight. She turned it over. "It's beautiful!"

"Yes." Mara explained how she believed that the crystals were some of the magic ones the Oathtakers created and used as weapons—the same kind that made up the windows of the main sanctuary building in Polesk.

"I can't imagine where they came from though," she said, "since no one seemed aware of an Oathtaker's magic ability to make them until Basha and I discovered it when we came back here to the palace to retrieve the great scepter. That of course, was when you two were just infants."

She looked off at nothing in particular, biting her lip. Then she said, "I suppose like so much of our lore, the information was simply lost through the ages." She glanced back at the twins. "Even Lucy, who as you well know is centuries old, didn't know about them."

Reigna looked the item over again. Handing it to her twin, she asked, "Where do you suppose it's from?"

"I'm sorry, I've no idea. It may have been an heirloom her mother gave to her."

Mara reached into the rosewood box and retrieved another item. "This also belonged to your mother," she said, placing it in Reigna's hand. "Dixon retrieved it after her death. I understand that she wore it at all times."

Inside the locket clasped to a chain that Mara had given her, Reigna discovered two miniature paintings. She showed them to Eden and to Vida. The picture on the left was of a man, that on the right, clearly one of their mother.

Pointing at the likeness on the left, Mara held Reigna's gaze. "That was your father, Grant. His portrait was never painted and hung on the wall here. As you know, he wasn't born of the Select. I don't know if the decision was made not to include it under those circumstances, or if they'd simply not managed to get one commissioned before his death."

Reigna examined the item closely. "I've always wondered what father looked like." She glanced at Vida. "He was very handsome."

"He was indeed."

"I couldn't agree more," Mara said.

Reigna handed the locket to Vida, who jumped when the sound of the murmuring rainfall on the windows, suddenly changed to a drumming. After perusing it, she gave it to Eden.

"I have another item here," Mara said, removing something more from the box. "This was your mother's wedding ring." She turned it around and around in her fingers. "Dixon also took this from her just after she died." She paused, closing her eyes. "I'll never forget how distraught he was . . ." She glanced back up. "He cared for her deeply, and I know he'd have done anything to have seen to her safety."

She held the ring out. "I've kept this all these years. I thought one of you might like to wear it, and the other, the locket," she said to the twins. Then she glanced Vida's way. "But of course, its up to you all what we should do with these pieces."

The twins looked at one another and then at Vida. They all nodded, as though each understood what the others thought.

"Actually," Eden said to Mara, "you should hold the ring for safekeeping."

"Yes, and I think that one of you two," Vida said to her sisters, "should make use of the hairpin, and the other, the locket."

"Are you sure?" Reigna asked.

"I'm certain."

Reigna addressed her twin. "That's fine with me. Which would you prefer, Eden?"

"Oh, please, don't make me choose. We could be here all night."

Reigna chuckled. "Fine. I'll take the hairpin then. But I do think we should keep these things safe in our lock boxes."

"Agreed."

Just then a knock came at the door, quiet in comparison to the now crashing thunder outside.

"Yes?" Mara called.

Lucy entered and approached. On the night table next to Mara, she set down a mug. "Some more tea," she said. "How are you feeling?"

"I think a bit better, thank you."

"Adele's come down with something now too, as have a few of the Oathtakers who've been helping with your children," she said to Vida, scowling.

"I'm so sorry, Lucy."

"Oh, never mind. It couldn't be helped, I'm sure." Then she glanced at the twins. "Actually though, I'm not sure the two of you should be spending time with Mara just now—or with your sister, for that matter. We don't need you coming down with anything."

"I'm fine," Reigna said.

"Me too," Eden agreed.

"Very well then, as you say," Lucy said. "So, what are you all up to anyway?"

She leaned over and glanced at the ring that Mara still held. "Oh, I see," she addressed the three sisters. "You're going through some of your mother's things."

"Yes," Vida said.

"These rooms here that Mara and Dixon are using, your parents used to share," Lucy said as she waved her hand to indicate their surroundings. "When we moved in, I went through them. I had some of your mother's things packed up for storing in the lower levels. Some day, if things ever settle down, we can go through them together."

"I'd like that," Eden said.

"Thank you, yes, so would I," her twin agreed.

Vida merely nodded and smiled.

"Oh," Mara said, jumping to her feet as a flash of lightning shone through the window, "there's one thing more I found amongst your mother's belongings, after her death. Maybe Lucy knows something about it."

She went to her closet and pulled out from the top shelf, a box. Upon returning, she placed it on the bed. She took off the top and folded open the crinkling tissue paper inside.

"Here we go," she said, pulling something out.

Lucy grinned. "That old thing?" She held her hand to her chest. "Oh, goodness, I didn't know you still had that."

"Old!" Reigna cried, running her hands over the softest, whitest cashmere cape, in a most intricate cabled weave. "Why, it's beautiful!" she exclaimed.

Eden nodded her agreement. "This was our mother's?" She picked up the item and turned it over. It's spotless. Gorgeous!" She turned to Lucy. "You laughed about it. Why?"

Lucy picked up a corner of it. "Your mother got this years ago, when she was even younger than the two of you are now, from a vendor at a market in a village not far from Polesk. The woman went by the name 'Skelly.' Great Ehyeh, but I'll never forget her! She told the wildest stories—and was believed to be mad." She locked eyes with one of the twins, then the other, all to the sound of rumbling thunder. "In any case, Skelly had followed your mother and I around, along with your mother's first Oathtaker, all day."

"What was his name again?" Vida asked.

"Her first Oathtaker?"

"Yes."

"Sheva."

"That's right," she said. "I remember him—vaguely."

"So, this . . . Skelly . . . What about her?" Eden asked.

Lucy sat at the edge of the bed. "Well, as I said, everyone thought she was less than sane. When we couldn't seem to shake her tailing us, Sheva stopped to ask some of the locals about her. The vendors told him that Skelly was harmless—but crazy. So finally, when she drew near once more, Sheva turned around to face her, a scowl on his face and his Oathtaker's blade in his hand."

As Lucy spoke, she stood and demonstrated what he might have looked like, an expression of intensity on her face. Then she burst out a great smile.

"Honestly, I thought the woman would jump right out of her skin, he so surprised her!"

Grinning, Mara took up her cup, blew on the tea to cool it, and then drank.

"So, what happened?" Eden asked.

Sitting down once again, Lucy draped the cape over her shoulder. She ran her hand against it, up and down, up and down.

"Skelly insisted on speaking with Rowena," she said. "When Sheva finally relented and allowed her an audience, she told Rowena that she recognized her as a seventh-born among the Select. Then she gave her this cape." Again, Lucy stroked it. "She said that her father had been an Oathtaker to a seventh, and that his attendant magic had included the ability to create enchanted artifacts." She laughed outright.

"But, Lucy," Mara interrupted, "you're able to infuse objects with magic."

"Yeeeessss, but according to Skelly, her father produced things of magic out of thin air." She shook her head and waved her hand about, scoffing. "That seemed . . . preposterous to me. Anyway, telling your mother that she had the gift of foresight," Lucy said to the sisters, "Skelly gave her this shawl and a . . . prediction, or . . . something."

When a crack of thunder sounded out, they all jumped, then quickly turned their attention back to one another.

Lucy removed the shawl from over her shoulder and ran it under her chin.

"Why do you do that?" Eden asked. "Rub it under your chin?"

She smiled. "Cashmere is warm, lightweight, and intensely soft. If you run it under your chin, you won't feel the least scratchiness." She leaned in and whispered, as though sharing a secret, "I confess, I've always loved the feel of it."

She handed the item to the twins.

As they ran their hands over it, Vida reached over to touch it, as well.

"It's so luxurious," Eden said. "Still, this Skelly must have said something about it, Lucy. Was that what her—prediction—was all about?"

A sudden gust of wind blew rain into a window that had been left open a crack. Lucy went to close it.

"Well," she said as she returned, "Skelly spoke mostly in riddles. Even so, I know her to have been right about one thing, at least. She told Rowena that she'd have a seventh daughter one day, and then, about the cape, she said—" Lucy stopped cold. "No, that's not right." Her brow dropped. "As I mentioned, she spoke in riddles. I remember laughing about it at the time, teasing Rowena that we'd seen and heard it all, so I'm sure I can recall her words accurately. Now, let me think here . . ."

She stood and paced, her hands pressed together and her index fingers to her lips.

A minute later, she turned back. "Yes, I remember it all now." Then she recited what Skelly had said:

Come one.
Come two.
Come illusion,
Come true.

Bear me now.
Bear me then.
Dare to sense me even when.

She shook her head, grinning. "Like I said, it doesn't make any sense."

"Maybe you're not remembering it correctly," Eden suggested.

"Oh, no, I'm certain I got the words right." Lucy cocked her head, thinking. "I wonder if Skelly was referencing the fact that Rowena would bear twins—you know, with the language: *'Come one. Come two.'* Hmmm. I suppose that's possible. Although what the rest of it all could mean is beyond me."

She paused, once again contemplating. "In any case, the old woman told your mother that this," she gestured toward the shawl, "was for her seventh-born. Of course, the mystery is in whether she did in fact mean just you, Reigna," she nodded at her, "or you also, Eden," she added, glancing her way, "in that you are the 'seventh seventh who is, but is not,' of prophetic fame."

Mara put her empty cup down. "Since Skelly told your mother that it was for her seventh-born, that may explain why she took it along with her when she left here pregnant with you two," she said to the twins. "So, I guess that betwixt yourselves, you'll have to decide what you'd like to do with it."

Chapter Ten

His anger rose, then spurt out like steam escaping a teapot, causing him to shake intensely. He knew he shouldn't reminisce, shouldn't dwell on things of old, but sometimes all the self-counsel in the world was for naught.

On his knees, he bowed down until his forehead rested on the floor. He thought about how, as a child, he'd been taught of forgiveness, of pardons, and of mercy. He'd tried that way, had intended to protect it at all costs—had even sworn to do so. It was Ehyeh's way. But eventually, he rejected it—when the cost became greater than what he wanted to pay.

When Daeva visited him in the darkest hour of his young adulthood and introduced him to a new way, he followed, delighted that the underlord offered an alternative— retribution . . . vengeance. Over the years, thoughts of how to see those goals come to fruition, festered inside. They caused him to gush imprecations. Curiously, those thoughts also offered a unique sense of . . . satisfaction. In truth, he'd grown most talented in the art of malediction—and best of all, he'd found the way to bring life to his own damning curses.

Try though he might to hold his memories at bay, they flooded down on him.

He scowled as he recalled how his father had abandoned him, and of how his mother had left him a victim. Momentarily nauseous at the thought, he drew his hand to his mouth, choking back his bile.

When an act of violence against his person robbed him of his childhood innocence, following which the violator manipulated him—convinced him that he had himself to blame—hatred was born. Initially, it was a hatred of himself that sat dormant for a time. But eventually, when confronted with yet another rejection, his burning self-loathing produced its inevitable byproduct: the detestation of others.

Well, Mother had been right about one thing. To hate someone was to wish death upon him. But wishes are flighty, ethereal sorts of things. To come to pass, they oft require a helping hand.

He stepped back in time to that glorious day that he felt certain would remain with him for all time. He recalled looking at the man who'd trespassed against him, and who stood at the doorway before him with his arm draped over the shoulder of a boy at his side.

"Master Mugger," he had said to him, with a bow, "I learned of your move here. I thought I would stop by to pay my respects."

Mugger, in his usual style, tottered, a consequence of his chewing bibulous nut—notwithstanding the earliness of the hour.

"Ahhh . . . it's you—my favorite student of all time!" He grinned, maliciously, showing off his red-stained teeth, compliments of his drug of choice. "I just returned from a journey that I set out on earlier today to retrieve my newest student."

He pulled the boy closer, a lecherous look in his eye. "I've hit the big time. This one," he leaned in and whispered, "is a descendant of the Hazarik. His mother has placed him in my care. I'm to teach him the basics of reading and writing." Putting his hands on the boy's shoulders, he leered down at him.

Oddly, the child wore a half grin. His brow rose as his eyes ran down the form of his new master's visitor.

"I see," the man said, recognizing a sense of camaraderie with the boy. Although not more than five, possibly six, years of age, his physique already held the promise of great strength to come. "Well, my congratulations to you, master."

Stumbling, Mugger slumped into a chair. Waving his hand toward the boy, he demanded that he fill a pitcher from a keg sitting on the counter. When the youth, following his master's command, grabbed the vessel, cockroaches scattered out from beneath it. He flinched at the sight of them, then did as his master bid him.

He returned with the ale, along with two earthenware cups, and set them on the table.

Mugger's guest gestured toward a nearby chair, a question in his eyes.

"Of course, have a seat," Mugger said before coughing up and then spitting out a mouthful of phlegm that left a dark red spot on the floor where it landed.

The man sat, then filled his former master's cup before his own.

"It's a pleasure to see you once more," Mugger said before taking a great swallow.

"Yes, master." He paused. "You know, along my way—quite near here, actually—I made the most . . . intriguing find. I wonder if you might accompany me to take a look." Knowing the man could not resist flattery, he added, "I could use your most profound expertise, as I have never come upon such creatures before."

"Ah! Where are they then?"

"Just a short walk from here."

Lumbering back to his feet, Mugger winced from the effort of lifting his own massive weight. "Well, let's be off then, before dusk sets in," he suggested. Tottering in his insobriety, he turned to his new student. "Come, boy."

The three set out. After making their way through an oak grove and across a fallow field, they came upon a rocky area. In its midst stood a rounded opening, like a doorway. Long shadows enshrouded it, as the sun now neared the horizon.

"This way, master," the man said, making an opening in the brush that partially camouflaged the path ahead. He gestured for his former instructor to proceed. "After you."

Once they all passed the threshold, he said, "Now, just yonder is a clearing with room to venture about, in the center of which is a pond."

The boy glanced his way, as though reading his intentions, and then followed Mugger.

The man watched the youth closely. He sensed that he possessed an absence of restraint—and abundant, innate intelligence.

A nearby murder of crows burst into flight ahead of them. Their cackling and cawing filled the air. The man almost smiled upon noticing bits of flesh hanging from the beaks of several of them. It only seemed right that they'd enjoy a feast, as over the past weeks, he'd made sport of capturing a few of them from time to time to feed his pets.

"Just there," he said, pointing to a pond as he dropped his satchel to the ground.

Mugger approached the water's edge. "It looks deep," he said.

"It is—quite. So please, do watch your step."

As the boy stood off, watching, the man neared Mugger's side. He got down on one knee. "There, do you see the movement in the water? Just there?" He pointed toward the middle of the pool.

Mugger's eyes narrowed. He shook his head. "Where? I don't see anything. What is it?"

"Occasionally, about this time of day, the most unusual creature ventures out for a look." Glancing up, he held Mugger's eye. "And here is the amazing part," he added, before pausing for effect. "It breaks the surface—and then . . . it flies into the night!"

Pulling back, Mugger scowled. "That's preposterous."

"You think so? Here. Squat down, just here." He patted the ground at his side. "The water is clear. Take a look for yourself." He leaned forward, luring his victim in.

Oh, but he is too large. Still, if I can take advantage of his drug-induced inebriation, get him in a vulnerable position . . .

"Oh, there it is!" he cried, pointing down into the water. "Quickly, master! Look!"

After spitting out another mouthful of his bibulous nut-stained saliva, Mugger crouched down. His eyes narrowed as he searched the waters. "I don't see anything."

"Stay here while I get you some bait to draw the creature out."

He stood, then walked away to retrieve his satchel. Upon his return, he rummaged inside it.

Mugger made as though to rise.

"Oh, no, master! As you always taught: patience is rewarded. Just a moment longer now."

He took a biscuit out of his bag. "Here," he said, putting it in Mugger's crimson stained fingers, "take this and throw it . . . just there," he pointed, "to the center of the pond."

"Just there?" Mugger gestured.

"Yes. Now, be ready!" With that, he stepped back.

Try though he might, he could not refrain from smiling over the trap he'd laid. Upon arriving in the area sometime back and discovering this inland pond filled with man-eating lampreys, he'd stuck around, feeding crows to the eel-like suckers, sporadically, so as to be certain they remained alive.

Preparing to toss the biscuit to the pond's center, Mugger leaned in. He drew his arm back and then tossed the bait, following through with his swing.

In that moment, his former student knew three things with utter certainty. First, when the bait hit the water, the lampreys would squirm about, revealing their true size, nature, and strength. Second, Mugger, not entirely sober, was off balance at the moment, which made him vulnerable. And third—there would never be another chance like this. So, taking no risk that this window of opportunity might be lost, the man stepped up, placed both his hands on Mugger's back, and then pushed.

He hit the water's surface with a mighty roar. His arms and legs thrashed about. As he groped for a rock at the pond's edge, which broke away and scattered into fragments, the previously hidden nest of lamprey surrounded him. He writhed, screaming, as the beasts wrapped their forms about him and then latched on with their funnel-like sucking mouths.

He shrieked and flailed about. "Help!" he cried. "Help! Help me!"

As his screams continued, the beasts pulled him farther away, then down deep into the pond's center. Above, the water seem to boil, bubble, and foam.

A minute later, a cloud of crimson, eerily reminiscent of the color of Mugger's teeth, rose to the surface.

He was no more.

His former student looked up to find the boy approaching.

When the child stood just feet before him, he bowed. "Master," he said, looking back up, "teach me." He smiled—a gesture that did not quite reach his eyes. "I am called 'Zarek.'"

Back to the present, the man glanced up into the mirror, calling on the underlord. When the spirit made his presence known, he prostrated himself. "Tell me," he said, "what shall be the price for my request?"

Oh, how he gloried in his time communing with Daeva and the other lords of the underworld, Akka, and Sij. Decades earlier, sometime after he'd first turned to them, the three spirits had favored him, intervened for him, in the form of a hex—a glamour—in exchange for a price. They'd required a simple thing really. He had but to take the life of a member of the Select—or to be more precise, of his charge . . .

Yes, and he'd been all too content to comply.

Thereafter, through the underlords' intervention, he had maintained a generally youthful appearance—at least to those incapable of seeing with more than merely physical eyes. Moreover, the magic provided that one with the power to read thoughts or to discern truth from falsehood, could not see through to his true self. Even so, his body was giving out. But now, with a new mission before him, he dared not appear weak. Hence, once again, he'd turned to the spirits.

The underlords named their price for his latest request. This time they required that he take the life of an Oathtaker who possessed the power to heal, and that he then use that person's blade to dig his grave. He thought the demand simple enough. He'd heard that the City of Light fairly burst at its seams with the lot of them these days. And once done, his strength would be restored—for a time, at least.

Then of course, there was the matter of his persona. He grimaced with the thought of having to learn how to smile again. Such expressions were foreign to him. But he'd best start practicing them—straight away—as the underlords could do nothing for him in that regard. A grim countenance could add years to his visage—and that, he could ill afford.

Chapter Eleven

With the grounds cleared, and the Oathtaker troops now divided into companies, Reigna marched to the center ring. "Attention!" she called, her breath turning to a billowing fog in the cold air. "Attention, everyone!"

The sounds of weapons clanging, of horses neighing, and of orders made, sounded out as the hundreds of men and women about her, struggled for a better view, but in due course, the crowd stilled.

"As your leaders have instructed you, we must all be in our best fighting form. An Oathtaker's blade is a mighty tool—but is insufficient in itself. We will fight for Oosa—to protect its people and their freedom."

She paused as the crowd whistled and applauded.

"We begin today, with sparring matches," she added. "We'll start with a review of the basics in various weaponry, but be advised that we haven't much time, so let's get the most out of what we do have."

Eden whispered something in her sister's ear.

Reigna nodded and then addressed the crowd once again. "Each company leader has arranged for your matches. When not engaged in one yourself, you should be taking note of good form. Each of you will depend on each of the others for information as to how to improve your skills. We are a team, but we can only perform at our peak when we are all at our personal best."

The crowd responded with hoots, calls, and stomping.

When the sounds died away, she continued. "There will be a healer on duty at all times. Today, that will be Kayson. He is right there," she pointed in his direction.

After the crowd acknowledged his presence, Eden stepped up. "My sister and I will engage with some of you from time to time. You're to treat us as any other contender. Understood?"

Once again, the troops responded with whistles and applause.

"Very well then," Reigna said, "let's get started."

The troops rummaged about, finding their places along with their leaders at each of the rings.

Jerrett, Bane at his side, joined the group with which he would train, while Velia headed off in another direction. Marshall, Basha, Raman, and Samuel—the others

Reigna had previously designated to lead groups—also got to business.

Quickly, the air filled with the sounds of shouting, grunting, and weapons clanging.

After observing for a time, the twins separated so that they could each engage in a match.

A short time later, exhausted from her efforts, Reigna found Mara as she prepared to spar. "Are you sure you're feeling up to this?" she asked her.

Mara nodded. "I'm not at my best, that's true, but maybe this will help sweat out the grippe." She smiled, wanly. "It's frustrating, as all the others who've been ill seem to be on the mend already."

"Yes, but most of them were children, and they do bounce back more quickly."

"Agreed."

"Don't overdo it now."

Skipping toward the center of the ring, Mara called over her shoulder, "I won't." Then she pulled up her sword and began her dance with the other contender.

As Dixon met Reigna at her side, she glanced his way. "She really doesn't look well," she said.

"No," he agreed. "But let's remember, we traveled for months to her old home. Then she rushed to find you and Eden in The Tearless. And no sooner did she return with the two of you to the City of Light, than we got caught up making plans there." He shook his head. "Early on, she seemed fine. But I noticed a few weeks later, that she was dragging."

"Yes," Reigna said, watching the skirmish before her as the crowd, now engaged, urged Mara and her challenger on.

"Then we were off to the compound, where we spent a couple weeks preparing for our journey here, to the palace." He scraped his boot along the frost on the ground as he patted out a rhythm on his thigh. "That in itself took some time. But, you know, I think the worst part is that she's been plagued by nightmares. She awakens almost every night trembling, and in a sweat."

Reigna turned and stared at him. "About anything in particular?"

"I think it's just the pressure of knowing the Chiranians are soon to make their way here. She's frightened for you girls. She dreams she's being chased by grut— that she's carrying you and your sister, as infants—and that she looses you."

"Oh, my."

"Yes, and with all this training and planning . . . Frankly, I think it's all just finally caught up with her—that she's just desperately in need of some good, nightmare-free, rest."

"She shouldn't be training today then," Reigna said, looking back out as Mara held up her hand to call a halt to her sparring partner while struggling to catch her breath.

"Tell *her* that!" Dixon exclaimed. "She won't hear of being left out."

Reigna grinned. "I suppose we should take comfort then, in the fact that she's still herself." She put her arm around him. "She'll be fine, I'm sure."

After a couple weeks of intense training, the inner circle convened as, once again, word had come in from Liam and Rafal.

Bernard moseyed about, fine-tuning his prior arrangements of several trays of treats set out on the conference room table. Behind him, Chaya made her way around with a coffee pot in one hand, and a teapot in the other, filling cups as requested. On reaching Marshall's side, he looked up and smiled at her. She met his unspoken greeting with a lift of her brow and a clenched jaw, filled his cup, and then moved on. Once she'd made her way around the table, she set the pots down. Then she and Bernard left the room.

Eden stood. "Everyone's here, so let's get started," she said, calling the meeting to order. Then she resumed her seat.

Lucy placed her magic compact on the table and opened it.

"We've made our way from Darth, to Fallique, where Zarek resides," Rafal was heard to say. "As of now, there's nothing much to report, although we learned of some soldiers—regular troops, not the succedunt—readying for a journey. It seems they're on their way to the border. After that, it's possible they'll try to enter Oosa.

"We think the nearest city of any size to the point they have in mind is Ethanward. Not far to the east from there, of course, is Polesk, and a half-day journey southeast from there, is the palace at Shimeron. With the sketchy details we've uncovered, we can't be certain of their plans. Still, we estimate the group at something under a thousand men. More, of course, could follow. We'll provide further word as it becomes available. Until later, then."

Lucy closed the compact and then slipped it in her pocket. "That's it," she said, addressing the twins.

"Thank you," Eden said. Then she asked each of those designated as training leaders, to report on how his or her group fared. Since Samuel was not officially a member of the inner circle, Jerrett reported for him, as well as for himself.

"So, it seems things are coming along nicely in that department," Reigna said when they'd all concluded.

"Thank goodness, as it seems there's no time to spare," Therese, sitting at Basha's side, commented.

"Right," Reigna agreed. She turned to Marshall. "I'd like you, and you, Raman," she glanced his way, "as well as Samuel, to take the companies under your control to the border, immediately. You're to make camp on this side of it, near Ethanward. That would get," she paused in thought, "five hundred Oathtakers, give or take, nearby to respond, in the event Zarek's troops try to cross the border there."

Marshall and Raman each confirmed his understanding with a nod.

"Together, we'll draw up plans for any extras you should take along to assist with your meal preparations, with your potential medical needs, and so forth."

"Very well. I'll let Samuel know," Marshall said.

Eden leaned in. "Also, Reigna and I have been talking," she said with a glance at Mara, "and have determined that a trip to the City of Light is in order for us."

"But we've only just arrived here," Mara said.

"Still, the training here can go on quite well without us now, and given the significantly greater number of troops in the city, we need to spend some time there, as well." When Mara opened her mouth to speak, Eden interrupted her with a raised hand. "No, Mara, you won't be joining us."

She pulled back, surprised. "Of course I'll join you. I can deliver you there safely with no loss of time." She looked from her, to Reigna, making eye contact with each of them, in turn. "Don't be ridiculous. I'll not have you traveling without me."

Dixon patted her arm. "Actually, Mara, the twins discussed this all with me."

She looked at him, her eyes narrowed.

"Hear me out," he said, his palm extended toward her. "You could use some rest—and Lucy and I could each take one of them, and then—"

"Absolutely not!" she cried.

"Mara—" Eden sought to interrupt.

"No." Mara stood, her hands on the table, leaning in. "I'm fine. What's a little grippe? Goodness, you'd think there was something seriously wrong with me." Huffing, she sat again. "I won't hear of your going without me."

As Dixon sighed in frustration, Reigna caught his eye. Then she turned back to her Oathtaker.

"You need some rest," she said to her. "You can join up with us when you're feeling better. But," she added, her finger raised when Mara looked about to speak again, "we need to get there as quickly as possible. We may not even be there long. Who knows? Still, we need to discuss with Dax and Aliza, how their training is going there. We all have to be ready to act when this threat moves into Oosa, putting the safety of more and more of our fellow Oosians at risk. And Mara . . . we don't want you to become truly ill."

"Perhaps they're right," Velia said, turning to her friend.

"Yes," Basha agreed.

Effie, on the tabletop, addressed Mara. "You should listen to your friends," she said. "They have your best interests at heart."

Mara sat up straight and folded her arms. "What is this?" she asked. "A conspiracy or something? Even my dearest friends plot against me," she added, glaring at each of Velia and Basha in turn.

"No," Velia said, "that's not it at all."

Sighing, Mara turned back to the twins. "I won't hear of it."

"Listen," Lucy said, "I've been at this Oathtaker business for a long time. I understand your—"

"No," Mara repeated.

Reigna stood. She glanced at each person around the table. Finally, she fixed her gaze on Mara. "I'm sorry," she said, "but you've been overruled. We'll leave first thing tomorrow morning. Dixon and Lucy will stay in the city with us, but Lucy will return here before long, to check on your progress. Once you're feeling better, assuming we haven't already returned here by then, you may join us. But until then—"

Mara stood. She took several deep breaths, glaring all the while.

"It's been decided, Mara," Eden said, holding her gaze, "and our decision is final. This time, like it or not, we're going without you."

Silent, Mara readied for bed. In her nightdress, sitting before her vanity, she untied the band that kept her hair tied back and threw it down. She shook her head, letting her dark tresses fall.

Dixon approached from behind. He put his hands on her shoulders.

Refusing to look at him, or even at his reflection in the looking glass before her, she pulled away, freeing herself from his hold. Then she commenced brushing her hair.

"Mara, please, don't be angry."

"Fourteen, fifteen . . ." She mumbled through gritted teeth, counting her strokes.

"The twins are right. You need some rest."

"Twenty-one, twenty—"

"Please, talk to me."

She slapped her hairbrush down, then turned his way. "How could you?"

He got down on one knee. "I'm worried about you. You haven't been yourself. You're not feeling well—and with all the nightmares, you're not sleeping well, either."

She turned back to the mirror. "Why don't you just have me replaced while you're at it, huh? Maybe you'd like to be the girls' Oathtaker." Her eyes flickered toward his reflection. "Or maybe one of the other Oathtakers who's currently uncommitted wants his turn? Maybe—" She stopped short, shaking her head, seething.

Dixon put his hands on her shoulders again. When she squirmed at his touch, he tightened his grip and then forced her around to look at him.

"Mara," he said, "you're not well, and in truth, you're not in your best form. When you spar, you're slow. And more often than not, you're left, after a match, in a gasping heap."

She clenched her jaw.

"Please try to understand."

"Leave me be, Dixon."

He put his hands over his face and rubbed it, then ran his fingers through his hair. "Try to see reason—"

She jumped to her feet. "Oh, I see. I'm weak. I'm slow. And now, it seems, I'm not in my right mind." She went to their bed, took up a blanket from the end of it, and then grabbed her pillow before marching to the door.

Dixon beat her there. He stood against it, barring her from leaving.

"Get out of my way."

He shook his head.

"I said, 'get out of my way.'" She breathed heavily. "I'm well enough to know when I'm not wanted."

He stepped forward, reached for her. "Please, don't go. I just want you well again."

She pulled herself to her full height. "Let me go, Dixon," she ordered, emphasizing each word.

Reluctantly, he stood aside.

As dawn approached, random flakes of snow tumbled through the air. Then, interrupting the peacefulness, a cock crowed. The sound of it, after which came the shuffling of footsteps down the hall, stirred Dixon from his sleep.

He turned over, reaching for Mara, expecting to find her at his side. Then his eyes flashed open as he recalled her having left the night before. Except for when she'd lost her memory and he'd taken her on a trip to her old home, he couldn't remember a time when she'd ever been so angry with him. Back then, she'd acted out of fear. Perhaps that explained things now, too. Perhaps she was simply afraid. Fear did seem to bring out the worst in her. It masked itself as anger. Still, he wished he could reason with her.

He ran his hand against the whisper-soft, empty sheets at his side, choking back a groan. He was lonely without her. The world was not right. Back when she'd lost her memory, he'd been miserable without her nearby.

But this is ever so much worse. This time, she intentionally left my side.

"Ahhh!" he cried as he sat up, threw his pillow at the far wall, and then fell back again.

He tossed the goose down filled comforter aside and sat at the bed's edge, his head in his hands.

Just then, a knock came at the door.

"Yes?" he called.

The door cracked open.

"May we come in?"

He grabbed a robe from a side chair and donned it. "Yes. Come on in, girls."

The twins, already dressed and armed, entered to the sounds of their weapons clanging. Having earned Ehyeh's favor while in The Tearless, each now emitted her own unique scent. Still rather new to Dixon, their fragrances caught his attention. He inhaled deeply and, despite his misery, smiled at the thought that they were now equipped for what might come their way.

They sat, one on each side of him, at the edge of the bed.

"We saw Mara downstairs," Reigna said, "sleeping on one of the sofas in the reception area."

He nodded. "She left here last night, angry with me. I couldn't reason with her."

When he turned her way, Reigna held his gaze. "I'm so sorry, Dixon but it can't be helped."

"I know."

"It's just a bit of the grippe, like she says," Eden added, "but we need her in her best form."

He sighed. "Are you two all ready to go then?" He grimaced, recalling that whenever he asked Mara that question, she responded with: "So long as you go with me." He doubted she'd do that now, given her anger with him, even if she was in fact, going along—which she was not. He cringed at the thought.

"We are. And you?"

"I packed last night." He took a hand of each of them. "You've eaten?"

"We were waiting for you," Reigna said, "and we're hoping that maybe Mara will join us."

At that moment, the door opened. Mara entered, then marched to the closet.

Dixon went to her side. When he reached for her, she pulled away

"Mara," he said, "please don't be angry."

She pursed her lips, then selected some clothing.

"Please," he repeated.

She turned to him, cocked her head. "Haven't you got somewhere you need to be?"

Eden approached her other side. "Mara, come have breakfast with us."

She turned back toward the closet, as though mesmerized with its contents.

"Come on." Eden put her hand on her Oathtaker's back. "We don't want to leave with you feeling this way."

She closed her eyes and shook her head. "What's the hurry? That's what I'd like to know. This illness will be over soon enough, and then I can take you myself."

"Time is of the essence. You know that." Eden stepped closer and wrapped her arms around her. "Let's go have breakfast together before we go."

"I can't eat. It'll just come back up anyway."

"See?" Eden pulled back and looked her in the eye. "That's just what we're talking about. Now, we know that you want to come along, but we need you well first."

Tears pooled in Mara's eyes. "It's so painful being without you. I'm afraid it'll just delay my getting better."

Smiling at her, Eden released her hold as Dixon put his hands on her shoulders. He turned her toward himself and then wrapped his arms around her. "We all understand," he said. "Now let's get you well, so that you can join us there."

Weeping now, she buried her face in his chest. "I'm so sorry. I—"

"Shhhh. Shhhh," he comforted her, tightening his embrace. Then he pulled back, put a finger below her chin, and tipped her head up. Winking at her, he smiled, wanly. "Get some rest here. I'll send Lucy back as soon as possible, and then when you're on the mend, you'll join us."

Leaning into him yet again, she nodded her agreement.

Chapter Twelve

He made his way through the palace, his walking stick striking the floor with each step, announcing his presence well in advance of his actual arrival.

The help staff scattered, anxious to be out of the way before he arrived.

After heading out the back doors, he limped along to the training grounds where Zarek leaned against a railing, watching his troops sparring below. To the emperor's right stood his secretary, Gonen, a man who moved jerkily, spasmodically. At his left, one of the succedunt soldiers held a chain, at the other end of which a grut strained to get loose.

In the center ring reserved for champions, a soldier fended off the advances of a new challenger, as his three prior contenders stood on the sidelines, nursing their wounds.

"Ooooh!" Zarek exclaimed when the champion took a blow to his side and staggered. Then, "Ha ha!" he guffawed, as the man, growling ferociously, charged, throwing his weight on his latest rival. "Ah! There he goes! He's down!" Zarek laughed, raising his hands in the air.

Glancing at Pestifere who neared him, he pointed to the champion and said, "That one must lead a battalion." Then turning to his secretary, he added, "Gonen, make note of his name. I'll want to speak with him later." Finally, looking back at his fighting forces, he commented, to no one in particular, "Men will follow one such as that."

"Yes," Pestifere agreed. Then, catching Zarek's eye, his brow dropped. "We must speak."

"Oh? What of?"

"I have a mission to see to."

"Another? You've only just returned."

The priest nodded. "It cannot be helped."

"But I've need of you here."

Pestifere wiped his brow. "I am of more use to our venture where I go."

Sighing, the emperor nodded. "Very well. But before you leave, we'd best go over our plan of attack. Now that most of our scouts have returned, some of our forward teams could head out soon. Possibly as early as in a fortnight or so."

"It may be beneficial to wait just yet—as I make further arrangements." Pestifere paused, in thought. "We can discuss things further this evening so that I may be on my way tomorrow, at first light."

He turned to go, but then stopped short and looked back. "Oh, you will be pleased to know that the underlords have provided the means for me to communicate with you while I am away."

"And that is?"

"Just as Lilith did in the days of old, I will summon their presence through a looking glass. They will then relay to you, all of which I inform them."

"Very well."

"As I said, I will provide you further details this evening." With that, amidst the sounds of clashing swords, of grumblings and cries of both pain and triumph from Zarek's fighting forces-in-training, Pestifere headed off to prepare for his journey.

CHAPTER THIRTEEN

Mara convinced Dixon, Lucy, and the twins, to wait until evening to travel. Believing they'd be safer arriving somewhere in the dark, as the risk of someone seeing them appearing out of nowhere would be lower, she urged them to head straight for Ezra's place, The Clandest Inn, where they intended to stay anyway. Besides, she reasoned with them, she wanted some time with the girls before they set off. After some discussion, they all agreed.

Unlike Mara, who could travel with both the twins at the same time, Dixon and Lucy each could take only one of them. Like Mara, they found their magic paths through swirls of color, with tints and hues, shades and tones, which eventually became, upon arrival, a solid scene before them.

Landing in the stables of the inn, hay and sawdust beneath their feet, the smell of horse in the air, the Oathtakers glanced at one another, both grinning broadly, clearly pleased with their traveling success.

Dixon approached the hostler on duty, the only person in sight. Fortunately, he was the same man he and Lucy had met weeks earlier when the two of them had delivered Liam and Rafal there to meet with Ezra before they set off for Chiran. Thus, he was spared the trouble of explaining how they had all appeared out of thin air.

"Destry, it's good to see you again." Dixon greeted the man with a handshake. "Back so soon?"

"We've business to attend. Is Ezra in?"

Destry brushed hay from his clothing. Then he grabbed a pitchfork propped up against the wall. "He's inside."

After making their way across the frost-laden grounds to the front door of the inn, their breath billowing in the air, they stepped inside. There, a familiar scene met them. Barmaids rushed from table to table, slapping cold ales down before the patrons. Meanwhile, a fiddler played a lively tune, accenting the up-beat, inviting dancers to join in the fun.

As Dixon's eyes scanned the premises, a barmaid approached his side. Plump, and boasting a generous bosom, her cheeks turned rosy when she smiled.

"Delighted to see you, Dixon!" she cried, poking his side.

He turned her way and smiled. "And you, Nancy." He leaned back for a good look at her. "You know, time never seems to tell on you."

"Ha! Well, Dixon, while I appreciate your flattery, the mirror tells me otherwise." She grinned, her brow raised.

"No, I swear. It's the truth." Then, looking over the place again, he said, "Things are busy, I see."

"Yes. As to the Clandest Inn, I would say that it is true that some things never change." Then turning to Lucy and the twins, as though seeing them for the first time, her brow lowered. "Goodness Dixon," she winked at him, "but I swear that every time I see you, you're in the company of some new and beautiful women."

Laughing, he introduced Lucy and the twins to her, just as Ezra and Celestine arrived on the scene.

After greeting Dixon, Ezra bowed toward Lucy. "If it isn't Lucy Haven in the house! Welcome back."

"Thank you." Smiling, she glanced about. "I see that the hospitality business thrives."

"Yes, as does the spy business, let's not forget." Then standing back, he turned toward the twins. "Gracious Good One!" he exclaimed. "I haven't seen you two since you were just young teens. Do you remember? Mara and Dixon brought you here for the festival one year."

"Yes," Reigna said. "We have fond memories of The Clandest Inn." She introduced herself, and then her sister.

"You look so much like your mother." The innkeeper shook his head as though in disbelief.

"Don't they though?" Dixon agreed.

"The spitting image."

Dixon brushed his fingers through his hair. "I'd forgotten that you didn't get to see them when we were all here in the city, after they journeyed into The Tearless. I'm sorry. We were just so busy preparing things before heading back to the compound. Then we packed our things up there and returned to the palace in Shimeron."

"Yes, you mentioned you were headed to the palace when you delivered Liam and Rafal here. Did your journey there go well?"

"It did, thank you."

Celestine stepped up to greet her cousin, Dixon, with a kiss to his cheek. Then she returned to her husband, Ezra's, side.

"What brings you here?" the innkeeper asked Dixon. Then his brow dropped. "Wait a minute. Where's Mara?" He glanced at the door, apparently anticipating that she might merely have lagged behind.

His voice kept low, Dixon explained how, in the interests of time, and in light of her illness, they'd left her at the palace.

"Oooh," Ezra grimaced, then with gritted teeth, acted out a flinch.

"Yes," Eden agreed, smiling, "she was none too pleased."

"Well, let's hope she's well soon."

The innkeeper turned and pointed toward a back hall. "I can set up your old and familiar quarters for you," he told Dixon. "But first, I hope you all have time for a brew. Yes?"

Dixon looked at Lucy and then at the twins, his brow raised in question.

"Certainly," Lucy said.

With Celestine's arm linked through his, and the others following behind, Ezra wound his way through the crowd to a table at the back of the room Once everyone was seated, he motioned for Nancy to bring drinks.

"So what brings you here?" he asked. He grinned at Dixon. "I'm reminded that wherever you go, trouble seems to follow."

"Ha ha ha!" Dixon laughed. "Well, hopefully not this time."

"When we were last in the city," Reigna said, "we left Galen Dax and Aliza Kensey in charge of the Oathtakers that stayed here to train."

"I'd heard that, yes," Ezra said. "You made excellent choices with those two."

"Agreed. In any case, we've come to see how they're faring, and to bring them the latest news we've received from Liam and Rafal who are now in Chiran."

"I'm happy to hear that they made their way there safely," Ezra said.

Lucy leaned in. She explained that Liam and Rafal reported of Chireniar troops they had reason to believe might enter Oosa before long, near Ethanward.

"Have you got anyone stationed in that general area?" she asked the innkeeper.

Grimacing, he shook his head. "Unfortunately, no longer."

"Why is that?"

Nancy arrived with a tray laden with food and drink. After leaning it on the edge of the table, she deposited a sturdy earthenware mug before each of the innkeeper, Celestine, and their visitors. Then she filled the steins with cold ale.

"Here you go," she said, as a rich malt scent filled the air, along with the spicy smell of hops. Next, she put before them all, a basket filled with slices of bread, a platter loaded with chunks of succulent hot, roasted pork, and a stack of plates, knives and forks.

"It's quite chilly out, and I thought a snack here, might help to warm you up," she added as, finally, she deposited a jar of a warm, spicy sauce in the center of the table.

"Yes, it seems winter is taking hold," Ezra said. "Thank you, Nancy."

Dixon inhaled deeply "It looks—and smells—great."

"I'll say!" Reigna exclaimed.

"Enjoy yourselves, now," Nancy said before whisking off to attend to other guests.

"Where were we?" Lucy asked. "Oh, yes, Ezra, you were going to tell us why you haven't any spies at the border near Ethanward."

He leaned back, nonchalantly. "The criminal element has run rampant in those parts for some time now," he said. "Quite a number of refugees have made their way into Oosa around that area. Many of the former locals moved on."

"We saw some of that when we passed through there on our way to Shimeron," Lucy said. She proceeded to explain how the girls' oldest sister, Vida, with her Oathtaker, Clarimonde, traveled with them from there, to the palace.

Dixon picked up the stack of plates, kept one, and then passed the others to Reigna, who sat to his right. She took one, handed the remainder to Eden at her other side, and then reached for the platter of shredded roast pork that Dixon offered her.

"From time to time, over the years," the innkeeper said, "Vida and Clarimonde provided my people with information. I'd begun to worry for their safety. So I'm glad to hear they're at the palace now."

"Yes," Lucy agreed.

"I actually lost two men to traveling marauders in that area, not long ago."

"I'm sorry to hear that."

"Yes, well, that's when I discontinued sending any more of my people that way. It seems that when control broke down, thieves took over the roadways. Had you not been in such a large group when you traveled through, you'd likely have fallen victim yourselves. My people just stay away now." The innkeeper scowled. "Unfortunately that means that we get little news from those parts."

"We arranged for some of our troops to head that way," Lucy said. Then she turned to the twins. "Let's not forget to have Effie and Fleet send some flits to join Marshall's camp there," she said.

"Good thinking," Reigna said. Then she glanced at the food. "Goodness, enough of business for now. Let's eat!"

Chapter Fourteen

Reigna swung her sword with all her force. On contact, the reverberation of metal-on-metal shook her. It vibrated through her being. Jumping back, her arm dropped from the weight of her weapon. Her thoughts momentarily fuzzy, her eyes unfocused, she took in a deep breath and then pulled her blade up again. Growling, she charged back into the fray.

"Stop. Stop! Stoooop!"

The force behind her too great to halt abruptly, she leaned sideways, then fell over, landing on her shoulder. She rolled, still gripping the handle of her sword with both hands. Sawdust billowed, filling her mouth and nose, choking her.

"Are you all right?" Dax ran to her side.

Coughing, she got to her hands and knees. She glanced up, panting. She coughed again, then spit out a mouthful of dirt and wood chips.

"Yes, I'm fine. And—I think I understand now." Her breath clouded up in the cold air.

"It's like I was telling you," he said, "you haven't the advantage of weight on your side. You'll need—"

"I know. I know." She put her hand out to stop him. "I know. I need to *dance* my way through, not *barge* my way through."

"Exactly. That's why I wanted you to see what happens when you charge like that, wielding the weight of a real, and not a practice, sword."

He reached for her hand. "Here," he said, helping her to her feet. "You're taller than the average woman, which is to your benefit in many ways, but you haven't the bulk of the average man to go along with it. Your strength lies not in brute force, but in finesse. Remember, you are an artist," he added, holding her gaze. "Use those skills you've been taught so well, and steer clear of allowing others to convince you to the contrary."

She hung her head, her chest still heaving. "Yes, I see. I just get anxious, I guess."

Lucy approached. She brushed sawdust and ice crystals off Reigna's arms and back. "Have you had enough for the day yet?" she asked her. Then she turned to Dax. "It's a good thing you stopped when you did. We can't have her hurt."

"I understand," he said. "Now, if the two of you will excuse me?" He bobbed his head, then walked off.

"Just give me a minute, Lucy," Reigna said, leaning over, her hands on her thighs, still gasping for air. "I'll be fine. And Dax has been careful. He was showing me—" She stopped short, startled, when glancing Lucy's way, she found her looking off into the distance with widened eyes and her mouth gaping open.

"What is it?" she asked her, standing up straight.

Lucy pressed her palm to her chest. "Ahhh . . . Oh . . . nothing." She shook her head. "Nothing."

"You look like you've seen a ghost."

"Do I?" She turned back. "Huh. Well, no matter."

Reigna stole a glance in the direction in which Lucy had been looking. "Did you see something—or perhaps, someone?"

"Me?" Her eyes flickered out again for the briefest moment. "Oh, no. No, never mind." She tucked her hair behind her ear in a sort of nervous gesture. "Now—"

"You'll forgive me for saying, that you appear to be working to convince yourself as much as to convince me."

After stealing another look away, Lucy commented, "Oh, it's . . . nothing. Now, let's get your sister and be on our way. Dixon is expecting us. Unfortunately, as I'm running late, I'll have to reschedule a meeting with Salus—a healer and an old acquaintance of mine."

They ambled across sanctuary's training grounds, toward the archery fields. As they approached each lane, the archer there awaiting a turn, glanced their way and acknowledged them with a wave or a curt bow.

Finally spotting her twin at the far end, Reigna picked up her pace, motioning for Lucy to do the same.

When they arrived, they found a woman, one of the arms-trainers, at Eden's side.

Eden stood, with the string of her bow pulled back and resting against the tip of her nose, and her hand anchored to the back of her jawbone. "Like this?" she asked.

"Yes, that's right," the woman said. "In truth, you have good form, but if you tweak the stance you've been using just a bit—just like you are right now—I think you'll discover that you're even better. So, go ahead now."

Eden focused. She adjusted her aim and then loosed her arrow.

"Bullseye!" Reigna cried out seconds later.

Her twin turned to her, beaming. "Reigna, you've got to try this!" she exclaimed. "Fabiana is amazing. A few minor adjustments and she's got me shooting like that!" She pointed at the target.

Smirking, Reigna held her hand up and out. "We've been over this, Eden. I'm no archer. I'll leave that to you, while I spend my time improving on those things relating to where my talents lie."

A man ran toward them. He stopped just feet away. "A report has come in from the border," he said, "and Dax and Aliza asked me to find you."

Eden handed her bow and quiver off to Fabiana, then grabbed Reigna's arm. "Let's go then," she said, setting off, motioning for Lucy to follow.

Back when Ehyeh tested the twins, while they were lost in The Tearless groups of Oathtakers traveled across Oosa, seeking to find all the remaining Oathtakers and Select in the realm that they could. Most of those they found agreed to meet in the City of Light, arriving there just days before the earthshaking that occurred when the twins found Ehyeh's favor and therefore, came into their powers. Since then, the City of Light in general, and sanctuary in particular, overflowed with the newcomers, as most had chosen to stay on so that they could train in preparation of meeting the threat from Chiran.

Lucy and the twins, now arm-in-arm, rushed through the crowds, across the portion of the grounds the Oathtakers had traditionally used to train young men and women who sought to join their order.

The facilities sat to one side of the main sanctuary building. At its other side sat a library and research center where, in days past, students attended classes and studied, in hopes of earning their Oathtaker credentials. They, as well as their instructors, stayed in the nearby dormitory, along with the occasional traveling sanctuary guest. A few oldtimers who'd committed their lives to Ehyeh's cause had also chosen to live on site. But now, the residence hall overflowed with all the recent newcomers.

When they reached the research center, Lucy came to a sudden halt. Surprised at her abruptness, the twins both stumbled.

Before fully falling, Eden regained her balance. She turned to Lucy, her brow furrowed. "What was that all about? I nearly tripped!"

Lucy stood stock still, gazing into the distance, her mouth opening and closing, but with no sound coming out.

Reigna grabbed her elbow and turned her around. "What is it?"

She dropped her head in her hands and shook it. "I'm sorry, girls. I'm just . . . distracted today, I guess."

"This is twice today that you've done this. Who did you see?"

"Who?" Lucy looked Reigna in the eye. "Ahhh, no one. I just—" She bit her lip. "I guess that sometimes the gravity of this all just leaves me . . . Oh, I don't know."

Eden scowled. "Never mind, then. Come on, let's go."

Before them a granite staircase rose to the front door of the research center. Bits of graupel, hail-like snow pellets, rested in the corners of the steps, each of which nature had frosted with a thin layer of ice.

"Get some gravel on these right away," Lucy ordered one of the attendants on duty, as she pointed at the steps and scowled at him. "We can't afford unnecessary injuries."

He bowed, acknowledging the order, then rushed off to attend to the matter.

While keeping their feet wide apart and moving slowly, deliberately, so as to maintain their balance, the twins and Lucy made their way to the door and then entered the building.

Crowds filled the hallway before them. Men and women dressed and armed for training, scurried about, making room for the on-duty healer, who just then ushered an injured man toward a nearby room designated as the infirmary.

"Oh, Salus!" Lucy cried on sight of the Oathtaker. "I'm glad I caught you. I'm afraid we'll have to reschedule."

"Certainly," he replied. "I'll wait to hear from you."

As Lucy and the twins continued on, the pack spread back, allowing room for them to pass. Thus, they marched through, to the end of the hall. Then they stepped into the conference room they'd reserved earlier as a meeting place.

"What is it, Dax?" Reigna asked, making her way forward, her footsteps clicking on the hardwood floor. Then she caught sight of two flits sitting on the table, on duty there for the day so as to rush communications about, should the need arise.

"Hello, Fugacious," she said to the first of them, "and Mercurial," she addressed the other as she slipped off her cloak and draped it over a chair. For whatever reason, she and her twin had taken to using the flits' full names whenever they spoke to, or referred to, one of them.

The flits returned her greeting, then acknowledged both Lucy and Eden.

Dax, his face buried in a stack of papers on the table before him, looked up. "Please, sit down," he said, "and grab some lunch." He gestured toward the fare before them.

"I am hungry," Reigna said as she grabbed a bowl and then scooped some rice into it. Atop it, she spooned some of the rich stew that she found. Thick with roasted chili and cumin-spiced chicken, corn, black beans, garlic, onions, and stewed tomato, its spicy, peppery aroma filled the air.

"Great Ehyeh, this smells amazing," she muttered as she topped the fare with shredded cheese, after which she filled another bowl with some stone-ground corn chips.

She sat, then mixed the stew and rice. Once through, she scooped some up with a chip and ate it.

"Mmmm . . . so, so good," she mumbled, her mouth full. "This almost puts Adele's cooking to shame."

Grinning, Eden got her lunch.

Lucy followed suit.

"I swear, Reigna, you're always hungry," her twin teased as she sat down.

"What? I can't help it!" Reigna held her free hand out, palm up. "Ever since freezing and starving in The Tearless, I've been like a bottomless pit."

She took another bite, then turned back to Dax, suddenly all business. "All right then, what's happening?" she asked him.

The door opened and in walked Dixon with Aliza Kensey.

"Good, you're here," Dax acknowledged them. "So, here's the situation," he said, once again addressing the twins. "A report came in just this morning that a company of about a hundred men neared Oosa within the last days. We understand they've set up a camp not far from Ethanward."

"We'd heard from Liam and Rafal that there were some Chirarian troops headed that way," Eden said.

"Yes, but until now, we'd had no credible reports of their arrival in the area."

"As you all know, we already sent Marshall and some of the others that way," Dixon said. "Hopefully, they'll be able to respond to an invasion, should one occur."

"Yes," Lucy said, "and for the record, I've intended to make sure that they have some good healers with them. I just ran into Salus, who I think is an excellent candidate to put in charge there. Do any of you know him?"

"I do," Dax said. "He's a good choice." Then, sighing, he pushed his now empty bowl of lunch aside. "But you know, in truth," he filled his teacup, "our greatest lack at this time, is of information from the Chiranian side of the border."

"Have you a plan of some kind to address that?" Lucy asked.

He glanced Aliza's way. "As a matter of fact, we do."

"Oh?" Reigna spoke up. "What's that?"

"I'd like permission to go there," Aliza said.

"Inside Chiran?" Reigna pulled back. "But, Aliza, we need you here. Also, it cannot go unsaid that as much as you—as all we women for that matter—are preparing for this threat, we know what a terrible place that would be for any of us."

"But I have an advantage."

Eden tapped her spoon on the table. "What's that?" she asked.

"My attendant magic."

Dixon leaned in. "Are you saying what I think you're saying, Aliza? That you want to mask yourself as one of them? That—"

"Liam and Rafal are already doing that—just as Marshall and Jerrett did in the past," Lucy said. "From their reports, they've managed to dress themselves like the Chiranian guards and to infiltrate their troops. I see no reason to risk your safety, Aliza, or for us to lose the advantage of having you here with us, training. Besides—"

"Wait, Lucy," Dax said, "I think you should hear her out."

Aliza sat with her hands tented open, tapping her fingertips together. "Listen, with my magic, I can make the Chiranian soldiers see exactly what I want them to see. Perhaps in doing so, I could get more relevant information. You see, I could take on the form—"

"Of Zarek, himself, if necessary," Lucy completed her sentence, her eyes wide.

Aliza bit the inside of her cheek. "It is possible. I could do that, although of course, my main goal would be to gather information. In fact, I'd prefer not to engage with anyone at all."

"How long could you keep it up? Using your magic to trick Chiranians, I mean. Surely, you'd need to stop to rest from time to time." Lucy shook her head. "Look, I haven't time to create another means for you to communicate with us. You can't use the compact I created because only a current or former Oathtaker to a seventh of the Select can use it. And the only other success I've had with such an item to date, was with the compass I provided Liam and Rafal when they left Oosa." She paused, tapping on the table. "No, it's too dangerous," she finally concluded.

"Hold on, Lucy," Reigna said, "we shouldn't dismiss this idea out of hand."

"I can keep my magic operating for long periods without needing a rest," Aliza said. "And you, Dixon," she continued, "could get me inside the border directly, so that I could get started right away." She looked at each of the others, in turn. "Perhaps I can cause confusion with the Chiranian troops that I meet up with. But best of all, if I go, I can get a good look at what's really happening in those parts."

"In general, Aliza, I like your idea," Reigna said, "but think about it. You say that what we lack, is information. However, even if you gathered some while there, you couldn't get it back to us. Moreover, in truth, I don't want to send you in alone."

"I wouldn't be alone."

Dixon stared at her. "You want me to stay there, as well?"

"No. Thank you for the offer, though," Aliza said, grinning. "Actually, I've already recruited a couple of willing assistants." She turned to the flits. "Fuggy? Merc?"

Fugacious spread his wings, then flew toward Reigna and Eden. Mercurial followed behind. Landing on the table before them, the flits bowed.

"With your permission, Merc and I would accompany Aliza," Fuggy said.

"Yes, and then, should the need arise, one of us could get word back to you quickly," his fellow flit added.

The twins shared a glance.

"Fugacious," Reigna said, "we depend on you flits here to—to get messages around between us."

He smiled at her halfheartedly. "Forgive me if I sound . . . presumptuous," he said, "but in truth, that is not the best use of our abilities."

She pulled back. "You don't think so?"

"Look," he said, "most of the time, around here," he waved his hand to indicate his surroundings, "you can assign one of your own kind to carry a message—just as was done today to get word to you that Dax hoped to meet with you here."

"So?"

"So you should take advantage of our real skills. They lie in our ability to go the distance—to make our way to and fro far more quickly than can one of your own kind."

"You are absolutely correct," Reigna said. She turned to Eden. "What do you think?"

"I guess the plan sounds good."

"As I think on it," Reigna added, "we've meant to get some flits to stay with Marshall and the troops stationed on this side of the border, as well. We should do that now."

"We'll let Effie and Fleet know that they should send some of our ranks off straight away," Merc said.

"Good," Lucy agreed.

"Well then, Aliza," Eden said, "if you're willing to go with Fugacious and Mercurial, I think we should allow for it."

"We're all agreed then," Reigna said, standing, her lunch bowl in hand. "Now," she grinned, "I need more of this . . . chili-soup, or whatever this is . . ."

Chapter Fifteen

Shivering, he wrapped his arms around himself. Cold had descended in the last weeks, and although he kept a fire burning in his quarters at all times, Broden couldn't seem to shake the chill, as he spent most of his hours in the unheated prison for women. From there, he oversaw the latest captures, and prepared caravans of the unlucky—those he'd have to send to the troops. It disgusted him. He forced down his bile, its acidity threatening its way up the back of his throat. The women's cries sounded out, morning, midday, and into the wee hours of the night, day after merciless day. They left him sick at heart, and with a constant headache.

Sitting at the table he used for a desk, in the room he'd designated as an office, Broden dropped his head into his hands. This was madness. He simply couldn't save them all.

But I can save some.

"What of this one, master?" Striver asked upon entering, his voice shaky.

Broden looked up. His heart sank. At Striver's side was a bound prisoner, trembling with fear.

"She's a child!" he cried, taking to his feet.

His tutor refused to look him in the eye. "You know your father, Zarek's, orders. We must fill the wagon. And, there's still room—"

Broden struggled to fight back a cry, then let it loose. "No. No!" He shoved the papers and files from the tabletop to the floor. "Not this one!" He clutched his middle, to suppress his visceral reaction. "There's still some hope, albeit little, for the young."

He approached the girl at Striver's side. "How old are you?" he asked, his voice hard.

She spat, then charged at him.

Striver held out the staff he carried for precisely this purpose, blocking her forward movement. Not allowed to wield weapons, it was all he had to help Broden to maintain order in the prison.

She grabbed it, then struggled to escape.

"He's trying to help you," Striver cried. "Stop now!"

She leaned over and bit his hand, bearing down hard, growling all the while.

He cried out in pain and surprise.

Broden shoved his tutor aside, breaking her hold. "Listen to him," he ordered. "I'm trying to save you."

She glared at him, seething. "You took my mother!"

Striver stumbled to regain his balance. He brushed on his pant leg, blood that trickled down the back of his hand.

The girl sobbed. "You took my mother!" she repeated.

Broden stood before her. "I'm sorry. I'm doing what I can, but I have my orders."

"Orders! Mother says you are all monsters."

"She has it mostly right, I'm sorry to say. I cannot save you all. But I can save some. I can save *you*. Or at least I can try."

He turned to address Striver. "Isn't there something? Some . . . provisions they require where the cart is going that we can fill it with? Help me out here!"

Carlie stepped up. "There's a trunk we could send," she suggested.

"What's in it?"

Tear pooled in her eyes. "Weapons."

"Ohhhh!" Broden cried, wiping his hand across his forehead. "Weapons that ultimately will be used against our own kind! This is utter madness."

He paced, rubbing the back of his neck, breathing heavily. Then he went suddenly still. His shoulders sagged.

"Great Ehyeh," he moaned, "I cannot do this any longer."

"You can do it for this one," Carlie said, approaching him and resting her hand on his arm. "How old do you suppose she is? Ten? Maybe?" Her eyes held his. "It's our only choice this time."

Broden turned to the girl. "What's your name, child?"

She stood mute, glaring.

Carlie stepped toward her and then knelt. "We're doing everything we can to help you," she said.

Her eyes flickered from her, to Striver, and then to Broden. "Clementine," she muttered.

"Listen, Clementine," Broden said, "I need your help if I'm to keep you from being sent off. What can you do? Do you have any special talents or skills? I need to find a job for you of such importance that—"

"You can't promise her that," Striver muttered.

"No, but I can promise to try!" Broden glared at him. Then he turned back to Clementine, willing himself to calm down. "Tell me," he said, his voice softer now, "what can you do?"

"Wait!" Carlie exclaimed. "You said Zarek is using children for casters. Why don't you tell him that you've grown fearful, and have chosen to put one into service for yourself?"

"Just let them take me," the girl said, holding her head high. "I'm strong. Save my mother instead. Please. She's all my younger brothers and sisters have."

Broden shook his head. "I'm sorry. I cannot."

"But . . . she may die."

Closing his eyes, he hung his head. "My dear, she's already well on her way."

Clementine fell to her knees. "Please. Please!"

Broden crouched down before her. He put his hand on her shoulder. When she looked up, he shook his head. "I cannot. But I will do everything I can to save you, Clementine. I promise."

The table was laden with all good things—roasted wild boar bathed in a dried cherry, red wine, and shallot sauce; sweet potato hash, fragrant with cloves; and carrots, fire-roasted. To top off the refection, the cook had provided hot fresh bread for sopping up the juices. The fragrances from the various dishes rose into the air, tickling the diners' noses.

Broden, as usual, sat next to Zarek, with Striver at his right. He hated leaving Carlie and the other slave women who assisted him alone with their guards, but he had no choice about attending this dinner meeting, as the emperor entertained a guest.

He looked at the woman who sat across from him. This was the first he'd ever seen Zarek with one of her kind. Although petite, she displayed boldness in her demeanor. Perhaps it was her raven hair streaked with gray, pulled up tight and held back, that gave her such an air of authority. *Or perhaps it's that deep widow's peak of hers*, he thought.

Grimacing, he watched as the taster, another child, partook of a bite from each item on the table.

When a minute later, nothing had happened, a guard directed the boy toward a back door, through which he stepped out.

"I must say, Emperor Zarek," the woman purred, watching the child, "your wherewithal never ceases to amaze me."

"Oh?"

When she grinned in response, Broden feared her skin might crack. Clearly the expression was a most unusual one for her.

"The boy," she said, gesturing with her fork in hand toward the door from whence the young taster had exited.

Zarek's brow rose. "Yes, Tanith, but then I give you credit for that." He laughed heartily. "Your plans all those years ago to raise some girls for sale here in Chiran was . . . brilliant! And to have initiated the venture with your own daughter . . ." He paused in thought. "Chaya was her name, if I remember correctly."

"It was, indeed."

Broden's eyes narrowed as he watched the exchange.

Tanith tasted the roast boar. "This is nicely done," she said.

"Hmmm, yes," Zarek agreed. "The chef who made this was captured seeking to escape Chiran—with his family. When we learned of his skills, we put him to use." Grinning, he leaned toward her. "The taster is one of his children, so you can trust me when I say that he is ever vigilant about anyone seeking to poison my food."

Broden cleared his throat, struggling to remain silent.

"Am I to understand that you are not in agreement?" Tanith asked turning his way, her eyes boring into him.

He pulled back and pointed at his chest. "Me?"

"Yes, you. I sense some . . . dissent."

"Oh, no, ma'am. In fact, I've my own taster now. A girl child of ten years or so."

Striver leaned in and addressed her. "Broden oversees the women's prison here."

Glaring at him, she lifted her glass of wine, examined its deep raspberry color in the candlelight, swirled it in her glass, and then sniffed at it. "So I heard," she said before tasting it. Then she turned to her host. "Really, Emperor Zarek, has it become the fashion to allow slaves at your table?"

"He is my son's tutor in all things Chiranian."

She sneered at Striver. "A tutor who hasn't learned not to speak in the midst of his betters?"

Striver's jaw dropped.

Struggling for words, Broden put his hand on his tutor's arm. Then, "I've given him the freedom to speak openly in my presence," he said, "so that he can inform me as to matters of which I should be aware—in the moment when the information may be of primary use to me."

Tanith put her fork down. "I see. Well, perhaps he should have taught you at the outset, how inappropriate it would be for him to directly address one of his superiors."

Broden turned Striver's way. "Make note of that," he said before turning back to Zarek's guest. "So, Mortal Tanith, what brings you here, to Fallique?" He used the title *Mortal* as a sly reminder to her, and perchance to Zarek as well, that she was of no greater significance than any other free Chiranian.

With her eyes narrowed, she once again tasted her wine. "Well, it so happens that I ran into Brother Pestifere some time ago. He suggested I take a look at the prison here. Now that I'm in charge of the one at Camp Cark, in Darth, I thought it would be prudent to follow his advice. So, here I am. I must say, Master Zarek," she added, glancing his way, "that I particularly appreciate your use of the grut here. Would that I had some in Darth."

"Perhaps we can arrange for that," he said.

Broden pushed the food around on his plate. Looking back up, he addressed Zarek. "Shall I conduct a tour for Mortal Tanith, then?"

Once again, her eyes narrowed at him, but she said nothing.

The emperor turned to his guest. "Broden has much to learn about Chiran, that is true. Still, I need someone in charge of the prison, and he convinced me that I should give him the opportunity to prove himself. So far, I've had no reason to regret my decision. He's managed to prepare numerous shipments of slaves. Why, just a short while ago, he even found room on one of the wagons to send more weapons your way."

"I see." Then turning to Broden, the corners of Tanith's mouth turned up into what might be deemed a smile, had the gesture reached her eyes. "I would like that then. A tour of the prison, I mean."

CHAPTER SIXTEEN

Rounding the corner, he used his free hand to pull his wool cape closer so as to hold out the cold. He'd always hated winter. He much preferred hot, dry days. They matched the deep burning heat of Daeva's presence within him. But some things couldn't be helped, and as it was time to render the service required of him, he'd have to bear the discomfort. After all, he'd soon need the full strength of youth.

Having spent time around the healers' quarters of late, he'd become familiar with a number of them—and it was a good thing too. It allowed for him to choose the perfect candidate—a small man who, it also happened, was an acquaintance of his from days of old.

When his cane unexpectedly slipped on a patch of ice, he stumbled, then quickly righted himself—but not before wrenching his back. Grimacing, he set out once again, his handicap now appearing even more pronounced than before.

He picked up his pace; he didn't want to be late.

He turned the next corner and seconds later approached The Swindler's Cup, a seedy pub. It hadn't been easy to convince his target to meet him here, as the establishment's reputation was well known. Still, he couldn't risk arranging an appointment at a place where the two of them might be seen together.

Inside, the regular patrons, most of whom were addicted to more than merely the spirits of alcohol, lounged in various states of delirium. An acrid smoke hovered in the air in layers around them.

He glanced about. "Ahhh, Salus, there you are," he said as he neared the corner table where he sat. "I feared I might be late."

Salus sat up straighter. "This place is—"

"Abysmal, yes, I know."

"Tell me again why we had to meet here."

"I wanted you to see this. I have discovered that it can be helpful for a healer to know the circumstances of his patient's life and . . . Well, I understand she spent considerable time here."

"She's an addict you said."

"Sola? Yes."

"And no doubt she prostituted herself to feed her habit."

Salus nodded at the establishment's keeper who approached with two ales that he slapped down on the table, after which he returned to the bar.

"I hope you don't mind," he said, "I took the liberty of ordering."

"Not at all."

Salus picked up his mug. Noticing something old and dried stuck to the rim of it, he grimaced, coughed, and then put it back down. "Never mind." He sighed. "What's she addicted to then?"

"Bibulous nut, I believe."

"Her teeth are red?"

"With what I can tell from those few she still has left, yes."

Salus shuddered. "As you well know, there's not much a healer can do with an addiction. He can't take the desire away—that's something the individual must, with Ehyeh's aid, conquer for himself. Or *herself*, as the case may be."

The man sighed deeply. "Yes, I know. Still, the physical effects can be devastating and I understand you have been particularly successful in cases like this. Not every Oathtaker-healer is."

"Yes, that's right."

"Surely then, there is something you could do to help."

"Possibly."

"I would not ask this, but she is—"

"Your sister. Yes, I understand."

The man hung his head. "Shortly after I left home as a young man, to train, I lost contact with Sola. She got caught up with the wrong crowd and . . . disappeared." He looked back up. "Then out of the blue the other day, right here in the city, I ran into her. She begged me to help her and . . . Well, I just cannot bring myself to stand by and watch her suffer this way."

"What have you done so far?"

"Not much. I sought to ease what discomfort I could, and then I moved her to a little cottage very near here. She is there now—at least I hope she still is. I told her I would bring help."

Salus stood. "No time like the present then." He pulled some coins from his pocket, selected enough to pay for the untouched ales, and then dropped them on the flyspecked table. One of them landed on its side, spun in place, gradually slowed, and then fell flat with a *clink*.

Together the men made their way out the door and down the street.

Minutes later, they arrived before a cottage set back from the street. Various shrubs planted around it had grown wild and now nearly hid the building from view. Smoke sputtered up from its chimney.

The man stepped to the front door, which sported flaking paint. A squeaky sound, along with the smell of woodsmoke and mildew, filled the air when he opened it.

He motioned for Salus to enter. "After you," he said.

After stepping inside, Salus stood with his hands on his hips. "Where to?" he asked.

Pointing at the fireplace, the man said, "Please, have a seat—just there. I will get her."

He stepped away, then turned back. "Oh, here, let me get your cape for you."

If I do this just right, I can disarm him before he even knows what happened.

With that, he reached for the Oathtaker's blade, grasped it firmly, and then drew it.

Surprised, Salus tried to spin around, but not before the man planted his cane between his feet, causing him to lose his balance. As he struggled to remain upright, the man pushed him against the wall with his left hand, and then plunged the blade into his back with his right.

Salus threw his head back. His eyes went wide as his next breath caught in his throat. As magic provided, the Oathtaker's own blade used against him, brought his immediate death.

Slowly, his body slipped to the floor. It landed with a thump.

The man grabbed the front of Salus's tunic and pulled. It took a minute for him to make his way across the room to a back door that led to an enclosed garden. Then, leaving the body just inside, he stepped out.

He approached the space he'd selected earlier for burying Salus, then dropped to his knees. Grinning maliciously, and holding the dead man's blade, he stabbed it into the nearly frozen earth.

Chapter Seventeen

Pulling her head down and closing her cloak more tightly, so as to keep out the gusting wind and sleet, Lucy made her way inside. She stomped her feet on the rug, then marched to the end of the hall. Stepping into the meeting room, she found Dax sitting at the opposite end of the long oak conference table that graced the center of the floor.

"Hello, Dax," she greeted him. "Dixon and the twins are with Professor Hadwin today, so I wondered if you could use some help here."

"Oh, no need to ask. I'm sure Reigna and Eden would like for us to get these plans together as quickly as possible. I'd appreciate your assistance."

"I've got this afternoon free. I had intended to meet with Salus about heading to the border, but he's nowhere to be found. So I'm going to return to the palace for a short time, while Dixon remains here with the twins. I want to check on Mara. You know, I'm surprised she hasn't shown up herself . . ." She shook her head and sighed. "In any case . . ."

She strolled to the hearth, then stood there quietly, rubbing her hands together to warm them over the crackling fire. Looking back over her shoulder, someone outside the window behind Dax, heading toward the building, caught her attention.

"Oh!" she gasped.

"What is it?"

"I'll be right back!" she cried.

She ran out of the room, down the hall and through the crowds, and then burst out the front door. Having thrown caution to the wind, when she reached the second step, she slipped. Her feet gave way beneath her, sending her tumbling down the remaining steps where she landed, sprawled out, her legs twisted beneath her.

"Oh, blast!" she groaned, pulling herself up to her elbows. Grimacing, she sat up, then brushed the snow from her face and sleeves.

"Can I help you?" came a man's voice.

Looking up, her breath caught her throat. She stared. Then, "Oh!" she exclaimed. "Percival! Percival Ferreolo!" Her eyes narrowed. "Is that you?"

"Well, hello, Lucy. I'm flattered you remember me. It's been quite some time.

Here, let me help." He reached his hand out to her.

Gripping it firmly, she thanked him, staring at him all the while. "When did you arrive?" she asked.

"Just a couple weeks ago. It seems word of all the Oathtakers and Select gathering here in the city finally reached my little corner of the world."

"Goodness, but I feel so ridiculous," she muttered.

"It could happen to anyone." He paused. "Well, anyone with two left feet anyway."

Chuckling, she stood, only to discover that having twisted her knee, she couldn't put all of her weight on one leg. "Oooh oooh, oooh . . . ouch," she moaned.

"Here, let me help."

Nearly carrying her, Percival assisted her to a nearby bench.

"I'm a healer, you'll recall," he said as he sat beside her, "although I've been told that my bedside manner is rather . . . unusual. Left to my own devices, I'm afraid I'm a bit . . . grim. But you know, over the years I've discovered that people who laugh, mend more quickly. So, while humor doesn't exactly come naturally to me, I . . . try."

She grinned. "Yes, as I recall, you were always a serious one."

"I was just on my way to report for duty." He motioned toward the research center. "It seems we're in constant demand these days."

Lucy looked at him closely, as though examining his every feature. "You know, I never noticed the resemblance before," she muttered.

"Resemblance?"

She shook her head.

"To whom?"

"Oh . . . never mind." Then, cocking her head, she asked, "Did you just come from that way?" She pointed toward the training grounds.

"Yes. Why?"

She pursed her lips, in thought. "And you've been out to the training grounds of late?"

"Regularly, since my arrival, yes. I'm surprised we haven't run into each other before today."

"Hmmm. Well, like I said, it's nothing." She winced from the pain when he lifted her leg to rest it over his thighs. "You just remind me of someone I knew way back when. In fact, the resemblance is . . . uncanny, really."

She rubbed her knee. "Now, do you think you could lend me a bit of healing here?"

"Certainly. Sprained knees are one of my specialties—and it's a good thing, too. We can't have you out of commission."

He placed his hands on her knee. "Just here then, is that right? I can feel the heat."

"Yes."

As he poured his magic into her, she felt the swelling around her knee reduce, and the pain lessen.

When he was through, she rubbed it and put her foot back down. She bent her knee a couple of times and wiggled her toes. "Thank you."

"Don't mention it." He stood, but then quickly resumed his seat. "Ahhh, Lucy . . ."

"Yes?"

"I . . . ahhh . . . Well, I . . ."

"Yes?"

He pulled his shoulders back. "I don't know if you're aware of this, but I've outlived two charges. Filip passed not long after I last saw you." He paused, sighing. "Then my next charge, Arvid, died just recently."

Holding his gaze, she nodded. "No, Percival, I wasn't aware of that."

"Actually, of course, Filip was still just a child when I lost him." He looked out at a crowd gathering near the building.

"Oh, yes, now I remember! Filip was very young when you first swore to protect him." She cocked her head in thought. "If I remember correctly, there was a Council hearing into the matter of his death."

He hung his head. "Yes, that's right. I was, of course, exonerated from any wrongdoing."

"Yes, of course."

"And then there was Arvid . . . Well, I'd never intended to commit myself once again, but he was in need, and I was there. It . . . seemed like the right thing to do."

"I see." She held his gaze. "This 'Arvid' you mention. I don't recall ever having heard of, or of having met, him."

"He was a loner. Rather like your first charge, Selene."

"You say he died recently?"

"Of old age."

"I see."

She sat quietly for a minute. Then, "Remind me what happened to Filip," she said. "I seem to recall something about an unexplained illness that wasn't healed in a timely manner, or . . . something to that effect, anyway. Is that right?"

He looked down. "Truthfully, it's . . . hard to talk about . . . even after all these years."

He brushed newly fallen snow off from the top of his head. "It was a shock. I don't think Filip's parents ever got over it, and I— Well, if I'd understood the true nature of what was happening—of the dangers . . . I might have done something differently, taken action more quickly, even though it's sometimes best to allow a malady to run its natural course. Still—" He stopped short, swallowed hard.

"I'm sure," she patted his arm. Then, rubbing her hands together to warm them, she sighed. "As much as we all try to do for the Select, some things, as you know, are beyond our experience or our control. You're not to blame. Illnesses happen. Accidents and injuries happen. Old age happens, for that matter." She hesitated, lost in thought for a moment, and then added, "My advice is that you pick up the pieces and move on. You've a whole new life ahead of you now."

Glancing down, he nodded. "Yes, I've thought to do just that—move on, I mean. So I wondered . . ."

Her eyes narrowed. "Yes?"

He turned to face her full on. "Do you remember, Lucy, some time ago, when a number of us Oathtakers here in the city, along with our charges, happened to meet up with you?"

"I do."

"We had a great time," he said, holding her gaze. "At least, I had a great time."

"It was fun, yes. I remember that we gathered for dinner. Goodness, I don't know if I've ever laughed so hard. But you! Well, it took some doing to get you to join in." She slapped his arm and chuckled, recalling her memories. "You were just so very serious, Percival. Even so, I seem to recollect that we got you to lighten up—eventually."

"I do try," he said. "As a matter of fact, I make it a conscious effort these days to be a bit more . . . lighthearted—to smile more often. I find that it helps to put others at ease."

"Yes, it seems I'm relearning that same lesson. So, what about that night?"

"Well, excuse me if I'm being forward, but . . . as you know, at the time I was—" He hung his head. "Well, I'd just sworn an oath to protect Filip. I was committed." He glanced back at her. "But now . . . Well, in truth, I'd like to spend some time with you. You know, now that I've been released from my latest oath and all. I mean—"

Lucy put her hand on his arm. "Percival, you're a good man, but I've never made it any secret that my focus is elsewhere— So . . . Well, if it's your intention that something might come of our spending time together, you'd only be disappointed in the end."

"I see."

She gazed up at the falling snow. "I'm sorry."

"Hmmm." He pulled his shoulders back and took in a deep breath. "Well then, as to your injury, there will be no wild dancing on the tabletops for you for a while." Though the comment was humorous, he didn't crack a grin.

She laughed. "Oh, goodness, how ever will I restrain myself?"

"Truly, I advise you to stay off of your feet for a bit." He looked toward the research center, and then back at her. "And watch those steps next time. They can be slippery. Even for those of us without two left feet," he added with a shaky grin.

She chuckled, then turned serious. "Yes, I'd ordered gravel to be thrown on them the other day. It seems we'll have to put someone in charge of keeping them maintained, going forward."

"I'll have someone see to them right away." He stood. "Well, I guess I'd best be on my way." He hesitated. Then, "It was really, really nice to see you, Lucy," he said.

She nodded and then, as he set off, glanced across the grounds once more. She hadn't expected that. She'd certainly been aware of Percival's interest those many years ago. But having committed himself to Filip, she'd made certain he knew the boundaries. She frowned as she recalled that she'd actually found it necessary to remind him of his duty. Then she thought about the past weeks. Was it he whom she'd seen that day when she'd been training with the twins? It certainly was possible. Funny how she'd never noticed the likeness between Percival and Petrus in the past.

Sighing, she grasped the edge of the bench, preparing to rise.

"Hello, Lucy."

She looked up. All the color drained from her face. "Uhhh, I . . . Ahhh . . ." She stuttered, searching for words.

"It has been a long time," the newcomer said.

"Ahhh, yes, it— It has been a . . . a very long time." She smiled, then bit her lip. "Wha— Ahhh . . . What are you doing here, Petrus?"

With the snow now falling in earnest, Lucy brushed flakes off from the bench at her side and then patted it. "Have a seat," she said. "Tell me—what's been happening with you?" Her eyes narrowed as she looked him over closely. "Still looking youthful, I see," she added, smiling. "So then your charge—Tam—he still lives?"

"Ahhh, no."

"I'm sorry." She looked down. "I understand the loss, which it seems by the looks of you, must have been a recent one. Yes? Unless of course, you were committed to another of the Select since I last saw you."

"Ahhh . . . It was a recent loss, yes." He took in a deep breath and then let it out slowly.

She looked him over carefully. "Truly, Petrus, you were always thin, but you're looking a bit . . . gaunt," she said. "Are you eating at all?"

He shrugged.

She patted his hand. "I know, it's hard, but it will get better—a bit, anyway—over time."

"So they say."

"You know, you're not going to believe this, but I've thought of you several times of late. I even just now visited with someone who, it seems, bears a striking resemblance to you."

He raised his brow. "Oh? Who is that?"

"One of the healers. Percival Ferreolo. He helped me with a sprained knee." She rubbed it, absentmindedly. "Anyway, over the past weeks, I actually thought I saw you here at sanctuary a couple of times."

He pulled back, his brow lowered. "But . . . I only recently arrived."

"Yes, it seems it was all a case of mistaken identity then." She pursed her lips. "So, tell me, where have you been? How have you been? How has life treated you?"

He lifted his hands, palms up, shrugging. "Where does one begin?"

Smiling, she folded her hands. "Just the highlights will do." She hesitated. "Where did you go after we— After I last saw you?"

"I . . . ahhh . . . Well, of course, I thought I should not be . . . close. You know?" He looked at her, held her gaze for long seconds, and then looked away. "So I was relieved when Tam's family decided to move to the western parts of Oosa. They were from there originally. Then, after Tam's parent's died, he and I just stayed put."

"I see." When a gust of wind whipped its way inside her cloak, she pulled it closed more tightly. "And now?"

"I questioned where to go after his death." Petrus glanced across the training fields. "I decided to come here—just to check out sanctuary. I had no idea the place would be so busy." He shuffled snow away from beneath his leather-booted foot. "And how about you? Are you committed to another of the Select?"

"Not to an individual member, no."

"Meaning that you continue in your venture to assist all of the Select—in your commitment to them as a whole—and to Ehyeh."

"Yes, that's right." She pondered, wanting to choose her next words carefully.

"Well—" he said, making as though to rise.

"You should stay," she interrupted him, reaching for his elbow, then pulling him forward in a silent invitation to sit back down. "There's no charge now keeping you from another venture. We could use your help here."

"We?"

"The ranking members of the Select—the twins—Reigna and Eden."

"I have heard something of them."

"They've just come into their powers." She frowned. "And goodness but what powers they are," she added, muttering.

"Oh?"

"Let's just say they are most . . . unusual."

"I see."

She watched him carefully, "Petrus, do you mind talking about Tam?"

"No, not at all. He . . . ahhh . . . he lived . . . to a ripe old age."

"He did, indeed. And now you have another lifetime ahead of you—and so many things to look forward to."

His eyes met hers briefly. Then he nodded and looked away. "Tell me of the twins," he said.

She explained about Rowena's having born the first-ever twins among the Select, and of Mara's role as Oathtaker to them.

"I'm here with them now—the twins, that is, and with Dixon, Rowena's former Oathtaker. They're married, you know. Dixon and Mara, I mean."

"Married!" he exclaimed. Then scowling, he pulled back. "How is that possible when she remains bound to her oath for the protection of her charges?"

"Ahhh . . . a magic exception, you might say."

"I see." Then, "Too bad there was no exception for us," he murmured.

She behaved as though she hadn't heard his comment. "I'll be leaving the city shortly to head back to Shimeron to check on Mara."

"To check on her?"

"She's not been well. I'm assisting Dixon here in seeing to the twins' safety."

"It sounds like you might be away for some time then. The palace is a long way off."

"Well, actually, I shouldn't be more than a couple days."

"Days?"

She grinned. "Attendant magic."

His brow dropped as he contemplated her meaning. "How is that?"

She shrugged. "Suffice it to say, I'll be back soon. In the meantime, like I said, you could be of service here."

"Hmmm." He pulled his shoulders back. "Shimeron, huh? I heard the first family abandoned the palace after Lilith's death."

"We returned there only a short time ago."

"I see." He stood. "Actually, Lucy, you know—I think I need to get myself in order before I can be of any use to anyone else."

"Understood." She paused. "Will you be in the city for long? Maybe when I return, we could—"

Just then came a commotion at the front door to the building. Lucy looked up to find Dax marching his way toward her, calling her name.

"I have to go," Petrus said. He took her hand and squeezed it. "When you return, I will find you."

With that, he turned and jogged away.

Chapter Eighteen

The lunch table held a bounty. The main course consisted of a winter root vegetable soup. Adele had roasted parsnips, carrots, turnips, sweet potatoes, pumpkin, and squash, then semi-mashed them along with a plentiful portion of cream and butter. Once done, she'd seasoned the fare with sautéed, caramelized onion bits, salt and pepper, and thinly sliced celery, after which she allowed the ingredients to stew together for a time, blending and magnifying their flavors. The savory scent of the resulting dish filled the air.

The children, having eaten earlier, returned to their lessons under Nina and Erin's supervision. Meanwhile, Lucy and Mara, along with Vida and Clarimonde, sat at table.

Mara dipped her crusty bread into her soup and then tasted it. "Mmmm," she moaned, "this is the perfect fare for a cold day. I'm glad to have my appetite back!"

"I'm just so relieved to see that you're feeling better," Lucy said. "Things have gone well in the City of Light, but the truth is that the twins miss you—and they need you. I think I've reached a new understanding with them, so they're more willing now than ever before, to share their thoughts with me. But in truth, they do their best work when you're with them."

Mara accepted the compliment with a smile. "Actually, things turned around for me in just the last days," she said.

"Oh?"

"It was touch and go for a time there. Just when I'd think I was on the mend, I'd suffer another bout. But finally, I'm feeling myself. What's even better, is that all of the children seem to be on the mend now, as well."

"That's right," Vida said. "There were a few cases of the grippe that held on longer for some of them—as did yours, Mara," she gestured her way, spoon in hand, "but everyone seems well now."

Clarimonde filled her teacup and raised it toward Lucy. "Your plan with the catswort tea helped," she said, "and Adele has burned sage and rosemary smudges throughout the palace on a few occasions. Consequently, we stopped most of the spread of the illness, and the children are now all well. So we've finally managed to get classes started for them."

"Thank goodness for that," Lucy said.

"I'd actually intended to make my way to the city within the next day or so," Mara said. "I miss the girls—and Dixon, of course. So you could fill me in, and then I'll set off as soon as I can get my things together."

Lucy explained about how the girls were working with the troops and insisted that the training was going well.

"In any case, for now, they've decided their efforts would be best spent there," she concluded.

"I'd like to see it," Vida said.

"The training?" Mara asked.

"Yes—and sanctuary. And the City of Light, for that matter. I've never been there, you know."

"It's quite the sight," Clarimonde said.

"What do you think, Lucy?" Mara asked. When she didn't respond, she turned her way, only to find her glancing off.

"Lucy?"

She started. "What?" She smiled wanly, then put her spoon down. "Oh, I'm sorry. What did you say?"

Mara watched her closely. "What do you think of Vida going to the city?"

Lucy shrugged. "Why not?"

"But—" Vida said.

"No, I think you should go."

Vida and Clarimonde shared a glance.

Just then, a knock came at the door.

"Yes? Enter!" Mara called.

Nina stepped in. She approached. "I'd like to know what you've heard about Carlie," she said.

"This is not the time, Nina," Lucy interrupted.

She glared at her, then turned back to address Mara once again. "Tell me."

"I'm sorry, Nina. Lucy says there's been no word from Liam and Rafal for some time now."

"Then *you* should go to look for her, now that you're feeling better. Carlie needs our help."

Mara sighed. "Nina, I'm sorry. I can't go." She reached for her friend.

Nina pulled away. "I might have known you'd leave her there. So long as you get what you wa—"

"That's enough," Lucy snapped.

Clenching her jaw, Nina stared at her. "One of you needs to go look for her. Or— Or I will!"

"I said 'that's enough.'" Lucy looked hard at her. "Now, we're doing everything we can for Carlie."

Nina sneered at her and then at Mara before stomping out.

"Isn't there something more we can do for her daughter?" Vida asked. "I feel so badly for her."

"So do I, but she's asking too much of me," Mara said, as she visibly tried to shake off the encounter. "Now, Vida, do you want to go to the city?"

"Practically speaking, Lucy, that would be difficult," Clarimonde said. "It's a long way off, and—"

"So? I'll take the two of you, one at a time, when you're ready to go."

"I'd love to go," Vida said. Then she shook her head and looked down. "But, I really should stay here, I suppose. The children are my responsibility, after all."

Lucy huffed. "We can manage the children quite well here. You should do it. You should go. You can visit sanctuary and spend some time with your sisters."

"Clarimonde?" Vida asked, her eyes wide, turning her way.

"If Lucy's willing—and if there's room for us there—"

"I'll see to it when I get there," Mara said. "That there will be room for the two of you, I mean."

"Perfect!" Vida exclaimed. She smiled broadly. "Goodness, I'm so excited! I'm going to go prepare some lesson plans for the children for while I'm away."

"Let's go then," Clarimonde said to her as she stood and took her arm. "I'll help you."

After they stepped out, Mara turned to Lucy. She bit her lip. "Poor Nina," she commented.

"Yes, but you're right. What she asks of you is too much."

"Still . . ." She tasted her tea, then put her cup back down. "Now, is everything really well, Lucy? You seemed . . . distracted earlier."

"No, everything is just fine." She stretched her neck to one side and then to the other. Then she smiled briefly at Mara.

"Out with it," Mara insisted.

She pushed her bowl away. "I . . . It's just—"

"Are the girls really all right? Is there something about them you're not telling me?"

"Oh, yes! Yes, they're fine." Lucy turned and looked out the window.

"So, what is it then?" Mara's brow dropped. "Is it Dixon? Has he been hurt or something?" She started to her feet.

Looking back, Lucy patted Mara's hand, encouraging her to sit back down. "No, I assure you, everyone is well. Now, you'd best get ready to set off. I'll stick around here for a time, then meet up with you again in the city when Vida and Clarimonde are ready to go."

Mara nodded. "All right," she said, then hesitated, "but first, Lucy, I wondered if I might speak with you about something."

"Sure. What is it?"

"I've been having the strangest dreams of late. They're troubling me."

"Dixon mentioned something of them, yes." Lucy filled her teacup, then took a drink, waiting.

"There are some I've had about the twins that— Well, I suppose it's just about my fear for their safety. Given everything that's happening, that doesn't seem so odd, I suppose." Mara's eyes narrowed. "But there's one that I just can't seem to figure out."

Looking over the rim of her cup, Lucy asked, "The same dream, repeatedly?"

Mara nodded.

"Well, as you know, your attendant magic includes oddities relating to your dreams. So, tell me about it."

Mara sighed. "All right. Well, there's this black forest. I mean, everything in it is dead. Logs from trees have fallen. The ground is desolate. Here and there a pocket of . . . I don't know . . . uhhh . . . steam, or smoke, rises. The sunlight can't make its way through it. And it smells ghastly—of sulphur, of charred bodies, of . . . death."

Lucy grimaced.

"Crows fill the skies above. They swirl about, watching for anything that breathes to come along. And then there's this one, clearly a male, that's larger than all the others."

"One of the crows."

"Yes. It's—I suppose—twice the size of the others. But here's the strangest thing. Each day it—" Mara paused, struggling for the right words. "I guess it *produces*—seeds."

Lucy pulled back. "I don't understand."

"It nests in the uppermost branch of the highest tree. Each morning it squawks as it springs up to another branch. Then it looks down and there, inside its nest, is a packet of seeds."

"How do you know they're seeds?"

"Well, that's where it gets truly strange. You see, one day, another crow comes along. It is clearly a female, although I can't tell you how I know that. As the master bird gathers the seed pack in its mouth and shakes it, the individual seeds all fall down to the ground, except that she—the female crow, that is—grabs one before it lands. From there, the dream follows that seed."

Lucy warmed Mara's cup of tea. "What happens to it?" she asked.

"The female crow takes the seed. She flies over the forest. Soon she drops to the ground near one of those beds of steam—or smoke—or whatever it is. She lets go of the seed and then waits there, staring at it. Notwithstanding its surroundings, the thing slowly sprouts. The moment it does, she caws loudly, then pulls it up and tosses it aside." Mara looked up and held Lucy's gaze.

"That's it?" she asked.

"No, that's all strange enough, but there's more."

"What happens?" Lucy leaned in closer.

"As she tosses it, this other bird comes along in a gust. Clearly female—although again, I don't know how I know that—its feathers are bright, colorful. It stands out amongst the surrounding darkness. That bird grabs the seedling and flies away."

"What happens when the crow catches her?"

"It doesn't. It doesn't even chase her."

Lucy cocked her head. "So . . . what's the problem?"

"The colorful bird takes the seed. She flies through the desolation, eventually making her way out. The next thing I know, others like her, surround her. They are in a place of sunlight and greenery. The bird opens her beak and drops the seedling, which by now, is nearly dried out."

"So . . . it's dead?"

"Oh, no! Then the first of the birds finds a spot in the earth where sunshine is plentiful and there is fresh water nearby. She pokes a hole in the ground with her beak. She struggles with the seedling until she can get its little root into the ground. Meanwhile, the other birds all go to the river. They fill their beaks and then, one by one, they return and drip the few drops of water they can carry, onto the newly planted seedling."

Mara took a drink of her tea and shrugged. "Then," she said, "the colorful bird flies off, leaving the little plant to the care of others."

Lucy put her cup down. "Is that all?"

"Almost." Mara paused, her brow furrowed. "The next thing I see is the seedling grown into a tall tree. I know it's the seedling because of where it stands in the forest. But now it is green and strong. Its foliage is . . . luscious. Its branches reach out and over the ground beneath it. One of them reaches all the way into the area of desolation. In those branches sit several nests, and in those, are more birds. They seem almost to laugh with delight." She looked up.

"And that's it?"

"That's it. What do you think it means?"

"Uhhh," Lucy sighed. "I'm sorry, Mara. I have absolutely no idea."

Chapter Nineteen

Much to Mara's dismay, she spent her first three days after arriving in the City of Light, utterly exhausted. Although she assured Dixon and the twins that she felt fine, she slept most of that time, and ate and drank only when someone awakened her to do so. When she finally regained her strength, she assisted them with training. The four of them coordinated their efforts with Dax. Their goal was to get as many of the Oathtaker troops battle ready, as quickly as possible, in anticipation of Zarek's likely invasion. They hoped it would not occur until at least the vernal equinox, when the weather once again became spring-like, but that time would arrive soon enough.

Following through with their plans to keep one another informed of their efforts, the leaders living in the city met with the twins on a weekly basis. Lucy delivered Vida and Clarimonde there, and then joined them each time.

Having just returned to the city once again, she headed to the conference room. Upon entering it, she found the twins already seated in their places at the head of the table. To their one side, sat Mara and Dixon. Lucy positioned herself in her usual place, at their other side.

Dax and several of the trainers were also already in attendance, as were Vida and Clarimonde, who'd taken an active interest in the twins' plans. They all sat visiting amongst themselves, as additional members continued to arrive. Meanwhile, staff from the dormitory kitchens delivered tea and cakes.

Percival entered. He waited near the door.

"Oh, thank you, Percival," Lucy said, standing to greet him. Then she addressed the other attendees. "I discussed matters with Mara and the twins. We all agreed that we needed someone in charge of the healers here, to keep order in their ranks. We asked around, and Percival's name is the one that kept coming up. So, going forward, he will represent their interests at these meetings." She turned back to him. "Please, have a seat."

He walked around the table, then sat in the empty chair at her left. "Lucy," he said, looking serious, "as always, it is good to see you." Then as though in afterthought, he added, "Your knee is as good as new now, it seems."

"It is," she said, smiling. "Thank you." Ever since turning him away, back when she'd injured her knee, she took careful stock of his attitude toward her whenever the two met up.

Just then, as the last of the wait staff departed, Reigna called the meeting to order. One by one, she asked each of the leaders for a report, ending with Lucy.

"So as we previously discussed," Lucy finally said, in conclusion, "Marshall and the others stationed near the border, have had a few minor skirmishes with a band of Chiranians camped nearby, on the other side."

"And I'm on my way there shortly," Dax interrupted, "to see things there first hand."

"I had intended to send Salus there as their healer-in-charge," Lucy said, "but—"

"Salus?" Percival interrupted.

"Yes, we were to meet some time ago to discuss the plan, but since then, I've been unable to find him. So, could you please select another worthy candidate?"

"Now that you mention it, I haven't seen him around of late. I'd assumed he'd taken some sort of leave. What do you suppose happened to him?"

"I've no idea."

"Right. Well then, I'll come up with a new candidate to send Marshall's way."

"Yes, and maybe you could ask around to see if any of the other healers have heard from him. He's usually so responsible. I can't imagine why he hasn't checked in with me."

"I'll do that."

Reigna addressed Percival. "Aside from the situation with Salus, have you had an opportunity as yet to assess how things are amongst the healers?"

"Well, as I'm sure you can appreciate, we're all kept busy. In truth, there are not that many of us. Consequently, I'm concerned with the numerous injuries that have resulted from all of the training going on. Frankly, we're wearing out. The healers are working long days and get little time off to rest up." He sighed. "If we prepare everyone for battle, but are unable to assist when the real threat arrives—"

"I understand." She turned to address the others. "Please, everyone, put word out that we need the assistance of any Oathtaker with even the least bit of attendant magic that grants them the ability to heal. We'll re-assign them to Percival's ranks." She turned back to him. "Kayson is a great healer, but he's currently at the palace. What do you think of our bringing him here?"

"You should leave at least one truly gifted healer in Shimeron," Lucy suggested.

"Perhaps you're right," Reigna agreed. "Well then, Percival, let's you and I get together later to see what else we might do to be of assistance to you all." Then, "Very well," she said, addressing the larger group, "it's time we turn our attention back to our plans for disrupting Zarek's war machine."

At that very moment, a bell rang outside the door. When Lucy went to open it, the flit, Fuggy, flew inside. He landed before the twins, next to Effie and Fleet, and then bowed. Aliza, now stationed just over the border, had made a practice of sending either him or Merc back, once a week, in an effort to keep the twins apprised of her efforts. Each time, it took them a couple days to make the trip, but in the interim, the flits rested.

"Oh, good, Fugacious, you're back," Eden said. "I'd begun to think you might miss this gathering."

"Yes, my apologies," he said, his voice quivering. He fluttered in the air, settled back down, and then rose once again.

"What is it? Is something wrong? You seem . . . agitated. Have the Chiranians invaded?"

He bowed. "We've seen nothing of that as yet. It's just that Aliza is so concerned about the many children seeking to make their way across the border, out of Chiran and into Oosa. She asked me to ask you for reinforcements—and quickly. For now, she's sending the young ones to Marshall's camp on the Oosian side of the border, but she's growing concerned with the sheer number of them."

Lucy leaned in. "I'll check with Marshall soon and make plans for him to keep moving them toward the city."

The flit nodded. "Good. Aliza says she hasn't the resources to continue to care for all the children that pass by her place. What's more, she's begun to find amongst some of the older teens—the boys, in particular—a certain . . . penchant, shall we say, for mischief."

"What does that mean?" Lucy asked.

"Well, she thinks they act as though they've been trained, as though—"

"As though they've been sent here, to Oosa, to distract us, and then to cause 'mischief' as you say, right here in our homeland," Reigna piped up, finishing his sentence.

Everyone looked her way.

"What would make you say that?" Dixon asked.

"It's the perfect plan, don't you think? If Zarek knows anything of our social order, if he appreciates the significance we place on the vulnerable, and in particular, on children, he knows we'll invite them in with open arms."

"Yes. So?"

"So, what if he's actually training some of them? In that event, we'd be opening our borders to the enemy." She glanced about at the others. "It's perfect, don't you think?"

Filling her teacup, Mara turned to Fuggy. "Is that what Aliza thinks is happening?"

"In truth, it is," he said. "This past week, there must have been twenty or thirty young men who arrived at the same time. These youths are ill-behaved and . . . Well, some of the younger children, upon sight of them, refused to go near them.

"And does Aliza think they harmed the children. Perhaps before they reached her?"

"Yes. She tried to speak to some of the little ones, but they refused to answer her questions. She thinks they're too afraid to talk."

Vida sat up straighter. "That is unacceptable. We must do what we can for them."

"I agree," Reigna said. "Have you a suggestion in mind?"

Her sister pursed her lips. Then she said, "Let Clarimonde and I go help Aliza."

"I'm sorry, but that's not possible."

"Why? We're accustomed to helping those children. Maybe we could get some information from them—get them to talk."

"We couldn't provide you with sufficient protection," Eden said.

"Yes and besides that, Vida," Reigna said, "I'd like to go myself to have a look around."

Eden turned her way. "Perfect. I was going to say the same thing."

"Is that wise?" Lucy asked.

"I don't like it," Dixon said.

Mara set her tea down. "No, I agree with them. The twins and I should get a firsthand view of things. We could go to Aliza's camp, check things out, and then return—all in short order."

"All right. I'll go with you then," Dixon said.

Reigna glanced his way. "Actually, Dixon," she said, "this time I think you should stay to see to things here."

"I agree," Eden offered.

He threw his hands up. "Very well. I've been overruled."

Lucy headed out of the research center and then made her way through the center of sanctuary grounds, ignoring anyone who called out to her. She rushed down the steps to the walkway that would take her to the river. With winter in full force, the waterways were frozen over and clear. She liked walking along their banks, stillness surrounding her.

She glanced behind to confirm that no one followed, then meandered along the ice-encrusted pathway. Eventually it made its way toward The Clandest Inn, where she stayed, along with Mara, Dixon, and the twins, whenever she was in town. She'd made a habit of extending her visits for at least a day. It gave her time for herself.

Coming to a bend, she stepped off the path, sidled her way around a stretch of ice, and then shoved from out of her way, a pine branch. Its clean, rich scent filled the air, reminding her, as it always did, of the smell of rosemary, although it was sharper and stronger.

Almost slipping, she slowed. Then she took back to the path.

A minute later, upon hearing footsteps coming from behind, she spun around. "Oh," she said, smiling, "hello!"

"I was beginning to think you might not show."

She cocked her head and grinned at him, her brow raised. "Don't be ridiculous. I'm running late, is all. I arrived just in time for my weekly meeting with the twins and the others."

"How are things going?"

"Quite well, Petrus. They're going quite well. As well as can be expected, anyway. Except, of course, that the twins have decided to visit the border." She frowned.

"Alone?"

"Oh no, of course not. Mara will take them. They want to talk to Aliza about what she's finding on the Chiranian side."

"I see." He held his arm out for her. "So, they leave right away then?"

Looping her arm through his, they started walking.

"No, but quite soon. Probably within a week or so."

"Good thing she can travel with them both," he said.

"Yes. Still, my having acquired the power to travel at all, has been a bonus. It allows me to go back and forth for meetings and," she glanced up at him, then looked away, "other things."

He nodded.

"You know, Petrus, I've said it before, but I'll say it again: we'd certainly appreciate your help. I know you have a good head for military-style operations. The twins could use you, especially now that Dax plans to head to Marshall's camp."

"Dax is leaving?"

"For a time anyway."

"Lucy, I just— I am not ready yet."

"I see." She looked out across an open stretch of water at a point where an underground spring fed into the river. There, the cool breeze lapped up the frigid waters into frothy, shallow waves.

"Did I ever tell you that Dax and I studied together?" he asked.

She stopped short. "No, you didn't."

"Talk about your unusual powers."

Lucy laughed. "Yes—or lack thereof."

They approached a bench and then sat. Lucy pulled her cloak tighter. "Brrrr," she said, shivering.

He moved close enough for their shoulders to touch, then glanced her way. "I am very glad you made it today," he said.

"Yes, me too. The twins decided to stay at sanctuary to meet up with Professor Hadwin again. Dixon's with them, but Mara headed back to the inn. Apparently, she and Dixon have something special planned for the evening."

"The twins are lucky to have the both of them."

"Lucky?" she repeated. "More like . . . blessed."

"So have you time then for dinner tonight?" He nudged her. "I found this great little—"

She took to her feet. "I'm sorry, Petrus. Like I said, I arrived late and I really should get to the inn now—or Mara will be asking after me." She frowned. "I don't want to raise any suspicions or have to make any introductions. For now, I appreciate our time . . to just . . . catch up. You know?"

"Sure." He stood.

"I'm sorry I don't have more time now, but I'll see you next week. Same time?"

"That sounds good, Lucy." He turned to go. "I will see you then," he added, glancing back over his shoulder.

She watched as he continued on his way.

As he passed from her sight, hearing footsteps from behind, she turned.

"Mara!" she exclaimed. "What are you doing here?"

She looked off in the direction in which Petrus had gone. "That's funny, Lucy. I was just about to ask you the same thing."

"Oh," Lucy scoffed, "whatever do you mean? And where'd you come from anyway?" Her words came in a rush. "I thought you left the conference center before I did."

"I did. But then I had to run back for something."

Taking her friend's arm, Mara set out. "I decided to take the scenic route back. This walkway holds dear memories for me—both sweet and melancholy." She paused, glancing about, considering that she was standing very near the spot where she and Dixon had been back when he'd first confessed his love for her, when the twins were infants.

"Anyway, I saw someone up ahead," she said. "I thought it might be you, so I rushed to meet up." She hesitated. "So, who was that with you? You seemed mighty . . . friendly." She smiled wanly at her old friend. "Is there something you'd like to share?"

"Oh, I . . . Nnnno . . . I—" Lucy stuttered.

Mara stopped cold. "What's going on?" She released her arm.

Lucy bit her lip. "I—" She swallowed hard, then sighed deeply. "Do you remember, some time ago, I told you about someone . . . special . . . that I knew years back?"

"Yes. Petrus."

Lucy held her gaze. "He's here. In the City of Light."

"And that's who you were with?" She glanced in the direction he'd gone.

"Yes. You see, one day when I thought I caught a glimpse of him, I ran out—"

"You still have feelings for him."

Shrugging, Lucy cleared her throat. "Possibly."

Once again, Mara looked off. "Lucy, is he free of his oath now?"

"He is."

She looked back. "Well then, if you still have feelings for him, maybe—"

Lucy made her way to a nearby bench and then sat down. "No," she said, twiddling her fingers, "it's like I told you before, it could never work." She sighed.

"Are you sure?"

She nodded.

"Do you think he still has feelings for you?"

She sat up straighter. "Possibly."

"What makes you think that?"

"Just— You know, the way he looks at me, the way he speaks."

"So, you've seen him more than once."

She pursed her lips. "Yes, Mara, I've seen him more than once," she said sharply, staring at her before turning away.

Mara sat at her side. "You shouldn't be seeing him at all."

Lucy turned abruptly to face her. "What? Whyever not?"

Mara frowned at her. "Because it's unfair to him."

"What are you talking about?" Lucy asked, her voice clipped.

Mara reached for her hand. Holding it, she patted it, then looked her in the eye. "My grandmother used to say that young people waste too much time, and that too often, they do one another harm. I'd have thought this was something that you, with your vast experience, would have figured out long ago."

"Again I ask: what are you talking about?"

"Grandmother told me that when I was interested in a young man, my main purpose was to determine, when I spent time with him, if he was the one I wanted to spend my future with." She tipped her head, narrowed her eyes. "She also said that the moment—the very moment—I determined he was not the one for me for the long term, that I was duty bound to release him."

"I'm not holding him to anyth—"

"If he has any feelings for you," Mara interrupted, "and you give him any reason to think he has a chance with you, then you are."

Lucy clenched her jaw. "I just . . . want to see him. That's all."

"What have you told him?"

She shook her head. "I haven't told him anything. When we first met up, I was on my way to the palace to check on you. I merely suggested that I'd see him upon my return. And so I have."

"You shouldn't see him."

"Why not?" She scowled at Mara. "I'm free. He's free."

"Because it's unfair. When you encourage him, you keep him from finding his proper future. You know, Lucy, you might not be interested in spending your life with him, but someone else may."

"Sometimes you confound me, Mara." Lucy folded her arms. "What are you talking about?"

"You're cheating him. And you are cheating any other woman out there who could be looking for him. For so long as he thinks he has a chance with you, he'll deem himself unavailable. Then, when—if—the right woman does come along, he may well miss his opportunity."

Lucy held her gaze. "Well, but maybe I should . . . make sure."

Mara pursed her lips. "You sound sure enough to me. Now, if you can honestly say that you might change your mind, fine. Then you go on seeing him. But if you're certain that you'll not spend your future with him, you must let him know that—and you must do so immediately."

Hanging her head, Lucy nodded. "I'll think about it," she said.

CHAPTER TWENTY

Zarek pulled himself back up from the floor, from whence he'd prostrated himself in the presence of the three lords of the underworld, and then took a seat.

"He hassss reported," Daeva said. "They are on their way. You musssst sssend ssssomeone for them, immediately."

"Even though it's too early to invade?" Zarek asked. "Whatever else happens, I want the prize—I want Oosa for my own."

"And you shall have it."

"But we don't want to put anyone else on notice."

"Concern yourself not with that. You are nearly ready for a masssssive campaign anyway. Sssso much is in placccce. The young men you had trained are already making their way into Oosa." As Daeva contemplated the idea, he laughed. Thick smoke rose up in the air. Then he added, "You have even managed to hide a few of your elite forcessss—thosssse who appear young enough to mix in well amongsssst the children—as they crossss the border. Once there, the ssssuccedunt will know what to do."

"I admit," the emperor said, "that I look forward to their deaths. Still, I—"

"Oh, no! No, you musssst not kill them."

"No! Why?"

"You musssst not cheat Brother Pestifere of the joy of witnessssing the event. He hassss worked long and hard for thissss. Indeed, I could not deny him the pleasure. So, I have promissssed him that he will not miss out. Ressssst assured, he will return ssssoon enough. Then you may use the great ssssword to take them all out."

Zarek scowled.

"It will only be for a time. Meanwhile, you will continue working toward your goal of ssssecuring your victory over Oossssa."

Zarek paced. "So, what do I do?"

Daeva laughed. "You must have your men capture them all. They mussst be certain the Oathtaker remainsssss unaware of what goessss on about her. They should knock her out—drug her if need be. That will do the trick. After relieving her of her blade, they are to keep her ssssseparate from her chargessss, and return here with the three of them."

Zarek shook his head. The chains of gold and silver hanging about his neck, jingled. "Yes," he said, "I understand—about her attendant magic power to travel away with them if she's able to touch them."

The underlord chuckled. "You know the prisssson cellssss that Brother Pestifere prepared at my direction?" he asked. "Have your men put the twins in one, and their Oathtaker in another. When they lock the Oathtaker up, they are to jam her blade in the locking mechanisssssm at its door. I ordered Pesssstifere to have each of them made out of an Oathtaker'ssss blade—that is, out of the blade of one who had not been true to his vow. Thus, those cellssss are now linked to my world—to Sinessssspe. And do not forget—I rule the underworld."

As Daeva paused, the air filled with smoke.

"The Oathtaker will be unable to retrieve her blade—unable to move it—unable to form any weapon that could assisssst her in escaping her confinessss. Trusssst me. It will keep her imprisssssoned. And for so long as she is unable to get her chargessss within her grassssp—she will do whatever issss demanded of her. She would never abandon them."

"And then I wait for Brother Pestifere to return," Zarek said.

"That issss right. Have patience, my son. Patienccccce."

Chapter Twenty-One

He sat back, then slowly exhaled. He should be grateful things were going so well. Now he just needed to keep his head down—although in truth, doing so was getting more difficult all the time—if he was to see to his plan to fruition. He'd smile, but his face hurt. The gesture still felt so foreign to him. Yet to fit in, he'd had to learn how to do it once again. He recalled a time when smiles and laughter had come more easily to him—but even then, he'd offered them, as often as not, to satisfy others, not himself. In any case, those days were long gone.

He bent over, dropped his head in his hands, and then rubbed his face brusquely. At times like this, times when he was alone and with little enough to do, he always found his thoughts wander—just as they did now.

In his mind's eye, he could see his young charge. He'd met his parents not long after he'd completed his Oathtaker training.

And not long before she . . .

The boy's father had almost fallen to an assassin, and so he'd traveled to the nearest city, hoping to find an Oathtaker who would be moved to swear to the protection of his young son. That's where he'd met them all.

And, foolish me, I agreed to do it.

He remembered his first meeting with the boy. He'd sworn to protect him because he'd been told that following Ehyeh was the way. He'd heard that he should do good works, please others, and advance the Good One's cause of life and freedom . . .

But then I changed my mind—because the cause did not advance me. I could follow no other path. I could not follow what—who—I loved.

"Grrrrr," he growled.

And that was when Daeva found me.

The child was nice enough as children went, he recollected. Although a typical boy, enjoying recreational pursuits, he'd also proven himself to be quite the scholar.

But he was not smart enough to know what was coming his way.

The man stood, then looked out the window. Sanctuary fairly glistened in the light of the early setting winter sun, and around it, bustling activity filled the grounds.

He drew the curtains closed and then returned to his brooding.

Daeva became impatient with me. I could excuse my delay no longer . . . And besides, she had rejected me.

He winced. In truth, she would never have had to have said a word. He knew where she stood.

Once again, his memories drew him back. He recalled everyday events: how he'd assisted his young charge in his studies; how he'd counseled him regarding all manner of outdoor living craft; and of how he'd accompanied him on rides through the forest and then returned him safely to his parents' home located on the River Nix that separated portions of Oosa from Chiran. Although Oathtaker to his young charge for only a short while, he'd quickly grown weary of the inevitable once Daeva pointed out to him that he did, indeed, have a choice—and that there was one way out—a payback of sorts.

And so, to free myself . . . I killed him.

His charge had taken ill. The sounds of the boy's sniffling and coughing grated on his nerves. Fortunately, with the child's parents having left to attend the late spring festival in the City of Light, he had all the time to act that he could possibly need.

He cleaned up after their dinner and then sat with a cup of lemongrass tea. Its rich green and sweet citrusy scent rose into the air. All the while, he mused, as he had over the past months, of the different means by which he might do the deed.

I could cause him to have an accident with his ride.

I could throw him from a cliff.

I could lace his tea with poison.

I could drown him.

I could . . .

But . . . no. He wanted the prize Daeva had promised him—the reward for taking his young charge's life with his Oathtaker's blade.

He tiptoed to the door of the boy's room and peeked inside. There the child slumbered, with his arms and legs all akimbo, as in his illness, he had trouble sleeping. His mouth hung open as he labored for each breath.

Placing one foot before the other, he proceeded cautiously.

The floorboards squeaked.

The boy struggled to open his eyes.

"Are you feeling all right?" he asked him.

Nodding, the child closed his eyes once again.

What am I waiting for? Daeva promised he would hex me so that others would forever see me as youthful looking. I should act . . .

As he couldn't risk that the child might scream or cause a disturbance of some other kind, it would be best if he covered his mouth. So, with blade in hand, he took a pillow from the end of the bed, ran his fingers over its smooth, whisper soft, cotton exterior, and then stepped closer.

Chapter Twenty-Two

As darkness surrounded them, interrupted only by the light of two three-quarter moons, they landed in a shallow patch of snow. Melting water trickled beneath its crusty surface. A breeze stirred up into the air, the fresh clean scent of the earth from portions of the ground recently freed from beneath their wintry blanket, the result of a week of mid-season mild temperatures.

Feeling odd, weak, Mara thought her knees would buckle beneath her. The sensation startled her. Traveling didn't usually cause such a reaction. Shaking her head to clear it, she released her hold on the girls. Then, struggling to remain upright, she spun on her heels, even as she pulled Spira from its sheath, in the event danger presented itself.

Satisfied when the moonlight revealed no cause for alarm, she leaned over, her hands on her thighs, laboring to catch her breath.

"Are you all right?" Reigna asked, resting her hand on her back.

"Yes." Mara shook her head. "Errrr, no . . . I— I don't know." She stood upright, then sucked in a deep breath. "I just need a minute, I think."

"What is it?"

She stepped out. "I'll be fine," she said. "Come on now. That's it—just there." She pointed toward light emitting from the window of a nearby cabin even as she fought for another breath. "Fuggy was to tell Aliza to expect us."

"Are you sure you're all right, Mara?" Eden asked.

"I'm . . . sure."

Lifting her sluggish feet, she brushed past the first in a line of scraggly cedars. Their newly fallen flat needles, wet from melted snow, cushioned her footfalls.

"Stay close," she cautioned, her words slurred together.

Reigna, just behind, glanced back at her sister who hesitated long enough to take in a deep breath of the rich, cedar-scented air.

Just then, the hoot of an owl sounded out.

Startled, Mara crouched. With Spira in hand, she scanned the tree line.

At that very moment, out from behind the evergreens, several men sprang.

She threw her blade at the one nearest her. "Run!" she cried. "Run "

As the man's knees gave way, Mara stood to her full height. She felt slow. She feared she'd crumble. Pulling on all her reserves, she staggered to the man's side to retrieve her blade. Once done, she fell to her back and then rolled away.

She fought her way back to her feet, just as another man came in at her, low on her right side. "Run!" she called out again as she stabbed at him, finding his soft middle. She felt his warm blood spurt out on her hand as he dropped.

Sucking in a great breath, she scrambled back to a fighting stance. Her feet unsteady, she swayed.

From all around came sounds of swords pulled free from their scabbards.

When yet another man charged her, Mara engaged. No sooner had she committed herself to thrust her blade than, out of the corner of her eye, she saw yet another come at her. This one wielded a wooden club.

"Go! Go, girls!" she cried.

He pulled his weapon back and then swung it around.

She looked up just as it connected with her head. When a resounding *thwack* sounded out, she dropped to the ground, unconscious.

As the twins both cried out for her, the attacker grabbed her arms. He turned her over and snatched her blade. After stopping for a second to admire its gleam in the moonlight, he stuck it in his belt. Then he took her arms again and dragged her away.

Reigna, having pulled her sword free, lost sight of where he went with Mara. Holding her weapon in both hands, crouched into a battle position, she danced in a circle, ready to meet an attack from any side.

Meanwhile, Eden, holding her bow with an arrow nocked, neared her sister. "They've got her. They've got Mara!" she cried.

"Let her go!" Reigna ordered.

"Ha ha ha! Such spirit!" one of the intruders taunted.

He, and three of his companions, all heavily armed, advanced. Then he struck with his sword.

Eden loosed an arrow that missed its target, as Reigna parried the man's attack. She grunted when he lunged, striking out at her again.

She defended against his move, feinting to her left. As she did, two of the men jumped between her and her twin.

"We're surrounded!" Eden cried as she grabbed a dagger sheathed at her waist and then stabbed at the man nearest her.

He jumped back a split second before she made contact. At that same moment, two more men rushed her from behind. One of them grabbed her free arm, and twisted it.

Arching her back, she cried out in pain.

He grabbed her other wrist and squeezed until her grip released and her weapon fell to the ground.

As he pulled her away, his arm wrapped around her neck, she kicked back at him, apparently seeking to make contact with his knee and thus, potentially, to cripple him. Instead, he placed his foot in front of her, tripping her.

Meanwhile, Reigna struck at her opponent. Their blades rang out in the still night air.

Then Eden landed with a *thud*, face down in the snow.

When her twin saw her fall, she drew back.

One of the men dropped to his knees, then straddled Eden from behind. After pulling her arms back, he proceeded to bind her wrists together. Once done, he dragged her back to her feet.

"Enough!" Reigna cried as she threw her weapon down. "Enough." She had no intention of leaving Mara, or Eden. Moreover, she knew she couldn't possibly fend off all of their attackers on her own.

Reigna's opponent and another man approached her. When the first of them reached her side, he wrenched her arms back and then tied her hands together. Meanwhile, the man who'd captured Eden, drew nearer, with her in tow.

"Well, well, what 'ave we 'ere?" Reigna's captor said as he looked from her to her sister. "Twins. *Select* twins. Why we've bin lookin' fer you fer some time." He leaned in. "Very 'commodatin' of ya tuh concede like that and all," he whispered at her ear, mockingly.

Then, as the man ordered that his comrades assist him, Reigna felt something flutter near her ear.

"Fugacious," she cried, upon recognizing the flit, "go for help!"

❦ ▬▬▬

Fuggy flew into the air. Then he watched things, below.

One man carried Mara, thrown over his shoulder, away and into the woods. The others led the twins off, prodding them onward with their weapons, steering clear of the crusty patches of snow that might tattle on their presence should anyone unexpected be in the vicinity. They chose instead to march on the ground from whence some of the former snow cover had recently melted.

No one said a word.

Before long, they reached a stream. The recent mid-winter thaw had melted most of its former ice cover near its banks. The water trickled, almost musically, its peaceful serenade at odds with the goings on.

From a nearby thicket, those of the men not carrying Mara, or leading the twins, pulled out two well-worn riverboats. No longer cautious to remain silent, they dragged them across the ice and rocks to the water's edge. The air filled with the sounds of pebbles grating against the bottoms of the vessels. Then came a splash when the men dropped them in. Once settled, the water licked at their sides in an almost soothing rhythm.

"Put her in 'at one, Pretty Boy. Right there," one of the thugs directed the man who carried Mara.

"Got it, Mad Dog," his comrade responded as he dumped Mara into the boat.

Mad Dog laughed. "Now, boys, we've a ways tuh go, so keep yer swords 'andy in the event we 'ave tuh chop through any ice on our way."

Fuggy flew in closer.

Reigna looked up. She gestured with a tip of her head, for him to go for help.

He shook his head "no."

"What do you want with us?" she asked their captors.

"Shut up!" Mad Dog ordered.

"But—"

"No more, or we gag ya."

She fell silent.

Eden leaned toward her sister. "I could kill them," she suggested. "Remember what Lucy said? On my word and at my touch—"

"No! You know the price."

"Yes, I suppose you're right. It could mean losing Mara. Besides—"

"I said, 'shut up,'" Mad Dog ordered. He approached. Then he grabbed Reigna's head, jerked it back, and stared into her eyes. "Ya wanna be gagged?"

She opened her mouth to speak, then closed it and shook her head as well as she could while subject to his hold.

"That's what I thought." He released her brusquely, glaring at her. With that, he turned to his men.

"Scarface, Shadow, and Hatchet," he glanced at one of his men, then another, and then another, "take 'er," he said, pointing to the boat in which they'd dropped Mara. "If ya see her comin' to, Scarface, get somma this down 'er throat." He handed over a canteen.

"What is that?" Reigna asked. "Please, don't hurt her!"

The man laughed. "It's just a li'l somethin' to keep her sleepin' soundly," he said. Then, "You, Pretty Boy, and you, Caveman, come with me," he ordered as he approached the other vessel.

With that, they were off.

CHAPTER TWENTY-THREE

They rode all night. Reigna and Eden fought to stay awake, to see where they were going, but from time to time, sleep overcame them. When dawn arrived, they found that someone had re-tied their hands while they slept, in front of them, rather than behind.

Two more full days passed as they continued on. Their captors traded off oaring and sleeping, but remained steadily on course. All the while, Mara remained silent and still. From time to time, one of the men dripped water into her mouth, but he did so with little care.

The dawn of the third day arrived. A cold misty rain filled the air. Gradually, it turned to snow.

"I have to— You know," Reigna piped up, directing her comments to Mad Dog. "Nature calls again."

He glanced her way, grinning. "I told ya before. There's nothin' stoppin' ya."

She grimaced. "But—" She crossed her legs tightly. "Please."

"Never mind. We're almost there. But we'll not stop a'gin 'til we arrive."

"Where are we going?"

"Huh," he scoffed. "Whaddus it matter?" He looked away. "Silence, now!"

Wiping an errant tear brusquely on her shoulder, she caught Eden's eye. Then she glanced up at Fuggy who still flew above them.

The flit drew closer. When he reached the twins, he landed on Reigna's shoulder. "Don't worry now," he said in his quiet, high-pitched way, "I'll make sure they don't see me."

"You should go," Eden whispered. "You need to tell the others what happened."

"Not until I know where they're taking you."

"But we need help," she mumbled.

"That's enough!" Mad Dog ordered as he glanced back at the sisters.

The twins fell silent and remained so, growing increasingly more uncomfortable on the wooden bench upon which they sat, and given the urge each felt to relieve herself.

Finally, around noon, they stopped.

Having fallen asleep once again, the sisters both jerked awake.

Eden turned to the boat in which Mara rode, still unconscious and gagged, just as Scarface reached for her and felt for her pulse. Satisfied, he nodded.

The men jumped out of the vessels, pulled them up onto the rocky shore to the sounds of rattling rocks beneath them, and then tied them to each of two nearby, tall, cylindrical-shaped rocks.

"Zarek's gonna wanna see this! Get word tuh 'im. Now!" Mad Dog ordered Scarface.

Immediately, the man flew off to follow the order.

Pretty Boy turned to the twins. "There's a bit of brush right there," he said, "where you can do your duty." He laughed as he approached Reigna and grabbed her arm. He pulled her out of the boat, then handed her off to Caveman's care. "Need any help?" he mocked her.

She scowled at him. "I can handle it."

Hatchet grabbed Eden's bound hands and pulled her out of the boat.

Pretty Boy turned her way. "And you?" he asked, as he drew nearer. "Shall I lend you a hand?" He leaned toward her ear and reached for her thigh. "I could pull your skirts up for y—"

She spat at him.

Pulling back, he balled his hand into a fist.

"Enough!" Mad Dog shouted at him. "Now, git those two over there," he ordered, nodding toward the brush.

Caveman and Hatchet led the twins away. Then they stood leering as the sisters squatted.

Before long, a company of succedunt soldiers arrived, all on horseback. They led along behind them, enough horses for each of Mad Dog, his men, and their captives, to ride. In their midst, rode the emperor, sitting tall in the saddle of his ebony stallion. When he came to a stop, the animal pranced in place, jerked its head up, and snorted.

As Zarek jumped to the ground, he threw his reins toward the man nearest him. Once done, he gestured toward another who pulled a bundle of black cloth out from his saddlebag before meeting him at his side.

The two drew near Mara and the twins' captors.

The emperor slapped Mad Dog on the back. "Well done," he said. Then, "Ha ha ha!" he laughed. "Just look who we have here!" He halted before the twins.

They glared at him.

"Where will ya keep 'em, master? Sir?" Mad Dog asked.

"I've got just the place in my prison. I'll keep the twins in one cell," he said as he looked them over, "while their Oathtaker," he added, approaching Mara and running his eyes over her unconscious form, "will find her new home in another." He glanced at the guard. "Is she still alive?" he asked.

"Yes, sir. Just passed out."

He grinned broadly. Then, "Oh," he whispered to Mara's sleeping form, "it's too bad you aren't awake to fully appreciate all the fun your good little charges and I might have together."

He took up the bundle of black from his guard and threw it at Mad Dog. "Cover them up and get them on those horses." He pointed at the extra mounts. "Oh, and tie her on," he added, tipping his head Mara's way.

Mad Dog caught the items. He opened them to reveal three black shrouds. He threw one over each of Mara and the twins, and then with the assistance of his men, saddled them up.

The sisters peeked through the slits in the coverings left for their eyes.

"Let's go!" Zarek ordered as he headed back to his stallion.

His guards opened a way for him and then allowed Mad Dog and his men to lead Mara and the twins through the now blustering snow.

⚬ ▬▬▬

The utter quiet felt thick, eerie.

Three block walls, and one with floor-to-ceiling iron bars, surrounded her. Outside them, jammed into the lock, was her Oathtaker's blade. A single barred window let in cold air and moisture, along with a bit of moonlight.

Mara pulled at the metal cuff on her wrist that was so tight, it pinched. Attached to it was a chain, which was attached at its other end, to the block wall behind her. Two more similar chains hung down from the ceiling at her side.

On the floor sat a pitcher, and next to it, a bent and dirty tin cup, and a similarly mutilated and filthy bowl. Around it, a fat roach crawled. Assuming the pitcher held water, and too thirsty to care how rank it might be, she knew she'd have to struggle her way to it—but not just yet. She hadn't the energy.

She sat quietly, waiting for her strength to return. She didn't know how long she'd been unconscious. She only knew that she was thirsty and ravenously hungry—and that her head hurt.

She wondered where the twins were. If she could get to them, she could magically travel away with them. Thus, she determined, she should free herself and then seek them out.

Then an idea came to mind. She'd used Spira once to pick a lock. It was when she'd traveled with the infant twins and found an old barn for refuge from a storm. Perhaps with her weapon, she could unlock her chain, and also, the door to her cell. Once done, she could find the twins. Then they'd all escape.

Too weak at the moment to get up, she determined she'd simply call her weapon to herself. *My captors shouldn't have left my blade within such easy reach. But then, they couldn't know that my attendant magic powers include the ability to move things.*

She concentrated, willing Spira to come to her.

Nothing happened.

Pulling back, she blinked repeatedly, in surprise.

She tried again, but still, nothing happened. Troubled by the phenomenon, she drew her knees up, and rested in a quasi-fetal position. She had to think.

Perhaps I could move the lock's tumblers, magically. Yes . . . that might work.

Oh, but I can't concentrate just now. I need a minute . . .

At that moment, came movement in a back corner under a damp and moldy bed of straw. Then a fat brown rat slunk out from beneath it. The rodent, its nose twitching, stared at her with beady eyes. When she flinched at the sight, it scurried along the edge of the cell toward the barred wall, and then disappeared through it.

"Blast," she muttered.

"Mara?" came a nearby voice.

"Reigna!" she rustled up, shaking her chain. "It was so quiet here, I assumed I was alone! Oh, I'm so glad to hear you. Are you all right? How is Eden? Have they harmed you at all?" She closed her eyes, dreading the answers to come.

"We're both fine," Eden said. "You?"

She rubbed the lump on her head. She could feel her swollen eye and assumed it was black and blue. But thank goodness the blow hadn't caused her to lose her memory again.

"I'm . . . all right," she said.

"You've been out for days."

"Days?"

"Yes. It was three full days ago that we were attacked."

"Hmmm. No wonder I'm so hungry and thirsty—and weak."

"How's your head?" Eden asked.

"It hurts, but it's all right, I guess." Again, she rubbed the lump on it.

She scrambled to her feet, stepped nearer the barred door and reached for it, but fell far short of actually touching it.

"I have a problem here. I'm chained and I can't reach my door," she said as she glanced into the pitcher of water, noticing in the scant light, an oily layer on its surface. She swallowed hard. Then, "Do you know who did this?" she asked as she filled her cup from it and then drank. Still shaking, some of the water ran out from the corners of her mouth and down her frontside.

"Zarek's men."

"Oh, no. So then . . . where are we?"

"In a prison in Chiran."

"I'm so sorry, girls." She groaned.

"Don't be ridiculous," Reigna said. "We all thought we should see things at the border for ourselves. Besides, you could just travel magically outside your cell. Right? Then you could come over here for us."

"Yes, of course. I'm not thinking clearly yet, I guess."

Mara closed her eyes, seeking the magic stream that allowed her to travel. She'd always found it before in various colors, but this time . . . there were none. She tried again. Still, she couldn't seem to connect to the stream.

She opened her eyes. On sight of Spira, she willed her weapon, once again, to come to her. But as before, nothing happened.

"I've got another problem here."

"What's that?" Eden asked.

"My attendant magic isn't working right. I can't travel—and my blade is stuck in the lock to my cell, but when I try to call it to myself magically, it won't come. I had thought I might use it to release the chain, free myself, and then unlock my door, but . . ." Then, as an afterthought she asked, "Are you chained?"

"No, thank Ehyeh."

"What's your chain connected to?" Reigna asked.

She looked behind. "A block wall." She touched it and, concentrating, peered into it with her attendant magic. "From what I can tell, its shaft is a part of the wall itself—almost as though they grew together." She sighed. "Of course that's impossible, but at a minimum, it runs deep. I see no way to loosen it."

"What about the links? Can you break them apart?"

Mara concentrated, but they remained fast. Then she lit a flare and examined it. "No. The links are forged together, leaving no gaps between them. There's nothing to try to pry open."

She closed her fist on her flare. On re-opening it, she expected to find a crystal in her palm—but there wasn't one. "Huh," she muttered.

"What?" Eden asked.

"I made a flare, but when I closed my hand on it, it didn't turn into a crystal."

"Try again."

She did. Again, nothing happened. "No. Nothing."

A long quiet minute passed.

"Why do you suppose those men didn't just kill us right off?" Eden asked, a cry in her voice.

Mara hung her head. "I don't know, but . . . you know, each moment alive offers some hope." She paused, contemplating. "Do you remember my telling you how things went with Lilith all those years ago? She refused to quit before she'd stretched things out to get the very most that she could. The time she took to do that turned out to be time on our side. Maybe Zarek will make the same mistake."

The twins said nothing.

"Truthfully, girls, it's interesting how often the force of evil does that. Waits too long, I mean. I guess that's because it's never satisfied." When the girls said nothing, she continued. "Zarek should have ordered his men to kill us—or at least me—right off. I can't imagine what he wants with—"

"We met Zarek when we arrived," Eden interrupted.

"What?"

"Yes, and as you know, he has the great sword. Imagine if he'd used it against us. Still, he didn't. Why not, do you suppose?"

Mara sighed. "I don't know. Anyway, we'll figure something out," she said, as much to encourage the twins as herself. Then, "Ahhh, it's rank in here," she muttered.

She looked behind her where a chamber pot sat. By the smell of things, it wasn't empty. She wiped at her nose, but couldn't clear her nostrils of the stink of it. She drew the back of her hand to her mouth, fighting back a gag reflex.

They all sat quietly for a time.

"At least we have Fugacious," Reigna finally said.

"He's here?"

"No. I tried to get him to set off for help right away when we were captured, but he insisted he needed to know where the men took us before he'd do that. When we arrived here, he finally flew off."

"When was that?"

"Earlier today."

Mara dropped to her haunches, rattling her chain. "I hope Dixon and the others don't come for us. Imagine if they were captured, as well." She rubbed her face with her hands, thinking. Her eye hurt. "We'll get out of this . . . somehow." Glancing down, she added, "They took everything from my belt. My extra knives, my crystals—"

"Ours, too," Reigna said.

Then Mara noticed her backpack on the floor nearby. "But they didn't take my bag. Do you still have your packs?"

"Yes," Eden said.

"Is there anything in them that we could put to use?"

"Not much," Reigna said. "We've got mother's cape, which is good, since it's cold in here. We're wrapped up together in it now."

"Anything else?"

"I'll look."

"Oh!" Mara cried as she dropped her hand in her pocket. "They didn't take the compact either! It's here in my pocket. I can get word to the others. Fuggy can tell them our location when he gets back to the City of Light—but in the meantime, I can at least let them know what happened. Maybe they'll have some ideas for us."

"Do it," Eden said.

Mara opened the compact. "Lucy," she whispered, hoping her friend would feel its vibrations on the other end and answer her. "Lucy!"

When no response came, she left a message that her friend would retrieve later. "Some of Zarek's men captured us immediately upon our arrival. It was almost as though they knew we were coming . . . But that's not possible. Is it? More likely, they simply recognized the twins as those Zarek has pursued all these years Don't you think?"

She fought back tears. "In any case, our captors stripped us of all of our weapons, including our crystals, and brought us here—to a prison in Chiran. For some reason, my attendant magic isn't working right. I can't call things to myself magically, travel, or make more crystals. Anyway, Fuggy is on his way back to you to let you know where we are. But don't come for us. It's too dangerous. We'll get out . . . somehow."

She closed the compact, then scooted closer to the wall. There she sat, leaning against it. She let her head fall back.

"Mara?"

"Yes, Reigna," she said.

"I'm afraid."

"Me too," Eden said.

Mara closed her eyes, willing herself to sound brave. "I know, but you're not to loose faith." She stifled a cry. "We're still alive. That has to count for something." When they said nothing, she said, "You should get some sleep."

"Can't," Reigna said.

"Do you remember what I used to do when you were little girls and you couldn't sleep?"

The twins said nothing.

"Do you?"

"Yes," Eden said.

"Well then," Mara said, "let's give it a try.

She thought about the tune of an old lullaby she'd sung to the girls the day they were born to get them to rest comfortably. It was the same one that had revealed her attendant magic that allowed for her to sing someone to sleep quickly and peacefully. It was the same one she'd sung to Dixon back when she'd rescued him from Lilith's grasp, so that he could sleep his way to healing.

And so, she began. "Hush, hush, close your eyes . . ." The words, tripping from her lips, brought back memories, both peaceful, and not so much.

Chapter Twenty-Four

Zarek, attended to by a succedunt soldier at each side, marched down the hall. The heels of the men's boots *click-clacking* on the floor, announced their presence. Behind them came another man leading a chained grut, its foul odor filling the air. Turning a corner, they all entered Broden's prison office.

He, sitting behind his makeshift desk, took to his feet even as the grut pulled on its chain, seeking to get closer. Meanwhile, Yasmin, Farida, and her sister, Ghazala, along with Mouse and Clementine, scurried out of the emperor's way. Then the women all stood against the back wall, trembling with fear.

Striver entered behind Zarek, made his way to Broden's side, and then, simultaneously with him, bowed.

"Broden!" the emperor called. "I need the assistance of a couple of your women."

"But I require their assistance here—to keep order." His eyes flickered their direction.

Zarek approached the women. Upon sight of Clementine, he reached for her. Cupping her chin, he lifted her face up.

Trembling all the while, her eyes remained downcast.

As he glanced back his son's way, he raised a single brow. "You . . . surprise me . . . son." He looked his guards' way, and then laughed before turning back. "I'd have thought this one too young for your tastes."

"Ahhh, no, you ahhhh . . . you misunderstand," Broden said. "She . . . is my taster. It's like I told you, I've grown concerned that someone—"

"Save it," the emperor interrupted, rolling his eyes. "I certainly don't care. You might as well put these young ones to use—however you can."

"Sir," Broden acknowledged, although the idea Zarek suggested sickened him—made him want to kill the man.

"I'll take the young one here and . . . that one," Zarek pointed at Yasmin.

"Ahhh . . . May I ask what you need them for?"

When the emperor smiled, Broden thought the man appeared truly happy about something, perhaps for the first time ever.

"I've a few new . . . special guests," he said. "Well, in truth, they are prisoners.

In any case, I require the assistance of your women to help to see to their needs."

"I can do that."

"No, Broden, these are, as I said, 'special.' Your women are merely to keep an eye on them—not conscript them for your . . . pleasure." He puffed his chest out. "But never fear, I'll have them returned to you each evening."

"Understood."

Zarek motioned toward Yasmin, then Clementine. "Let's go," he ordered.

The two stepped forward, their eyes never leaving the grut.

"Ahhh, the beast won't hurt you," the guard who held its chain said as he pulled back on it. "I'll see to that."

"Yes," Zarek added, "so long as you don't step out of line, you should be fine. Although . . . the beast does have a special affinity for the Select." He grinned at Broden. Then, "Let's go," he ordered once again.

With their eyes looking to the floor, Yasmin and Clementine both acknowledged his order with a nod and, with that, they were off.

"What was that all about?" Striver asked after they departed.

Broden bit the inside of his cheek and rubbed the back of his neck. "I don't know. But I'd sure like to find out. Do you think you could follow them? Discreetly? Find out where they go?"

"I can try."

Without further ado, Striver set off.

To the taunts and jeering of the troops they passed along the way, Yasmin and Clementine followed Zarek and his guards. They wound through rooms they didn't recognize, and down hallways, along a route that Yasmin began to think felt decidedly circuitous.

Finally, Zarek marched into an area immediately recognizable as a prison. The smell of used chamber pots, of sweat, and of mildew, assaulted her. She fought back a gag reflex as Clementine covered her nose and mouth with her hands.

"Stay by the door here," Zarek ordered the guard with the grut. Then he continued on, waving for the women to follow.

Soon, he halted before a cell. Gesturing toward it, he said, "You're to keep an eye on these two and report anything you witness that seems out of the ordinary." He grinned.

Looking inside, Yasmin immediately recognized the prisoners as sisters, due to their similar size and hair color, but their faces were so dirty that she couldn't tell them apart. They sat against the back wall, clinging to one another.

Zarek gestured toward the next cell and then approached it.

"You'll do the same for the one in here," he said.

Yasmin looked in the cell. The woman inside sat in a corner, silent, but glaring. Her one eye, black and blue, was swollen almost shut. Her hair tangled about her face as she whipped her head the emperor's way. A heavy chain attached to her wrist at one end, and to the block wall at the other, jingled.

"Now . . . I suspect they're feeling rather . . . vulnerable—that things are at the moment, futile even. That could make them unpredictable. So watch yourselves. In fact, my guards will be keeping their eyes on you and listening to everything. You're not to speak with the prisoners.

"I'm giving you this assignment since you," he nodded at Yasmin, "have proven yourself . . . trustworthy . . . when it comes to your prison duties." He turned to Clementine. "As to you, just do as you're told." He crossed his arms. "Should you need them, the guards will assist you. Also, someone will arrive after dinner each evening to escort you back to your rooms." He glared at them before turning to go.

"Oh, one more thing," he said, glancing back. "Discussions—including with your master—about anything you see or hear here, or about anything that goes on here, are prohibited. Is that understood?"

"Yes sir, Master Zarek, sir," Yasmin said. "But—" She glanced out at the grut.

"The beast will remain there," Zarek said. Then he leaned in, as though sharing a secret. "It's my added insurance that these prisoners do not escape."

"Yes, master."

With that, Zarek turned on his heel and marched away.

Yasmin approached the guard posted just outside the hallway that led to the prisoners' cells to ask him for the prisoners' food.

He stepped away. Moments later he returned with a bucket of gruel and a ladle. "Come back in a minute," he said, "and I'll have water for you."

She set the gruel on a table situated outside the cells and then returned to wait for the guard. A minute later, he brought to her, a bucket of skanky water.

Yasmin marched down the hallway, put the water down, and then grabbed the bucket of gruel. She went to the cell housing the two prisoners. There, she dropped to her haunches, reached through the bars for the two misshapen tin bowls that sat inside on the floor, and pulled them closer. Then she poured a scoop of gruel into each.

"Ahhh," she cried, her hand to her mouth, as she nearly gagged upon sight of a worm wiggling in it. Then, swallowing down her disgust, she repeated the procedure at the other cell. Once done, she pushed the bowl as far inside as she could.

She stood and then, "Oh!" she cried, as a rat ran across the top of her feet before disappearing down the hall. Her hand to her chest, she willed herself to remain calm. When her breathing settled, she returned the bucket of gruel to the table and grabbed the one filled with tepid water.

She approached the sisters' cell and once again knelt down before the iron bars. "You'd best eat quickly," she whispered. "I just saw a rat. You don't want to invite those scavengers in to stay." She filled the sisters' cups.

"What's your name?" she heard Clementine ask the woman in the other cell.

"Clementine! They're watching us!" Yasmin cried through gritted teeth.

"But—"

She rushed to the girl's side and grabbed her wrist. "Keep silent," she ordered as she marched her away. Then, returning to the cell, Yasmin filled the prisoner's cup before walking away again.

After several minutes, noting that none of the prisoners had touched their rations, Yasmin returned to the cell that held the single inmate, and squatted down.

The prisoner stared at her.

"You should eat," she whispered.

"Take it away."

"But—"

"Take it away. As you said, we don't want the rats getting it. But the truth is that I'm not that hungry—or thirsty." Her eyes flickered toward her bowl and cup. "Not just yet, anyway," she added.

Yasmin reached for the bowl, then paused.

"Take it away."

"What'll I do with it?" she whispered as she stole a glance toward the guard. "They'll know you're not eating."

The prisoner's brow rose. She shook her head. "Empty it in a chamber pot where it belongs." With that, she turned away.

After Yasmin did as she'd been bidden, she approached the other cell. "You should eat," she repeated.

One, then the other prisoner, turned away. "Throw it," they said, in unison.

"Well?" Broden asked as he entered his rooms after working in the women's prison all day, to find Striver. "Where did he take them?"

The tutor shook his head. "I don't know. I followed them down a hallway and through one of the grand rooms, but there were too many guards stationed along the way after that. As it was, I had to hide so they wouldn't catch me. Then I made my way back here, to your rooms, to wait for you."

Just then, the door opened. A guard ushered Yasmin and Clementine in. "I'll be back for you tomorrow morning," he said, before slamming the door shut behind them.

Broden rushed to their side. "Are you both all right?" he asked.

Each acknowledged, with a nod, that she was fine.

"Where'd he take you?"

Yasmin scowled. "I'm not sure. The route was so . . . convoluted. I felt like we were going in circles. Then, when we were through for the day, they blindfolded us before bringing us back here. That trip was shorter."

"So there must be more than one way there . . ." Broden paced. "How many prisoners are there? And, what's so important about them anyway?"

"There are three of them." Yasmin approached the table, filled with a spread of food, and then turned back. "I don't know what's important about them, but they'll starve if left to the rations allotted them."

Striver stepped up. "You and Clementine should eat," he said. Then, "Is the prisoners' food really that bad?" he asked.

Turning away, Yasmin held her hand to her mouth, as though willing back her bile. Then she cleared her throat.

"It is, yes," she said. "They refused to eat any of it—told me to empty their bowls in a chamber pot where the gruel belonged."

"Yasmin!" Clementine cried.

When she looked the girl's way, her eyes went wide.

"What?" Broden asked them.

"We're not to speak of what we saw to anyone—including to you," she said, realizing the import of Clementine's warning.

He looked the girl's way. "Well then, you'd best keep things to yourselves."

"Thank you. Now, before we can eat, we really should clean up. Come on, Clementine."

The girl neared Broden. "I'm scared," she said.

He put his hand on her shoulder. "Shhh . . . shhh, it's all right," he tried to assure her. "You know I can't make you any promises—but I'll do my best to keep you from harm."

He approached a window and looked out at a regiment of guards, marching on the snow-spotted lawns. High above, a single sliver moon shone as the sky was turning to dusk.

"Striver?"

His tutor approached. "Yes?"

"We have to figure out where the guards took them," he whispered, "or better yet, get Carlie in there. She'd tell me whatever goes on, no matter the danger."

"You have to be careful, here."

Broden bit his lip. "I know. I'll think of something."

"Good night, Yasmin, Farida, Ghazala, Clementine," Broden said, nodding at each of them in turn. Once they departed and closed the door behind, he turned back to the table where Striver and Carlie sat. He grabbed the teapot, joined them, and then poured three cups. The sweet apple-like scent of chamomile rose into the air.

"Carlie," he said leaning forward, his brow furrowed, "I have to find out who Zarek's prisoners are."

"How do you intend to do that?" She patted his arm. "Broden, you could put Yasmin and Clementine in even greater danger than they already are."

"I know." He hung his head. "But my bigger concern is putting *you* in more danger."

"Me?" She pulled her hand back. "Why? How?"

"Carlie, my little Mouse—" He stopped short.

"What?" Her eyes narrowed.

"I can trust you." He held her gaze.

"Broden," Striver interrupted, "we talked about this."

She looked at each of them in turn. "You've talked about this?" She stood, shaking her head, her brow furrowed and her arms folded. "You are the only thing that stands between me and those animals, Broden." She glared at him. "Are you suggesting what I think you're suggesting?"

He stood before her, cupped her elbows in his hands. "I need to get you in there."

"No."

"Carlie, please. I know you're brave—even more so than you think you are. You've withstood so much here already."

"I said, 'no.'"

"There has to be a reason Zarek is keeping those prisoners secret," Striver said.

"Yes," Broden agreed. "Mouse, listen. What if Jerrett returned here, to Chiran, with others, and the Chiranians captured them? You know he must have told Lucy about me. Maybe he didn't think I was a traitor after all, and he decided he needed help to rescue me. Maybe he brought Velia along, or Lucy—or both of them—and they were captured."

She pulled free of his hold. "Broden, you're reaching here."

"Please, at least think about it. If the prisoners include anyone we know . . . Listen, this could be our means to get you out of here."

She closed her eyes and shook her head. "This is crazy."

"Carlie," he said, putting his arms around her, "I wouldn't even consider risking it if I didn't think . . ." He pulled back. "Listen, Zarek is awfully pleased with himself about these new prisoners."

She nodded.

"It's true we've never seen him like this over anything before," Striver agreed.

"That's right," Broden said. "So there has to be something special about those he's holding."

"But Broden," she said, "I—"

"I need to know who it is. Please, Mouse, at least consider it. I don't know how we could make it happen, but if you're willing, and if an opportunity presents itself, we could at least try."

Chapter Twenty-Five

After Fuggy left Mara and the twins at Zarek's prison, he returned to Aliza's camp, near the border, to report what had transpired. He discussed with her whether they should send Mercurial to the City of Light to inform the others, but it was Fuggy who had all the pertinent details. So, concerned something might go missing in the translation, they agreed he would head there himself, after a day or so of rest. Finally, he took off, only to arrive just in time for the next meeting of the leaders. It was then he discovered that Mara had already managed to get word to Lucy, via the magic compact.

As Dixon paced, Dax repeatedly rapped a quill against the edge of the table.

"Dax, kindly stop that tapping," Lucy said. "It makes it difficult for me to think. And Dixon," she added, turning his way, "would you please sit down? We all need to concentrate, to figure out a plan here, and . . ."

She slapped her hands on the table, startling them both. "Honestly, the both of you are getting on my nerves."

Dax dropped his quill. He folded his arms and leaned back, sighing. "I can't believe this happened," he said. "We should never have allowed them to go."

"Do you think we have a leak, like Mara suggested?" Percival asked.

The other attendees turned his way. "No. She was just . . . She wasn't serious," Dixon said as he took his seat.

"Still—"

"I can't believe that," Lucy said. "No, it was just— Zarek got lucky is all. You know he's had his thugs out looking for the twins for decades. And they certainly are easily recognizable. That's got to be it. Don't you think?"

When no one responded, she turned to Fuggy. "What can you tell us about what happened?" she asked him.

Fuggy's wings drooped as he reported all that he'd seen and heard. When he got to the part about the thugs threatening Mara and the twins, Dixon shot to his feet.

"We have to get them out of there!" he cried.

"We need a plan, Dixon. That's what we're doing here," Lucy reminded him. "Now, please sit back down. Let's get to work."

He resumed his seat. "We should send someone after them," he said. "We can't just wait around here while Ehyeh-knows-what is happening."

She patted his hand. "What do you propose then?"

"I'll go."

She scoffed. "And leave—"She stopped short, shaking her head. "No, Dixon, there's got to be another way."

"I'm going."

"I'll join you," Dax said. "We'll check in with Aliza at the border, then make our way."

Lucy scowled. "Mara said not to go."

Dixon patted a rhythm out on his thigh. "I don't care what she said. I'm going."

"And if you're captured as well?" Lucy asked. "Or Dax? Come on, Dixon, it would be a fool's errand."

"Then I'm a fool." He turned to Dax. "Get your things together."

Lucy sat up straighter. "Dixon, I need the help of at least one of you for awhile. We need to reassign duties here if you're going to be missing for a time. So if you insist on going, I suggest that you send Dax now to Marshall's camp. He was going to head there anyway to check on things. Then, after we've worked things out here, you can meet up with him."

He groaned. "How long is that likely to be?"

"You should be able to make it in a week or so. Then the two of you can simply walk cross the border from there. That way, you'll get a truly good understanding of how things are working."

"And leave Mara and the twins that whole time?"

"Have you got another suggestion?" she asked. Then, "We need a plan before you do anything!" she snapped.

"Fine." He turned to the flits. "Fuggy, you join Dax. Merc can go with me, later." Then he addressed Effie and Fleet. "We need the flits spread out more. Aliza needs more of them with her to carry messages as they come in. We're not getting information quickly enough."

"Very well," Effie said. "We'll prepare some of our best to go."

Through the falling snow, Percival jumped ahead to open the door for Lucy, even as the gusting wind slammed into it.

She stepped inside and then stomped her feet on the rug. Turning his way, she exclaimed, "Oh, Percival! Thank you."

"Sure. Don't mention it." He moved away as a group of trainees headed his way. Then he caught up with her again. "Where are you off to?"

"Dixon and I just met with Professor Hadwin. He's been studying *When the Two*

May Overcome, and wanted to go over some of his findings. Now I'm going to see Dax off."

"Any further word from Mara?"

She scowled. "Yes, she messaged me again, via the compact. She says the conditions are deplorable, and the food, inedible. Unfortunately, she has no information about Zarek's plans for them all."

She pulled him aside as another gathering of trainees headed out, their boots *click-clacking* on the hardwood floor.

"I don't have the heart to tell her that Dixon and Dax are soon headed to Chiran," she said, shaking her head. "Honestly, I don't know what those two are thinking."

"We're going to need more help here, you know," Percival said.

"Yes—and I've just the person in mind." She sighed. "Unfortunately, I've been unable to recruit him as yet."

"Well, you'd best get at it."

"Yes. Where are you off to, by the way?"

"The same place you are. Dax said your hands are too full, so he's handing some of his plans off to me before he leaves. But I hope you manage to recruit this person you mentioned—and quickly—because I won't have time for following through on any of them. Our ranks of healers are spread too thin as it is."

"Come along then, let's go."

They wound their way through the crowds to the conference room. Upon arrival, they found Dixon and Dax.

Dax had stacked his backpack, extra weapons, and foodstuffs, near the table on which sat Effie and Fleet, Fuggy, and several additional flits. He stood looking out the window. Upon sight of Percival, he motioned for him to approach.

Lucy greeted the flits. "So, who have we here?" she asked Effie.

"This is Spectral, Evanescent, and Scintillation," Effie said as she motioned to each of the first three flits in turn, "but we call them Spec, Evan and Cindy."

Fleet then introduced two others. "And this is Prismatic and Ethereal," he said.

"Don't tell me," Lucy said, "you're called 'Prissy,'" she gestured toward Prismatic, "and you're 'Ethel,'" she said to Ethereal.

The flits grinned.

"That's right," Effie said. "And this is Blink," she added, gesturing toward the last of them.

Lucy nodded her greeting to them all. "So, you know what you're to do then?"

"Yes," Spec spoke up. "We'll only head back this way if we have something critical to report."

"Very well."

Dixon approached. "Dax is ready to go. One of the flits should stay with him at all times. The others can head straight to Marshall's camp."

Lucy turned to Dax. "You know where you're headed then?" she asked him.

He met her at her side. "Yes. I'll check things out at Marshall's camp, and then, when Dixon arrives, the two of us will hike to Aliza's station together."

Holding his gaze, she sighed. "I wish you wouldn't go," she said. Then she turned to Dixon. "And I certainly don't like the idea of your leaving. Are you sure I can't change your minds?"

"Quite," Dixon said.

"Very well." She addressed Dax again. "Percival mentioned to me earlier that you're leaving the plans you've been preparing, with him."

"That's right."

"I have a recruit in mind for working with the defense plans and those we're preparing for circumventing Zarek's war machine."

"Oh? Anyone I know?"

"As a matter of fact, I understand the two of you studied together. Petrus Feoras."

His brow dropped. "I don't remember a . . . Wait!" he exclaimed. "Yes, I do. A quiet, serious man, as I recall. Is that right?"

"I suppose that's right."

"I wouldn't have taken him for a military-operations type. Still, I think he was in the class below me, so I was already gone by the time he earned his credentials."

"Oh, he's quite gifted."

"And his powers?"

She chuckled. "I understand he's nearly immune to pain. He can withstand far more than you might imagine."

"Interesting. How was that discovered?"

She cocked her head. "You know, I don't recall. But I do remember some discussion about how he tested his powers. It seems he could take an extraordinary amount before feeling anything."

"Hmmm. Well, in any case, the work will require careful attention to detail. Has he a charge?"

"He did have. He was just a boy when Petrus first swore his oath. That was decades ago—shortly after he completed his training. And his charge is only recently deceased."

"I see." Dax tapped on the stack of reports he was leaving behind. "Well, do as you think best."

"I will."

Just then came a knock at the door. Dixon opened it.

Percival jumped to his feet on sight of the visitor. "Kiera, what is it?" he asked.

She brushed her tightly curled, cocoa colored hair from her face. "I'm sorry to interrupt," she said, "but you did ask us to let you know right away, Percival, if we heard anything of Salus."

"I'm about through here. You can wait for me outside and I'll get your report shortly."

"No, wait," Lucy said. "I'd like to hear your news too, Kiera."

"Really, Lucy," Percival said, nodding her way, "I can take care of it."

"Thank you, but I'd like to hear what Kiera has to say." She turned to the young woman. "Go on, then."

"Well, an Oathtaker by the name of Willow, one of the arms-trainers, stopped by the healers' quarters earlier today. It seems she'd left the city for a time due to a family emergency and only just returned. She was looking for Salus. I told her that he hadn't been seen for some time and that we had no idea where he'd gone off to."

Lucy approached. "And?" she asked.

Kiera's brow dropped. "Willow was perplexed. She said that she and Salus are planning to be married, given that neither has a living charge. The day she left, Salus was headed out to visit someone in need of assistance with a healing. He was late in returning, but Willow had to be off, so she left a note for him, letting him know that she'd see him upon her return."

"And?" Lucy asked again, urging her on with an uplifted hand.

"And when she returned, she found the note where she'd left it—untouched."

"Did she know where he was headed?" Percival asked.

"Yes. It seems someone had asked him to meet him at a pub called 'The Swindler's Cup.'"

"Ahhh . . ."

"Did Salus mention to her who the friend was?" Lucy interrupted.

"Not that Willow could recall."

"When was this?" Percival asked. "Did she say?"

"As near as I could tell from my conversation with Willow, it was about the same time as anyone around here recalls having last seen Salus."

"Thank you," Lucy said. "You may go now."

After Kiera stepped out, she turned to Percival. "I've heard of this place, The Swindler's Cup. It's a sleazy little pub frequented by addicts. Let's the two of us go there, see what we can find out."

"I'm sorry, Lucy," he said, his head hung low and shaking, "but I'm so overextended. You'll have to take someone else along with you."

"It won't take us long," she said dismissively.

"But—"

"If we leave now, we'll be back in time for a late dinner," she said. Then she turned to address Dax. "So then, if you still insist on going away, I guess you'd best be off," she said.

Through the gloaming, lamps bordering the roadways guided Lucy and Percival as they trudged through the snow. Fortunately, it was not so deep as to impede their progress.

"I do hope we can hurry up with this," Percival said.

"It won't take long," she assured him as they turned a corner. Then she came to a sudden standstill.

Ahead of them, no streetlamps offered them guidance, the consequence of having been broken.

"Hoodlums," she muttered.

"What's that?" he asked.

"From this point on, the area is replete with gangsters, addicts and—"

"We should turn back," he interrupted. "You could return tomorrow in the daylight. It would be much safer."

She scowled. "Come on, we're almost there."

At that moment, a man came staggering out of a door at their right, above which hung a sign that read "The Harlot's Alehouse." He bumped into Lucy, then grabbed her arm.

"What 'av we 'ere?" he asked, his words slurred.

She pulled free and then reached for Vivacitas.

"I think we should turn back," Percival said as he, too, armed himself.

"Be off with you," Lucy ordered.

"Jus' lookin' for a bit o' fun," the man said. "What else'd ya be 'ere fer?"

She looked him square in the eye. "I said, 'be off!'"

He sneered at her, but then seemed to notice for the first time that she was armed. Glancing Percival's way, swaying unsteadily on his feet, he grunted before moving on.

"Lucy—" Percival tried once again.

"It's right there," she said, pointing to the next establishment.

Seconds later, they stepped inside The Swindler's Cup. They both coughed from the smoke hovering in the air.

Lucy marched to the bar, behind which stood a man pouring drinks into four glasses set before him, none of which appeared to have been cleansed after their last use.

He looked up, furrowed his brow, and then continued pouring.

"We're looking for someone," Lucy said.

He scoffed. "Aren't we all?"

"A friend of ours, an Oathtaker and healer by the name of Salus, was headed here some weeks ago. Do you recall having seen him?"

He turned to a woman who stood at his side. Her hair resembled a rat's nest. Her shoddy dress was disheveled, leaving one shoulder bared almost to her breast. He instructed her as to which of the tables she should take the drinks and then turned back.

"I don't know why you're asking me."

"Because this is the last place we know he was headed," Percival said.

The barkeep laughed. Then motioning his way, with the bottle still in hand, he muttered, "You should know, given that you accompanied him." With that, he filled another glass, and in a single gulp, finished it off.

Percival stepped back. "What?"

Lucy turned his way. She stared at him.

"It's a little guy you're looking for, this Salus, right?" the barkeep asked.

"That's right," Lucy said, meeting his eye once again.

"Well, he's the only Oathtaker I've ever seen around here—except for your partner there who met him here, and then left with him," he said before consuming another shot.

"You're mistaken," Percival said.

"Fine. If you say so."

Percival leaned in and whispered in Lucy's ear, "As you can see, he's as much an addict as his patrons. We'll get nothing more here."

Nodding, she let out a heavy breath. "I suppose you're right." Then, leaving a tip on the counter, she addressed the barkeep one last time. "Thank you for your help," she said.

Chapter Twenty-Six

Snow had fallen for ten days straight, and there were no signs that it was likely to let up soon. Deep piles of it, around which ran slippery walkways, dotted the campground. To add to the residents' discomfort, their clothing was cold and damp at all times, and the smell of woodsmoke from the various fires they kept burning, day and night, filled the insides of their tents and wagons.

Marshall and Dax had spent the past days, since Dax's arrival, going over plans for the camp given the numerous children that Aliza had sent its way. With the assistance of a few civilians who had traveled there from the palace with the Oathtakers, including Nina's sister, Erin, and Chaya, they kept the children clothed, fed, and warm. They'd even arranged for the resident Oathtaker with healing powers, whom Lucy had sent Marshall's way a short while back, to see to their medical needs. Even so, Dax was convinced that they needed more troops from the City of Light to assist. Thus, he sent one of the flits to Lucy with a message to that effect. Having just accomplished that, and as he and Marshall rounded the corner of the tent reserved as a cafeteria, they came face-to-face with Chaya.

She stopped dead in her tracks. Then, "Good morning," she said.

"Good morning," Dax responded while Marshall merely nodded, acknowledging her greeting.

"A half dozen more young ones arrived just after dawn," she said.

"Their ages?" Dax asked.

"In their teens. All young men, really." Chaya shuddered. "In truth, they give me the creeps."

"Oh? Why is that?"

Her eyes flickered Marshall's direction, then back to Dax. "They're inside now—eating," she said, gesturing toward the tent. "But earlier, I had to get a couple Oathtakers to stop the infighting amongst them. Unfortunately, these youths will take no direction from Erin or me."

"Oh?"

"We're 'just women,' they tell us."

"Hmmm. So, what were they fighting about?" Marshall asked.

She sighed. "Everything and nothing. They pester each other, take food from one another . . ." She shook her head. "They act just as I've seen most Chiranian troops behave—like bullies."

"Wasn't there enough to go around?" Dax asked.

"Food?" she asked. "Oh, no, there's plenty—for now, anyway. Another wagonload arrived just this morning. But these . . . *boys* . . . show no gratitude whatsoever—and they are never satisfied."

Marshall rolled his shoulders back. "Let's have a look then," he said.

Chaya led the way inside the tent. There, sat several tables. Around one, a motley group of young men had congregated.

The clear eldest amongst them stood as the newcomers approached. He put one foot on the bench before him, and then leaned forward.

"What's this?" he asked, chewing on a long thin scrap of wood.

Marshall turned to Chaya. "We'll take it from here," he said. He watched as she set off. Then he turned back and addressed the young man. "We're just stopping in to have a look. When did you arrive?"

"Earlier today."

"I see. Where was your home in Chiran?"

The youth grabbed a piece of bread from the basket before him and chewed off the end. Once done, laughing, he threw the remainder at one of his lot. Then, rolling his eyes, he asked, "Why do you care?"

Marshall stepped up. He took a handful of the young man's tunic and pulled him closer.

As the others appeared ready to get to their feet, Dax cautioned them to stay put.

"Why do I care?" Marshall asked. "Perhaps because it's through my efforts, and those of my people, that you're sitting here filling your ungrateful bellies."

Scoffing, the youth struggled to free himself.

Marshall shoved him back into his seat, then glared down at him. "You boys will cause no further disturbances. If you do, I'll deliver you back to Chiran myself. Have you got that?"

Just then, the tent flap opened, and Dixon stepped in. "Good, I found you," he said.

Marshall acknowledged his presence with a nod. Then he turned back to the youths. "I'm ordering extra guards to keep an eye on you. Don't forget what I said." With that, he and Dax headed Dixon's way.

"You've arrived!" Dax greeted him.

"Yes. Just now."

"It's good to see you, Dixon," Marshall said.

"And you."

At that moment, Chaya stepped back inside.

Marshall turned her way. "I'll have some Oathtakers guard them," he said to her. "If you have any further problems, just let me know."

"Are you leaving now?" she asked, her eyes downcast.

"Leaving?"

"With Dixon."

"Oh, no. He and Dax are headed out soon. Why do you ask?"

She just shook her head. Then she retreated.

"So, Marshall," Dixon said, "you've brought Dax up to date here?"

"Yes, that's right."

"Good. Then you won't mind my taking him away. We leave immediately."

The Oathtakers stepped through crunchy snow, as a cold cedar-scented breeze blew toward them. Seconds later, two squirrels, dancing around an enormous oak, beat their way up the tree. Then all went still.

The men pulled their blades out as they looked about for any danger.

"Nothing," Dixon said.

"Right," Dax agreed, "but keep your weapon handy."

"This is where Mara and the girls were captured," Fuggy said. Around him flew his fellow flits, Spec, Evan, Cindy, Prissy, Ethan, and Blink. Together they and the Oathtakers had made their way successfully across the border from Marshall's camp to where they now stood.

The flits fluttered about the Oathtakers as they trudged through more snow and then made their way down an icy path that led to the cabin in which Aliza stayed.

Before they could knock, Aliza opened the door. Growling, she fell back into a fighting crouch, her blade, Gloriam, in hand.

"Oh!" she cried a second later, upon recognizing them. "I wasn't expecting you two!" She stood to her full height and re-sheathed her weapon. Then, "Welcome, Commander," she said, nodding Dax's way, "and Dixon," she greeted him. "I see you've brought some company with you."

The men entered, the flits following.

She closed the door behind them all.

Mercurial, the only flit who'd still been with Aliza prior to her guests' arrival, made his presence known when he also greeted the visitors.

"Have a seat—and something to eat," Aliza said, gesturing toward the table. "Tell me—what's been going on? I'd begun to worry. I've heard nothing since Fuggy last headed to the city. I'd have sent Merc out, but he was my only remaining option in the event of an emergency."

The men sat. Then they explained to Aliza all they'd learned from Mara's communication via the magic compact.

"It's just devastating!" she cried. "All three of them captured."

"Yes," Dixon said. "So we're going after them."

"Is there no other way? Honestly, we can't afford to lose the two of you, as well."

"Without the twins, we've lost most everything anyway," Dax muttered

Sighing, Aliza stood. She paced. "I feel so responsible. If only I'd been here at the time . . . I might have heard them out there when they arrived. I might have helped."

"Where were you?"

"I'd received a report of a half dozen children preparing to cross the border not far from here. I set out to meet them, and to direct them on to Marshall's camp for help." She shrugged. "But when I arrived at the place, there was no one there. What's more, those living nearby knew nothing of any children in the area."

The men exchanged a glance.

"Is that a common occurrence?" Dixon asked. "I mean, for someone to deliver such a report to you? And who would do that anyway?"

"It's not unheard of for some local to let me know of something he sees." She sat down again. "But I'd never met this man before."

"Maybe we do have a leak," Dax suggested, glancing Dixon's way.

Dixon looked off. "It's difficult to imagine, but I suppose it's possible . . ." He turned back. "Aliza, are you finding your efforts here to be of much use?"

"Honestly, no. As I had Fuggy report earlier, without assistance right here, I can't really tell, of those seeking entrance into Oosa, who represents danger. Worse, there's not much I can do to stop anyone even if I do suspect harmful motives."

Dixon sat up straighter. "Then . . . come with us," he suggested. "We could use your help. Perhaps we could make our way into the prison where Zarek is holding Mara and the twins more easily if you used your magic as a mask to help us gain access."

"I suppose I could."

"You could pretend to be escorting us to the prison."

"Yes, that could work."

"What of us?" Merc asked, as he fluttered forth, then landed on the tabletop.

"We'll take three of you along for sending messages back," Dixon said, "and leave the others of you here until we return. Or, if you prefer, you could wait for us at Marshall's camp."

Aliza turned to Dax. "What do you think, Commander?"

"I think it's a plan," he said, "provided that going forward, you refer to me only as 'Dax.' We don't want to raise any suspicions."

"Well then," Merc said to his companions, "I'll go along with them. Why don't you join me, Spec and Evan?"

CHAPTER TWENTY-SEVEN

Overwhelmed, and feeling she required direction, Lucy spent the afternoon in the inner prayer room of sanctuary. The faithful—numerous members of the Select and their Oathtakers—filled the space. She relaxed to the sounds of their prayers and supplications. Their worshipping had always raised her spirits, and today was no exception. In truth, however, it also made her miss some of her old friends. In particular, she longed to see Leala and Fidel. Their insight was often just the thing she needed at times like this.

"Perhaps I should head back to the palace for a spell," she mused aloud, "so that I can visit with them. There's little I can do here, after all." With that, she headed out to the vestibule.

When she was ready to leave the building, she watched out the window at an unexpected winter rainstorm. It made everything slippery when it froze to the ground.

A minute later, when the downpour momentarily let up, she stepped out, keeping her head down.

"Lucy!" someone called.

She turned to the sound. "Oh, it's you, Percival."

He neared, then stood, his thumbs looped inside his leather belt. "I was wondering, Lucy, if you might like to catch a quick dinner tonight." He shuffled his feet. "I have to go over some of Dax's plans yet this afternoon, but—"

"I'm sorry," she interrupted, "but I . . . shouldn't."

He looked up and held her gaze for long seconds. "Are you sure I can't talk you into a good meal and a night of music? I know this place that grills the best steaks you've ever had. And the music!" His eyes widened. "The owner is a gifted fiddler and— Well, you could even dance on the tabletops if you like." Smirking now, as though satisfied with his attempt at humor, his brow rose. "Come on. Say you'll join me."

She shook her head "I—"

"You know, Lucy," he said, "I've no intention of giving up."

"Ahhh, well, I—"

He pursed his lips. "My momma didn't raise a quitter." With that, he turned to go. Glancing back, he waved feebly. "I'll see you soon."

Grinning and shaking her head, she watched as he sauntered off. Then she headed out to follow her ritual path toward the river. She needed time to think—to focus.

Before long, she arrived at the river's edge. With the sun now peeking through the clouds, she stood just where the underground spring fed into the waterway, keeping the area immediately around it, from freezing. The water lapped on the shore, making a mesmerizing, slapping sound, and rattling the rocks gathered there. They sounded as though they were chattering to one another.

She looked up. She couldn't wait for the gulls to return, to fill the air. She loved that time of year when they flew together in circles, swooping and diving, as though dancing at the prospect that spring was on its way. It was the picture of happiness.

But there will be no happiness in Oosa if something isn't done—and soon.

"Lucy?" A man called as he neared her side.

She glanced his way. "Oh, hello, Petrus."

He drew his pursed lips to the side. "I have not seen you for some time now. Is there something wrong? Or . . . have you been avoiding me?"

She exhaled audibly. "Avoiding you? Oh no . . . not exactly. I've just needed time to think."

"I see." He looked down. "I can go." He turned away.

"No!" she exclaimed, grabbing his arm. "Please don't."

He turned back, slowly.

She caught his eye. "Petrus, I—" She swallowed hard. "I'm sorry. It seems I owe you an apology."

His brow dropped. "What? Why?"

"Well, a while back, someone pointed out to me how . . . selfish I'd been—in seeing you."

"Selfish!" He frowned. "What are you talking about?"

"Yes. Listen, I—" She rubbed her forehead. "In truth, I'm confused. You see, I don't think this thing between us— This—whatever this is—can go anywhere."

He said nothing.

"I was flattered, Petrus, that you sought me out, and I . . . Well, I allowed for more than I should have."

He scowled. "You make no sense."

"It's just that I don't want you to get the wrong idea. We—you and I, together—" She dropped her gaze. "Well, it could never work, Petrus."

"I see."

"You know my mission." She glanced back. "And the truth is, that I don't want to lead you on, but—" She stopped short.

"But?"

"But I need your help."

Shaking his head, he stared at her. "I see."

"Please, Petrus, I'm not asking for me."

"Oh no, of course not."

She sighed. "Now you're angry."

"No, Lucy, I am not angry . . ." He sighed. "But then I suppose that I am not all that surprised, either."

"I just . . . can't."

He nodded. "So what is it you think I can help you with?"

She watched him closely, sensing his anger in the furrow of his brow and the set of his jaw. Then she told him about the situation with Mara and the twins, and of Dixon and Dax's recent departures.

"Dax left, too?"

"Yes. So you see, we need someone who can help to work out a plan for rescuing the twins—someone who also can assist with Dax's plans for upsetting Zarek's war machine. I think you're the right man for the job."

He said nothing.

"Please, Petrus, I've seen the way your mind works. I know this would be the perfect position for you and— Well, in truth, we need you." She wrung her hands. "Dax turned his plans over to the best person we currently have for the job, but he's a healer." She shrugged. "And, frankly, that's where we most require his talents."

Petrus stepped away, and then paced, his boots sloshing through the ground cover of mixed snow and rain.

After a long quiet minute, he finally, turned back. "Fine," he said, although he refused to look her in the eye. "I will do it."

CHAPTER TWENTY-EIGHT

Basha hadn't intended on making her way to the border, nor of exposing Therese to the risks there, but when Marshall informed Lucy and the others in the City of Light, of the urgency of the situation, she relented. Two hundred and fifty Oathtakers accompanied her to his camp. None of those troops, trained for warfare and now in top fighting shape, had living charges of their own. Thus, she told herself, they could assist in keeping Therese safe. Further, Effie and Fleet had commissioned a number of flits to travel with her. They would provide the means for her and Lucy to communicate regularly. Still, she worried, since after she'd informed Trumble of her intentions, he insisted that he and his charge would accompany her as well. Despite her cautions to the contrary, he felt certain that Felicity's connection to the twins would be of help to her and his other new-found friends and colleagues.

Given that the palace was situated fairly close to the border, within days after setting out, Basha and her entourage arrived at Marshall's camp. It was situated at a spot approximately a league—the distance a person could walk in an hour—from Chiran. There, they would set up their accommodations.

Her first order of business was to find Marshall, who assured her that his company would assist her group in getting things in order. Then she addressed those under her command.

"Let's get to it!" she ordered. "Everyone to their assigned duties!"

The air filled with the clamoring of weapons and tack as those tasked to see to their mounts, did so. Others set up tents. Still others quickly prepared campfires expecting the night would grow colder. Meanwhile, several people attended to preparing dinner for the lot of them. Finally, those designated to keep an eye out for potential danger, spread out, along with some of Marshall's troops, in all directions. They would act as sentries, changing out for freshly rested replacements every few hours.

After informing Marshall of her plans to scout out their surroundings, Basha and Trumble set out on foot for a better look at the area.

"Marshall confirmed that a number of young men have been making their way across the border near here," Basha said. "He believes they may have been trained by the Chiranian guard."

"That may account for some of Felicity's recent troubles," Trumble replied.

"Oh? She's having problems?"

"Nightmares—about the men in black—again. I suppose that was to be expected. After all, you will recall that she tried to warn us about the possible capture of Mara and the twins."

"Yes."

Basha winced as she recollected a spell Felicity suffered shortly before Mara and the twins had set out on their mission. Out of the blue one evening, the girl had crumbled into a heap on the floor of the palace dining room. Everyone present had rushed to assist her, but not even Trumble could ease her pain. Hours later, she still sat, nearly comatose, staring into space, trembling and weeping. When she finally spoke the next morning, she simply repeated the same phrase, over and over again: "The trap is sprung. The trap is sprung!"

Unfortunately, as Trumble was unable to decipher her meaning, Basha had not provided Lucy with advance warning. Later she learned that it was the very next day that Zarek's men had taken Mara and the twins captive, quite near where Basha now stood. Since then, Felicity had suffered long spells during which she refused to communicate with anyone.

Basha worried for the girl; she looked deathly. Her eyes were sunken and red, and ever-present dark circles graced the hollows beneath them. Moreover, she often refused to eat, and she'd dropped weight. She looked less like a sprite—and more like a ghoul—by the day.

"I wish you'd stayed back at the palace with her," Basha finally said. As much as she enjoyed Trumble's company, she also realized that his nearness to her presented its own difficulty, namely, staying true to her oath; he moved her as no other man had ever done. Moreover, it put Felicity in harm's way. "It would have been safer," she added.

He glanced at her. "What? And miss out on all the fun?"

When her eyes met his, she smiled. "I'm concerned for her, but I'm glad you're . . . That is, we can certainly use your assistance here."

Just then, Trumble ducked down behind a nearby tree trunk. He grabbed Basha's elbow and pulled her toward himself even as he directed her attention, with a nod, at something ahead.

Dusk had descended, making visibility difficult, but then Basha made out movement before them. Keeping her eyes on it, she crouched down at his side. From there they watched as three young men made their way toward them. The last in line held a rope. It was tied at its other end, around a young woman's neck. Repeatedly stumbling, the gag over her mouth muffled her cries. All the while, her captors talked and laughed as though nothing was amiss.

When the group came within a few feet of the hidden Oathtakers, the leader spoke. "The border's just that way," he said, pointing. "We'll be able to deliver her tomorrow."

Another of the youths chuckled. "We've still got tonight then," he said.

Basha's stomach turned. There was no mistaking the young hoodlum's intentions.

"Ha!" the leader laughed. "I don't know. She's worth more to us if we deliver her . . . unhandled. Still, I suppose we could take less for this one—make the most of our time with her while we can."

Trumble caught Basha's eye. Then he glanced toward the first of the youngsters as he soundlessly unsheathed his blade, Amora. Looking back at his cohort again, he pointed toward the last of the hoodlums.

She understood his gesture. He would take out the first of the youths, she the last. Once done, they would see to the remaining captor.

Quickly, she unsheathed her blade, Honora.

He lifted one finger and mouthed the word, "One," then another as he mouthed the word, "two," and finally, he held up a third finger as he whispered, "three."

Immediately and simultaneously, the Oathtakers jumped out from their hiding place and threw their blades. So unexpected was their attack that when each of their targets fell, the remaining youth stood frozen for a moment. Then, once he'd processed the situation, he reached for a weapon.

By that time, Trumble was once again armed. He threw his blade. It found purchase in the young man's chest.

He dropped. His screech mingled with the muffled screams from the woman he and his comrades had held captive.

Basha retrieved Honora and then ran to the girl. "I've got you," she said. "Everything is fine now." Quickly, she removed her gag.

The girl's piercing scream rent the air.

"Quiet!" the Oathtaker cautioned, holding her hand over her mouth. "There may be more out there! Do you understand?"

Her eyes wide, her breath heaving, the girl nodded.

"Good." Basha released her. Then she slipped the rope off from around her neck, and cut the bindings at her wrists.

"Oh, thank Ehyeh you've come!" she cried.

"Do you know if there are any more of them out there?" Basha asked, her eyes scanning the line of trees ahead.

"I'll look around," Trumble offered. Then with Amora in hand, he turned away.

"I haven't seen anyone else for a few days now," the girl said.

"What happened?" Basha asked.

The young woman, likely in her mid-teens, pointed at her former captors. "They nabbed me and told me they intended to deliver me to 'Succedunt.'"

Basha cringed.

"You've heard of it?" she asked. "This 'Succedunt' place, I mean?"

"It's not a 'where,' it's a 'who,'" Basha said. She proceeded to explain to the girl who the succedunt were.

She covered her mouth with her hand. "I had no idea what they were talking about. Oh, thank you for coming!"

Just then, Trumble returned. "I didn't see any more," he said, "but we'd best get back as quickly as possible."

"Right." Stepping away, Basha motioned for the girl to follow. "I'm Basha," she introduced herself, "and this is Trumble," she added, tipping her head in his direction.

"I'm Nadine," the girl responded. "Where are you taking me?"

Basha explained how they'd come to stay near the border in the event the Chiranians invaded Oosa. By the time she was through with her story, they'd arrived back at camp.

"You can stay with us here tonight," she said, "and then make your way back home in the morning."

The girl stopped cold. "But I haven't a home to go back to. It was just my older sister and me—and she went missing several weeks ago. When those young men took me, they burned our house down." A tear trickled down her cheek. "I suppose they must have been the same ones who kidnapped my sister." She paused, in thought. "Goodness! I need to rescue her!"

Basha shook her head. "I'm sorry, but you shouldn't even try. You heard them. They intended to sell you. No doubt they sold your sister already—and there's no way to know where it is in Chiran that she might be now."

The girl choked back a sob. "May I stay here with you then?"

"Truly, that's not a good idea. It really wouldn't be safe. But we can give you directions to somewhere that might be."

She took the girl's arm and headed toward her tent. "Don't worry now. We'll help you."

<hr>

After grabbing a quick meal, Trumble saw Felicity to bed. Then he returned to the main bonfire in the midst of camp where Basha sat. As he neared, the frozen ground crunched under his footsteps.

She glanced his way as he sat down a few feet away. "Is she sleeping?" she asked him.

"Yes. Raiden's keeping an eye on her."

"Good."

At that moment, Therese arrived. She sat at her Oathtaker's other side.

Basha put more fuel on the fire. As sparks flew up into the air, she asked her, "Is Nadine all right?"

"Yes, I think she'll be fine. I left her with Chaya and Erin. They'll add her to the others for whom they're making arrangements. Marshall says they've been sending a group off about every other week."

"Good."

"Yes. Some Oathtakers will escort them to a nearby city. Then they'll work with the sanctuary there to arrange for homes for the youngest of them, and to find work for some of the older ones."

For a moment, all was quiet.

"They'll set out first thing tomorrow morning," Therese added.

Basha sighed. "Marshall says that they've seen this before—young Oosian women taken captive for sale in Chiran."

"It's disgusting."

"It certainly is," Trumble agreed.

Just then, a scream sounded out.

"That's Felicity!" Basha cried as the three all jumped to their feet.

They ran to Trumble's wagon, skirting their fellow campers along the way. As they neared, Basha pushed through a group congregated nearby.

Upon their arrival, Raiden jumped down. When he caught sight of Trumble, he visibly relaxed.

"What is it?" Trumble asked.

"I don't know," Raiden said, shaking his head. "She was sleeping peacefully, but then she screamed suddenly. She's in there now, crying. Great Ehyeh, she sounds so desperate. She's . . . inconsolable."

Trumble stepped up at the back of the wagon and entered it, Basha, at his heels. Once inside, she made a flare. She used it to light a nearby lamp.

Felicity sat, staring into nothingness, weeping uncontrollably. Her shoulders shook with the fury of her despair.

"Felicity?" Trumble called her, as he took her hands.

Her eyes wild, she turned his way. "You have to help her," she pleaded

"Who?"

"Ella." A cry escaped her.

"Who is 'Ella'?" he asked.

She closed her eyes. "She'll waste away. Someone must rescue her."

Basha stroked the girl's hair. "Shhh . . . Shhhh, now," she said.

Felicity reached out for her. "Will you help her?" she asked.

"Who?"

"I told you. Ella. She's too weak." She pulled back, then looked again at her Oathtaker.

Trumble pressed her shoulders back. "You need to sleep now," he said. "We'll do what we can for Ella."

Moments later, Felicity closed her eyes. The spell having passed, she drifted off to sleep.

"Who is she talking about?" Basha asked.

Trumble shook his head.

"Has she done this before?"

"She asked me to pray with her last night for 'Ella,' and I did, but like I said, I've no idea who she's talking about."

Basha was baffled, as she also, knew of no "Ella" to whom the girl might be referring.

"Is there anyone in Little Creek by that name?" she asked.

"No. To the best of my knowledge, Felicity has never met anyone by that name."

"Huh. Well, she's resting easy now, anyway." Basha turned to go. "I'll ask around to see if anyone knows who she might be talking about. I suppose it could be one of the children we've taken in."

"Good idea. Thank you."

Chapter Twenty-Nine

Huddled low together in the midst of a birch grove, Dixon, Dax, and Aliza, watched and listened to the commotion below, as the flits fluttered over their heads.

A half dozen succedunt soldiers, all on horseback, led along a string of prisoners roped together in a line, stumbling along their way. One man fell, then struggled back to his feet so as not to be dragged along.

The leader pulled his black hood back and hooted into the air. "This is as good a place as any," he cried as he pulled out a sword with a long curved blade and raised it in the air. His mount prancing, he turned it back toward the end of the line of captives.

The prisoners, all covered in dirt-encrusted, shredded clothing, stood shaking before him, as he rode up and down the line.

"So, we've some believers of Ehyeh in our midst," he said, chuckling.

The Oathtakers exchanged glances, then turned their attention back to the goings on.

"You even have your own sanctuary," the man mocked. "As you're aware, Zarek doesn't allow for that." Suddenly serious, he glared at each of the prisoners, in turn. "So, we've confiscated your goods—and your women," he added, to the hoots of his cohorts.

One of the prisoners rushed toward him, pulling on the ropes that bound him, causing those of his fellow abductees nearest him to fall to their knees.

The succedunt leader laughed. "That's right," he said, "on your knees!" Then he called out to his fellows, "It's time!"

Like a carefully choreographed dance, each of the other guards pulled out a similar sword with a curved blade. Their weapons glistened.

"We have to do something," Dax said.

"They're going to kill them!" Aliza cried.

As the guards, now armed, prepared to dismount, Dixon turned to her. "You need to make them think you're one of them," he said.

"I— Sure—"

He rummaged in his pack, then pulled out two ropes. Quickly, he tied one to the other, leaving three exposed ends. He tossed one to Dax.

"Wrap that around your wrists—loosely," he ordered. Then he tossed another end to Aliza. Finally, he wound the last end around his own wrists.

"This is crazy, Dixon," Aliza said.

"Tell them you've been sent with orders to round up all those you can, to march them back as slave labor for a new program Zarek has put in place. Now, there are only a half dozen of them. When we get close, take one out with your blade. Retrieve it quickly, then get another. Now, hurry!" With that, he jumped to his feet.

Aliza engaged her attendant magic. She didn't know how she would appear to the guards, but she knew each would see her as someone with authority over him.

She rushed forward, with Dixon and Dax behind, behaving as though she pulled them along.

"That's enough!" she cried when she neared the Chiranians.

The soldiers all turned her way. One by one, they lowered their weapons.

"I'm taking your prisoners from here," she said.

They exchanged glances.

"I've been ordered to round up additional slaves. Now," she looked the guards over, "hand me that rope."

One of them turned back toward his mount to retrieve the end of it. As he did, she reached back for her blade, even as Dixon and Dax dropped the ropes from around their wrists, so as to do the same.

She threw her weapon, then rushed forward to retrieve it from the chest of the dead man in which it now protruded. Meanwhile, each of her cohorts did likewise.

Commotion erupted as the remaining guards held up their swords. Then, clearly confused, they dropped them again.

Focusing on the man who'd gone to retrieve the rope that bound the prisoners, Aliza threw her blade at him. When it met its mark, he dropped to his knees. Seconds later, he fell to the earth at the feet of his mount.

Whinnying, the gelding danced in place.

Meanwhile, both Dixon and Dax killed another of the soldiers. A *thud* sounded out as each body fell to the earth.

When the Oathtakers had vanquished all of the guards, Aliza disengaged her magic.

Dixon retrieved his weapon from the last man he'd killed. Then, taking up the end of the rope that bound the prisoners together, he approached them.

"Thank Ehyeh!" one of the men cried.

"Where did you come from?" another asked.

Dixon started at one end of the line, cutting each man free, as Dax did the same from the other end.

Meanwhile, Aliza addressed the prisoners. "Where did they take your women?" she asked.

"They locked them in our sanctuary, then led us out here," one of them said.

"Did they leave any guards over them?"

"No. They told us they were going to go back for them. But we've heard tales of their doing this in other villages. Sometimes they lock the doors and then set fire to the place."

"I see."

When all the prisoners were free, Dixon met Aliza at her side. "Go home now," he said to the men. "Release your women."

One man dropped to his knees, then prostrated himself. "Thank you," he cried.

"Get up," Dixon ordered him. "Go free your women."

He stood. "How can we ever thank you?"

"You don't owe us any thanks." Dixon re-sheathed Verity. "Now, tell us about this sanctuary of yours."

"What do you want to know? Our village has always served Ehyeh. Our sanctuary has stood there for centuries."

"I'd advise you not to use it for now. It's not safe."

"We know that, but we're faithful—"

Dixon held up his hand. "Listen, you can be faithful followers without a sanctuary. My advice to you is to burn the building down yourselves. If you value your lives, put on a show of your loyalty to Zarek."

The man glared at him. "But—"

"We won't be here to save you the next time. Do what you can to protect yourselves. If the succedunt think you're behind Zarek, perhaps they'll leave you alone. Now, I'm not suggesting you do anything contrary to Ehyeh's interests, I'm merely proposing that you don't make it obvious that you support them. Only then can you be safe."

"One thing's for sure, you're not Chiranians," the man scoffed.

Dax neared him. "Oh? Why do you say that?"

"Because here in Chiran, no one is safe. When violence and savagery are glorified, it's just a matter of time . . ." The man shook his head. "They've already taken most of our children," he added, a cry in his voice.

"What?" Aliza asked.

He looked back at her. "They train the boys to help them. They . . . use the girls."

She grimaced. "Where did they take them all?"

"We heard something about a prison in Darth." He shrugged. "But we don't really know."

Dixon sighed. "And things are the same elsewhere here, in Chiran?"

The man nodded. "They are."

"Well, go then. Save those you can."

With that, Dixon approached the now-dead guards' mounts. Then he led three of them back to where his fellow Oathtakers stood. He handed the reins of one to Aliza, and those of another, to Dax.

"Thanks," she said.

"I've got it," Dax added.

"Let's go then," Dixon ordered.

Chapter Thirty

Things couldn't be going better. Still, so much depended on him. He completed his report to Daeva and then, deep in thought, paced.

The underlord's goal was to turn all mankind to his cause—not because he had any particular affinity for the people, but because he harbored resentment and hatred against Ehyeh. Now, with his plan having been in operation for decades, success finally neared.

Memories drowned the man's thoughts.

Oh, dear, his poor innocent little charge was dead. The thought almost made him smile. Having accomplished the deed, he waited for the child's parents to return—and then did away with them as well.

His next order of business was to ask around about Mugger. Upon discovering that the man had moved to Chiran, he set off in pursuit of him.

He thought back to that day at the swamp, with his former tutor. He'd delivered to the man exactly what he'd deserved. But he'd never anticipated finding Zarek there.

Finding the child had been a bonus.

Born a descendant of the Hazarik, of a family of succedunt warriors, the boy's mother neglected him, just as the man's own had neglected him. The child crimped her style. So she'd pawned him off on the first person she could find who would board him. Little did she know of, or perhaps she simply didn't care about, Mugger's long history of molesting young ones.

The man shook his head to dispel the thought. His own mother had been just like Zarek's. She, too, had pawned off her spawn without ever looking back, refusing to listen when he'd tried to tell her the truth. He recalled a visit he'd made to her once. He couldn't have been more than twelve or so.

"Mother, about Mugger," he had said. Although difficult to find the necessary words, he'd proceeded to tell her everything.

But she didn't believe him—or couldn't be bothered to believe him. Perhaps she simply didn't want the truth. It might obligate her to take him away—to see to his welfare for herself. No, it was easier for her to deny the evidence he'd set before her.

And so, she did.

Oh, I hate her.

And love her.

Just like Lucy.

"Grrrrrr!" he growled. No matter how many times he'd told himself that his mother was an evil woman, and that she'd deserved what he'd done to her, he couldn't help that he still had feelings for her.

He paced, allowing his thoughts to wander, once again.

Yes, Zarek was a bonus.

He thought again about how the child had approached him, following Mugger's death. "Teach me," the boy had said.

He told him he'd think about it—that he would have to earn his way. So, first things first: he had to determine how far the child would go.

"See that house, right there?" he'd asked the boy.

He nodded.

"I want you to go to the door and knock. When she answers, here is what you are to do . . ."

Smirking, he watched his memories unfold once more in his mind's eye.

Zarek approached the house and then, hesitating, looked back. Upon getting a nod of approval, he knocked.

A woman answered. Then the two conversed quietly for a minute before she invited him inside.

That's when I followed. I crouched below her window and listened.

"So, you just moved here with your mother," she said. "Well, I had a boy of my own, very like you, once upon a time." Her chair squeaked from her massive weight when she sat. "And you say she's offering free herbs to women who find themselves in a . . . precarious situation? Hmmm. Why would she do that?"

"She wants to show her goodwill—to build up her clientele. Here," the boy said as he reached into his pack, "she said you could try this tea."

A moment passed in silence. He envisioned the boy handing the item over.

"You should taste it now," the child said. "She wants to be certain that it meets with your approval. She says she can adjust it, if need be."

Once again, the chair squeaked, presumably as the woman stood. Moments later, shuffling footsteps retreated, then returned. Next came the sound of water sloshing into a cup.

"How strong does it have to be?" she asked.

"Oh, just let it steep for a bit."

Seconds later, he said, "Go on, you can try it now."

For a minute, there was naught but silence. Then came the sounds of a great gasp.

"What's wrong?" the boy asked, a smile in his voice.

The cups and saucers on the table rattled as she clutched its edge.

And that's when I entered.

Her hands to her throat, she looked up, her eyes wide. "Help," she cried. "Hel—"

He stepped up. "You need my help, Mother?" He smiled—it was a humorless gesture.

Staring, she stumbled into her chair. It crashed to the floor.

"What is it, Mother?"

"Hel—"

"You want my help? Well . . . let me think now." He tapped his finger to his lips. "What did you do when I asked you for help? Hmmmm . . . let me think."

Her eyes opened wide.

"Does it hurt, *Mother?*" he mocked her.

She grabbed his arm and pulled him, choking and gagging all the while.

"Yes, I see that it does. Hmmmm, let me see what I can do for you.'

As he looked at Zarek who sat watching, expressionless, he pulled out a dagger. He held it before her. Its glistening blade, the length of his forearm, boasted an extremely sharp edge.

"May I?" the boy asked, stepping up and reaching for the weapon.

He pulled back and stared at the child. Slowly, his lips turned up into a smile. "Next time—I promise," he said, before turning back to the woman. "So, here is all the help that you will get from me, *Mother.*" And with that, he thrust his blade.

CHAPTER THIRTY-ONE

Desert sands surrounded her. They glistened orange-brown in the blazing sun. Granules stuck in her nostrils and to her parched lips. She could even feel them on the roof of her mouth.

After readjusting the cloth that bound one of the babes to her frontside, she grabbed the handle of the basket in which the other rested.

Her eyes burned. She closed them to cut off the glare—but just for a second or two. She dared not fall victim to a desert predator.

She dragged one foot out of the sand and stepped forward. Then came another. Over and over again, she repeated the procedure. Soon, her muscles burned.

She reached for her canteen and shook it, but then recalled that she'd emptied it earlier.

Glancing up, once again, she found a pool of water ahead. Its glistening aqua stood out against the color of the sand, mimicking that of the cloud-clear sky above her.

She picked up her pace. She'd fill her canteen there.

For some time, the pool seemed to recede and grow thinner with each step and then, quite suddenly, it disappeared.

At that very moment, a hissing sound met her ears.

She looked down to find a snake, its red, brown and white scaly skin, standing out from its surroundings. It slithered along the sand in zigzagging motions before coming to a sudden halt an arm's length away.

She grabbed her blade and threw it, cutting the serpent in two.

She stepped forward, retrieved her blade from out of the sand, and then, relieved, closed her eyes.

Opening them again a second later, she found before her, two buzzards. Choking back a cry, she pulled her basket up closer, even as one of the flying predators jumped toward her.

Once more, she threw her blade. When it found its target, the beast disappeared.

She rushed ahead, took up her weapon from the desert floor, and then aimed for the other buzzard. It, too, vanished on contact.

She retrieved her blade as before, and then—

A grut, just ahead, advanced.

She stared at it even as a howl came from her right. She spun that direction to find another such beast. Then, when yet another yipping sounded out, she spun another quarter turn, to find another.

With one more sound, and one more turn, came one more beast.

They all advanced.

She was doomed. She couldn't save them. She couldn't even save herself.

She opened the blanket that covered the infant in the basket and gulped back a cry upon sight of the little one wasting away. She had to hurry. She had to beat back the threat. She had to find water. She had to find refuge.

At that moment, the beasts attacked.

Mara awakened with a start.

She cried out. Then realizing where she was, she took in a deep breath of relief.

The stench that surrounded her nearly choked her. She drew her filthy hand to her mouth. Unable to control herself, she gagged when her stomach lurched. A sour bile rose up the back of her throat.

"Mara, are you all right?" Eden asked.

In the dark of night, the only light came from a single half-moon currently peeking in through her barred window. Catching her breath, Mara glanced at the bug-infested straw at her side just as a rustling came from beneath it.

"Mara?"

She grabbed the strap of her canteen and whipped it out.

A fat brown rat, skittered out. It ran toward her, but then, suddenly, it shifted direction. It slinked its way against the far wall. Then it stopped, its usual twitching nose momentarily stilled, and its beady eyes staring.

"Mara? What is it? What's going on?"

"Just another rat." She exhaled audibly. "How is it that they don't bother you two over there?"

Left unguarded during the late hours, seeking time to speak freely, Mara and the twins often stayed awake through the nighttime, choosing instead to sleep during the day. Besides, that way Mara could better keep the vermin that continually assaulted her, at bay, given that they were particularly active after evenfall.

"Oddly, so long as we stay huddled up together and covered with Mother's shawl, they stay away," Reigna said. "Anyway, we thought maybe you were sick." The clicking of her heels on the floor sounded out as she approached the bars of her shared cell.

"I am. Or—I was."

"You have to eat, Mara," Reigna said, her hands on the bars before her. She hung her head. "The food is disgusting, I know, but it will keep you alive."

Mara groaned.

"Don't you think?"

"I suppose you're right, but I can't keep that gruel down."

"Just eat the bread then. It's stale and hard, but . . ."

"Yes, I know, you're right," Mara said, still watching the rat as it chose that particular moment to dash toward the bars and then run away down the hall.

Slumping back against the wall, her chain rattled.

Reigna sighed. "Still no luck with the locks?"

Mara closed her eyes as a rush of guilt came over her. *How could I have let this happen?*

"No, none. They're unlike any lock I've ever seen. There are no tumblers within them, to move."

"There have to be," Eden said. "You'll figure it out." Then she addressed her sister. "I'm going to sleep for a bit."

"Fine, but make sure you cover with the shawl so the rats don't get you," Reigna said.

She turned her attention back to their Oathtaker. "In any case, Mara, it's not like we'd know how to get out of this building if you freed us anyway." She sighed. "You know, maybe you should ask Lucy to send someone for us after all. I mean, how long do—"

"I've considered it," Mara interrupted, "but— Oh, I don't know. I feel so . . ."

"Stop it. There's no way you could have anticipated that someone would be at Aliza's place." Reigna pondered. "You know, I'd sure like to know how that happened though. I mean, like we discussed earlier, it was incredible timing."

"Agreed."

Just then, the sound of stomping filled the air.

"What now?"

"Another rat," Mara said as, having frightened the pest, it ran away.

"Oh. Well anyway, maybe you should send Lucy a message. You know, to test this idea."

"That there's a traitor in the midst?"

"Yes."

"What have you got in mind?"

"Well . . . maybe she could tell the others that Liam and Rafal reported that they would be at a specific place, at a predetermined time. Then she could wait there, to see if someone shows up."

"And have Liam and Rafal caught up in this? I don't think so." Mara pulled her knees up. She crossed her arms above them, then rested her head on them.

"No, they wouldn't go. Lucy would go—to spy things out. Then if someone turned up there with the intention of interrupting Liam and Rafal's supposed plans, Lucy would know that there's a leak."

Mara closed her eyes, thinking over the plan. "That could work."

"What do you think, Eden?" Reigna turned toward her sister. "Eden? Eden!" she cried.

Mara jumped to her feet. "What is it?"

"Eden!"

"What's happened?" Mara cried.

"Wh— Wh—" Reigna stammered.

Mara bit her lip, waiting for more.

"What is it?" Eden cried. "What's wrong?"

"Oh, gracious Ehyeh!" Reigna exclaimed. "Oh, dear Good One!"

Mara pulled on her chain. As usual, it gave nothing. Stopped dead in her tracks, she strained as far forward as possible, causing the band at her wrist to bite into her flesh. She winced from the pain of it.

"What is it?" she cried. "What's wrong?"

Reigna breathed heavily. "It's all right." Then, "Wooooo," she exhaled slowly.

"What happened?"

"It's all right. It's all right," she repeated.

"What is all the fuss?" Eden asked.

Her twin pursed her lips. The moonlight sparkled in her eyes as she held her sister's gaze.

"What is it?" Eden asked again. "I was sleeping."

"You— You disappeared."

"Wh— What?"

Again, Mara pulled at her chain. "What's happening?"

Reigna turned back toward the bars. "Mara," she whispered, "Eden disappeared."

"I most certainly did not," her twin said.

Turning back again, Reigna grabbed her wrist. "You did. You disappeared."

Eden stared at her. "What are you talking about? I curled up, covered myself with the shawl to keep the rats off—like you said—and then was drifting off to sleep when, suddenly, you yelled for me."

"Give me that thing." Reigna took the cashmere shawl from her sister. She turned it over in her hands. "Don't you find it interesting," she said, frowning, "that everything in this cell is utterly . . . filthy, yet this," she shook the shawl in her hand, "is as white as the driven snow?"

"Uhhh . . . So?"

Reigna turned back toward the bars. "Mara, can you remember the verse that Lucy shared with us about Mother's shawl?"

Mara, stunned at the inquiry, shook her head. "Ahhh . . . Let me think . . ." Her hands to her face, she rubbed it. "Ahhh . . . I think it was something like '*Come one. Come two. Come illusion . . .*'" She paused, concentrating.

"'*Come true.*'" Eden said.

"Yes!" Reigna exclaimed. "That's right. But there was more."

"You're right," Mara said. "The next line was . . . ahhh . . . ahhh . . . *'Bear me now. Bear me then . . .'"* She patted her forehead. "I'm thinking."

"It was something about sensing," Eden suggested.

"Right!" Mara exclaimed. *"'Dare to sense me even when.'"*

"Oh, gracious Good One!" Reigna exclaimed. "I understand." She draped the shawl over her sister's shoulders.

"What are you doing?" her twin asked.

"Now cover your head," she said.

Her eyes narrowed, Eden pulled back.

"Put it over your head. Let me see if I can *'sense you even when.'"*

"All right." Eden took a handful of the shawl at each side, then slowly pulled it over the top of her head.

"Ahhh!" Reigna's hands flew to her mouth. "You're . . . gone!"

She removed the shawl. "What?"

"All right then, let me try."

"Are you saying what I think you're saying, Reigna?" Mara asked.

Once again, Reigna approached the bars. "Mara, Eden disappeared. I swear it." She turned back to her sister as she took the shawl and put it over her own shoulders. "You see me now?" she asked.

"Yes," Eden said.

As she pulled it over her head, she asked, "And now?"

Eden gasped.

"What is it?" Mara called out.

Reigna uncovered herself. She and her sister stood, staring at one another.

"It's true, Mara," Eden said. "When one of us puts the shawl over her head, she . . . disappears."

Mara's mouth gaped open in surprise. "Girls," she said, "you must use care. Do not do that when anyone else is around. That shawl could be your way out of here."

Chapter Thirty-Two

Cold, the twins huddled in the corner as the woman overseeing them, and who they now knew as Yasmin, stepped to the bars. She untied something that hung around her neck, then dropped it in their cell. Once done, she headed Mara's way. There, she repeated the procedure.

"You gave them some food," the girl who accompanied her whispered. "Good for you. I just wish we could help them more."

"Hush, Clementine," Yasmin admonished as she turned back toward the sisters' cell. "You've been warned—and you know what Broden said."

Reigna's head jerked up at the sound of her cousin's name. She elbowed Eden and then, after catching her eye, inched toward the bars. She picked up the item that Yasmin had dropped there—a kerchief wrapped around something. Uncovering it, she discovered fresh bread.

"Who is this Broden of whom you speak?" she asked as she handed it to her sister. "I thought we were Zarek's prisoners."

"He's his son," Clementine said.

"Hush!" Yasmin scolded the girl again.

"His son?" Reigna said. "What's his role here? He wasn't with those who captured us."

Yasmin scowled at her. Then, "He's in charge of Zarek's prison for women, if you must know," she said through gritted teeth. "Now, silence!"

At that moment, the *click-clacking* of footsteps, making their way closer, sounded out.

A man neared Yasmin. "You've been warned not to speak to the prisoners."

"I didn't, sir," she said. "I just told them they'd best eat their provisions before the rats do."

As he looked into the cell, Eden slowly moved the bread under the shawl over her shoulders. After staring at her for a long minute, the guard finally retreated.

"If this—Broden—is in charge of the prison," Eden whispered to Yasmin, "why haven't we seen him in here?"

"He's—" Clementine murmured.

"Hush!" Yasmin scolded her, yet again. Then she reached beneath the wrap she wore and removed two canteens. Walking past the cells nonchalantly, she dropped one inside each, tossing the one for Mara far enough to land softly on the bed of mildewed straw within.

Mara's chain jangled as she retrieved the item. "Yasmin, come here," she whispered.

"I can't," she muttered.

"Come here, or I'll make a fuss and attract the guard's attention."

Tentatively, Yasmin approached. "What do you want?" she mumbled through gritted teeth, careful to keep her lips from moving.

"Why did you bring us this food and water?"

Bowing her head so as to remain discreet, she whispered, "Because what they leave for us to give to you is unfit."

"And you have a heart."

Yasmin glared at the prisoner. "I'm just like you."

"I see." Mara pulled on her chain. "We have to get out of here," she said.

"There's no way out."

"Maybe you could help us."

"I can't."

Mara nodded. "Yasmin, what can you tell us about Zarek's son?"

Just then, the guard returned. "Hey!" he shouted. "Back away."

Surprised, Yasmin jumped.

"I see I was wrong about you. You're not to be trusted after all," he said.

"No! I—"

He grabbed Yasmin's wrist with one hand, and Clementine's with the other. "You've been warned," he seethed.

"It wasn't us. I swear," Yasmin said. "It was the prisoner who spoke."

He looked in at Mara, then back at his captives. "Well, it won't happen again," he said.

When the guard entered his office, towing Yasmin and Clementine along, Broden jumped to his feet.

"What is it?" he demanded to know.

"They've been warned—repeatedly," the man growled, "not to speak with the prisoners. But this one," he added, jerking on Yasmin's wrist, "has continued to do so anyway."

Broden's eyes flashed from her, to Clementine, then back. "I see," he said. "Well, leave them here with me then."

"Zarek ordered no contact. Since she can't be trusted," he pushed Yasmin away, "I'll take her." He gestured toward Carlie.

Her eyes opened wide in fear.

He approached the guard. Then standing before him, his arms crossed, he said, "That one was my father's gift to me. She only goes if I say so."

"Fine. I'll take that one then," he suggested, designating Farida with a pointed finger.

Biting his lip, Broden glanced at Carlie. He wanted her to go, in the event she might recognize Zarek's prisoners.

She closed her eyes slowly. With a sigh, she nodded, almost imperceptibly.

"Never mind," he said. "Go ahead. Take her." He tipped his head Carlie's way. "I have need of the other one's assistance. I'm preparing a caravan of prisoners to send out today."

"Fine by me." The guard turned to Carlie. "Empty your pockets," he ordered.

Having seen the guards do the same with Yasmin and Clementine, the order didn't surprise her. She complied, setting out the items from there—a tie for her hair, and a dirty handkerchief—on the table before her.

"Let's go then."

When she stepped his way, he removed a bundle of black cloth from under his arm. "Put this on," he ordered.

She opened the item to discover a shroud, without slits for her eyes. She draped it over her head. "I can't see."

He grabbed her arm "Never mind. This way."

As he dragged her along, she fought her rising panic. She hadn't felt so vulnerable since she'd been nabbed from the compound. Shaking with fear, she concentrated on where her feet were going, willing herself not to trip.

They made one right turn, then another. The patterns of the floorboards beneath her steps changed, but nothing more. Then she thought back to something Yasmin had mentioned about Zarek's special prison, early on. She'd thought she'd been taken there via a circuitous route.

Just then, they rounded yet another right turn. Was this just another entrance into the same prison where she worked with Broden every day?

Suddenly, the air filled with the squeaking sound of a door opening. A most foul odor followed. She tried not to breath through her nose, but then the thought of taking the stench in from her mouth left her nauseated.

Finally, they halted.

The man ordered her to remove her shroud. Once done, he pointed down a hallway lined with cells. Barred windows high up in some of them allowed scant light in, as the sky was overcast with heavy gray clouds.

"In the last two cells down there," he said, "you'll find the prisoners. Now remember—I'll be here the whole time. And you can trust me when I say that the last woman got off easy. It won't happen again. There will be no talking to them. Understood?"

"Yes."

"You will not communicate with them in any way."

"I understand."

He turned to his side where a bucket of bug-infested gruel sat on a table, along with a loaf of stale bread. He handed the items to her.

"You give them their food," he said, "and you report to me, anything that you think is significant. That's it. Understood?"

She nodded.

"I'll be watching you at all times."

"I understand."

"Get at it, then." He pushed her.

As her eyes adjusted to the darkened space, and her nose to the foul odors, she made her way. The first cells she passed were empty, but finally, she approached the first of the occupied cells.

Upon her arrival, a rat dived past her. She jumped out of its way, then looked up.

And that was when she dropped the bucket.

The guard rushed toward her. When he reached her side, he pulled his hand back, as though to strike her, but then seemed to think better of it.

"Damned clumsy, witch!" he cried. "Look what you've done!" He pointed at the mess.

"I'm sorry! There was a rat and—"

"Never mind." He glanced in at Mara. "The prisoners will be fine without food until tomorrow." He turned back. "Now clean this up!" he ordered, throwing a rag at Carlie before marching off.

She watched until he reached the end of the hallway before looking into the cell again. She held Mara's gaze for a long moment. Then she squatted down to clean up the mess.

Gracious Ehyeh, but it stinks. How could anyone be expected to eat this?

Holding one hand over her nose, she mopped up the last of the spilled gruel. Then she put the rag in a bucket next to the nearby table.

Dreading what she might find, she proceeded to the next cell.

"Dear Good One!" she muttered under her breath, a hand over her mouth, upon sight of the twins.

"Shhhh . . . Carlie," Reigna whispered. "We don't want you in any trouble."

She nodded.

"Are you all right?" Eden asked, her voice nearly inaudible.

Carlie's eyes flashed toward the guard before she nodded again, faintly.

"Never mind about the food. It's inedible anyway."

Biting her lip, Carlie glanced up again, only to find the man staring at her.

She pulled back, then stood at the wall opposite the cells from whence she could see into both. Her thoughts in a turmoil, she leaned her head back, rested it against the wall, and closed her eyes. She had to tell Broden. She had to get him in here.

Dear Good One! Would he even know what to do?

Chapter Thirty-Three

Lucy sat back, watching the other attendees. With Dixon, Dax, and Aliza, all missing, the group of leaders remaining in the city had grown rather small. Consequently, she'd brought Jerrett and Velia back to the city with her from her recent trips to the palace. Now they assisted with training and planning.

She felt she knew all the attendees so well. Surely, it wasn't possible that one of them was a traitor, she mused. Besides, how could someone possibly get word to Zarek so quickly? Still, she had to admit, it was strangely coincidental—or else contrived—that so shortly after Mara decided to leave for Aliza's with the twins, they were all taken prisoner. So, since she'd asked for her assistance, Lucy would do the deed. Even so, she couldn't wait to report back that all was well within their ranks. Thoughts to the contrary were too painful to contemplate.

She turned her focus back to the proceedings.

"So," Percival was saying, "we're putting the healers on half-day shifts, starting immediately."

"That sounds good," Lucy said before turning to Petrus. "How are the plans coming along for interrupting Zarek's supply chain?" she asked him.

"Ahhh . . . Well enough, I guess."

"Excellent. Now, toward that end—" She turned her attention to her paperwork before looking back up. "There's one last thing for today."

"Oh?" Jerrett asked.

"Yes. Mara messaged me again."

"Great Ehyeh," Velia muttered, "is she all right?"

"In truth, she didn't sound good. Still," Lucy said, before clearing her throat, "she says it's time we intercept some of Zarek's plans."

Pausing, she tapped on the table. "Liam and Rafal reported to me just days ago that they'd discovered some succedunt storing a cache of food and weapons in a dried up well in the center of a little abandoned town just south of Fallique. Apparently, the succedunt troops act rather independently," she added offhandedly. "In any case, when I told Mara about what they'd heard, she insisted we destroy the goods."

Percival sat up straighter. "How?"

Jerrett stared at her. "It could take weeks to get some of our special forces there."

"Well, fortunately for us," Lucy said, "we don't need special forces. We just need Liam and Rafal."

"Oh?"

"They know where the place is—and they carry crystals, which they can use to blow up the cache."

"Where are these goods, did you say?"

Lucy picked up a nearby scroll. A crinkling sound filled the air as she unrolled it to reveal a map.

"The place is called Wylie," she said as she circled something on it. "Here," she passed it to her right, "you can all take a look at it."

Velia set down her quill. "So you'll tell Liam and Rafal to go there and destroy the goods?"

"I already did. Fortunately, they were close. They expect to arrive there overmorrow, between midday and dusk. Immediately thereafter, they'll return here, to Oosa. They've found no clues as to Carlie's whereabouts, and frankly, I can't justify their remaining in such danger themselves any longer."

"That was a fortunate discovery—about the stored goods," Petrus offered as he surveyed the map that Jerrett handed him.

"It was, indeed."

"Well, it sounds good to me," Jerrett said. "I only wish I could be there with them for this mission. I'd like to destroy some of Zarek's things myself."

Lucy chuckled. "It would be deeply satisfying, wouldn't it?"

Lucy had communicated back and forth with Liam and Rafal before the meeting with the other leaders. She'd insisted the men identify a deserted place close enough to the city of Fallique for some of Zarek's men to reach there on short notice. Fortunately, they'd come up with Wylie, a ghost town, which they described to her in minutest detail. Once done, Lucy instructed them to return to Oosa.

Now that her meeting was over, she set out.

Her magic journey went off without a glitch, but already she grew weary of waiting as she crouched down inside a deserted gristmill. She peeked out of its dirty, multi-paned front window. The cracks in one panel looked like a hastily spun spiderweb. She picked at the gummy substance that held the glass in place, and then wiggled the shards free. As a consequence, even more cold air gusted inside.

If no one showed up, she couldn't be certain there was no traitor in their midst. After all, it could just be that the person couldn't get a message to Zarek in time, or that his men couldn't get to Wylie in time. But if Zarek's guards did show up, she could be fairly certain that there was a leak in their system—either that someone was careless with their information, or that they hosted an outright betrayer in their midst.

And then what would I do? Oh, gracious Ehyeh, I sincerely hope that's not the case.

Shivering, she drew her wrap tighter, even as a gust of wind shook the building's rickety exterior and then worried its way inside through the one missing windowpane and the cracks in the others. It whistled, eerily.

She looked out again.

Nothing.

Having arrived late the night before, to be certain she got there before anyone else, she was cold to the bone—and tired.

With her teeth chattering, she stood and paced. It was nearly noon already, yet she'd seen no sign of anyone.

She glanced out again to find snow falling. She watched in silence for several minutes as it grew heavier, but still, no one showed. She contemplated heading home, then dismissed the idea. It was too soon.

Just then, a faint jingling caught her attention.

She got down on her haunches and looked out.

For a long minute, she saw nothing through the snow-filled air. Then out of the misty flurries, a band of four guards, all dressed in black from head to toe, neared. They soon arrived at the center of the ghost town.

This doesn't mean anything. They could just be passing through.

The man at the front directed his gelding around the abandoned city square. Although the snow-covered ground muffled the sounds of the equine's steps, its leather tack and metal hardware crunched and jingled. When he brought the animal to a halt, it pranced, whinnied, and jerked its head up, repeatedly.

"See anyone?" he asked his cohorts.

Lucy couldn't hear his comrades respond, as they all faced the other direction.

"You," the leader said, pointing at one of his men, "check it out."

The man dismounted. He approached the well that sat in the midst of the town square, just as Liam and Rafal had described it to Lucy, then tied his mount to a nearby post.

Lucy inhaled sharply. *It can't be!*

Looking down, he released the rope attached to a bucket hanging above it. After it dropped to the bottom, he drew it back up. Then, "Nothing," he said.

"Check out the buildings," the first of the men ordered.

The man that he addressed headed to an abandoned apothecary shop, even as two more of the gang dismounted.

The leader looked around the square. "I'll ride out a distance to see if anyone is still on the way here, or if someone might have heard us approaching and left before we arrived," he said. With that, he set off.

So, it's true, Lucy thought. *We have a leak. Well then, I'd best get to it.*

She took up her bow and an arrow from her quiver, and then turned back to the missing windowpane. She'd get the leader later, when he returned. In the meantime, she'd see to men just outside.

After tying their horses up, one of the soldiers headed toward a former blacksmith shop.

Lucy took aim.

The air held the heavy cold wetness of late winter. It was the kind that settled deep in one's bones. Shivering, she exhaled slowly, her breath fogging the air, willing herself to still. With one more breath, her shivering now brought under control, she released her shot.

The man went down, landing with a thud.

As another of the men approached what had once been an inn, he jerked around at the sound. Not having seen the source of the shot, he cried out for his cohort, then dashed back toward his mount.

As he struggled to saddle up, Lucy took aim and shot for the second time. She hit his leg.

Notwithstanding his injury, he pulled up, then grabbed the reins.

As he turned his mount away, Lucy shot again. The arrow landed in the center of the man's back.

"Uffhhhhh," he groaned as he dropped to the ground.

At the sound, the third man came running back from the apothecary shop where he'd headed earlier. Upon sight of his fallen comrades, he spun back around.

Meanwhile, Lucy reached for another arrow. She nocked it, pulled her arm back, took aim, and then released her shot.

He fell to the earth. Snow billowed into the air around him.

She dropped her arms. Now she just had to wait for the leader to return.

Seconds later, came a sound at the door. Slowly, the handle turned.

The leader must have turned back and then identified the place from whence Lucy spied.

She grasped her blade, Vivacitas, and crouched.

The door blew open, slamming against the wall.

She threw her blade. As always, it met its mark.

The succedunt soldier dropped to the floor with a last rattling exhale.

She approached, grabbed Vivacitas, and pulled. Once her weapon was free, she stepped over the dead man and out of the building, and then headed for the well.

Looking down into it, she dropped a crystal. She had to make it look as though Liam and Rafal had destroyed some cache of goods in the event anyone looked into the situation later.

As she stepped away, the crystal hit the earth below and exploded, throwing bits of rock and sparks into the air. Lucy ducked. Then, reaching for her magic, she returned to the City of Light.

Chapter Thirty-Four

Looking up at the three-quarter moon, the only one currently gracing the sky, Lucy decided it was time to return to the palace for a visit. She'd informed the other leaders of Liam and Rafal's report that, having arrived at Wylie earlier than expected, they'd destroyed the cache. Now came the hard part: to identify their leak. She knew it couldn't be Jerrett or Velia. They'd both proven themselves beyond reproach time and time again over the years. But that still left a number of other options. She decided she'd start with emphasizing to them all, the importance of maintaining confidentiality. Perhaps it was a simple matter of someone's carelessness. Gracious Ehyeh, but she certainly hoped so. In the meantime, she needed time to think.

She ran to the dormitory in search of Vida and Clarimonde, so as to inquire whether they wanted to return to the palace. They did not. So with nothing else to keep her around—for now anyway—it was time to go.

Seconds after spinning her magic, she landed in the vestibule of the palace. She glanced up as Bane bolted toward her, growling, his hackles raised.

Her hands up, she ordered, "Down, Bane!"

The wolf slowed, then circled her, sniffing at her feet.

"Go on," she ordered as she pointed down the hall that led toward the kitchen where he stayed in a room next to the larder.

Having recognized her, the wolf dropped his tail and then panted, offering her his strange canine smile.

"Oh, it's you!" Adele said, as she entered. "I thought I heard some commotion."

"Yes," Lucy said. "Goodness, but is he always so . . . so—"

"Aggressive? Protective?" Adele completed her question. "Yes, to both. I have him stand guard when I'm busy."

"I see."

"Why are you back so soon? We didn't expect you for a few days yet."

"I just need some time to think," Lucy said with a sigh. "Are Leala and Fidel still up?" she asked as she headed toward the kitchen.

"No," Adele said, following behind. "They both went down for the night some time ago. Is there anything I can do for you?"

Lucy entered the kitchen, then approached the larder. "Probably not. I've just had such trouble sleeping of late. Too much on my mind, I guess." She reached in and grabbed a labeled bag of herbs. "Oh, good."

"What is it?"

"My valerian, hops, and lemon balm mix," she said, bouncing the bag in her hand. "I could use some of this." She dropped it on the counter. "Is there still hot water on?"

"Always."

Adele went to the hearth and filled a cup from a pot of water that hung over it, then brought it to Lucy. "Here you go."

Lucy pulled out a stool and sat. She opened the sack, and then rummaged for a tea ball that sat on the counter nearby, just out of easy reach. Once in hand, she filled it.

Her eyes narrowed as she pulled back, looking closely at the tea. Then she drew it nearer and sniffed it, expecting the almost putrid smell of valerian the weedy scent of hops, or perhaps, a whiff of citrus. Her head cocked, she sniffed again.

"What is it?" Adele asked.

"This isn't my valerian tea mix." She dropped the tea ball on the counter, scowling. "Honestly, Adele, what is this?" she asked, grabbing the bag and waving it in the air.

"I— I'm sorry, Lucy. I know I told you that I'd have Barbara Jo help me with organizing all the herbs, but we just haven't had time."

"Look, if she's not working out for you, I can find someone else."

"Oh no, she's the best help I could ask for! The thing is that she's also responsible for cleaning—and that's taken most of her time and attention of late."

Lucy frowned. "Still, we discussed this all weeks ago, Adele."

"Yes, but with all Vida's children here now—and without her and Clarimonde here to assist with them—" Adele sighed. "Well, it's been hectic, to say the least."

Her jaw clenched, Lucy shook her head. "This is important, Adele. The wrong thing taken by someone, or something used by someone at the wrong time, could be . . . deadly."

"I'm sorry."

Lucy went back to the cupboard. "I'll just use chamomile, I guess." She rummaged about, finally pulling out another item. "It'll help me to relax, even it if it's not nearly as effective a sleep inducer."

She slapped it on the counter, resumed her seat, emptied the tea ball of its former contents, and then filled it from the bag of chamomile. All the while she held her jaw tight.

"I'm sorry," Adele tried again.

"Never mind. I guess I'll just do it myself."

"I'll get at it tomorrow. I promise."

"No, I'll do it."

"Lucy—"

She sighed. "It's all right, Adele. I know I promised you more help. I'll see what I can do about that. It's just that—" She grabbed the sack and waved it again. "We depend on the proper medications for the proper purposes. This is chamomile. I can tell by the look of it and by its characteristic smell—of apples. It is generally harmless—but in the hands of someone with allergies to certain types of plants, it could cause respiratory problems. That could be dangerous."

She dropped the bag, then swished the tea ball in her cup. "As to valerian," she said, "it is a powerful sleep inducer—but once again, it can be dangerous. Taken the wrong way, at the wrong time, or in the incorrect dosage, it can cause nausea, headaches, and even dizziness—all of which could prove seriously problematic."

"I understand."

"Besides," she huffed, "keeping these dried things in bags—in a kitchen— Well, that's just— It's not good practice. If they get moist, they could mildew, and that could cause another set of problems altogether."

Adele nodded.

"Look," Lucy said, waving her hand toward the larder, "this cannot go on. So I'll get to it tomorrow." She scowled. "I suppose, in truth, I'm probably the right person to do it anyway, as I'm well versed in herb-lore. That way I'll be certain it gets done correctly." She caught Adele's eye. "If you'd like to learn a bit about it, you can assist."

Adele smiled, falteringly. "I'd like that."

"Good." Lucy swallowed the last of her tea. "We'll get started first thing in the morning."

⁂

"Have we got enough glass jars?" Lucy asked as she stood examining the items on the table.

"I believe so," Adele said.

"Very well then, let's get at it."

Lucy started removing items from the larder shelves, handing them off to Adele, who in turn handed them to her assistant, Barbara Jo, who then set them on the table.

"There are a few more left," Lucy said as she paused to look over the pile of goods. "Can you move those jars over a bit farther to make more room?" she asked, pointing.

"I'll do it," Barbara Jo offered.

Having returned to the larder, Lucy continued emptying it. Finally, she handed the last items to Adele.

"That's it," she said as she proceeded to the table and then, with her hands on her hips, stood looking at it all. "What a mess."

"It looks about like it did right after the raid on the compound," Adele agreed, grimacing.

"Well then—" Lucy glanced Barbara Jo's way. "You make the labels. Please be certain they're legible." Then she turned to Adele. "I'll identify the items. You will put them in the jars. There's a wide mouth funnel there to use to keep the mess down."

"Understood."

"Wash and dry it out well after each item. We don't want one jar contaminated with what belongs in another—and we don't want any moisture getting into any of the jars. It could mold."

"Got it."

Lucy grabbed the first bag. "Do you know how these got so out of order?"

"After the raid on the compound, things were in a shambles. I think some of these," Adele said, holding up a handful of the bags, "just got tagged with whatever someone thought was correct."

"That's terrible."

"Yes, and it wasn't until back when the children were ill, right after we arrived here, that I became aware that there was anything wrong."

"Hmmm. So, they've been like this for several months now. Gracious," Lucy muttered. "All right, well . . . this label says 'bay laurel.'" She opened the bag and removed a few long, narrow leaves. Still green, but very dry, they cracked in her hand. "This is bay laurel, all right." She handed the item off to Adele to jar, as Barbara Jo made an identification tag.

"I use it in stews," Adele said as, having filled the vessel, she placed a cover on it. Then she wrapped the label, tied to a leather cord, around its top.

"That's right," Lucy said. "Now here's . . . dried borage flowers." She handed the next item over after sniffing at it. "Fortunately, it was marked correctly." Then, "It's good for colic, cramps, and urinary disorders, among other things," she added.

As Adele and Barbara Jo completed jarring the item, Lucy handed over another. "Dill," she said. "There's no mistaking its look or smell. See these little green bits?" She put some in her hand and held it out. "These are leaves. The plant itself is almost . . . fern-like." She passed the bag off.

"What's it used for?" Barbara Jo asked.

"Medicinally? Mostly to calm the digestive system. But it's also great for adding flavor to foods—especially fish."

She moved to the next one. "This is lavender—another easily recognizable look and scent. It's got a clean, floral fragrance. Well, so far, so good."

"I use it for cleaning," Barbara Jo said. "Now and again, I'll bruise a handful and leave it in a stuffy room to help freshen it up."

"Yes," Lucy agreed, "there are a lot of great uses for lavender. Cooking. Cleaning. You can use its essential oil in candles for a good scent, or for a quick and powerful remedy for a burn, and its dried flowers in soaps give them an exfoliating quality."

Opening the next bag, she took a look, then sniffed at it. "Yes, this is tarragon." She offered it to Adele. "Can you smell something a bit like anise?"

Adele agreed that she could.

So the women worked through the morning. Although they found a few mislabeled items, most of them, to Lucy's satisfaction and relief, had been marked correctly.

After taking a short midday break, they continued.

"What are you all up to?" Leala asked, as she entered the kitchen.

Lucy looked up. "Just getting some order to things around here." She paused, biting her lip. Then, "Say, are you and Fidel available for dinner this evening?" she asked.

"I am, and so far as I know, Fidel's got nowhere else to be. He's no spring chick, you know. He doesn't get around so easily these days." Leala chuckled. "Why do you ask?"

"I'd just like to discuss some things." Lucy turned to Adele. "Maybe we could finish the rest of these tomorrow," she suggested.

"If you don't mind, Lucy, it would be best to wrap this up. I've got a lot of things I need to see to, and truth to tell, I'd appreciate having this mess out of my way."

"No, you're right, of course."

Barbara Jo picked up one of the bags. Glancing at the label, she scowled. Then she opened it and sniffed. "Ewww," she said. "What is in this?"

"Hand it over," Lucy said.

She did.

Lucy read the label and smiled. Then she took a whiff of its contents. "Yes, this is right," she said. "Dried magic frog juice."

"What?" Adele asked. "I've never heard of such a—"

"Actually," Lucy said, laughing, as she pulled a stick out from the bag, "on each of these sticks, is dried frog venom. It comes from a far off land and thus, is quite difficult to acquire."

"What does it do?" Barbara Jo asked.

"Some say it's an antidote for snake bites. Others say it can help with fatigue, and even certain addictions. It's also an extremely powerful pain killer." She dropped the stick back into the bag and handed it off. "It must be kept dry and free of mold. So let's get it jarred."

As her assistants set out to do her bidding, Lucy grabbed the next bag. "Oh, here's another one you'll like. It's called 'Talking Rock Orchid.'"

"'Talking Rock?'" Barbara Jo repeated.

"Orchid. Yes. It can be used for gum disease. Hence, it's name." She handed it off.

"All right then, next we have—" She picked up another item and read the label. "'Bee balm.'" She reached inside the bag and pulled out some of its contents. "No, this label is wrong." She sniffed. "Right. This is . . ." Her eyes narrowed.

"What?" Adele asked.

She sniffed again. "Oh, I know. It's crushed feverfew leaves." She handed the item off for labeling. "Bee balm can have a bit of a minty or even peppery smell. It can be used to help with symptoms like sniffles."

"And feverfew?"

"It's got a musty, sometimes bitter, smell."

"Yes, and it's used for headaches," Leala piped in.

"That's right," Lucy agreed. Then, whilst Barbara Jo prepared a tag and Adele filled a jar with the herb, she readied the next one.

"This says 'lemon balm,' but it's actually marigold. The first is for upset stomachs, among other things, the second is for sunburn and other skin conditions. It also can be used for gastric problems and joint pain." She paused, in thought. "I recall that my mother used to make an infusion of it for women to treat . . . female infections. You know?" She pursed her lips, then looked back at the others. "In any case, like we discussed with chamomile last night, some people can't use marigold. If they take it internally, it can make them wheeze—cause difficulty with their breathing."

"Good catch," Leala said.

"Now, here's one marked 'parsnip root,'" Lucy said, grabbing another bag. She opened it and sniffed at the contents, then stopped cold, scowling. "Wait. This isn't parsnip root. This is . . ." She reached in for a pinch, then dropped it in her other palm. She stood, staring at it.

"What is it?" Adele asked.

Her gaze danced Leala's way. "Take a look," she said to her, handing the bag over. Then she turned back to Adele. "Do you recall the type of tea that Saga regularly requested?"

"Yes. She drank parsnip root tea—for her arthritis. She told me so herself. She brought some along with her to the compound, but she ran out."

"And do you know . . . Did you give her some of this?" Lucy asked, taking the bag back from Leala whose brow was furrowed.

"I don't recall that I did." She frowned. "Wait a minute. If memory serves, I asked Barbara Jo to do it."

"Yes, I got her tea for her," Barbara Jo said. Then her gaze danced from Lucy to Leala. Noticing the look in their eyes, she stepped back. "Well, that's what it was marked. Right?"

"Yes."

"So, yes, I . . . I must have."

Lucy and Leala exchanged a glance.

"Why? What's wrong?"

"Look," Lucy said, "it's not your fault."

"What? Oh, gracious Good One!" Barbara Jo drew her hands to her cheeks. "What is it?"

"It's . . . hemlock," Leala said.

"Wh— Hemlock? Oh, no! You mean I— I killed Saga?" She dropped into a nearby chair.

Lucy put her hand on her shoulder. "Look, it was an accident. You couldn't have known. I don't blame you. No one would."

"I killed her!" Barbara Jo muttered. "I— I murdered someone!"

"Stop it!" Lucy scolded. "You did not take her life with premeditation. It was an accident. Nothing more."

Barbara Jo sat with her mouth hanging open, her eyes wide.

"Come on, we're not through here yet," Lucy said. "Like Adele said, we need to wrap this up."

"But—"

"Barbara Jo—enough. It was an accident. It could have been at anyone's hand. Now, I don't want to hear any more about it. But we do have to do everything possible here to make certain that something like that doesn't ever happen again. Understood?"

Slowly, she nodded.

"Good." Lucy turned back to the remaining herbs. "Now, here's another." She read the next label, opened the bag, and then sniffed the contents. Suddenly, all the color drained from her face. Her hand to her mouth and her eyes wide, she sat down—hard.

"What is it, Lucy?" Barbara Jo asked.

"Oh, gracious Good One!" she exclaimed.

"What, Lucy? What is it? What happened?" Adele asked.

Lucy dropped the bag, jumped to her feet, and then ran from the room. She had to get word to her. She had to inform her of the mistake.

Oh, dear Good One! No, no, no!

She'd known, when the twins were in The Tearless, before heading to the City of Light, that she'd likely meet her there. Concerned that the tea she needed might not be readily available in the city, and knowing she'd likely be out of the supply previously provided to her, Lucy had taken some along with her from the compound shelter.

But it was marked wrong. I gave her the wrong thing!

She rushed through the vestibule and up the staircase. She'd pack her things immediately, and then head back to the city. Maybe Velia could counsel her on the matter.

Chapter Thirty-Five

Every night after the guards returned Carlie to Broden's quarters, the two of them discussed the state in which she found Mara and the twins. They sought ways to communicate with the three of them, but they didn't want to risk Carlie's safety by having her carry a written missive. Should she attempt to do so and get caught, Broden, also, would be in added danger. In the end, it was a risk they were unwilling to take.

"Maybe Mara can just read your thoughts," Broden suggested. "Or maybe she already has."

Carlie shook her head. "I don't believe so. I do recall that mind reading was a power that simply came over Mara from time to time. To the best of my recollection, she didn't 'exercise' it so much as she 'experienced' it."

"I see."

"You know, Broden, as I said before, there's something odd about the place. Her magic must not work in there."

"Why do you say that?"

"Well, why else would she stay there? Why wouldn't she just travel out of there, magically? And because she should be able to pick any lock by moving its internal parts, but she hasn't. Besides, as I told you, her blade is jammed in the lock, yet she hasn't retrieved it—with her magic, I mean. She couldn't get it any other way since she can't reach it."

He paced, pondering.

Just then, the door opened and Striver entered. "Any changes?" he asked.

"None," Carlie said. Then she turned Broden's way again. "Whatever else, though, we have to get them some decent food on a regular basis. What the guards leave for them there is completely inedible."

The door of the women's room opened. Yasmin, Farida, Ghazala, and Clementine, entered.

"Like I told you before, I brought them food," Yasmin said, "the day they released me from further service there."

Broden's eyes shifted to her. "You're lucky you didn't get caught," he said. Then he frowned. "Listen, I don't want any of you getting mixed up in this. You should go now."

"No," Yasmin said. "Now, Mouse," she said turning to Carlie, "there is a way to get food to them. Pack it in a cloth, tie it up, and then put it under your clothing. You don't want to have to slip it off over your head, because the guards would notice that. You want to be able to untie it from around your neck." She paused, watching Carlie's reaction. "They check your pockets before they take you there each day, but if you carry food in there the way I said, they won't know."

Carlie shook her head. "Broden's right, Yasmin. You shouldn't be involved in this."

She glared at each of them in turn. "You're not serious. Right? I mean, if I was in there, I'd sure want you to take the chance of bringing me something edible. Now, I don't know what those women all mean to you, but if you don't do like I'm suggesting, they could die in that prison."

His eyes closed, Broden bit his lip. Then he looked back at her. "You're right."

He headed to the table and looked over the assortment of bread and dried fruits and nuts.

Yasmin met him at his side. "Mouse will have to be able to drop the things into the cells without being seen. Here—"

She picked up a nearby cloth. With her teeth, she made a tear in it. Holding it at each side of the cut, she ripped it in half. Then she tore each of those halves into two more pieces.

"Wrap some food up into each of these," she said as she dumped some biscuits onto one cloth, and some nuts onto another. Once done, she tied them up.

"You can drop these packages into the cells," she said as she turned to Carlie. Then, "You know the woman who's chained?" she asked.

"Yes."

"You'll have to be sure to throw hers in sufficiently far for her to reach."

Broden helped Yasmin finish filling, and then tying up, the other cloths. Then he handed them to Carlie.

"And what of water?" she asked.

"The guards never questioned my canteen," Yasmin said, "although I never drank from it myself. Tomorrow, carry two, so you can leave one in each cell. Then just take the empty ones back out when you leave for the day."

Nodding, Carlie clenched her jaw. She was grateful for Yasmin's idea—and for the first time in a long while, she didn't feel completely powerless.

Chapter Thirty-Six

Mara kept a vigilant watch out for rats while the twins cuddled beneath Rowena's shawl, the magic of which forbade the creatures from reaching them.

For some time, they all sat silently.

"Thank Ehyeh for Carlie," Eden finally said. "I needed something decent to eat and drink."

"Yes," Reigna agreed.

Mara?" Eden called out. "Did she bring food and water to you, as well?"

She sat up straighter. "Yes."

"Any luck with the locks yet?"

She sighed. "Still none."

"Hmmm. You know, if you can't free yourself, there's no getting out of here for any of us."

"I've told you two. If you ever get the chance, cover with that shawl and make your exit."

"Not without you," Reigna said.

Her sister moved the shawl away from her shoulders and stood. Her boots clicked on the floor as she stepped to the bars.

"Mara?"

"You sound troubled, Eden. Are you well?"

"I guess. But . . ."

"What is it?" Mara pulled forward. Her wristband tightened.

"Do you think Carlie could bring something else—other than food—for me?"

Mara sighed. "I don't know. From all we've been able to tell, she's every bit as much a slave as we are. She helped us today, but she's yet to speak to us . . ." Her voice trailed away to nothing. Then, "What do you want from her?" she asked.

Eden paced, each footstep audible as the dirt ground into the rock beneath her feet. "I need some . . ." She went quiet again.

"Some what?"

She returned to the bars and gripped them. "It's my moon cycle, Mara," she whispered. "Do you think she'd bring me some clean rags?"

"Mine, too," Reigna said, approaching her sister's side. "You know ours always coincide."

Mara pulled back, her mind in a jumble. Then, shaking, she brought her hand to her mouth. "Ahhhh!" she cried.

"What is it?" Eden asked, her voice worry-laden.

"Oh, dear Good One, no," Mara muttered. "No, no, no."

"What? What's wrong?" Reigna asked.

Mara's tangled thoughts raced. How long had it been since her memory had been restored? How much time had passed since she'd found the girls and taken them to the City of Light? Gasping now, she struggled to recall details.

"What is it?" Eden asked again. "Please, Mara, you're scaring us!"

She'd returned with the twins to the city. Then, her memory fully restored, she was reunited with Dixon. She could remember a moon-cycle coming several days later, but . . .

Her hand again at her mouth, tears welled in her eyes. She groaned. She felt her middle. Notwithstanding the minuscule rations they'd lived on for the past few weeks, she felt bloated.

She concentrated, but couldn't think of another cycle since she'd been reunited with Dixon. How long after that was it before she'd started to feel ill? How long was it before she'd traveled to the City of Light where the girls were training?

"Oh, great Ehyeh," she moaned.

"What?" the twins asked simultaneously.

"Oh, girls," she said, panic making her voice shake. "You know, at the palace, when Vida's children brought us the grippe?"

"Yes," Eden said. "What of it?"

"And I was sick for weeks?"

"Yes."

Mara choked back a cry. "Oh, gracious Good One!"

"What? Please, Mara, you're really scaring us," Reigna said.

"I don't think I was just . . . sick."

"What are you talking about?" Eden asked.

Now, gasping for breath, Mara cried, "Oh, Reigna, Eden! I— I think I'm pregnant!"

Mara wept for hours, as sleep eluded her. She was certain now. She'd not been ill when she'd returned to the palace—she'd been suffering from morning sickness. It explained everything: the long weeks during which she felt constantly nauseous, the fact that she was so tired all the time, and why she exhausted so quickly while training. It even explained her itchy skin and her heightened sense of smell. For weeks, the mere whiff of something unexpected had made her stomach lurch and her head spin.

But how could this have happened? When Dixon had taken her from the compound to travel to her mother's home, Lucy was unaware of the true situation. No doubt, she thought Mara was adequately protected—and she was. Since Dixon was a stranger to her at the time, she'd not been intimate with him. But then . . .

She thought back to the day when she'd been reunited with Dixon after the hearing. That was when Lucy had given her some barrenseed tea. Mara recalled thinking it tasted a bit different than usual, but she hadn't had any in all the while that her memory had been lost to her, so that fact didn't particularly trouble her.

She concentrated on what happened after the hearing. Lucy had marched up to her and insisted that they meet in private. When they found their way to a conference room, she'd rustled inside her pack.

"Here," she'd said, removing a bag of something.

Mara reached for the item. "What is this?"

"Barrenseed tea." Lucy scowled. "I expect you weren't drinking it during your travels?"

"Ahhh, no, I . . . I guess I wasn't."

"Is there any cause for concern, do you think?" Lucy clenched her jaw. Her eyes seemed to bore into her.

Mara stood tall. "First of all, Lucy, it's really none of your concern." She shook her head. "But in answer to your question: no, there is no cause for concern."

"The two of you have been traveling—alone—for some time."

Mara stared at her. "Honestly, Lucy, there are times . . ." She folded her arms and stepped away, then turned back. "As you are well aware, I had no memories of my past. Dixon was a stranger to me. And I don't find myself . . . intimate . . . with strangers—ever." She huffed. "So you can put your mind at ease."

"When I learned the truth about how you'd lost your memory, I thought you might not be protected. I brought that with me," she said, pointing at the tea, "so that I could get it to you when I met up with you, as I assumed that eventually, you might need it."

Again shaking her head, Mara looked back up. "It's like I said, Lucy, it's none of your concern."

"Well, I'm just trying to help. You're the one who asked me—"

"Forget it." Mara marched to the door. "Now, if you'll excuse me."

Yes, she'd been angry. But she'd used the tea that Lucy gave her—religiously. She'd made a morning cup of it every day since she'd been reunited with Dixon.

There'd been times in the past when she'd not been particularly regular in her moon cycles. Usually that was when she'd been greatly stressed. But she was certain now that she indeed, carried a child. It explained so much—her rounded abdomen, for example—notwithstanding the small rations on which she'd been living. It even explained the strange feeling she'd experienced from time to time in the past week or so. It was . . . ephemeral . . . a fleeting thing—like a butterfly gently brushing its wings inside her.

Now, she understood.
The child had quickened.

Dusk having just settled, she found it odd that she perspired so profusely, given the coolness of the night. Still, the load she carried was significant—almost too much to bear. Her arms, back, and knees, ached.

Sweat ran down at her temples. It tickled—in an irritating sort of way. More trickled down at her hairline, then ran into her eyes, fogging them over. She tried to brush it away at her shoulder, but the movement caused a shift in her weight that left her unbalanced.

She fell, intentionally twisting on her way down, as she dared not land on the little ones for fear of crushing them.

Grimacing upon landing on her left forearm and hip, she choked back a sob. A shot of pain jolted through her lower back, but that wasn't the worst of it. It was her elbow that spasmed. It tingled all the way down to her fingertips, leaving her arm numb. She rubbed it in an effort to relieve the sensation.

Fortunately, the babies hadn't awakened. She had to keep them quiet or they'd all be discovered. With one of the little ones tied to her frontside, the other resting in the basket on her arm, she sat up. She'd stop for a minute to catch her breath, but knew she mustn't take long.

She looked out. A distant stream sparkled in the moonlight. Above it, bats flew in quick, broad circles, dipping sporadically, then with faint flutterings of their wings, rising again. Every few seconds, they repeated their jerky, almost spasmodic, maneuvers.

For a moment she considered stopping longer, but then decided against it. They were in the open. Besides, if she could get more distance before morning, she might actually outrun their pursuers. And fortunately—for now at least—the babies slept. She had to get them to safety, and she had to do so soon.

On sight of a long sturdy stick on the ground nearby, she grabbed it. It would help her to walk. Planting it firmly in the ground, then grasping it for leverage, she rustled back to her feet. Once done, she rearranged the items she carried, then placed one tired foot in front of the other.

Time passed slowly. Each step required greater effort than the one before.

Finally, as dawn brushed the morning sky, she came upon a cave. She glanced inside, hoping she'd discovered a refuge.

But then came an unexpected sound from behind.

She looked back.

They'd found her! How could that have happened? How had they made their way so close without her knowledge?

She opened the covering of the babe in her arms and stole a glance. Goodness, but the infant did not look well. So tiny, so fragile . . .

Wait. Did she? Or did I imagine it?

Gracious Ehyeh, don't let it be. Don't take her.

She picked up the infant's tiny hand and placed it at her lips. She closed her eyes momentarily, afraid to look, then opened them again to watch for the babe's breath.

There it was—the slightest rise and fall of her chest. But in the faint morning light, her skin looked almost . . . blue. Surely, she couldn't survive much longer.

"Ahhhhh," she cried. With that, she awakened and sat upright.

"Mara?" Reigna cried.

Breathing hard, she put her hand to her chest.

"Are you all right?"

"Yes. I'm— I'm fine."

"What happened?"

"Just a . . . a nightmare." She paused. "I'm so sorry, Reigna. I fear for you two—and it's all my fault."

"Please Mara, that's not so."

She closed her eyes, but when the image of the nearly dead child met her consciousness, she opened them again. She couldn't look at it.

Oh, Ehyeh, what have I done bringing the twins into this?

She choked back another cry upon recollecting that it was not only her charges in danger—so, too, was her own child—*Dixon's* child.

She wept with the realization that she'd failed on every front.

Chapter Thirty-Seven

Leading their mounts behind, as the uneven ground made the going treacherous, they traveled through a marshland, encrusted with ice. From time to time, one of them broke through, causing water to rush up unexpectedly. Their boots drenched, and their feet nearly frozen, they nevertheless drove on until dusk when they happened along an old farmstead, its buildings aged and battered. The barn's door hung on rusted hinges, while a single cracked window graced the building's frontside.

Avoiding the house itself, in the event it might be inhabited, the Oathtakers, along with the flits, Mercurial, Spectrum, and Evanescent, entered the barn. There they found several empty stalls. Some old damp hay, frozen to the floor, crunched beneath their steps.

An orange striped tomcat looked up as they entered. The hair on its arched back stood up as it spat at them before running off.

"Why don't you leave your mounts here and then check around for some dry hay and fresh water?" Dixon asked Dax and Aliza. "These horses need to eat and drink."

He bent down to examine a cut on the front leg of the gelding he'd been riding, the result of sharp edges of ice they'd meandered through. Then, "I'll have to get some lavender oil balm on these cuts, I see," he commented.

As his cohorts headed up a rickety ladder to the loft above, Dixon grabbed a pitchfork and shovel, then mucked out a stall. Once done, he led into it, the mahogany bay gelding he'd ridden. Then he approached the next stall to clean it out.

"Watch out below!" Dax called out.

A second later, from above, a bale of hay, and then another, dropped to the floor. Each landed with a resounding thud.

Dixon looked up. "Is it dry?"

"It is," Dax said as he headed down the ladder. He stopped suddenly. "Watch the third rung here, Aliza," he called out. "It's loose."

"Got it. Thanks. I'll be right with you. I just have to get my pack."

"Good thing," Dixon said as he entered the next stall. "That it's dry, I mean."

He scraped from the ground and then shoveled up, a pile of the old hay. He dumped it outside the unit.

"We could lose good horses to mold in wet hay," he commented.

"It should be fine," Dax said.

Just then, the cracking of splintering wood, followed by a muted scream, and then a loud crash, sounded out.

Dixon and Dax ran to the source, just as Aliza, having broken through the floor, landed face-up next to a bin of grain. Several planks followed behind, one hitting her soundly on the head. Specks of hay and billowing dust rained down on her.

"Ohhh," she cried.

"Are you hurt?" Dixon asked, crouching down at her side.

"Ohhh . . . Ohhh . . ." She moaned. "Ahhhh . . . I went back for my pack and the floor gave way." She grimaced. "Ohhh."

"Let's take a look." Dixon leaned over her. He felt each of her legs. All seemed well. He picked up her right foot and moved it around. "Does this hurt?"

"I can't tell. I hurt everywhere."

He lifted her other foot and repeated the procedure. When she didn't cry out, he took her left elbow.

"Ahhh!" she cried. Her body jerked upward.

He pulled her sleeve up. One glance was all it took. She'd broken her arm halfway between her wrist and elbow. The bone poked out through her skin. His gaze flickered toward Dax who, standing nearby, bit his lip.

Aliza watched the exchange. "Great Ehyeh, but it hurts." Tears streamed down her cheeks as she tried to sit up.

"Wait. Stay. Don't move," Dax said, holding his hand out.

Her eyes widened. "What is it?"

Dixon pulled back. "Aliza, you broke your arm. The bone is . . . Well," he said, looking down, "neither of us is a healer—so that's not good. That means I'll need to take you back."

"No, Dixon! Please, don't. We can't leave Dax here alone. He has no magic to protect him." She wiped away an errant tear. "If someone finds him, we could lose him."

"I really should take you back."

"Please, please, don't."

He pulled his shoulders back, and sighed heavily. "All right, if you're sure."

"I'm sure."

"Well then, I guess I'll have to set your arm myself."

She choked back a cry. "Will it hurt?"

"Yes, I won't lie. It's going to hurt. Quite badly, I'm sorry to say—and we've nothing much to dull the pain." He turned to Dax. "There's a flask of spirits in my pack. Would you get it?"

"Oh, dear Good One. What have I done?" Aliza asked, lying back, her tears now flowing freely.

"You're going to be fine, but if you're staying here, then I can safely say that we won't be going anywhere for some time."

She covered her face with her other hand and moaned. "It hurts so much."

Dax returned with two flasks. "Here's yours—and one from my pack as well," he said, handing them to Dixon. Then, "I'll go find some ice," he added as he walked away.

"Good idea." Dropping the flasks, Dixon watched him exit, then turned back to Aliza. "Do you think you can sit up?"

She nodded.

"Wait." He pulled his cloak off and wrapped it around her arm. "All right, then. Here we go." He put a hand behind her back to assist her.

Groaning, she sat up, then leaned against the bale of hay that Dixon put behind her. "I can't lift it," she said. "My arm, I mean."

"Yes, I know," Dixon said, "that's because of the break."

Dax returned with his arms full. "There are icicles hanging from the lowest part of the north side of the roof over there," he said, gesturing with a tip of his head. "I broke off a bunch—and I can get more if needed. Also, I found a water pump."

"I'll need the ice here," Dixon said, patting the floor at his side. Then looking about, he spotted a weathered wooden bucket. "You could fill that," he added, pointing at it. "If we wet some cloths and then wrap them over ice, we can put them on each side of her arm. We don't want to freeze it—but it could help to dull the pain for when I set it. It'll also keep down some of the swelling that's sure to follow."

Dax nodded as he put the ice down.

"Oh—also, see if you can find a flat board about this big," Dixon gestured with his hands. "I'll use it as a splint after I set her bone."

As Dax set out with the bucket in hand, Dixon grabbed one of the flasks.

Seconds later came the sounds of shuffling footsteps from near the barn door. Convinced they did not belong to Dax, Dixon jumped to his feet and reached for Verity. But before he could do more, Aliza spoke.

"I've got this," she whispered to him. She turned her magic on so that she would look and sound to their visitor as someone with authority over him. She didn't need to know any more. His own imagination would fill in the gaps.

At the door stood a man in aged and ragged clothing. The wrinkles in his skin were like those on the mug of an old bloodhound. Staring at Aliza, his mouth opened and closed repeatedly, as though he was at a loss for words. He licked his puckered, chapped lips.

"What?" she asked him, her voice clipped.

"I— I didn't expect you back, is all," he said.

"Why wouldn't I come back?"

He stood, stammering.

"Well?"

"It's just that when you left Mother and me, Father, you said you'd never return."

Despite her circumstances, Aliza had to stifle a grin. Apparently the person the old man saw as someone with authority over him, was his long-lost father.

"Well," she groaned, fighting to get each word out, "have you taken good care of the farm in my absence?"

"I have, Father."

"Good." She glanced away, then turned her gaze back on him. "But I don't see any livestock."

"Zarek confiscated it all."

"I see." Aliza grimaced in pain.

"Are you all right, Father?"

"Yes." She swallowed hard. "Now, off with you," she said, tipping her head toward the door. "And don't come back in here. I'll find you when I'm ready to see you."

The man turned away. A second later, he glanced back for another look.

"Go on," she urged, then watched him walk away.

When he was gone, she released her magic, dropped back her head, and closed her eyes. "Can we just get this over with? I don't know how long he's likely to obey my orders."

"That is an amazing gift you have," Dixon said, grinning.

She shook her head. "All right, what do I do?"

He handed her a flask. "For starters, drink this."

She took a swallow, then pulled back. "Ugh!"

"Just drink it."

She blew out her breath and lifted the flask again. She took another swallow, then started to lower the vessel once more.

He pressed it back up. "Now."

Grimacing all the while, she followed his directions.

"We'll hold off on that one for now," he said, pointing at the other canteen, "since we'll need to put some on the wound itself to guard against infection."

She closed her eyes. Once again, tears streamed down her cheeks.

"You're going to be all right," he said.

Just then, Dax returned. "Here's some water," he said, "and a flat board I found."

"I expect it's quite dirty," Dixon commented.

"Well . . . it's not clean."

"Hmmmm. All right . . ." Dixon hesitated, thinking. "Listen, can you build a fire? You should keep it small, but we could use some boiled water to clean her wound and to disinfect these rags before we wrap her arm in them. Also, we could cover the board with some of them before laying her arm on it."

"Sure." Dax stepped away.

Dixon went for his pack, then returned to Aliza's side with it in hand. From inside, he removed two cotton cloths. After using his blade to make a tear in one of them, he split it in two, then dropped both halves in the bucket. Once wet, he wrung the excess water out from the rags. Then he wrapped icicles into each of them.

"The fire is started, and I've got a pot of water on to boil," Dax said upon returning. "Now, if you don't need me here, I can water the horses."

"Good," Dixon said. Then he removed his cloak from around Aliza's arm and, once done, placed an icepack on either side of it.

"I'm cold," she said, her teeth chattering.

"Likely, you're going into shock," he said. "Let's get you back down and cover you with my cloak here."

As he pushed the bale of hay away and then helped her to recline, Dax returned with another bucket of water. He set it on the floor before his mount.

"Dax," Dixon called.

"Yes?"

"Is the water boiling yet?"

"I'll check." He walked out and then returned a minute later. "Just about."

"While we wait, could you clean out another stall and put some fresh hay in it? We'll need to get Aliza down and warm before long."

Several minutes passed as Dax shoveled old hay out from one of the stalls. Then he retrieved a fresh bail, cut the twine that held it together, and spread the bedding out.

"This is ready," he said. "I'll go check on the water now."

A minute later, he returned with a pot of boiling water. He set it down.

Nodding, Dixon dropped several cloths into it. Then he turned Dax's way. "I need you to sit behind her and let her lean against you. I want you to hold her at her elbow—firmly." He looked his friend in the eye.

"What are you going to do?" he asked.

Dixon bit his lip, then turned to Aliza. He leaned in. "Aliza, like I said, this is going to hurt. I'm going to pull on your arm just above your wrist here, to pull the bone back. Then I'm going to have to twist it to get it back in place."

The spirits having taken effect, she merely groaned.

"Have you got her?" he asked his friend.

Dax nodded.

"All right then—on the count of three. One," Dixon took her wrist in one hand, "two," he grasped her arm just below her elbow with his other hand, "three."

Quick as a flash, he pulled and, before her resulting scream died away, twisted. Then observing that she'd passed out, and that her arm appeared to be set correctly in place, he let his breath out slowly.

"Now what?" Dax asked.

Dixon opened the remaining canteen of spirits. "Now, I pour some of this on it, splint it, and then wrap her arm up in these cloths."

"Anything I can do?"

"Yes, you can lay her back, now. Then I suppose you should put the fire out. We'll eat some of our dried foodstuffs. They're in my pack. I'll be with you as soon as I get this done."

Minutes later, he crouched down to pick Aliza up off the ground. Then he carried her to the stall that Dax had prepared for them all. Finding a spot thick with clean hay, he put her down.

"Here," Dax said, passing over a loaf of semi-stale bread and some dried meat.

As Dixon sat, the flits—Mercurial, Spectrum, and Evanescent—flew near him. They hovered at his shoulder.

"That was amazing," Spec said.

"Oh, I'd almost forgotten you were here," he commented.

"Where did you learn to do that?" the flit asked.

He shrugged. "Just observing over the years." He dropped his head in his hand and rubbed it. "Listen," he said, looking back up, "I think it's time we sent one of you back to report to Lucy."

"I agree," Merc said.

"Tell her what happened." Dixon let his breath out slowly, audibly. "If an infection sets in, I may not have any choice about bringing her back to Oosa, but I'd like to honor her wishes, if possible."

"I'll go," Spec offered.

"Fine." Dixon brushed breadcrumbs from his clothing. "We're not far from Fallique now. Please just get to Lucy and back as quickly as possible. Maybe she'll have some ideas for us in the event Aliza's wound does infect." He patted his thigh. "I wish we had a healer here with us."

"Maybe Lucy could deliver one here."

"I'd rather she didn't. We've enough problems as it is."

"Shall I leave now?"

Aware that the flits were ready to set out on their missions at any time of day or night, Dixon nodded. "Sure. Tell her everything. And please—hurry."

"I should be able to get there within a couple days. Then I'll need a couple more to return." The flit fluttered his wings. "I'll see you soon."

Dixon leaned back against the wall and closed his eyes. "Right. We won't be going anywhere for some time."

With that, Spec flew away.

Chapter Thirty-Eight

"You don't dare go, Lucy," Jerrett said.

"He's right," Velia agreed.

Frowning at them, she sighed. "If an infection sets in, we could lose her. It's been days already." Her hands on the conference table, she leaned in. "Although, I suppose, truth be told, there's not much I could do anyway. That's why I asked Percival to stop by here. I want to know if there's anything I can tell Dixon to do, via Spec, that might help since he doesn't seem inclined to just bring her back here." She scowled.

"Are you sure that's wise? Telling Percival anything, I mean?" Jerrett asked. "What if he's . . . you know."

"Our leak? Of course, that's possible, but what choice do we have?" she asked, her hands raised, palms up. Then she dropped them, huffing, as her shoulders sagged.

"I don't like it."

She sat, then drew a circle in the dust on the tabletop. "I'm just going to tell him that Dixon, Dax, and Aliza, are in trouble, but I won't say where they are. I'll only ask him questions in a general sense."

"Where exactly are they?" Velia asked.

Lucy picked up a scrolled map. As she unrolled it, a crinkling sound filled the air. After putting weights on its corners to hold it flat, she grabbed her owl feather quill, dipped the end of it in a pot of ink, and then circled a place on it.

"Right here is where Spec says they are—in some old barn on an abandoned farmstead."

Jerrett sat back. "If you're sure," he said.

"I am. Now, I'm going to get Percival." She went to the door and opened it.

Percival nearly fell inside.

"Oh!" she cried, surprised. "I was just on my way to find you."

He approached, his stride firm and determined. "Spec found me. He said there's an emergency that you need help with." He glanced from her to Jerrett, and then to Velia. "So . . . what is it?"

Lucy told him of the predicament in which their fellow Oathtakers found themselves.

"Maybe you and I should go," Percival said. "You could deliver us there."

"No, but thank you." Her eyes flickered toward her friends, then settled back on him.

"Is that the place there?" he asked as he motioned toward the map.

Lucy grabbed it and rolled it back up. "Listen," she said, "I just want to know if there's anything Dixon could do to help with any infection, should one set in. Apparently, the bone broke through her skin—and they were in an old . . ." She paused. "Well, they're not in a sterile place, let's just say."

"Sugar," Percival said.

She pulled back. "What?"

"Sugar. If the wound is open, pack it with sugar. Dixon could mix honey with it as well."

Her eyes narrowed. "Sugar? I've never heard of such a—"

"Nevertheless, it works. Pack it with sugar, then flush it daily and repack it. It will draw the infection out."

She stared at him, as though expecting him to break out a big grin. "Are you sure?" she asked when his expression remained stone-cold sober.

"I'm certain. The remedy dates back centuries. For those without healers readily available, it's been used frequently—and with great success."

Lucy stood and paced again. "Dixon should have some sugar in with his general supplies," she muttered. She turned back. "How much would it take?"

"He just needs enough to make a sludge of it. Pack it in and around the wound, and then leave it open—or cover it. It doesn't really matter."

"That's it? You're sure?"

"Yes, I'm sure."

"Well," Velia piped up, "you know, if Dixon doesn't have any sugar with him, it's usually fairly easy to get. So it seems the perfect option."

"Huh. All right. Thank you, Percival," Lucy said to him. Then resuming her seat she added, "That's it for now."

He stood and stepped toward the door, then turned back. "Ahhh, Lucy . . . may I have a word with you?"

"Certainly." She met him at his side.

He looked down, then glanced back at her. "I wondered if you might join me—"

"Thank you, Percival," she cut him off, "but no."

He made as though to say more, then clamped his mouth shut and nodded. "All right then," he said. "Jerrett," he nodded his way, and then, "Velia," he added addressing her. With that, he made his way out.

Before the door fully closed, Spec flew up from the tabletop whereupon he'd been sitting.

"Oh!" Lucy said, surprised at his sudden movement. "Well, you know what you're to tell Dixon."

"If that's it, then I'll be off," the flit said.

"That's all," Lucy said, "but do have one of you report back again as quickly as possible."

"Consider it done." With that, he flew to the door, waited for her to open it for him, and then sped off.

He watched and listened through the hole in the wall as Lucy, Jerrett, and Velia, left the conference room. It had proven to be an excellent place to go when he sought information. From it, he'd learned all about Mara's powers, including of her ability to make crystals from her flares that could be used as weapons. He'd warned Daeva about them before Zarek's men captured her and the twins, so that if they were carrying any at the time, the men could confiscate them. He was also relieved when Daeva assured him that she'd be unable to make any more of them, or make use of any of her other magic in a manner that would allow her to break free from her cell. He smiled at the thought. Then he scooted nearer the door leading out from his hiding place.

He brushed his sleeve across his face when the dusty air tickled his nose, recalling that he'd almost sneezed from it earlier. He frowned, considering the catastrophe that might have been. Fortunately, he'd not succumbed.

Placing his ear to the closet door, he listened. Hearing nothing, he turned the knob, opened the door a few inches to the eerie sound of squeaking hinges, and then peeked out.

Nothing.

He made his way out of the closet and then to the doorway that led to the hall. Once again, he put his ear to the door.

Just outside, Lucy visited with Jerrett and Velia as the three of them passed by.

He looked out as they left the building. Then he shimmied around the corner to the conference room door. Quickly, he turned the handle, opened it, and then stepped inside.

Ahhh!

The rolled up map sat in the same place where Lucy had left it. He was grateful for the chance to get a good look at it, as it would provide him with the information he required.

Lucy really is slipping. She'd just made another foolish, grievous, error.

Hearing boots clicking in the hallway, he pulled away from the table. Seconds later, the footsteps moved on.

Turning back to the map, he unrolled it. Then, after noting the markings on it, he quickly rolled it back up and returned it to the place where Lucy had left it.

He made his way to the door, then cracked it open. Finding the hallway empty, he stepped out.

Barely able to contain his glee, he rushed through the building and sanctuary grounds to his room.

Upon arrival, he entered, closed the door behind, and locked it.

He made his way to stand before a mirror that hung on the wall. Then as he'd done numerous times in the past, he called on the power of Daeva.

When the underlord arrived seconds later, he gloried in the pain that came of the spirit's heat. It was ecstatic; it left him momentarily speechless.

Finally, getting a grip on himself, he relayed all that he'd learned.

Chapter Thirty-Nine

Dax placed a fresh cold compress to Aliza's forehead. "Her temperature is still rising," he said. Then, turning to Dixon, he added in a whisper, "I'm afraid if you don't take her back to Oosa, we could lose her."

Having started a campfire earlier, and then boiling water over it, Dixon put a pot of it on a nearby shelf before crouching down beside his friend. Covering his face with his hands, he tapped his fingertips to his forehead.

"Arrgghhh!" he cried. He jumped to his feet, then stopped and patted out a rhythm on his thigh. "Spec should be back any time now," he said. "Maybe he'll have something for us. Above all, I'd like to honor her wishes of staying with us, if that's possible."

"He left four days ago."

"Yes, and he knew we needed him to hurry back."

Aliza fidgeted. Then, slowly, her eyes opened. She stared at Dax as though unable to identify him.

"How are you feeling?" he asked.

Groaning, her eyes closed again.

Just then, came a flutter at Dixon's side.

"Oh, Spec! Thank the Good One!" he cried upon recognizing the flit.

"I got here as quickly as I could." He flew nearer Aliza. "How is she?"

"Not well, I'm afraid," Dax said.

"Did Lucy have anything for us?" Dixon asked. "As we'd feared, her wound has infected."

"Yes." Spec landed on the hay mound that served as Aliza's pillow. Then, "Sugar," he announced.

"What?"

"Sugar. You're to make a poultice of it, then pack it around the open wound. It will draw out the infection."

He pulled back. "That's—"

"Wild. Yes, Lucy would agree. But that's what Percival said to do."

Dixon wiped his hair back with his fingers. "Well, I know he was a trained healer even before he became an Oathtaker. So he should know what he's talking about." He paused. "All right then, we'll give it a try."

"It would be great if you can mix it with honey, as well," Spec added.

Dixon grabbed his saddlebag. "I usually carry some sugar with my standard supplies," he said as he dumped the contents out. "Yes, here it is." Holding a cloth bag that was tied up with a string, he tossed it, and then caught it in his other hand. "So . . . honey, huh? Where would I get that?"

Once again, Aliza's eyes fluttered open. At the same moment, the man who'd come to the barn the day the Oathtakers had first arrived, stepped inside.

She looked his way. Somehow recognizing the potential danger to them all, she summoned her strength to turn her magic on.

The man stood still, clearly bewildered. "Father," he said, "I thought you were going to come to see me."

"And I will." Aliza's glazed-over eyes glanced Dixon's way, then turned back to the man. "But I'm not well just now. I need honey. Get some, give it to these men, and then go away."

He bobbed his head.

"Do you hear me?"

"Yes, Father."

"Go now." With that, Aliza's eyes closed and her head fell to the side.

"Follow him, Dax," Dixon ordered. Then he proceeded to remove the bandages from Aliza's arm. "Ughh," he muttered as the putrid odor of the infection that had settled in, rose into the air.

Her wound wept a green-yellow puss.

He dipped a clean cloth into the hot water and then washed it. Tender though he sought to be, it broke open at his touch.

Dax returned and rushed to his side. "I've got it."

"Good. Find a bowl. Mix a quarter-cup or so of the sugar with enough honey to make a poultice," Dixon directed him as he continued cleaning the wound.

A minute later, when Dax handed over the mixture, Dixon's eye caught his. "Let's hope this works," he said. With that, he packed the sludge, as well as possible, inside Aliza's open wound. Once done, he loosely wrapped clean bandages around her arm.

"And now, we wait," he said to his friend.

Morning arrived. A cool breeze wafted into the barn door.

Dixon, having stood guard through the night, went to Aliza's side. With a hand to her forehead, he checked her fever. It seemed to have abated some. He went about changing her dressings, then awakened Dax to stand watch, so that he could rest for a time.

Hours later, he woke again. When he saw Aliza rustling nearby, he rushed to her side.

"Aliza?"

Her eyes opened. "Dixon."

"How are you?" he asked as he felt her forehead.

"I'm not sure. A bit better, maybe."

Dax stopped grooming his horse, a task he'd chosen to do simply out of a need to keep busy. He stepped up. "I just put another pot of boiling water there," he said, pointing at it. "I'll go pump some more fresh drinking water now."

While Dixon explained to Aliza about the poultice he'd put on her arm the night before and again earlier that morning, he unwrapped her bandages.

"Oh, goodness, this does look much better than it did yesterday," he said.

"Let me see." She tried to sit up.

Pressing his hands to her shoulders, he shook his head. "I don't think that's a good idea."

She closed her eyes and let her breath out slowly. "Dixon, you may have to remove it." She swallowed hard. "My arm, I mean."

He grinned. "Don't be ridiculous. If it gets that bad, I'll take you back to Oosa. Anyway, Spec brought us information from Lucy. We tried it last night, and again early this morning, and things look better now. So, let's just get a fresh poultice and dressing on this again." Then he smiled at her and added, "You're going to be fine."

After cleaning out the wound once again, he made a fresh honey and sugar sludge, then packed it again. As he wrapped it up, she fell into a deep slumber.

Just then, the sound of crunching gravel carried to his ears.

"Dax?" he called.

When his friend didn't respond, he stood.

The sounds came again.

He headed to the door. "Dax?" he called again, drawing his blade.

Then, at the precise moment he stepped out, something came crashing down on his head.

His knees buckled, and he fell to the ground.

✦

"Hurry, Scarface, git that shroud over 'er 'ead," came a raspy voice. "Can ya believe these 'eathen women, goin' about uncovered?" He growled out his disdain.

"That's twice we've outwitted 'em, Mad Dog."

"Not so bright, are they, Pretty Boy?" He laughed. "But it helps when they 'ave a leak they don't know 'bout," he whispered. Then, squatting down, he looked over his shoulder. "Gimmee a hand 'ere."

When Aliza stirred in her sleep, Mad Dog grabbed her injured arm and pulled her up into a seated position.

Struggling beneath the heavy black cloth the men had placed over her, she screamed in pain.

"Hold it!" he ordered.

Her next cry fell to a whimper as her body went limp. She'd dropped once again, into unconsciousness.

"Caveman!" Mad Dog hollered. "Ya need tuh help us."

The men picked her up and carried her out of the barn. Then they put her on the back of a horse and tied her on. Once done, they saddled up.

Slowly, Dixon came back to his senses. His head spinning from the hit he'd taken, and feeling unsteady, he struggled for clarity. Upon realizing he sat on a horse and that his hands were tied before him, he looked around for Dax.

"Where are you taking us?" he asked when his eyes lit upon his friend astride a nearby gelding, similarly bound, and just then regaining consciousness.

Mad Dog's hearty laugh was accompanied by Pretty Boy's giggling. "You'll see soon enough," he said. He scowled at the Oathtakers. "Now, if there's any more outta either of ya, we'll gag ya." With that, he grabbed his reins and those of the horse to which they'd tied Aliza on, and then set off.

His cohorts followed, leading Dixon and Dax behind.

When Evan fluttered near his shoulder, Dixon whispered. "Go! Inform Lucy. Now!"

"Why not just escape, Dixon?" the flit asked. "Disappear magically. Perhaps you could take them by surprise."

Dixon shook his head. "They took all the weapons I had on my belt, including the crystals," he whispered. "Worse yet, they took Verity. Without my blade, I've not much to fight with. Besides, I couldn't rescue both Dax and Aliza. There are too many of them. I'll have to bide my time, wait for the right moment."

"No talkin'!" Mad Dog ordered.

"Get to Lucy," Dixon said to the flit. "Take Merc with you."

Mad Dog turned back for a look. When he saw nothing, he turned away again.

"And have Spec follow us," Dixon added.

Most of the time while they traveled, Aliza remained unconscious. Her moments of clarity were few and far between.

Meanwhile, although Dixon and Dax watched closely for any opportunity to escape, their captors guarded them too closely and at all times. So, since their blades had been taken from them, and their hands were bound, the Oathtakers offered little resistance.

At nightfall the next day, without food and with only scant water in the interim, they entered the city of Fallique. Hundreds of warriors filled the roadway before them. They mocked the prisoners as the men guided them in.

Before long, they approached the back door of a building made of cut stone, attached to the rear of another building. Bars ran up and down its windows. Burning torches in holders embedded in its exterior walls, lit the area, emitting the thick scent of pitch. At each side of the door, a succedunt soldier stood, holding a chained grut.

None too gently, the men assisted Dixon and Dax from their saddles. Then three guards surrounded each of them.

At that moment, Aliza, regaining consciousness, tried to sit up.

One of the men untied the ropes that held her to her saddle and pulled her down. She landed on the ground with a thud, her broken arm beneath her. As she cried out, he grabbed her other arm and dragged her to her feet.

Her expression couldn't be seen under the black shroud they'd placed over her head, but her crying and panting sounded out.

Dixon called for them to stop.

Seconds later, Aliza's knees buckled. She sagged back down to the ground. Once again, she'd passed out.

"Pretty Boy, get the door," Mad Dog ordered. "And you, Scarface," he motioned to another man, "get 'er." He pointed at Aliza, and then waited while the man took her up and flung her over his shoulder.

Spec fluttered near Dixon's shoulder, looking very much like a lightfly in the flickering, burning torchlight.

"Quickly," Dixon muttered, "get word to Lucy of our whereabouts."

The moment the flit flew off, the men ordered Dixon and Dax to march. At their heels, Scarface carried Aliza. Dixon was grateful that at least for now, she wasn't whimpering in pain.

Inside, the smell of wet hay, old urine, and other assorted odors assaulted the Oathtakers' nostrils. Dixon coughed, nearly choking on them.

Before them, cut-stone steps led up a flight and then around a bend. Hungry and thirsty, Dixon struggled to garner the energy required to make his way up them.

"Hurry!" Mad Dog ordered.

The guards half pushed, half dragged, the Oathtakers up the steps. At another landing, they turned and headed down a hallway. Soon, they turned yet another corner.

Before them, Pretty Boy opened a door, while Mad Dog went to the head of the pack and then motioned for his comrades to follow him inside.

If the place without stunk, the one within was even worse. Panting for a breath of less than fetid air, Dixon coughed repeatedly.

"You—in there." Mad Dog pushed Dax into a cell. As the Oathtaker sought to regain his footing, the thug closed the door and then jammed Dax's blade into the lock.

He approached the next cell. "In there," he ordered his men.

They pushed Dixon in. He stumbled, then landed hard on his shoulder. Wincing, he made his way back to his feet even as Mad Dog closed the door and then repeated the procedure he'd carried out at Dax's cell, this time jamming Dixon's blade into the lock.

"What are you going to do with her?" Dax asked, looking at Aliza, still in Scarface's arms. "She's hurt. She needs help."

Mad Dog stepped to a cell opposite from Dixon and Dax, one visible to them both. He grinned at them. "That's a shame for 'er," he said. With that, he looked at Scarface and jerked his head toward the inside of the cell.

The man walked in, squatted halfway down, and then deposited Aliza on an old, damp bed of straw. As she hit the floor, a fat rat shimmied out and toward the door, then ran down the hall.

The men closed and then locked the door. Once done, Mad Dog jammed her blade into the lock.

When he was through, he returned to stand outside Dixon's cell. "Come here," he ordered.

He approached.

"Put your hands through."

He complied.

Mad Dog cut the ropes at his wrists, even while instructing Pretty Boy to do the same with Dax's.

The second Dixon's hands were free, he reached for Verity.

Mad Dog laughed. "Yer blade is right 'ere," he whispered, "and right 'ere, it'll stay." He held Dixon's gaze. "Might as well get comfortable," he added, grinning, before he and his men retreated.

Nightfall having already arrived before the men delivered the Oathtakers to the prison, there were no guards in attendance after Mad Dog and his men left.

Simultaneously, Dixon and Dax, each still holding his weapon's handle, pulled, but to no avail.

Dixon's first thought was that he'd simply travel, magically, to get outside his cell. Once done, if he could reach Aliza, he could take her to safety. Then he could return for Dax. The plan might mean leaving their blades behind, but he figured he'd worry that that detail later.

He closed his eyes to summon his power, but felt no change. He saw no lights or colors like those that had always accompanied his magic traveling powers before.

Opening his eyes, he discovered that he hadn't moved. Startled, he sat down—hard. "I can't travel out of here, Dax! So now what?"

"Dixon!" Mara called out, having recognized his voice.

"Mara?" He jumped back to his feet. Grabbing two of the bars, he tried, unsuccessfully, to see down the hall. "Is that you?" He pulled, but the bars were so solid, they didn't even rattle.

"Yes!" she cried. Her chains jangled as she got to her feet. "Oh, Dixon! Was that Dax I heard?"

"Yes, he's here with me. Aliza, too."

"Oh, gracious . . . I told you not to come for us!"

"We didn't 'come' so much as we were 'delivered,'" he said. "We didn't know this was where they were taking us. Anyway, are you all right? And where are the twins?"

"They're here. In the cell next to me."

"Dixon," Eden called out, "what happened?"

He and Dax told Mara and the twins all that had transpired.

"Aliza's hurt? Oh, dear Good One! How is she now?" Mara asked.

"I'll light a flare—see if I can get a good look."

Dixon did. Then he reached out with it and peered into the cell across the way into which Scarface had dumped her.

"It's hard to tell," he said. "She's still unconscious."

"Listen," Dax said, "they've jammed our blades into the locks of our cells and we can't get them loose."

"And I tried to travel out of here, but couldn't," Dixon added.

"Oh goodness, then whatever is barring my magic here is barring yours, as well," Mara said. "As to your blades, like I told Lucy before, they did the same with mine. I've tried to retrieve it, magically, but it won't budge."

"Magically?" Dixon asked.

"She's chained," Reigna piped up. "She can't reach it. And she's been unable to break loose."

"You didn't mention that, Mara, when you messaged Lucy," he said.

She didn't respond.

"Dixon, can you see how Aliza's wound looks now?" Eden asked.

"No, it's wrapped." He closed his fist over his flare, then opened his hand. "What's this?" he asked.

"What?"

"I put my flare out, but there's no crystal."

"Yes, I suspected as much," Mara said. "I'm not able to create one either."

He sighed. "Well, in any case, I'm growing concerned with Aliza's wound. We were captured two days ago, and I've not been able to put a fresh pack on it since."

He proceeded to explain the sugar-poultice remedy that Lucy, at Percival's suggestion, had urged them to try.

"So she wasn't able to trick your captors into thinking she was someone else," Reigna said. "What a shame."

"She's been unconscious most of the time since she was injured," Dax said. "And now that we're here, that particular attendant magic power isn't likely to be effective." He sighed. "Oh, and by the way, they took all our other weapons, as well," he added.

"Ours too," Mara said.

"What more can you tell us about this place?" Dax asked.

Mara told them everything she knew, including about how of late, Carlie had been in charge of them on a daily basis.

When Dax asked who Carlie was, Dixon reminded him that she was Nina and Jules's daughter, and about how Jerrett had determined from his earlier trip to Chiran, that she was with Broden.

"Do you think she's still with him?" Dixon asked Mara.

"Yes, based on something another woman who'd been guarding us earlier, told us."

"What do you suppose is Broden's role in all of this?"

"The woman told us that he's in charge of the prison. Beyond that we don't know anything. But Carlie has been bringing us decent food and fresh water, secretly." She paused, in thought, and then said, "Tomorrow, I'll make sure she gives the canteen she usually gives to me, to you. Maybe you can get it to Aliza so that she can clean her wound when she awakens."

"Mara," Eden said, "I don't think that's a good idea. You need that water."

"Shhh," she scolded.

"But Mara—"

"No more," she ordered.

"What's she talking about, Mara?" Dixon asked.

"She—" Eden started.

"Nothing," Mara called over her. "I can do without water for a day."

"Let them take ours then," Reigna suggested, clearly having concluded that Mara didn't intend to share her news with Dixon just yet.

"No." Mara sighed. "You two have to stay strong. I've already told you, when— if—you get a chance, you must make your escape." As an afterthought, she explained to Dixon and Dax about Rowena's shawl.

When she was through, all were silent for a time.

Then, "This isn't just about the two of us any longer—or you," Eden said. Her comments were clearly directed Mara's way.

"That's enough, Eden."

"Mara—"

"I said, 'that's enough.'"

Dixon, still standing near his bars, spoke up. "What aren't you telling me, Mara?"

She dropped back to her haunches, then leaned against the rock wall. Just then, her stomach turned over. With a moan, she struggled to hold back her nausea.

"What is it?" he asked.

She gained control of herself. "Nothing, Dixon," she whispered. She'd been getting sick again—regularly. But she didn't want the twins to know. "I'm fine."

"You're not telling me something. I can hear it in your voice."

She stifled another moan. She'd had a lot of time to think on things. Once again, it seemed that Ehyeh had managed to allow for her to suffer. The thought made her both sad, and angry.

"I told you," she said when she finally got her breath back, "I'm fine."

Dixon groaned. "Do you think there's anything Carlie could do to help us?"

Mara swallowed down another fit of nausea. "Please don't involve her any more than she already is." Breathing heavily, she wiped away a tear, brusquely. "Nina will never forgive me as it is."

"You had nothing to do with her capture." Exasperated, he patted his thigh. "You know, Carlie may be our only hope in here. Or, our only hope of getting *out* of here, as the case may be."

As Carlie stood near the door to the prison, she thought back to the previous night. Broden had paced, his gate quick, his arms folded, and his jaw set. He'd stopped suddenly and turned to her and Striver.

"Mara and the twins have been here for weeks now," he'd said. "I have to get in there."

"Listen, maybe we should write Mara a note, after all," Carlie suggested. "We could put it in with some food I carry in. I've been going there daily, and so far, the guards have yet to search me beyond having me empty my pockets."

Broden grabbed her elbow. "We cannot risk your getting caught with a missive." He shook his head. "No. Bringing them food is one thing—but not that."

She held his gaze. "You know, you were right to get me in there in the first place, or we wouldn't even know about them. If not for the food and water I've been bringing them, they might already be dead." Her eyes searched his. "Please, Broden, I want to do it. I'm tired of being just another prisoner. If we can help them, then maybe they can help us. If not, perhaps I'm ready to die in the attempt."

Broden dropped her arm. "Please, don't talk like that. Please. Let me think on it."

He paced, then said, "For now, let's get some food wrapped up for you to bring to them tomorrow."

Back to the present, the guard removed the black shroud from over Carlie's head. Once done, he did the same with Clementine, who of late had been accompanying her there, daily.

"Fold out your pockets," he ordered.

They complied.

After confirming they carried no contraband, he stepped back. "There are some new prisoners for you to look after today," he said, glowering at them. "Need I remind you that you're not to communicate with any of them?"

"No, sir," Carlie said.

When Clementine didn't answer, he grabbed her arm roughly. "And you?"

Whimpering in pain, she tried, meekly, to pull away. "No, sir. I won't say anything, sir."

Tipping his head toward the pot of gruel, he addressed Carlie once more. "Take that," he said. "You can come back for the water when you're through." Then he pushed Clementine.

As the girl stumbled to regain her balance, Carlie rushed to her side "Are you all right?"

She rubbed her arm. "Yes."

The two started down the hall. Arriving at the cell of the first of the new prisoners, Carlie glanced inside, where she found a lone man. He'd managed to reach a bar that ran overhead. He hung from it, then pulled himself up, dropped down, then pulled back up again. Dark of skin and eye, his clothing tattered and filthy, and with bruises decorating his face, his muscles bulged as he pulled back up, yet again, demonstrating his enormous strength. Never having previously met the man, however, Carlie had no idea of his identity.

With her hand on Clementine's shoulder, she moved on, as she noticed an occupant in the first of the cells on the opposite wall. Once again, she glanced inside. There, she found a woman, struggling to sit up. A splint on her arm handicapped her movements. Through the bandages wrapped around it, spots of blood, now dried and turned brown, stood out. The woman commenced unwrapping her wound. Once again, Carlie did not recognize the prisoner.

Then she glanced inside the cell to her left. She stopped cold.

The prisoner stared at her.

Dixon! She opened her mouth as though to speak, then clamped it shut once again.

He tipped his head at her.

Carlie continued until she stood before Mara's cell. Her eyes narrowed as she witnessed her wince. Troubled, but seeking to be discreet, she moved on to the last cell even as she untied two of the packs of food that hung from around her neck.

She put the bucket down. Then, squatting, she acted out spooning gruel into the twins' bowls while she tossed the food packs inside for them. When she stopped to loosen one of the canteens at her waist, Reigna held her hand up.

"No. Please, Carlie," she whispered, "bring our water to the new woman prisoner if she's awake, or to Dixon, if she's not."

Carlie nodded, then headed back to Mara's cell. There, she got down. She grabbed the other pack of food she carried and threw it inside, all the while pretending to fill Mara's bowl. Then she tossed in her remaining canteen, making certain it would land on the bed of straw.

"No." Mara grabbed the vessel and reached out with it. "Please, bring this to the new woman prisoner—to Aliza."

Shaking her head, Carlie turned away. Then she set about filling the bowls of the remaining Oathtakers, dropping the last canteen of fresh water, the one originally intended for the twins, into Aliza's cell.

She couldn't wait to get back to tell Broden all.

Chapter Forty

The flit, Evanescent, dropped his wings and bowed his head. His story now complete, he glanced back up. Merc remained silent, at his side.

"Yes," Lucy said, "Mara messaged that Dixon, Dax, and Aliza, were brought to the prison."

In frustration, Jerrett sprang to his feet. He paced.

Just then, a knock came at the door.

Lucy opened it. "Oh, hello, Petrus," she greeted him.

His brow furrowed. "You look . . . troubled, Lucy. What happened?"

"I'm not ready for our—" She stopped short. "Actually, you should step inside. We could use your help."

She and Petrus made their way to the conference table as Jerrett was addressing Evan. "And they covered Aliza with a black shroud or something," he said. "Is that right?"

"Yes."

"But her magic doesn't depend on *her* seeing *others*. It depends on *others* seeing *her*."

"She was in awful pain. She wasn't even conscious."

"The poultice didn't work?" Lucy asked.

"Well, they'd only managed to get one on her arm the night before, and I believe Dixon changed it once—maybe twice—some hours later. It did seem to be working, but . . ."

"So, you think she just didn't have the strength to use her power."

"That's right."

"What is this?" Petrus asked.

Velia explained Aliza's unusual magic powers to him. Then, sitting up straighter, she said, "I think Jerrett and I should go to Chiran—to see what we can do."

"No!" Lucy cried. "We've lost too much to Zarek already."

"Well, what do you propose then? We can't just sit here." Velia frowned.

Petrus leaned forward. "What exactly happened, may I ask?"

Lucy closed her eyes and shook her head. "It seems we have a traitor in our midst, Petrus, as a consequence of which, we've not only lost Mara and the twins, but we've now lost Dixon, Dax, and Aliza, as well."

"Oh . . ." He pulled back. "How do— Why— Are you sure? I mean, what makes you think that? What happened?"

She explained all that had transpired.

"So, who is the traitor? Do you know?"

Her lips tightened into a thin line. "I wondered earlier, but I'm certain now. It's Percival." She ground her teeth. "I'll get the Council to sign off on an order to arrest him the minute we're through here—before he can give away more of our information. We'll get him to talk."

"Why do you suspect Percival?" Velia asked.

"Other than you and Jerrett, he was the only one who knew of Aliza's condition. Also, he saw the map on which I'd inadvertently marked where she, Dixon, and Dax, were hiding out."

"But that was just a glimpse that he got."

Sighing, she stood and approached a window. Stopping to look out, she said, "Yes, well, after Mara informed me of what happened, I did some looking around."

She turned back to her cohorts. "It seems there's a closet in the room just to that side." She pointed at a wall and then approached it.

"See this hole here? I found clear evidence of someone having recently been in the closet on the other side. From there, a person could see and hear everything that goes on in this room."

"But even if someone spied from there, it doesn't follow that it was Percival. It could have been anyone," Jerrett argued.

"No, I think Percival went and sat there after we excused him that day and then listened in on the rest of our conversion."

"So Percival has some connection to . . . Zarek?" Petrus interrupted.

"It seems that way." Lucy sat down again. She tapped on the table, repeatedly. "He must have. It's the only explanation. Look, I don't know all that much about Percival's past. He claims to have served two Select." She hesitated, pondering. "I knew of Filip from decades ago—and I know there were serious questions surrounding his death. Then, shortly after arriving here, Percival told me that he'd also served someone by the name of 'Arvid' who recently died of old age. Still, I don't recall any Select by the name of 'Arvid.'"

"But I remember Percival mentioning that he was headed out for a meeting with you," Petrus said. "That was just a week ago or so. Right?" His eyes narrowed. "How could he possibly have gotten word to anyone in that short a period? More likely it was just . . . happenstance. Yes?"

"No, I don't think so," Lucy said. "Those hoodlums knew just where to find Mara and the twins, and later, Dixon, Dax, and Aliza. And clearly, they understood the conditions sufficiently well to know how best to overtake them all."

She pounded the table in her frustration. "As to their dealing with Dixon's ability to travel, I suspect they thought he'd remain with them since after knocking him unconscious, they took all of his weapons, including his blade. It seems they rightly assumed that once he came to, he wouldn't try to escape—that he'd bide his time waiting for the right opportunity—given that he couldn't take both Dax and Aliza at the same time. But now that he's in the same prison where Mara's at, his magic doesn't work either!"

She stood and paced. "But there's more."

"Oh?" Jerrett asked.

"Some time ago, one of our healers, Salus, went missing. Do you remember my mentioning that?"

Her cohorts all nodded.

"Well, the last anyone knew, he was headed for a seedy little pub called 'The Swindler's Cup.' I asked Percival to go there with me, to see if we could trace Salus's steps, so as to determine where he might have gone. Percival tried to refuse going—said he was too busy to accompany me. But I think the real reason is that he was responsible for Salus's disappearance."

"What?" Velia cried. "What would make you think that?"

"Well, the barkeeper there said that he recognized Percival as the person who'd been there with Salus. Of course, Percival denied it. He suggested that the man was too inebriated to be trusted." She sighed. "But now I suspect that there was something more going on. I think he was with Salus there. Perhaps Salus had discovered something that Percival wanted to keep hidden." She closed her eyes and shook her head. "I'm afraid Salus may have been the victim of foul play."

A long quiet minute passed.

"Do you want help with the questioning?" Petrus finally asked.

She drew in a deep breath. "Actually, I'd like it if you just took it over. Above all, I'd like to know how he got word to Zarek so quickly."

Petrus nodded. "All right. I can do that."

"But what of rescuing them all?" Velia asked. "What do we do about that? I mean, isn't that the most important thing at this juncture?"

Lucy pulled her shoulders back. "Yes," she said. "We need to formulate a plan."

Jerrett bit his lip. Then, "Suppose Velia stays here, but that I go—with Bane," he said. "You could deliver him there, Lucy, and then me. I mean, Bane's no Oathtaker, but he's a powerful weapon—and my magic connection to him could prove valuable."

"No, Jerrett, I want you and Velia to stay here."

His eyes narrowed. "If I didn't know better, Lucy, I'd think you were scheming. I can see it in your eyes. What is it?"

Her gaze rested on the table, as she bit her lip. Finally, she looked back up. "I'm going," she said.

"What?" Velia cried, rushing to her feet. "Not you! Lucy, everyone here needs you. You have the most information, the most experience, the—"

"I'm going."

Petrus glanced around the table at each of the others. Then he turned Lucy's way. "I have an idea."

She turned to him, her brow raised.

"Let me question Percival. I have been known to be a pretty effective interrogator. Maybe I can get some information that would prove truly helpful."

She leaned in, scowling. "You think I should just wait?" she asked.

"Yes," he said, one finger raised, "but only long enough for me to determine if Percival can tell us anything more that we will need."

"That 'we' will need?"

"Yes. I want to accompany you."

A half dozen Oathtakers, at Lucy's direction, made their way to the sanctuary dormitory. Heavily armed, they entered the building, directing anyone in their path to move aside.

They made their way down the narrow stone floored walkways of the first floor, peeking around each corner before turning down the next hall.

Upon arriving at the door to Percival's room, the Oathtaker in the lead, Idaleen, stood at one side of the door to his room, while her first assistant, Ozel, stood at the other.

She turned to the remaining members of her crew, nodding at them to signify that they were about to enter. Then she caught Ozel's eye. With her hand on the wrought iron door handle, her brow rose.

Ozel signified that he was ready.

In a single breath, she threw the door open and rushed inside. Her team barreled in at her heels.

There sat Percival, at a vanity, a mirror before him, bent over and writing in a book. Startled, he dropped his quill and bumped his pot of ink. It turned over, spilling great blotches across his manuscript.

Reaching for his weapon, he turned toward the ruckus.

"Stop right there, Percival Ferreolo," Idaleen cried, "by order of the Council!"

His mouth moved as he searched for words. Slowly, he put his hands down.

"Keep those hands in sight!"

He followed her order. Then, "What's going on?" he asked.

"By order of the Council, you are under arrest."

His hands started to drop. "What?" His eyes widened.

"Hands up!" She repeated her order.

He complied. "I— I don't understand. What's this about?"

She and Ozel approached him, one at each side.

"Slowly now, put your hands forward and together," Idaleen ordered.

When he did, Ozel removed from a bag hanging over his shoulder, a magic band. He wrapped it around the prisoner's wrist, and then stepped back.

Percival scowled. "Would you care to explain what this is all about?" He raised his arm. "What have I done to deserve this? To be banded?"

Idaleen grabbed his upper arm and then pulled him to his feet. "You," she said to the two of her assistants who stood closest to the door, "lead the way Ozel and I'll take his sides. You follow immediately behind," she instructed the remaining members of her troop.

When Percival tried to pull away, she gripped his arm more firmly.

"I don't understand," he said. "What's this all about?"

"We're following orders," she said. "You'll be informed of all the details in due course."

They made their way out of the dormitory and walked across the grounds toward the conference center. As an early-spring, heavy rain, had just ceased, the air smelled clean and earthy from spots where the snow cover had melted away. Along their way, several bystanders stopped to gawk, but no one interrupted the entourage.

Unable to control his path, Percival stepped through a puddle of greasy mud. "Could you at least use some caution here?" he asked.

"My apologies, sir," Idaleen said. "We'll use greater care." She guided him around another puddle. "Our purpose is not to pronounce a judgment, or to exact a punishment—merely to arrest."

When they arrived at the conference center, they stepped inside. There they found Lucy, Jerrett, and Velia, awaiting them.

"Lucy!" Percival cried. "What is this? Tell them to set me loose!"

"I will do no such thing."

His head cocked. His eyes narrowed. "But—"

She stepped closer. "I wouldn't have thought it of you, Percival," she seethed.

"What are you talking about?"

"A traitor—right here in our midst."

His mouth dropped open. "I— I don't know what you're talking about."

She turned to Idaleen. "The guard downstairs will direct you to the room we've reserved for questioning," she said.

"Lucy," Percival interrupted. "I haven't done anything."

She stepped closer, glaring at him, her mere presence cutting him off from saying more. "Save it, Percival," she snapped. "We're investigating all of your claims now."

"My claims?"

"Take him away!" she ordered.

Hours later, Lucy and Petrus arrived at the room in which the guards held Percival. Upon sight of them, the men stepped aside.

"Any trouble?" Lucy asked.

"None," the lead guard responded.

"Very well." She took in a deep breath. "You can open the door now."

Once done, she stepped inside, Petrus at her heels.

"Lucy!" Percival cried as he jumped to his feet.

"Sit down," she ordered.

His eyes flickered from her to Petrus, then back again. "What's this all about?"

"I said, 'sit down.'"

He sat.

Petrus pulled out a chair for her, then one for himself.

Sitting, Lucy stared at Percival, her lips in a thin line, her jaw clenched tightly. "So, we've been looking into your records." She pulled out some papers from the pack hanging over her shoulder. "Why don't we start with Filip?"

"Filip?"

"Yes. You remember Filip. Your first charge?" She glared at him.

"Wh— What of him?"

She turned a page over. "I've been reviewing here the questions about his death—you being alone with him at the time, and his being so young, and so ill and all," she said. "And given your powers as a healer."

Percival's brow dropped. "But . . . the Council looked into all of that years ago. They determined that he'd only been ill for a matter of hours when he died." He shook his head. "What's this all about, anyway?"

She tapped the tabletop. "Fine then, we won't talk bout Filip—just now anyway. Tell me about Arvid."

He raised his hands, palms up. "What of him? What do you want to know?"

"Well now," she said, glancing once again at her records, "here's something interesting. It seems none of the Council members recall an 'Arvid.'"

"So?"

"So, there's no record of a Select named Arvid."

His eyes narrowed. "But Lucy, it was only recently that a census of the Select was conducted. He died shortly before that. Prior to that, no one had any idea about the Select remaining in Oosa, their names, or where they lived."

"So you stand by your claim—that you served this . . . 'Arvid' until he died of old age."

Percival looked down. "Of course. Why would I make up something like that?" He glanced back her way and tapped at his chest. "Just look at me. Clearly, I've aged little since I first met you—which means that my claims are true. I started serving Filip shortly before that, and then, following his death, Arvid became my charge. And, as I told you before, he died only recently."

"So you say."

"But what else would account for my continued youth?"

"Ehyeh only knows," she said.

He put his hands to his face and rubbed it. "Uhhh. I just—" He sat up straighter and squared his shoulders. "What is this all about anyway? You mentioned something about treason. What is it I'm accused of having done?"

Lucy stood and paced. "Go ahead, Petrus, tell him. I can't bring myself to speak to him any longer."

Petrus leaned in. "When Mara and the twins were captured, someone suggested we might have a leak. Then, when Dixon, Dax, and Aliza, suffered a similar fate, it became clear who that leak was—or is."

Percival looked from one of his visitors to the other. "You think it was *me*?"

"I know it was you," Lucy said. Then, when he opened his mouth to speak again, she held her hand up, signifying that she was not through.

"Outside of me, Jerrett, and Velia, no one knew where Dixon and the others were. But, of course, you stole a glance at the map we were using. I suspect you then hid in the closet in the next room to get the other details you required. Interestingly, within hours of Spec's returning to them all, they were captured. So I can only surmise that you got word to your comrades in time to do that. What I'd like to know is: how did you do it? What dark magic are you mixed up with, anyway?"

Percival stared at her. "What closet? What other facts? You think that I, somehow, got word to someone about all this?"

"Not just to 'someone.' To Zarek, himself," Petrus said.

Lucy stood. "You'll get your hearing, Percival. On that, you needn't fear. However, we require information from you—and we require it now. We need to know everything about which you've informed the enemy." She glanced her cohort's way. "Petrus will lead the interrogation," she then added.

"Lucy, I swear, I've told no one anything of a confidential nature."

She approached the door, then called over her shoulder, "Get on with it then, Petrus. I'll be preparing my things to go."

"Wait! Lucy!" Percival cried. "Where are you going? Hear me out!"

She turned back.

"I swear—it wasn't me."

Her lips pursed, she turned away again, and then stepped out.

•••

The Council members sat around the table located in a secret part of sanctuary.

"Well, we've heard your evidence, Lucy," Piers Hamilton said. "But—what if you're wrong?" A businessman best known for opposing everything, and for always asking difficult questions, he stared at her.

"I'm not wrong."

"What if you are?" he repeated. "Look, Percival denies any knowledge of this."

"Of course he denies it." She slapped a handful of papers down on the table. "You didn't think he'd just spill everything without a fight, did you?"

Eben Taft, the well known scientist, leaned in. "You know, Lucy," he said, "I'm inclined to agree with Piers on this one."

"As am I," Skylar Hadwin spoke up.

She glared at each of them in turn, then looked at the legal expert, Heather Larkspur. "Well?" she asked her.

"I believe you can keep him banded and held for now, out of an abundance of caution," she said, "but you haven't much to go on here. In truth, you've little more than suspicion, so you must use care in how you question him."

Lucy shook her head. Turning to Mildred Crane, best known for her work with issues relating to health and healing, she scowled. "Well, I'm sure I don't need to ask you for your thoughts," she muttered under her breath.

The woman pulled back. "Excuse me?" She pursed her lips. "Why wouldn't you ask me?"

"Because you always agree with whoever seems to have the most support on his side at any given moment."

"Well!" she exclaimed.

"Look," Piers interrupted, "I agree with Heather that we can and should hold Percival, but let's use care with the interrogation tactics that we use. We mustn't get ahead of ourselves here."

Skylar addressed Lucy. "Do you recall our discussions about the book *When the Two May Overcome* that you brought to me?"

"Yes."

"Do you remember how it cautions against acting rashly? How it emphasizes that things are not always what they seem? I think the words are something like . . ." He put his fingers to his forehead. "Let me think."

"*Beware the obvious when you ought follow the obscure,*'" Lucy recited.

"That's right!" he cried. "That warning is repeated, again and again. I've thought all along that it pertained to Broden's situation."

"You mean that his appearing guilty, since he's with his father, Zarek, is too obvious? So, perhaps he's not?"

"Right. Just as Percival's guilt seems too obvious."

"I'd like to think that all of that is true," she said. "It's so hard to imagine Broden having turned to the dark side." She paused, shook her head. "Fine, then. I'll have Petrus continue questioning Percival. But if he can't come up with anything shortly, then I'm headed into Chiran myself."

"We can't stop you," Piers said, "but I recommend you reconsider. We've suffered enough losses already." He held his jaw tight, then added, "You know, if the twins don't survive this—"

"Ah!" Lucy cried. "How can you even say that?"

"Because, it is possible—and you know it. Now consider this: should that occur, we'll need to go up their line to their next eldest sister for the next ranking member of the Select."

"Adamina?" Skylar asked.

"Yes," Piers said. "She was the sixth-born. And as much as I'd prefer not to have another sixth leading the first family after Lilith did so—although illegitimately—we may need to seek her out."

"Now who's getting ahead of himself?" Lucy muttered.

He tapped on the table with his quill, staring at her all the while. "I propose we put together a plan of action," he said. "At this point, only you and Dixon know the whereabouts of Rowena's other daughters, and he's already been captured. What if something dreadful happened to you, as well?"

Lucy stood. She paced for a minute, then approached a nearby portrait and appeared to study it. "I don't like the idea of disclosing where they all are," she finally said. Then she turned back. "But I agree it may be necessary to make some sort of arrangements."

"From a legal standpoint, I suggest we exercise extreme caution here," Heather Larkspur said. "Perhaps the information could be locked up somewhere, allowing this body to retrieve it only if we all agree that we should do so."

Shrugging, Lucy said, "I could live with that, I guess."

Heather patted her hair bun. "Then again, there is another issue to consider, and that is that none of us is getting any younger." Sitting ramrod straight, she paused, pursing her lips. "What if something should happen to any of us?"

Stepping back to the table, Lucy sat, She rubbed her face with her hands. "I don't like it, but I agree with you all about this. So, I've a proposal. I'll put the information in a lock box that can only be opened on the approval of any three of this Council."

"How will you do that?" Eben asked.

"There is a magic trinket that I created that should do the trick. Once we complete the process, the box will only open when any three of you—collectively—place a hand against a side of it." Looking around at the other Council members, one by one, she held the gaze of each, momentarily. "I will, however, add a fourth requirement."

"Oh?" Eben asked. "What would that be?"

"I'll add that along with the agreement of any three of you, the box will only open if one of Mara, Jerrett, Velia, or Basha, also places his or her blade on the fourth side of the box."

"Why one of them?" Heather asked.

"Dixon and I already know where Rowena's other daughters are, so we'd have no need to access the information. Then of course, Mara is an obvious choice. As to the others? I chose them because they've spent so long with the twins—with me. They've proven themselves loyal, time and time again." She glanced at the others. "So . . . will that be acceptable?"

They all nodded their agreement.

"Very well then. I'll complete the matter before I leave for Chiran."

"And where will this box be kept?" Skylar asked.

"For now, with Jerrett and Velia."

Chapter Forty-One

As the Council members stepped out through various hidden passageways to their assigned sanctuary offices, a knock came at the door. Lucy made her way through the room of marble floors and pillars, and past numerous paintings hanging on the walls, to answer it.

Velia stepped inside. "Sorry I'm late."

"No. Your timing is perfect."

She glanced around. "I've never been in here."

She stepped around a pillar, examined the nearby paintings, and then looked up at the ceiling mural that depicted scenes from one of the most important books of history and prophecy: *The Book of the Blood*. She studied it for a moment, then turned her gaze once again, to the walls. There, she noticed what looked like a window to a room situated near the back that did not let in any light.

"Is that where witnesses go when they give testimony?" she asked.

"It is."

"I see. So, that's where I was when I testified for Mara all those years ago."

"That's right."

Cocking her head, Velia looked hard at Lucy. "So, what am I doing here?"

Lucy took her elbow and directed her to the conference table. There, she offered her a seat, then sat to her right.

"Well?"

"I've looked for some time now, for an opportunity to speak with you—in private. I have something we need to discuss, and I can't take the chance that anyone might overhear." She drummed the tabletop with her fingertips.

"What's troubling you, Lucy?"

She sighed, then looked down. "Mara's . . . pregnant," she said, as she glanced back up, her eyes tear-filled.

Velia pulled back. "What?"

Lucy wiped her eyes dry, then told her all about the mix-up with the herbs at the compound.

"After Mara regained her memories, when I met up with her in the city, after she rescued the twins from The Tearless, I gave her what I thought was more barrenseed tea.

"But . . . it wasn't."

"No."

"Oh, great Ehyeh!" Velia ran her fingers through her hair, then tucked a stray sprig of it behind her ear. "She told you this, via the compact, did she?"

"No. In truth, I'm not sure, based on her communications to date, that she even knows."

Velia pulled back. "But then— How do you know this? I mean—" She shook her head. "Honestly, Lucy!" She stared at her. "What makes you think she's pregnant?"

"Think about it, Velia. Think about how sick she was—every day, for weeks— but not constantly. And she was tired—all the time." Lucy went through all the symptoms she felt certain indicated that Mara was pregnant.

"I hate to admit it, but I think you might be right," Velia said as she stood and then paced. "And she's stuck in that prison. Lucy, you have to tell her!"

"I was hoping we might do that together."

"What? Now?"

She nodded. "I brought the compact with me. I don't often carry it because, as you know, I don't want others to learn of it, and of its power. Moreover, she's made sure I know not to try to reach her during the daylight hours when the guards watch over them all. But we could reach her with it now."

Velia sighed deeply. "Gracious Ehyeh, I hope you're wrong. I mean, I'd love it for Mara—to have a child. I think she's long wanted one of her own, but . . ."

Lucy bit her lip. "I don't know if there's anything she could or would do differently if she knew, but I feel I must tell her."

"And you've mentioned this to no one else? Dixon doesn't know?"

"I spoke about it briefly with Leala and Fidel shortly after I discovered what had happened with our stock of herbs. Unfortunately, Basha was already at the border, or I'd have asked her what she thought I should do. I wanted to speak with you when I returned, because I know that the three of you are the best of friends, but I just haven't had the opportunity until now. And— Well, as to Dixon, he'd already left with Dax. It didn't seem right to share that kind of information via the flits."

Velia sat down again. "Yes, I think that was right. Besides which, it wasn't really your information to share." She paused. "All right, go ahead then, try to reach her."

Lucy removed the compact from her pocket. She opened it and called out, "Mara?"

Far away, in a prison in Chiran, the action alerted the Oathtaker when the compact vibrated. As nightfall had descended some time earlier, the twins slept soundly in the next cell, beneath their mother's shawl. Dixon and Aliza also currently slept, as Dax kept watch for them in the meantime, for marauding rats, killing off as many as he could so that they wouldn't return at a later time.

She opened the compact.

"Mara!" Velia cried on sight of her face therein. Tears sprang to her eyes. "Goodness, it's so good to see you!"

Her eyes flickered away momentarily, then turned back. "You too, Velia, and you, Lucy," she whispered. "It's good you waited for dark to contact me. Thank you for that. But please, keep it down. Most of the others are sleeping. I don't want to awaken anyone."

Lucy nodded. "I'm happy to see that your bruises are gone."

Mara patted her cheek, then rubbed it. "Yes, they are."

"Mara, how . . ." Lucy swallowed hard. "How are you feeling these days? I mean—has the grippe returned?"

Tears sprang to her eyes. "It—" She breathed in deeply, in an effort to keep from outright weeping. "Whhhhuuooooooo," she exhaled slowly, then sucked in another breath. "Lucy . . . it . . . wasn't the grippe."

"No?"

"No." Mara covered her eyes with one hand and shook her head. Then, looking back into the compact, she bit her lip. "Lucy, I'm— I'm pregnant."

A tear rolled down Lucy's cheek. She brushed it away. "I thought that might be the case."

"I've no idea how this could have happened. I used the barrenseed tea faithfully, I swear!"

"I know, Mara. I think I can explain."

Her eyes narrowed. "You knew? How?"

"I didn't know, but I came to suspect as much." Lucy explained about the mix-ups with the herbs.

"Then it really is true," Mara said. Her gaze turned to Velia. "You've never miscarried, right?"

"No. Why do you ask?"

Mara swallowed hard. "I've just been quite sick again of late and—" She stopped short.

"And?"

"And I've been having cramps."

"I see."

"I think I'm losing the child, Velia." She choked back a great sob. "Oh, what'll I do? What'll I tell Dixon?"

Tears rolled down Velia's cheeks. "He doesn't know about any of this?"

She shook her head.

"Do the twins know?"

She nodded, then explained how the discovery had come upon her. "I can't believe the thought hadn't occurred to me earlier. But as soon as Eden mentioned her moon cycle, I just . . . knew."

"Listen, Mara, you have to tell Dixon."

"I can't." She swallowed hard. "I should never have taken the girls to the border. I—"

"Stop it," Velia ordered.

Mara stared at her, her brow lowered. "He'll blame me. He should blame me!"

"I said, 'stop it.'" Velia looked down, pausing, then turned back up. "Dixon loves you, and he knows the risks an Oathtaker faces. He cannot and will not blame you for being who and what you are. Those are amongst the very things that endear you to him."

Mara sucked in a breath. "He knows something is up. The twins were going to tell him!" she exclaimed. Then she brought her voice back down. "I can't even see him, Velia, to know how he reacts. I don't know what to do."

"You should tell him." She looked, via the compact, deeply into her dear friend's eyes. "Tell him, Mara. If nothing else, he'll be able to grieve with you."

She closed her eyes. "I'll think about it."

"Tell him. Do it as soon as you can."

Hearing something in the next cell, Mara looked that direction, then turned her attention back. "I'll think about it."

"We're doing everything we can from this end," Lucy added. "We think Percival is wrapped up in this—although we're not sure just how. He's undergoing questioning now. So, we'll be sure to keep you informed."

"Take care of yourself," Velia added.

Mara nodded. "Thank you." With that, she closed the magic trinket.

Rustling sounds filled the air. Mara jerked her head toward their source.

"Were you talking to Lucy?" Dixon asked.

She sucked in a breath. "Yes." She paused to collect her thoughts. "What all did you hear?"

"Just the end. I thought I heard Velia, but of course, she'd have needed Lucy to reach you."

"It was Velia, yes. The two of them contacted me."

Now shuffling sounds came from his cell. Mara imagined him standing and approaching the bars.

"What did they want?" he asked.

"Just to get an update."

"I see. Then what was Velia talking about when she said 'you should tell him.'"

Mara swallowed hard, seeking to hold her tears at bay. "Oh, I'm—" She paused. "I'm supposed to tell you they have a leak on their end."

For a long moment, he was quiet. Then, "There's something more," he said. "I can tell. I can hear it in your voice. I can feel it."

"Dixon?" Reigna called out.

"Reigna, no!" Mara exclaimed, jumping to her feet.

"What do you know about this, Reigna?" he asked. "What don't I know?"

"Mara, you have to tell him," Eden chimed in.

"I— I can't."

"If you don't, we will," Reigna said.

Bitter, salty tears, ran down Mara's cheeks. "Please, please don't. It's not the right time." She sucked in a sob.

"Mara," Dixon said, his voice soft. "I don't want the twins to tell me. I want *you* to. I can hear that something is terribly wrong." He paused, sighing. "I love you. You know I do. I want to share whatever pains you. Please . . . tell me."

She leaned her free hand against the wall as she cried so hard that her shoulders shook. "Please, don't make me."

"I can't make you, Mara. But I wish you would."

At that moment, a sharp pain went through her middle. Her knees buckled when she gasped from the shock of it. She struggled to stay upright.

"Great Ehyeh!" he cried. "Tell me what's wrong!"

After several long seconds, she caught her breath. "Dixon, I don't know how to tell you something that—" She stopped short, overcome with weeping.

"Please. I don't understand what's wrong."

She cried out when another pain struck. Holding her middle, she waited until it subsided, shaking all the while. Then she said, "I'm trying to save you from despair." The pain now subsiding, she dropped to her knees. Once done, she sat on the floor, and leaned against the wall.

"I don't understand."

Mara took in a heavy breath. "I'm trying to spare you, Dixon. I'm—"

"By shouldering whatever is bothering you all by yourself? I'm sorry, Mara, but I don't want to be saved from that pain only to experience another worse one— that of your suffering silently and alone." He went quiet for a minute. "Did they— Were you—"

"No," she interrupted. "I'm not sure how or why they spared the girls and me such indignities, but they did."

"What is it then?"

"Please tell him, Mara," Reigna said.

Mara bowed her head. Then she reclined, curled up into the fetal position, and wept.

Chapter Forty-Two

He marched down the hall, his son in his wake. Behind them came several succedunt soldiers, one leading a chained grut along the way.

"Where are we going?" Broden asked, keeping watch on the beast.

Zarek turned his way and grinned. "We're going to visit some prisoners of mine. You've been . . . reluctant to swear your allegiance to Daeva. Perhaps, if you see what it is you are up against, you'll change your mind."

"What prisoners?"

"You'll see soon enough."

They made their way around another corner, took another turn, and then headed down yet another hallway. Broden assumed they were bound for the portion of the prison where Mara and the others were held.

Before long, they passed Zarek's quarters. A minute later, the emperor came to an abrupt halt.

Broden almost ran into him, then stepped back.

"Any changes here?" the emperor asked the attending guards.

"None. The newest woman prisoner appears to be on the mend."

Zarek glanced Broden's way. "Come along then," he said, grabbing his elbow. With that, they headed down a hallway.

Moments later, they stood outside a cell situated on the outer wall of the building. Broden glanced inside. He didn't recognize the man within, but he surmised it was one of the prisoners about whom Carlie had informed him.

"Meet Dax," Zarek said, "the Commander of the Oathtakers' fighting forces."

Dax approached the bars. "You'll die for this," he threatened.

Zarek threw his head back and laughed. "Oh? Exactly whose army do you think will accomplish that? Ha ha ha!"

Dax growled.

Zarek, ignoring him, strutted toward a cell on the opposite wall. "And here is his second-in-command, Aliza. She possesses a unique magic, I'm told."

"Oh?" Broden asked.

Zarek explained her attendant magic power to take on the form of another.

As Broden bit his lip, Zarek turned to the cell to his left. He motioned toward it. "Now, I believe this might be an old friend of yours," he said with a grin.

"Dixon," Broden muttered.

"Yes, that's right," the emperor said. "Perhaps you'd like to fill him in on your position here as head of the prison." He turned to the Oathtaker. "My son here, Broden, helps see to the women we send off to a special concentration camp in Darth. We're busy building more like it in other places here in Chiran. Indeed, I have a mind to prepare one to house only Oosian women who've come our way." He watched for a reaction, but got none. "He's been instrumental in our cause, you might say."

Dixon glared at Broden.

Broden wanted to shake his head to negate Zarek's claim, but the man's gaze rested on him.

"Come along then," Zarek said, clearly enjoying himself.

When they arrived at the next cell, Zarek pointed toward Mara. "Ah! The great Oathtaker to the ranking members of the Select," he said. His eyes narrowed as he looked more closely at her. "Hmmmm, you don't look so good," he said. "What do you think, son?" he asked, turning his way.

"Yes, you're right. She doesn't look well."

"One less to concern ourselves with, should she meet her demise." Zarek smiled, then moved on.

Seconds later, as he stood before the bars of the last cell, he motioned Broden forward. "And last—but surely not least—we have the current ranking members of the Select themselves—cousins of yours, if I'm not mistaken." His brow rose as he tipped his head, watching Broden. "So, what do you think?"

Momentarily speechless, Broden pulled to his full height. He contemplated how to play this. If he appeared supportive of Zarek's actions, perhaps the man would give him greater access.

"I . . . congratulate you . . . master," he said.

"Oh, please, call me 'Father,'" Zarek said with a chuckle. "Just think. We've gutted their attempts to fight back and we haven't even engaged in a full-scale invasion yet."

His eyes still on the twins, Broden nodded. "So, what are your plans? What's held your hand against them thus far? Why do you allow them to live, anyway? Why not just kill them?"

The emperor pursed his lips. Then, "It's all in the timing, Broden," he said. "As you know, Brother Pestifere is away just now and— Well, I simply could not rob him of the satisfaction of seeing all his efforts and plans come to fruition. But you can be certain we won't have long to wait now."

"I see."

Broden stepped back toward Mara's cell. There he stopped to examine her blade stuck in the lock of the barred door. "What's this?" he asked, pointing at it.

"I see the same at the door of each of the other Oathtakers, as well."

Kicking away an errant rat that scampered toward him, Zarek laughed. "I thought you'd never ask." He leaned in and smiled at Mara. "Those locks are connected straight to Sinespe." He turned back to Broden. "The Oathtakers' blades make them unbreakable."

"I don't understand," Broden said.

Zarek's brow rose. "They cannot escape," he said. "No magic powers to travel will take them away. And no magic powers to move things will allow this one," he gestured toward Mara, "to retrieve her blade. Indeed, there is no magic they can practice that will help them out from behind these bars."

She perked up, waiting for more. It was the first clue as to why her attendant magic had not allowed for her to do the very things he mentioned.

"Nothing short of an earthquake would open these locks without my say-so," Zarek added. "So I've decided that— Well, perhaps I should put you in charge here, after all. You've done an excellent job with the women's prison, to date. And here, you'd have a constant reminder of my strength—of the surety that I'll win this battle."

Broden's heart skipped a beat. He knew now that there was no helping his friends escape. Still, the Good One did operate in mysterious ways. Perhaps there was something . . .

"Very well," he said, "I'll do it."

⁂

She recalled a time, long ago, when she'd followed a passage from a barn, into the earth, ultimately discovering a magic artifact. Then, as now, bones were scattered on the ground all around her.

Patting the back of the child bound to her frontside, she put down the basket holding the other infant, then crouched next to it. She grabbed a handful of the smaller bones. Unlike those in the cave of her recollection, these included not only those of humans, ranging in age from the youngest to the oldest, but also those of animals, from the smallest of rodents, to what she surmised, was a big bear.

She got back to her feet, lit a flare, and continued down the passageway. Some of the smaller bones crunched beneath her feet. She had to keep going. She had to find her way out.

A second later she halted when she thought she felt a breeze across her shoulders, but on looking around, found no evidence of an opening, so she kept on.

Soon, she came to a fork in the path.

She peeked down in each direction, but could make out no discernible differences between the two. Thus, she determined that she'd stay to the right. If it forked again, and she stayed right each time, she'd know which way she'd gone if she had to turn back.

Suddenly, out from the surrounding stillness, came a low, throaty whine. A deep, grating growl, followed.

She stopped in her tracks.

The sound came again, and this time, a horrific odor accompanied it. She recognized the smell. It was that of a grut—of death, of decay, of Snespe, the underworld.

She had to think. Should she back out and try another path? Or might the beast be guarding the way out? Surmising that could be the case, she continued on.

Suddenly, the growling, whining sound met her ears again. This time it rose in volume to a great howl.

She grabbed her blade, then paused to peek in at the little one in the basket. So still, it frightened her.

And at that very moment, the beast attacked.

Mara, awakening with a scream, sat up, shaking.

"What happened?" Dixon called out, his voice worry-laden. "Are you all right?"

Once again burdened with cramps, she winced with the pain of one, then took several deep breaths to calm herself.

"Mara?"

"Yes?"

"Are you all right?"

"Yes, I— I'm fine."

"You don't sound good," Reigna said.

"She's right," Dixon said. "Are you ready to tell me what's going on? Even Zarek noticed that you don't look well."

"Tell him, Mara," Eden urged.

"I'm fine, Dixon," she said, her voice clipped. She swallowed hard. Then, "Aliza," she continued, "how is your arm?"

"Actually, it's . . . Well, I've continued to pack it with the sugar Dixon threw my way earlier and the clean water Carlie has given me. It seems the infection is gone now—thankfully."

"Good," Dixon said. Then, "Nice try, Mara," he commented.

"You know," she said, "from what Zarek said, we've no chance of escaping here. I think I should inform Lucy of the facts. She and the Council could put someone else in charge and move forward with the plans we discussed before we left Oosa. We all may be casualties of this war, but the good people of Oosa needn't be." Just then, she cried out as a pain bit deeply, taking her entirely by surprise.

Dixon jumped to his feet. "Mara!"

Eden called her name. Then, "I think I know what's happening," she said.

Mara still recovering, didn't respond.

"What *is* happening?" Dixon asked.

"Tell him, Mara, or I will."

She said nothing.

Finally, after a long minute, Eden spoke again. "She's pregnant, Dixon, and unless I miss my guess, she's miscarrying."

"Oh, Eden," she cried, "you shouldn't have—"

Dixon, struck dumb by the news, staggered. "Ahhh . . . Oh, dear Ehyeh, is it true? Mara?"

Hot tears streamed down her cheeks. "Yes," she whimpered.

He dropped to his knees, rested his head against the bars. "Oh, Mara, I'm so sorry."

"You've nothing to be sorry for," she whimpered. "It's my fault. I should never have—"

"Stop it!" he ordered.

He stood, turned, and paced, then approached the bars again and grabbed them. "Please do not take responsibility for the wrongdoing of others. This is not your fault."

"Mara?" Reigna said.

She didn't answer.

"Mara, perhaps I could save the child."

She sat up in a rush. "What?"

"If I could touch it, I could save it. Maybe Carlie would— I mean, if you lose it, maybe she'd—"

"No, Reigna," Dixon whispered.

"What?" Mara cried, clearly distraught.

"She can't, Mara. You know the price."

"But this is our child she's talking about!" She couldn't believe Dixon would stop short of doing whatever it might take to save their infant. Shocked, she dropped back, then leaned her head against the cold wall.

"Gracious Ehyeh, I hate to say it, but Mara, if you think about it, you know that's not the answer."

She sobbed. How could he turn down the one thing that might save their little one? It was unthinkable that he'd refuse what Reigna could do.

"Mara," he pleaded, "even if she could save our child— What would she save it to? For?"

When she said nothing, he continued. "Mara, you said it yourself. We can't escape. And— And, you know, a child could not survive in here. Its only hope is in you."

Mara curled up into the fetal position. She thought about everything he said. Finally, she said, "Please, don't say anything more, Dixon."

Everyone was quiet for several minutes. Then, out of the blue, Mara's cramps having dissipated, she started in a whisper, to sing an old lullaby.

"What are you doing?" Reigna asked.

"You all should rest," she said. Then she turned back to her song. She sang louder, but gently.

A minute later, certain the others slept, she stopped.

"Mara?"

She started. "Oh! It's you, Dax."

"What just happened?"

Recalling his power that made magic ineffective on him, she hung her head. "They're all sleeping," she said. "It's part of my attendant magic. I just . . . I couldn't talk about it any longer."

She contemplated for a moment, then asked, "Dax, if no magic works on you, then how is it that you can't escape your cell?"

"Because my door is locked as might be any other door—and I can't unlock it. The fact that the mechanism is reinforced with magic doesn't really matter."

"I see."

They both sat quietly for a time.

"You know," he said, finally breaking the silence, "if you could pick our locks with your magic, then you could use that power you have to put others to sleep to keep anyone else from standing in our way of escaping."

She huffed. "No. Don't you see? You would stay awake, but so long as Dixon, the twins, and Aliza, heard me, they'd fall asleep."

"Not if they knew it was coming. If they were prepared, they could cover their ears, or plug them with something."

"So they'd stay awake while the guards fell asleep."

"Right. Then you could take the girls from here, and Dixon could take—"

"Only one of you. That would still leave either you or Aliza behind." She sighed. "Anyway, nice thinking, Dax, but there's still the problem of the locks."

"Right."

"You should get some sleep now," she said.

"No. I'll keep watch for the others."

"Suit yourself, then."

Chapter Forty-Three

"But what if you ended up in the worse possible place?" Jerrett asked. He glanced at Velia, who sat at his left, seeking her agreement.

Lucy sighed. "I've traveled to Chiran before," she said. "The last time I went, Ehyeh protected me. He delivered me to the abandoned town of Wylie—the exact place I needed to reach."

"Perhaps because you knew where you wanted to go."

"Yes, and when Spec returned, he told me where the prison is located. He pointed out its precise location on a map."

Basha, whom Lucy had retrieved from near the border days before, so that she could attend the meeting, sat at Velia's other side. "Lucy," she said, "I beg you to reconsider. We can't lose any more."

The four of them had decided to meet together with Skylar Hadwin to discuss options. As the most renowned scholar in all of Oosa, Lucy hoped he could help them to devise a workable plan of action. She'd also wanted Fidel to join them, as his expertise was in prophecy. Thus, she'd returned to the palace earlier that very day to ask him to join them and, when he agreed, brought him back to the city with her. Now, he sat nearby.

"Have you discovered anything helpful from your studies?" she asked him.

He leaned in. "There are vague references in *The Book of the Blood* here," he said, waving a copy of the book in his hand. "I'll look for them."

"And," Skylar piped in, "there are some things here in *When the Two May Overcome* that might pertain." He motioned with the black book that he held.

"What do they say?"

He opened the book, its leather cover crinkled with age. He turned to the first of several pages marked with a black satin ribbon.

"This one says something about 'deliverance,'" he said.

"Read it, please."

The professor turned the page over, then back again, its rustling sound filling the air. "This part discusses magic trinkets. It says, *'In those days when deliverance is sought, trust not illusion when I am born.'* I'm sorry," he said when, looking back at her, she grimaced, "that's all there is to it."

Lucy stretched her shoulders back. "So, what's it about?"

"Well," Fidel piped up, "frequently, when analyzing prophecy, we translate the term 'deliverance' to 'rescue.'"

"That's right," Skylar said.

"So, it could read, *'when rescue is sought, trust not illusion when I am born.'"* Lucy stood, then folded her arms. "I seem to recall something about a magic trinket—and being born—and the used of the term 'illusion.' Hmmm."

"If you could remember what that was," Basha said, "it might help."

"Wait!" Lucy cried. "It was about Rowena's old shawl. Do you remember it, Basha?"

"Oh, yes, I do."

"The words that came with the shawl mentioned something about being born. But maybe it wasn't about something being *birthed.* Maybe it was about its being *worn!"*

"Do you think?"

"Mara told me that the twins had discovered that they could disappear when they covered themselves with it. So, I think that's it." She looked at each of the others, in turn. "I suppose, somehow, in a rescue attempt, they're to make use of it. What do you think?" she asked Skylar.

He shrugged. "I don't know."

"What else did you find then?"

Fidel turned the pages of his book. "Here's something," he said. "This one speaks of the twins, of that I'm certain."

"Oh?" Basha turned his way.

"Yes, and it, too, mentions deliverance—which we're assuming for the sake of our discussion, means 'rescue.'" He looked down, squinted, and then read: *"Before evil claims all, the seventh seventh and she who is but is not, may seek deliverance. Pray for faith, that the bowels of the earth may heave.'"* He looked back up at her.

"Any idea what it means?" Basha asked.

"Sorry. None whatsoever," he said.

"Maybe it's a reference to when the twins chose Ehyeh. Do you remember how they sought escape from The Tearless? Then, when the moons aligned, the earth shook so violently?"

"Yes," Lucy said. "Well then, it seems that that prophecy was already fulfilled."

"Still, there may be hope for Chiranians in general," Skylar suggested.

"What makes you say that?"

"Listen to this." He turned the pages of his book, and then read out loud:

Shall the tree determine the circumstances of its seed? A miniature kernel, containing its own survival, in itself is neither good, nor evil. That from which it is derived determines not the kernel's end. Consider, rather, the ground in which it sprouts, the purity of the water sprinkled upon it. Even when germinated in darkness, yet in clear light, it may thrive. Even when cast in the ashes, when transplanted to nourishing soil, it may live. Even that which emerges, surrounded by acidic waters, may find new life at the base of a fresh spring well.

He closed the book.

"I don't understand."

"The book is about the twins overcoming," Skylar said. "I think it's cautioning us against seeing all Chiranians as evil. If they could be shown the way of life and freedom, through our example, they may follow."

"I see. Still, there's nothing useful there for us regarding an escape plan." Lucy sighed. "Is there anything else?"

"No," Skylar said.

"I've one more here," Fidel said. *"Lose not faith when deliverance is sought. The despot inevitably offers the seed of his own destruction.'"*

"So," Lucy ventured, "we're to wait for Zarek to make a mistake of some kind?"

"Perhaps he already has," Basha said. "He should have killed them all, straight away. Instead, they've—we've—been given time to seek their rescue."

"Well," Fidel said, tapping on his book, which now sat on the table before him, "there's nothing more here."

Velia leaned in. "Lucy, without more information, are you still planning to go Chiran?" she asked.

"I feel I must."

"Alone?"

"Actually, no." She picked up her quill, then put it back down. "I've decided that Petrus will join me, as he suggested."

"Don't you think he should stay here? After all, isn't he working on our defensive plans?" Jerrett asked.

"He is. But his viewing things there up-close could ultimately be to our benefit." She glanced at each of the others in turn. "I can see you don't support my plan, but I feel I must see it through."

"When will you leave?" Basha asked.

"Shortly. I'll keep you informed. But for now, I need to check in on how the investigation into Percival's actions is coming along."

She strutted down the hall. When she arrived outside the room in which Percival was held, she nodded at the Oathtaker guards. One of them opened the door for her. Its squeaky hinges sounded out.

Lucy stepped inside.

Percival sat, Petrus facing him.

She glanced at the men, then pulled up a nearby stool. She addressed Petrus. "Anything?"

"No, sorry," he said, scowling at the prisoner. "Nothing."

"Percival," she said turning his way, "the Council has determined that we've not enough evidence to exact any punishment."

He sighed with relief.

"However, they agree we do have enough to continue to hold you."

He shook his head. "I've done nothing."

"Let's hope that's the case. Still, I'd like to hear you explain how it is that we found this," she said, handing him a book, "in your rooms."

"You— You searched my rooms?"

"Yes. So, can you explain that?" She pointed at the book.

He turned the item over. "I— I've never seen this before. I know that there's a copy or two around. I think I've even seen you studying one, but—"

"You deny that was in your room?"

"I do."

"Hmmm. And I suppose you can't explain this either."

She handed him a map. Someone had designated on it, the same place she'd noted earlier, where Dixon, Dax, and Aliza, were staying in the barn. Another marking showed the town of Wylie, the place to which Lucy had traveled earlier, after setting a trap to determine if they had a leak in their ranks.

He took the item and perused it. "I've never seen this map before."

She stood, tapped her foot. "Very well then, Percival. Until we can get to the bottom of this—"

"I'll remain in custody? But Lucy, the troops need me."

She leaned in. "Don't think too much of yourself," she seethed. "Now, I'm told that the Council is willing to offer some leniency here. Perhaps life imprisoned, rather than the death penalty—"

"I've done nothing!" he persisted.

"I can't help you, Percival, if you are unwilling to help yourself." With that, she turned to the door and then made her way out.

The crowd consisted of a group of nearly thirty Oathtakers, many with the ability to heal. The charges of some, accompanied them. The room erupted with their collective shouts and exclamations.

Lucy pounded her fist on the desktop. "That is enough!" she ordered. When silence ensued, she continued. "The evidence supports this."

"I refuse to believe it," came the voice of someone from the back of the room.

"Percival Ferreolo is one of the best of the healers. He healed my Oathtaker from a terrible injury. If he meant to do harm, why would he prove so helpful in keeping our troops in such good fighting form?"

"I understand, Joed," Lucy responded. "Still, wouldn't you agree that his assistance would prove as good a way as any to divert the attention of you all away from him?" Her gaze scanned across the room. "And from the looks of things, the plan worked."

"He is not a traitor!" Joed insisted. "What is this 'evidence' of which you speak anyway?"

Frustrated, Lucy rubbed her temples. "We searched his rooms. There, we found a map of Chiran—one unlike any I've ever seen before. It was quite detailed—and on it were markings of . . . significance."

"So?"

"So, we also found a copy of *Serving Daeva*." She paused, letting the others take that fact into account. "How else would you account for that?"

Joed stepped to the front of the room. "Those are the very things we've been using in our efforts to design a plan to oppose Zarek when he invades," he said. "Percival, as you well know, was left with Dax's materials when he left the city. Those items are no different from the ones that all of us use and study here every day. We make the best use of resources of that nature that we can. So, if that's your evidence, you might as well take me into custody right now, as well." He held his arms out, his hands close together, inviting her to bind him.

"That's right!" came cries from some of the others, a few of whom joined him, their hands also held out.

"Turn Percival loose!" someone demanded.

Lucy stared at Joed, her jaw set.

"Look," he said, putting his arms down, his hands still fisted. "You have no evidence. If you think what you found is incriminating, then take me into custody. For that matter, why don't you arrest my Oathtaker, as well?" he added glancing at him over his shoulder.

"Joed, don't be—"

"Ridiculous? Is that what you were going to say? I have maps and books in my quarters. You'd best get there quickly so that you can confiscate them and then arrest me, too."

She sighed. "Be reasonable."

"I am being reasonable. Percival has admitted to nothing, yet you use the flimsiest of evidence to hold him. The healers need him," he said, pacing. "Percival knows more about healing than anyone here," he added, coming to a halt, "including remedies that require no magic power whatsoever. You know, when the real war hits, there won't be enough magic to go around."

"Yes!" someone in the audience exclaimed.

"Agreed!" cried another.

Once again, shouts and exclamations sounded out, and once again, Lucy pounded the desktop. Then, "Has Salus returned?" she asked.

The din continued.

"Has Salus returned?" she repeated, louder this time.

As the ruckus died down, Joed spoke up. "No," he said, clearly confused as to the question, his brow furrowed.

Lucy held her lips tight, then tapped the table. Finally, when she had everyone's attention, she said, "There is evidence that Percival was the last person known to have seen him."

Joed took a step back. "What are you talking about?"

"I was informed that Salus headed for a seedy little pub one day. I understand that he hasn't been seen since. I took Percival there with me to investigate, notwithstanding his efforts to avoid going. In any case, the barkeep recognized him as the man who met Salus there. And he said that they left there—together."

"Surely he was mistaken."

"That's what I thought—at the time. By itself, that information didn't convince me. Eyewitness accounts are, after all, notoriously unreliable. However, I think otherwise now."

She reached into her pocket and pulled out a slip of paper. "We also found this in Percival's room." She opened it and then held it out for everyone to see. There, was written: *"Meet Salus at The Swindler's Cup, at evenfall."*

Eyes squinted and mouths dropped open in surprise.

"With all that has transpired, we must consider that Salus came into information that Percival did not want out," Lucy said.

"Why reach that conclusion?" Joed asked. "Isn't that a bit far-fetched, even with that so called evidence?" he added, pointing at the slip of paper Lucy held.

"Perhaps. But if it was your Oathtaker purportedly last seen with Percival, wouldn't you want to get to the bottom of all this?"

When no one responded, Lucy stood. "We'll take your concerns into consideration, but in the meantime, for the safety of us all, I insist we act with caution. Percival remains in custody." With that she reached down, slapped closed the book that sat before her, and then made her way out.

Chapter Forty-Four

Broden marched down the hall, Carlie and Clementine at his side. Two succedunt soldiers accompanied them, one in front, and one behind, apparently as a consequence of Zarek not wholly trusting his son.

As they entered the area of cells in which the emperor held the Oathtakers and the twins, Broden addressed the men. "You can go now," he said.

One of the succedunt shook his head. "We stay," he said. "Zarek's orders."

Tipping his chin up, Broden headed for the last of the cells—the one housing the twins. He looked inside, then motioned for Carlie and Clementine. "See to them," he said.

"How could you?" Reigna asked, glaring at him, disappointment and anger in her voice. "You're one of us. How could you?"

Feeling the eyes of the guards on him, his brow rose. He bit his lip and then said, "You know nothing about me."

She drew to the bars. "I know you're a coward and a traitor," she seethed.

Eden stepped behind her sister, grabbed her arm and pulled her away. "Leave him, Reigna."

Just then, Carlie returned with the bucket of gruel.

Reigna snapped her arm free from her sister's grip. Then, once again staring Broden down, she pointed Carlie's way. "How could you treat her as you have? What happened to you?"

Eden chimed in. "We always believed in you, Broden. We've always had faith in you. Tell us this isn't what it looks like."

Broden, pulling to his full height, noted the guards watching him closely. Then, looking Carlie's way, he nodded. "Get on with it," he ordered.

Carlie and Clementine saw to filling the prisoners' bowls with their daily gruel. Unfortunately, with the succedunt keeping such a close eye on things, they were unable to leave with them all, the packets of food that Carlie had brought along.

Meanwhile, Broden approached Mara's cell. Signs of pain laced her face and sweat stood out on her brow as, on her hands and knees, she panted. Clearly, she was in great pain.

"What's wrong with you?" he asked. He struggled to keep concern out of his voice. He didn't dare make the guards suspicious.

"She's miscarrying if you must know, Broden," Reigna, having overheard, cried out. "Because of you, your father, and his monsters, yet another life will expire." She choked back a cry. "How could you?"

Broden glanced at one of the guards now standing before him. "Well, I guess that's the price that comes with defying Zarek's plans," he said, dismissively. Then, looking back at Mara, he struggled to keep his emotions in check.

He stood and moved on, briefly glancing into each of the other cells. Once through, he turned back to the succedunt guards. "You can go now," he tried again.

"No. We're to stay at your side."

"I see. Well, I'll assist with the chores then." With that, he headed for the bucket of water.

When they returned later to Broden's quarters, he ordered all the women, but for Carlie, down for the night. Then he convened with her and Striver. On the table before them sat a carafe of wine and three brass drinking vessels, all of which Striver filled.

"Now what?" the tutor asked.

"If I could just get alone with them—just for a minute—perhaps I could convince them of my innocence," Broden said.

"They all looked at you like they wanted to kill you," Carlie said, patting his hand. "I'm so sorry. I wish they knew. I wish we could tell them."

"I need a plan. Something to get the succedunt off my back."

"Maybe there's a way to—" She stopped short. "Oh, never mind."

"To what?" he asked, sitting up straighter.

"It's— No. It's not an option."

"What?" he persisted.

She closed her eyes and sighed, then looked back at him. "If there was trouble in the women's prison, they might have to call all the guards to assist."

"But we're no longer working there—in the women's prison," he said.

"No. But Striver and the others are."

Just then came the squeak of a door opening.

"Master?" someone called.

Broden rushed to his feet as Yasmin, Farida, and Ghazala, made their way out of their room and toward him.

"May we speak with you?" Yasmin asked. Then her eyes skipped in Carlie's direction. "And to *Carlie*?" she added.

His eyes narrowed, he looked at her, then at Carlie, then back again. "What did you call her?"

"I called her by her name."

"Ahhh," Broden stuttered, "sure." What had Yasmin heard between them, he wondered.

"I recommend that you use us. Use me, Farida, and Ghazala."

He looked at each of them in turn. "I don't understand," he said.

"May I?" she nodded toward the fourth and last chair at the table.

"Yeeessss," he drawled.

"You've always told us to call you by your name."

"Yes."

"And you've always treated us with kindness."

He shrugged. "I've treated you as best I could under the circumstances."

"Well then, *Broden*," she emphasized his name, "we want to help."

"Oh?"

She leaned in. "Look, if not for you, Ehyeh only knows what would have become of us by now."

"Ehyeh!" Striver cried.

"You don't think we could have spent so much time around Broden and not discovered that much at least, do you?" Farida asked. "Of course, he's a follower. And because of his example, we've all become followers, as well."

Broden rubbed the back of his neck. "I can't allow you all to put yourselves at risk," he said.

Yasmin rested her hand on his arm. "We already are—at risk." She paused. "Look, the troubles here in Chiran may or may not be things that can be resolved. I don't know. But I do know that they aren't your responsibility—nor should it be up to the Oosians to help the common people of Chiran. Yet if we're ever to know true freedom, it won't come from our countrymen, it will come from yours. That's why we need to help you."

He stared at her.

"The concept of freedom was lost from this place too long ago," she said. "No one remembers what it is, or what it's like. They can't appreciate that they don't really live, because they never really have lived. But we," she pointed at herself, then gestured toward the other women, "have seen you. We've watched you. We've come to appreciate what freedom might be—and that's more than we've ever experienced before."

"Still—" He tried to interrupt.

"No . . . Broden," she said, pausing at the sound of his name, "these people Zarek has imprisoned are important to you—and to Carlie. That makes them important to us. And the truth is that even if you don't sanction us to follow through with our plan, we're going to. We *choose* to do this. We choose to exercise the freedom to do it. So unless you intend to act against what we know you believe in, nothing you say will change our minds."

A long quiet minute passed. Finally, "You have some sort of proposal?" he asked.

"Yes."

"Go on then."

"When Zarek brought you to the prison where he's holding your friends, he put new guards in charge of the women's prison. We assist them in preparing wagons for transport just like we did when you worked there. When the right time comes, we'll make a commotion. Perhaps shout that someone has escaped."

He stared at her.

"If they think there's trouble, they'll call for reinforcements. Meanwhile, you could have a few minutes alone with your friends."

Broden stood and paced. "If you end up in trouble, I won't be able to help you."

Yasmin held his gaze. "It'll work. I'm sure of it."

He sighed, nodding. "Very well then, I've got some ideas of my own. But we mustn't act rashly here. We need to take the time necessary to plan this all out well in advance. We won't get a second chance. Now, listen up."

Chapter Forty-Five

Lucy stood with a pack over her shoulder, Petrus at her side. "I'm going to return Basha to Marshall's camp at the border, and then I'll come back here," she said to him. "I hope we can leave shortly after I return." With that, she took Basha's hand, and disappeared.

Seconds later, they arrived in the midst of Marshall's camp.

"Guards! Guards!" someone shouted out. Then came more cries from all sides. Confusion reigned as people ran toward the original plea for help.

Basha grabbed the arm of one of the nearby Oathtakers. "What's going on?" she asked as she headed with him toward the sounds, Lucy at their heels.

"I don't know!"

They ran with the others. Soon, they reached the source of the commotion.

A young man stood near several barrels of water that the Oathtakers had filled at a nearby spring. In his hand, he held a bag.

"Put it down!" Trumble growled.

"It's nothing," the teen said.

"I said, 'put it down.'"

Basha pushed through to the front of the crowd. "What is it, Trumble?" she asked when she met him at his side. "Was that you who called for a guard?"

"Yes. I think that's poison in the bag he's holding." He gestured toward the youth.

"Who is he? Why would you think that?"

"He's one of the young men who recently come across the border from Chiran." He bit his lip. "And it's about something Felicity said." He took another step forward. "Put it down," he ordered once again.

"I'll take it from here," one of the guards said as he slapped Trumble on the back, then walked toward the youth.

"What did Felicity say?" Basha asked.

He turned her way. "You know how simple she is, how her words sometimes relay the impression of something happening, even though those words may not be wholly accurate?"

"Right."

"Well, just minutes ago, she awakened from a nap, crying out, repeatedly, 'Don't drink, don't fuddle! Don't drink, don't fuddle!'"

Basha's eyes narrowed. "I don't understand."

"Neither did I, at the time. But then I came out here to fill a pitcher with water. That's when I saw that one," he pointed at the young man, "wandering around the barrels here. Clearly, he was watching to be certain no one saw him."

"And?"

"And I thought about what Felicity had said. You see, if she saw someone delirious from poison, it might well appear to her that he'd been drinking spirits—that he was inebriated, 'fuddled.'"

Just then, Marshall approached Basha's side. "What's happening?" he asked.

Basha and Trumble relayed all they knew as they watched guards surround the youth who then dropped the item he held. He feinted going around one barrel, then another, drawing his pursuers every which way. Then, suddenly, he sprang out.

Whuuufff! He fell to the ground when one of them tackled him below his knees.

The youth twisted around and kicked, trying to free himself. A second later, he was armed.

"Watch out!" Basha cried. "He has a knife!"

The guard let go his hold, then pulled back, even as four more Oathtakers drew nearer.

"Back!" the teen cried, once again on his feet.

"Put your weapon down," one of the men ordered. "We don't want to hurt you."

He and his cohorts all took another step closer.

"Back!" the youth cried again. "I didn't do anything!"

"Keep him there," Marshall ordered.

Lucy headed to the water barrels. Spotting the bag the youth had dropped, she stooped down and grabbed it. As she looked back, the youth darted, once again seeking to free himself, even as the guards stepped closer to him.

"If he runs, stop him!" she cried. "But don't use your Oathtaker's blade. We may need to question him." She opened the bag and, holding it several inches away, sniffed. Then, "Bind him!" she ordered.

When the youth once again tried to run, one of the Oathtakers flicked a knife at him. It landed in the meaty part of his thigh. As he looked down at it, a crimson patch of blood shown out. Then, as he grabbed the blade to pull it free, several guards descended on him, simultaneously. One took one of his arms, while another held the other.

"Hold it," the first of them ordered him.

Marshall, Basha, and Trumble, made their way to Lucy's side.

"What's in the bag?" Basha asked.

"Ground castor oil beans."

"Are they poisonous?"

"Very." Lucy turned to Trumble. "Good catch," she said. Then she addressed the men who held the teen captive. "Lock him up," she ordered. Turning back, she asked, "How old do you suppose he is?"

"Fifteen, sixteen, maybe," Trumble said.

"We need to discuss the situation of allowing people over the border," she said. "Now!"

"But they're just children!" Basha exclaimed. She, Trumble, Marshall, and Lucy, along with the troop leaders stationed with them at the border, sat gathered around a table in the tent reserved as a cafeteria.

Lucy let her breath out slowly. "I don't care."

Basha glared at her. "You do too care, Lucy. I know you do." She crossed her arms. "Why are you taking this position? Why are you pretending to be so heartless?"

Lucy turned to the troop leaders. "Is this the first incident you've had of this kind?" she asked.

"Ahhh, no," one of them responded.

"That's why," Lucy said.

Basha turned to them. "What other incidents are you referring to?"

Trumble leaned in. "While you were away with Lucy, several of our men were out on patrol. Do you remember that young woman you and I rescued when we first came here?"

"Nadine? Sure. What of her?"

"Nothing about her—exactly. As you know, we directed her to a place of safety. But our patrols came upon several additional groups of young men seeking to do the same as had her captors."

"Kidnapping women."

"*Oosian* women. Yes." Trumble sighed. "The abductors are young Chiranian men who made their way into Oosa. Now they capture our young women with the intention of selling them as slaves in Chiran." He shook his head. "This must stop."

"He's right," Lucy said.

"So what exactly is it that you recommend, huh, Trumble?" Basha asked. "Lucy is suggesting that we turn all the children away. Is that what you want to see done? They'll die there, in Chiran, with no one to watch out for them."

"Basha," Lucy interrupted, "Zarek knows enough about our ways to understand that we value life, and that we seek to protect the youngest and the weakest."

"Yes, but now you're suggesting that we're *not* to do that—that we're not to follow the very essence of our calling." She sighed heavily as she ran her fingers through her hair. "So what if Zarek knows our ways?"

"So what? So he's using that information against us."

"May I speak?" one of the troop leaders asked.

"Certainly, Coye," Basha said. "What is it?"

"We had another incident while you were away. Unfortunately, the young man got away, so we were unable to question him afterward, but all the evidence suggested that he was—" He stopped short.

"That he was what?"

"That he'd been harming the children. The really little ones."

Biting her lip, Basha looked away. "What evidence?"

Lucy put her hand on her friend's. "Aliza told us she believed similar things were going on."

"What evidence?" Basha persisted.

"Someone came in with a group of children one day. Well, they weren't all children, exactly."

"Spit it out, Coye."

"There was a group of five boys, likely ranging in age from ten or so, up. We thought the eldest might be about fifteen. All the others seemed to look to him for direction. In any case, now we're not so sure how old he was.

"When they made it to the tents where we keep the children before we send them on to other safe places, the boys all stepped inside. Several of the younger ones who were already there burst into hysterics.

"I was standing to the young man's left when he lunged for one of them. I sprang out behind him, warning him to step back, but he didn't. The next thing I knew, he was armed."

He glanced about, hesitating. "I'm sorry, but at the time I carried only my Oathtaker's blade. I didn't want to use it on him. What if I had the facts wrong? I didn't think I should act as judge, jury, and executioner. So I hesitated and . . . Well, that's when he got away. I'm not sure it was the right decision since he'd been headed for one of the youngest ones there."

"You were right," Lucy said, "not to use your blade on him. I find no fault in your reasoning."

"Still, the child he was after was . . . terrified."

Basha, biting her lip, looked down and sighed.

"Listen," Lucy said, "I think Zarek is training young men to cause us harm. I also believe that he's trying to get his youngest looking warriors across the border so that they can cause problems for us right here in Oosa."

"We can't send all of the children back," Basha insisted.

Lucy's shoulders slumped. Then she asked, "Have you all noticed anything untoward coming from the young women who've managed to make their way here?"

"Not many have made it here," Trumble said.

"But of those who have?"

The leaders exchanged glances.

Trumble shrugged. "No," he said.

"Then here's our compromise," Lucy said. "You may let all the young women of any age in—unless or until we find we should act otherwise. But you must turn away any male child you have good reason to believe is over twelve years of age. Then, Marshall, I want you to set up some sort of . . . I don't know. Someone needs to school these young ones in our ways. I'm not sure we can change the minds of the oldest of them, but we can certainly try."

Basha stared at her. "But you still intend to leave all the others victim to Zarek?" she asked. "That's— It's barbaric!"

"Basha," Lucy said, "to whom do you owe your first duty?"

"Oh, great Ehyeh, Lucy," she muttered, shaking her head.

"Tell me."

"To the Good One and to my charge, Therese, of course." Basha's voice was clipped.

"When we allow those young men inside our borders, we increase the dangers to Therese—and to every other member of the Select—and to every other Oosian. This is hard, I know, but it is necessary. War is an ugly thing."

"So we sacrifice them for our safety?"

"It's like Dixon always says, we cannot take on blame for the wrongdoing of others. If the Chiranian system is so flawed as to cause them harm, we can do what we can to save some, but not at the risk of sacrificing our own safety to Zarek." With that, she got up, and walked away.

Chapter Forty-Six

Gnarly brambles covered the way before her. If not careful, she would trip on their roots. Here and there, in their midst, pits of rotting debris stood out. From time to time, one spontaneously burst into flame, filling the air with a thick black smoke that made her eyes itch. She wiped them, then turned back to business

Once again setting down the basket in which one of the little ones rested, she started hacking through another section. As she slashed with her blade, the plants' jagged thorns cut through her garb and into her skin, leaving criss-crossed bloody hatches behind.

She paused to pull a thorn out from her arm. Almost the size of her fingernail, its curved end, reminiscent of a fishing hook with barbs at its end, had caught deeply in her flesh. Sweat glistened on her brow as she struggled with it. Its poison quickly made her skin turn red. It burned. She knew she had to hurry before more of it made its way into her system. The last time that had happened, she'd been left unconscious for a time. Fearing for the infants' safety should that occur again, she grabbed the barb's end in her teeth and then pulled.

She cried out, tears running down her cheeks, when it came loose.

Blood trickled down her arm, then dripped to the ground, feeding the angry bush. New growth instantly sprouted where the drops landed.

She bound a cloth around her wound. She couldn't allow her suffering, her life force, to nourish the enemy.

The plant's poison, now in her mouth, choked her. She coughed and spit before opening her canteen, filling her mouth with water, and then spitting it out. After several more such washes, the irritation on her tongue lessened.

She recapped the vessel, then continued hacking away. Just then, through an opening in the wall of thorns, she thought she saw a flicker of green. Though tiny, it encouraged her to move faster.

She chopped more, until sweat ran down her frontside where the other child was bound, then stopped momentarily to review her progress. The tunnel that she'd made was not quite large enough to squeeze through without taking the risk that more poisonous barbs would catch her, so she slashed away some more.

Once satisfied, she peeked into the basket. The babe did not look good. Fearing for the lives of both the little ones, she grabbed the basket, swept her cape over it, and hunched down. She had to clear the top sufficiently, as she'd be unable to help herself if a barb made its way into her backside.

Her first foot landed just on the other side of the opening. The ground felt different—not hard and dry. Rather, it was almost spongy.

Once her other foot passed through, she stood and looked about. She had, indeed, landed in a clearing devoid of the brambles.

Then she beheld the strangest sight. One branch, reaching forward from out of the area of desolation, a branch from what appeared on looking back to be from the highest bush therein, had canopied out from its surroundings and into the clearing. At its end grew a small green bud that rested on the ground.

She approached, then examined it carefully, finding it strange.

She opened her canteen and trickled a few drops of water on it. Within seconds, the tiny seedling grew. She cocked her head, thinking, then watered it some more. Another branch grew, and then another. Almost immediately, out from the soil at her feet, sprang yet another green seedling, this one no doubt connected to the roots of the first. Then came more.

Soon a clover colored patch filled the space and started pushing up against the edges of the wasteland. In turn, the gnarly bushes started to shrink away. It was as though the bramble from within, a despot among despots, had created the seed of its own undoing.

At that moment, from out of the stillness, came a grunting, hissing sound. It reminded her of a dog barking.

She turned toward its source. There at the edge of the clearing, sat a black vulture, eyeing her. Seconds later, the air filled with more coughing, as a hoard of its mates, neared.

Just as she prepared to sweep her cape over the basket, one of the beasts flew into her, knocking her over.

She scrambled to get back to her feet.

The beast neared, its sharp, curved beak open to snatch up the babe.

And Mara woke, screaming.

"Are you all right?" Dixon cried.

She struggled for breath as a searing pain stabbed through her middle. As they were coming more regularly, she was now sure; there was no longer any question. She would lose her child. She choked back a cry as a strong contraction gripped her. Then gasping, on her knees, she bent forward, her hands held firmly on her center, as though willing the child to stay put.

"Mara!" Dixon cried. "What's happening?"

She caught her breath. "I'm so sorry, Dixon."

She glanced toward the window. Dawn would arrive soon, and with it, the first day in some time without the ever-present company of her unborn. She'd earlier calculated that it was likely somewhere between its twenty-second and twenty-fifth weeks of gestation.

"Please, don't be," he said.

She cried. "I'm so sorry."

"Broden and Carlie will be here soon," he said. "Do you think there's anything they can do? Maybe if we begged them for help . . ." His voice dropped away to nothing.

At that moment, Mara felt something trickle down her inner thigh. Shaking, she lifted her skirt.

Blood. It glistened.

"No, Dixon," she said, "it's . . . too late."

"Are you certain, Mara?" Reigna asked, her voice barely above a whisper.

"Yes." She choked back a sob. "I'm bleeding. It won't be long now."

"I love you, Mara," Dixon said. "Whatever else happens, know that I love you."

She longed for his words, even as they pained her. When another contraction came, then subsided, she responded, "I know, Dixon. I— I'm just so sor—"

"Shhh. Shhh."

Yet another pain racked her being. When it subsided, she felt something warm and wet, and for a moment, she smelled blood mixed with an almost earthy scent.

She reached down and then took into her hands, a fully formed infant, so small that it fit, all curled up, in the palm of her hand. She estimated that its weight approximately equaled that of her blade, Spira.

"Ahhhhhhh," she wept.

"Mara?" Eden called.

"She's . . . beautiful."

"She?" Dixon asked, a cry in his voice.

Mara pulled her pack toward herself. She rummaged in it for a towel, then wrapped the babe in it. She sat with it in her arms, rocking, weeping, silent.

"She?" Dixon finally asked again.

"Yes. It . . . was . . . a girl."

"We're so, so sorry," Reigna said.

For a moment, she wished the others would just leave her—ignore her. She didn't have the mental or physical energy to engage with them, to respond.

Just then, the guards entered. Broden, at the front of the pack, carried a bucket of water. Carlie followed, carrying the gruel. Behind them came a handful of the succedunt who stood in the middle of the hall from whence they could oversee things.

Carlie approached the twins' cell.

Reigna rushed toward the bars. "Carlie," she whispered, "please help. Mara has miscarried. Please, you must get her to give up that baby. Please. Please, bring the infant to me."

Eden grabbed her sister's arm. "No, Reigna."

"Please, Carlie, please," Reigna begged. "Bring her to me."

"What's going on there?" one of the guards asked.

Carlie filled the twins' bowls with gruel. "Nothing," she said, before stepping away.

Upon approaching Mara's cell, she peered inside. There Mara sat, cradling something in her arms. Seconds later, she keened with grief.

"What's going on?" the guard demanded to know. He approached the cell and looked inside.

"I believe she's miscarried," Carlie said.

"Oh?" He turned to Mara, a smirk on his face. "You'd best give that up—and the sooner the better—before this place smells of death."

She turned his way. Though too exhausted to so much as glare at him, in that moment she swore to herself that when the opportunity arose, she would kill him. So she took a long and careful look, committing his image to her memory.

"Leave her be," Broden said, patting the guard's arm. "I'll take care of this."

"Have it your way," he said, stepping away.

Broden crouched down. "Mara?"

She looked at him.

"Are you all right?"

Her eyes narrowed as she watched him.

"Leave her alone!" Reigna cried.

He hung his head, then looked back up. "May I see?"

She held her dead child even closer and backed further away from the bars.

"Please," he said. "He's right, you know. I mean— Well, I'm— You're not going to be able to keep it in there with you."

"It is not an 'it!'" she cried. She looked down at the infant. Tears streamed down her cheeks. "It is not an 'it,'" she repeated. "It is a 'she.'"

"May I see her?"

"Her name is 'Mariella,'" she offered, as though only to herself. Then she whispered, "Shhh, little Ella, it's all right."

"Can you let me have Mariella—Ella—now?" His voice remained soft, melodic.

Shaking her head, she neared the wall, all the while holding the infant closely. "Ella is mine," she whispered.

He bit his lip. "That's fine then, Mara, you just let me know when you're ready."

He stood, then ran his hand across the top of his head and rested it at the back of his neck. Unable to speak openly to her, as the succedunt soldiers made that impossible, he set about his duties.

Throughout that and the next long day, Mara sat in her cell silent, holding Mariella tightly to her chest. Although Dixon tried several times to get her to give up the infant, she refused to respond to him, or to engage with anyone else.

As the sun neared the horizon on the afternoon of the third day, Carlie, walking down the hallway, peeked inside Mara's cell as she placed the bundled Mariella on the floor and pushed her toward the bars. Once done, she fell back in a heap and wrapped her arms over her head.

Carlie got down on her knees and reached inside. Her fingertips barely touched the wrapping. She pinched a bit of it and then pulled. When the bundle was close enough, she picked it up. Removing the draping from over the infant's face, the sight of the child struck her, momentarily, dumb. Somehow, she hadn't imagined the perfection she'd find there.

Tears rolled down her cheeks. "You're right, Mara," she whispered. "Ella was beautiful. Just like her mother."

"Hey—ahhh, Mouse," Dixon whispered, using the name Broden used for her, "please, may I see her?"

"What's this?" a guard asked stepping closer.

"I just want to see my child," Dixon snapped.

He grinned. "Sure thing." He turned to Carlie. "Let 'im see."

She brought the bundled infant to him and handed her over.

Dixon opened her wrappings and looked. Tears filled his eyes. Taking her tiny hand, he examined her fingers. Moments later, his shoulders shook with grief as he brought her to his chest and held her there.

"That's enough now," the guard ordered. Turning to Carlie, he added, "You and Broden will need to dispose of it."

Dixon glared at the man. Then, after taking a final look at Ella, he handed her back to Carlie.

"Thank you," she said.

"Wait! Mouse!" Reigna cried. "Mouse!"

When the guard shrugged at her, she stepped toward the twins' cell, the bundle in her arms.

"Please, give her to me." Reigna held her hands out, between the bars of her cell.

Eden grabbed her sister and pulled her away. "You can't, Reigna."

"Oh, yes I can! Mara has lost enough as Oathtaker to the two of us." She struggled to pull free. "This is one thing I can give to her—and it's not too late. The sun has not yet set on this, the third day. But if I'm to act, I have to do so quickly."

Confused, Carlie watched on, as Reigna finally extricated herself from her sister's grip and returned to the cell door. "Give her to me, Mouse," she said again.

"Listen!" Eden cried, clutching her arm again. "Please, Reigna, listen to me. I want you to think about this. Mara's body—her womb—was the safest possible place on earth for Mariella. It was the one place to which Ehyeh could call forth her new spirit to grow—to prepare her for the world." She paused, swallowed hard. "Reigna, it's not easy to lose a child—or even intentionally to rid oneself of one. That's because a mother's body—her womb—is intended to be, is *designed* to be, a haven. A *safe* haven."

She dropped her head and shook it, then looked back up, and whispered, "If Mariella could not survive there, how long do you think she could survive out of there? Please, listen to me. You would be crazy to think of doing what you're considering."

"Leave me be, Eden."

"Please," she pleaded, in a voice so low that no one else could hear, "I beg of you. Consider the cost. Someone would die. *Mara* could be the one we lose."

Reigna glared at her twin. "So you're thinking only of us? Of yourself?"

"Or Dixon. Have you considered that? How would Mara feel if he paid the cost?"

Once again, her sister pulled free of her grip.

"Please, Reigna, you cannot do this. What if you brought her back, only for Mara to experience the loss of her all over again? What then?"

"I was given this ability for a reason," her twin snapped.

"Yes," Eden agreed, wiping away an errant tear, "but maybe the reason was to test you—to find out if you'd venture to take on Ehyeh's own power over life and death. Maybe He gave it to you to determine if you'd use it. Maybe—just maybe— you're not supposed to. Have you considered that possibility?"

Reigna turned away. With tears now flowing down her cheeks, she dropped to her knees, then turned and sat with her back against the wall.

"What do you want me to do?" Carlie asked.

Eden crouched down at her sister's side. "Tell her, Reigna. You know what she should do. Tell her."

She hung her head. Then, "Take her away," she said. "Just . . . take little Ella away." She gulped back a sob. "But please, please see to it that she gets a proper burial."

━━◆━━

A week passed after Mariella's death, each day bringing the same routine. Mara took the clean strips of cloth that Carlie had managed to leave for her, and bound them close to herself to soak up her remaining loss of blood. As the days passed, her discharge lessened. Even so, during most of that time, she sat silent, morose.

But on the morning of the eighth day, she awakened with a renewed commitment.

She'd never been a quitter. She'd never been a whiner—although truth to tell, the past year or so did not stand as particularly convincing testimony to that fact. Even so, she was not one of those people who was happy being miserable. And so, she'd determined, it was time to move on.

Several times over the course of the day, she dropped down to the floor and exercised her waning muscles, pushing herself up, then dropping back down, over and over again. She would renew her strength, no matter the cost.

When nighttime finally descended, and Broden, Carlie, and the succedunt guards left the prison, she called out to the others. "Listen up!" she said.

The sounds of her cohorts' shuffling filled the air.

"Are you all right, Mara?" Dixon asked. She'd said next to nothing over the past days.

"I'm fine. I'm sure the grieving will never go away, but it's time to turn my attention—our attention—elsewhere. Today is the eighth day since—" Pausing, she swallowed hard, then continued. "Today is the eighth day. The day of new beginnings. Now, we're going to get out of here. We just need a plan."

"I'm so sorry, Mara. I should have saved her," Reigna whispered.

"No, Reigna. You did the right thing. Ultimately, little Ella could not have survived here."

"I'm sorry too, Mara," Eden offered.

"I know. But I'm going to be all right. Now," she said, taking in a deep breath and squaring her shoulders, seeking to sound stronger than she felt, "as I was saying, we need a plan."

"Well, of course, the first order of business is to get these cells open," Aliza said, banging her tin cup on the bars. "Perhaps I can convince one of the guards that he should follow my orders and open them."

"I doubt that would work," Mara said, "since they are all well aware of your true identity." She paused, then added, "I sure hope Lucy gets some answers on our leak."

"Yes," Dixon agreed.

"And you're right—about my use of my magic," Aliza said. "Truth to tell, I've tried—unsuccessfully, I'm sorry to say. The guards just give me a strange look and then move on."

"All right then," Mara said, "for the sake of our discussion, let's assume we manage to get out of our cells. Then what would we do?"

"If there are guards here at the time, Mara," Dax said, "as I suggested to you earlier, you could sing them to sleep. If everyone knew in advance, a cue that you would use to indicate that you were about to do so, they could be ready for it."

"Ready for it?" Reigna asked.

"Yes. You'd all have to cover your ears so that you wouldn't hear her and fall to her magic. Of course, I wouldn't be subject to it in any case."

"And try to make our escape in broad daylight? I don't think so," Dixon said.

"If the opportunity arises, we try to make our escape no matter the time of day or night," Dax said. "We need to prepare for any eventuality."

"Reigna and I could get away under Mother's cloak."

"No," Mara said, "I'll take you girls with me."

"If we get free," Aliza ventured, "you have to get the twins to safety first, Mara. Then Dixon should take Dax with him."

"No," Dax said.

"You are more important to Oosa's troops than I am," she argued. "They need you. You'll find a new second-in-command. I'm afraid I'll be a casualty to this war," she ended in a whisper.

"No, you will not. I'm the commander here, don't forget."

"I've only one problem with that," Mara said.

"What's that?" Reigna asked.

"I would never be able to face Nina again if I had the chance to see Carlie to safety, but failed to take it."

"Then take her in my place," Eden said.

"No!" Mara exclaimed. "That is not an option."

"Dixon, if you can, you should take her instead of me," Aliza suggested.

No one said anything.

"Dixon?"

"Fine, Aliza, I will." Then he asked, "Should we plan, Mara, to meet up somewhere afterward?"

"Mara," Reigna interrupted, "we could always go to the place where we first met Zarek. You know—by those two rocks at the stream. Our captors tied the boats to them."

"No, I'm sorry. I wasn't conscious. Remember?"

"Oh yes, of course, that's right. Well in any case, if you headed out from the city gates and went straight west, you'd find it. From there the river runs to an area near Aliza's former camp."

"Actually, I think we should all head for Marshall's camp. That way, we'll know everyone—" She swallowed hard. "That way we'll know that everyone we could get out safely, made it." She paused and then said, "If we should have to leave either or both of you, Dax and Aliza, Dixon and I will come back for you as soon as possible."

Then, "What of Broden?" Eden asked.

"Eden—" Reigna started.

"I refuse to believe that he's doing any of this voluntarily."

"We've seen nothing to suggest anything to the contrary," her twin argued.

"And how, exactly, would he let us know that? They watch him continuously."

"I'm sorry, Eden, I just don't trust him."

For a moment, no one said anything.

Then, "Once Aliza and I are out of here," Dax piped up, "her magic will again be of use."

"True," Aliza agreed.

"Now," he continued, "back to plans. What signal, Mara, will you give when you intend to make the guards sleep?"

Mara watched as a cockroach ran up the wall at her side. She grabbed her pack and flung it at the creature. When it fell to the floor, she stomped on it, repeatedly, not quitting until certain it was dead. Then she kicked it away, out of her sight.

"Cockroach," she said by way of explanation. Then, "I'll hit the bars hard, three times, with my tin cup here," she said as she struck the bars with it, but not too loudly.

"Got it," Dixon said.

"It's a plan," Dax agreed. "Now, what about these locks and these bars?"

With that, they all went silent.

Chapter Forty-Seven

Lucy had intended to drop Basha off and then head directly back to the city, but events at the border camp delayed her. Each day brought new dangers, problems, and warnings. Now, dawn not having even arrived, yet another descended upon them all.

She jerked up at the sound of screaming.

"Stop him! Stop him!" someone shouted.

"Hurry!" another voice called out.

Sitting up, Lucy grabbed her boots to don them. Then, thinking better of the delay it would cause, she jumped down from the wagon that had been allotted her, and ran toward the commotion. Soon, several more Oathtakers came running out from their wagons and tents, joining her. As they lit flares to help guide their way, they all rushed toward the sound.

The screams of horses filled the air.

"This way!" someone cried.

When Lucy arrived at the center of a newly formed crowd, she found Trumble with his arms around a child, trying to keep him from getting loose. The boy struggled, kicked his legs with wild abandon, and then tried to bite his captor.

Basha stood nearby. "He's not going to hurt you!" she cried, her comments clearly directed at the child.

"What is it?" Lucy asked as she approached.

Trumble, having managed to get the child under control, glanced her way. "Can you believe this? He's just a kid!"

Several more Oathtakers drew near.

"What's happened?" Lucy asked.

Trumble asked one of the newcomers to take the lad and to keep him restrained. Then he motioned toward the line of horses.

"What's happened?" Lucy repeated her question.

"I'll show you."

He headed off, down the line of squealing mounts, all prancing in place and pulling at the ropes that tied them down, their eyes wild. Soon, he pointed down at three horses on the ground. A pool of blood surrounded them. The beasts tried to rise, screaming and snorting in their efforts.

"Take them down," Trumble ordered the Oathtaker standing nearest him. Then he watched as the man quickly and definitively slit the equine's throats, bringing each, at last, to rest.

"The . . . boy . . . hamstrung them," he said as the third of the three beasts exhaled for its final time. I—" He dropped his head in his hands.

"You what?" Basha asked.

"Felicity awakened me, crying." Trumble got down on his haunches and patted the thigh of one of the now-dead mounts. Then, looking up at her, he asked, "You know how she spent days crying for someone she called 'Ella?'"

"Ella?" Lucy asked.

"Yes," Basha said.

"Who's that?"

"We've no idea who she was talking about."

"I see. What happened then, Trumble?" Lucy asked.

"Well, finally, I thought I'd managed to get her to concentrate on something else and . . . Basha, she's been riding your mare, Nightingale, right?"

"Yes."

"Well, Felicity told me I had to save Nightingale so that she wouldn't 'rain red.'"

Basha pulled back. "What? 'Rain red?'"

"I don't know how I put it together so quickly, but I guess my years with Felicity have given me some insight into how her mind works. I concluded Nightingale must be in danger, so I ran out here."

"And?"

"And I was so concerned with the horses' safety that I almost missed the fact that the perpetrator was just a boy. I saw him down here and came running this way. Right off, I found the first two mounts here, already on the ground. The third fell seconds later." He squared his shoulders. "I nearly used my blade on the boy as he ran. Thank goodness I realized he was just a child before I—"

"Threw Amora at him," Lucy said.

He nodded.

"How old do you suppose he is?" Basha asked.

"I don't know." He shook his head. "Ten? Twelve? Maybe?"

"You did the right thing," Lucy assured him, "but clearly, this cannot go on."

Basha stroked his arm. "I hate to admit it, but she's right."

He looked up at the next horse in line—the one that would have been the child's next target had he not intervened in time. It was Nightingale.

"I have to let Felicity know that she's all right," he said, patting the mare's rump. With that, he walked off.

Basha stepped to Lucy's side. "We need more troops here."

"Yes. I'll return to the city tomorrow and send more reinforcements this way before I journey into Chiran. But even more, we need to figure out what to do with all the little ones already here. I can see that this is one problem that it will take time to resolve."

He leaned in closer, gazing into the looking glass at the hollowed-out skull of his lord and master. He gloried in the heat emanating from the spirit. It burned into him, causing a pain that left him feeling euphoric. He longed to return to Chiran, where he belonged. He hated being away.

"It is soon time," he said.

"Zarek will be ready." The underlord released a burst of heat.

The man shuddered from the impact of it. Then, "There will be no room for mistakes," he said.

"Have no fear. Now, what hasss she ssssaid?"

"She has been away, so I have learned little of late. But I know how her mind works. If she gets her hands—"

"Not to fear. She will not get near the twinssss."

"What is Zarek's plan?"

"She will be taken into immediate cusssstody." Pleased with himself, the underlord laughed. "Resssst assured, she will have no opportunity to causssse harm."

"They have made it all so easy." The man shook his head, disdainfully.

"They are arrogant. They are weak and undisssssciplined. They say they are willing to die for their causssse, yet they take every measure to spare anyone from doing just that. By contrassssst, Zarek seeks to do my will, and he is willing to shed life for the furtherance of it."

"They value life too much," the man commented.

The underlord laughed. "Yesss, to their detriment. Asssss a consequencccce, we have already experienced great successesss at the border. I long to share all with you."

The man leaned back, directing his attention toward the sound of footfalls in the hallway. As they died away, he turned back.

"Soon," he said.

When Lucy arrived back in the city, she was so tired that she managed only to order a thousand troops to head to the border to assist Marshall and Basha, post-haste. Then she told Petrus they'd not head for Chiran until she was sufficiently rested. She had to keep her wits about her. Finally, a couple days later, she was prepared to go.

She stopped on her way to her final meeting with the other leaders before leaving, to see Percival. Stepping inside the scantily furnished room in which the authorities held him, she noted its single bed, bookcase, and dresser and mirror, before which Percival sat. On its top sat a bowl and pitcher of water for cleaning up.

Percival rose, then stepped toward a nearby table.

"Lucy," he greeted her, his voice clipped.

"I understand that you've yet to admit to any wrongdoing," she said.

"It wasn't me." A sheen of sweat glistened on his brow.

"So you say." She stepped nearer. "Yet your breaking into a sweat upon the mere sight of me is not a good sign, Percival. Are you nervous for some reason?"

"Huh. No. It's just . . . warm in here. Spring has finally arrived, but the guards won't unlock my windows to allow any fresh air inside."

"They can't allow for your possible escape." She approached the mirror and glanced at her reflection. "You will remain here until further notice," she said.

He sighed. "I need to get back to work."

She turned back to face him. "I don't have time to argue with you. I just thought you deserved an update."

He nodded. "Thank you. I appreciate it."

"When I return, I'll look into these matters further."

"Yes, I understand you're leaving again. I overheard one of the guards mentioning that you're headed for Chiran—with Petrus. But . . . that can't be. Right?"

Smirking, she shook her head. "I don't know how you're getting information to Zarek and his troops, so I'd be a fool to concede anything to you," she said.

"It wasn't me."

"Like I said, I'll look into this further upon my return."

"Fine, Lucy."

"Good. Until later, then." With that, she retreated.

Minutes later, upon arriving at the conference center, she headed down the hall. On her way, Joed, the man who'd spoken out on Percival's behalf earlier, drew to her side. Meeting her gait, stride for stride, their heels clicked on the hardwood floor, in unison.

"Are you going to release Percival now?" he asked.

She stopped short. "No, Joed, I am not."

He remained fixed to her side. "He is innocent. I'm convinced of it."

"If that's the case, then the truth will win out in due course."

Shaking his head, he sighed.

"Now, if you'll excuse me." With that, she opened the door to the meeting room and then stepped inside.

Jerrett and Velia, along with several leaders of the Oathtaker troops, stood to greet her.

She looked about. "Where is Petrus?"

"He hasn't arrived as yet," Jerrett said.

"I told him to be ready to go."

"I'm sure he'll be here soon." He pulled a chair out for her. "Are you sure we can't convince you not to go?"

She waved her hand at the chair. "I'm sure. I've no more time to waste here."

Velia patted her arm. "Have you been in contact with Mara?"

"Briefly. She sounded terrible, but was unwilling to share any details with me. In any case, Professor Hadwin agrees that I should at least get a look at what's going on there. My plan is to do just that. Of course, I'm hoping I'll be fortunate enough to get my hands on the twins. If that's possible, perhaps I can return here with them—or at least with one of them."

"I suppose it's worth a try."

Just then the door opened, and Petrus stepped inside.

"Oh good, you're here," Lucy said. "Are you ready to go?"

"I got your message earlier." He pulled on the bag hanging over his shoulder. "Why did I need to pack this? I thought you said you would deliver us directly to the prison."

"Yes—but sometimes traveling doesn't work the way one intends." She paused. "At least now that spring has arrived, we can manage all right if we do have to spend some time in the wilderness."

"Well, in any case, I am ready."

"Good." Lucy turned to address the other attendees. "As you know, I made arrangements for secreting away, information about the whereabouts of Rowena's other daughters in the event anything should happen to me. Have you any questions?"

"None," Velia said. "But Lucy, you should know that Jerrett and I won't be here in the city when you return."

"Oh?"

"We've decided we'll assist Marshall and Basha at the border."

"I see." She shrugged. "Well, if you think that's the right plan of action."

"We do," Jerrett said.

"Very well then." She stepped toward Petrus. "We'll grab a quick dinner and then, as I mentioned earlier, we'll leave shortly after dusk."

"Mara is unaware we are coming?" Petrus asked.

"That's right. Like you said, if she knew, she might act differently. I wouldn't want her inadvertently tipping off the guards that something is in the offing."

"Agreed."

"You were right, Petrus, to counsel me accordingly. Besides, she'd probably just try to talk me out of going."

She grabbed her pack. "So, are you ready then?"

"Yes."

"Good. Now, you won't feel anything," she said, taking his hands, "except perchance a slightly heady feeling. You'll probably see what looks like lights and colors, and then—hopefully—we'll land inside the prison. Mara says the guards leave at dusk, which settled a short while ago, so all should be quiet there when we arrive." She paused. "Listen, Petrus, as you know, if I get a chance to take one or both of the twins out of there, I intend to do just that. In that case, I'll do what I can to return for you later."

He nodded. "I agree with your plan—and rest assured, I understand the risks."

"Here we go, then."

With that, Lucy spun her magic. Surrounded by lights and colors, she noticed something different from any time she'd traveled before, namely, black streaks intermingled with the clear and vibrant colors she usually saw. She puzzled over the difference, determining that perhaps her magic sensed the danger of the place to which she headed and sought to warn her. Still, she remained focused on her destination.

Moments later, as her feet landed, she opened her eyes.

And that's when she felt it.

Chapter Forty-Eight

Overcome with frustration, Broden growled under his breath. He'd tried everything to gain an opportunity to be left alone with his friends, but over the past few days, even more of the succedunt soldiers attended him at the prison, than previously. They took up positions along the walls, one man standing a mere shoulder's distance away from the next. There they remained, hour after agonizing hour.

Not for the first time, he wondered why Zarek even bothered to have him there. Perhaps it was just to show him the futility of refusing to swear to serve Daeva. In any case, the only thing he and Carlie managed, was to provide the prisoners with their food. And unfortunately, because of the added guards, they'd not been particularly successful in bringing additional—and actually edible—rations to any of them. Still, Broden hoped that soon, he'd have the chance to speak privately with the twins, Mara, or one of the other Oathtakers.

He glanced up at the scant light coming in from the barred window in Mara's cell. Dusk was descending; it was time to leave for the day.

He grabbed the buckets of leftover gruel and water sitting nearby, then carried them out to the hallway leading away from the prison. From there, someone would take them to be refilled for the next day.

Marching back to where Carlie stood, just outside the twins' cell, he said, "It's time to go, Mouse."

He turned back around, nodded to the guards at his sides, and then stepped away. Seconds later, he realized something was amiss, as he'd expected Carlie's footsteps from behind, but didn't hear them.

Turning back, he found the guards barring her way.

Her fear-filled eyes flashed up at him.

"It's time to go," he repeated, taking a step back toward them all.

Two more men approached, flanking Broden. Each grabbed one of his elbows. "Let's go," one of them ordered.

He flung his arms out to release their hold. Then, "Come on, Mouse," he said, reaching for her.

She tried to step around the guards, but they refused her passage.

Broden watched as another guard lit torches dipped in pitch that lined the walls. He was confused. They'd never done that before.

The flames flickered and popped as the acrid smell of their burning filled the air.

"Let her go," he demanded, pointing at Carlie.

"Not this time," the lead guard responded.

Broden's eyes narrowed. "Is there something I should know?"

"No."

Carlie held his gaze, her eyes wide.

"Let her go," he tried again.

"Not now. We need her assistance."

"For what?"

"Never mind. We'll return her to you—safe and sound." He grinned at his cohorts. "In short order," he added.

"Go, Broden," she said.

He looked the men over carefully as he addressed them. "Very well then, but don't forget that she belongs to me. Zarek has ordered that no one else is to touch her."

He marched up to the leader. When he was close enough to smell the man's breath, he said, "You'd best return her unharmed." With that, he turned on his heels and headed out.

A few quiet minutes passed.

Then suddenly, out of nowhere, Lucy and Petrus landed in the midst of the hallway, between the cells, at a spot visible only to the twins and Mara. They watched on as, in a flash, several of the succedunt soldiers descended on them.

One struck Lucy over the head, even as Mara screamed for her to "Watch out!"

An almost inaudible whimper escaped Lucy's lips as she dropped to the floor.

Carlie struggled for a better view, but guards stood before her, not allowing her to see past them.

At Lucy's side, Petrus fell to his knees. "Leave her alone!" he cried. "Please! Don't hurt her!"

One of the guards grabbed his arm. "You're coming with us," he ordered, pulling him to his feet.

"Let me go!" He struggled to free himself.

"Now!" The man pulled at him, then dragged him away.

No sooner did they depart, than two other men neared Lucy.

"Check on her," one of them ordered Carlie.

Shaking, she crouched down at her side and then felt for her pulse. "She lives."

"Open that one!" he ordered one of his comrades, gesturing toward a cell situated across the hall from the twins and Mara.

The man did as bidden.

"Get her in there," he said to Carlie.

She dragged Lucy inside. Once done, she left her on the bed of filthy straw on the floor. "Now what?"

"Remove her blade and hand it to me. Hurry!"

Carlie removed Lucy's blade. She glanced at it, apparently considering whether she should use it. But of course, that would be folly. It's magic wouldn't work for her—and even if it could, she'd never be able to take down all the guards.

"Now!"

She handed it over.

"Now remove all the items from around her belt."

She followed his order.

"Careful. Bring them to me."

When she reached his side, he snatched the items from her hand.

"Out!" he ordered.

The moment she stepped out of the cell, he closed the door and jammed Lucy's blade in the lock. "Our work here is done," he said.

Then the men, with Carlie in their midst, marched out of the prison.

"Lucy. Lucy!" Reigna called. "Lucy, wake up!"

Slowly, she rolled her head from side to side. Then she put her hand on the spot where she'd been struck.

"Great Ehyeh," she mumbled, trying to sit up before falling back again.

"Are you all right? Lucy!" Eden cried.

She rubbed her head. "What happened?"

Fuming, Broden marched to his quarters. Upon arrival, he found his tutor, along with Yasmin, Farida, Ghazala, and Clementine, waiting for him.

"Where's Carlie?" Striver asked.

Audibly blowing out his breath, Broden shook his head. "They wouldn't let her leave with me."

"Why?"

"I don't know, but something's up." He paced, then stopped dead in his tracks. "If they hurt her, I swear—"

"She'll be all right," Striver tried to assure him.

"Listen, we need to move forward with our plan as quickly as possible," Broden said. "I've got to get my friends alone—even if only for a minute. They think I'm on Zarek's side in all of this. I need for them to know the truth!"

"We're ready with the plan," Yasmin said.

Broden stood, one hand on his hip. He wiped his other hand over the top of his head. "I wish I could offer you safety."

"This is more important, Broden."

"Still, I'd feel better if I knew for certain that the crystals would work for you." He held Yasmin's gaze. He was grateful he'd carried some of the miniature weapons when captured from the compound, and even more so, that he'd managed to hold on to them all this time. Even so, there would be no opportunity to test in advance, whether they'd work for her and his other friends.

"If not, we'll come up with something else," Striver offered.

"No matter what happens," Broden said, "if they catch you and take you hostage, I won't be able to do anything about it." He choked back a cry

"We know, Broden," Yasmin said. "It's all right."

"You should use the resulting confusion to make your way to safety," he suggested.

"There is no safety here in Chiran."

He growled in frustration. "Fine. Let's go over the plan again then."

Striver directed Broden to a table. Before him, he placed a sketch that he'd made of the women's prison.

"We've determined that the place where Zarek is holding your friends is probably right about . . . here." He tapped on the drawing. "Now, when we get an opportunity, we'll throw a few of the crystals to cause explosions. From what you told me about these weapons, you should hear the commotion from where you're stationed."

"That's what we discussed, yes," Broden agreed, nodding.

"How big are the explosions, did you say? How far away do we need to be?"

Broden pointed toward the door. "No closer than from me to there, for sure," he said.

"So, that's about . . . six, maybe seven full strides," Farida said.

"Yes, that sounds about right." Broden turned back to Striver. "Show me where you'll throw them."

The tutor looked his drawing over. "We don't want to hurt any of the women prisoners unnecessarily, but we'd like to take out as many of the guards as we can and cause as much other damage as possible." Once again, he tapped on the map. "You see here?" he asked.

"Yes."

"Some weapons arrived today. They're in a wagon that will stay there until guards arrive the day after tomorrow to unload it. The remainder will be sent to the border."

"That was fortuitous—that they just arrived, I mean."

"Yes, and," Striver grinned, "there's more in storage right about here." He pointed at another spot on the map.

"More weapons? Since when?"

"Earlier today, several other loads arrived."

"Yes," Yasmin said, "and tomorrow three wagonloads of women who were captured near the Oosian border are due in, as well. The guards will march them past the building right here." She showed him the place.

"With your help," Broden said.

"Right. As always, I'm to assist with keeping the women calm and directing them inside until they're due to depart again."

"But the guards might see you if you throw a crystal."

She knelt at his side. "I don't think so. They are very small, these weapons of yours. When I'm sure the guards' attention is diverted, I'll throw one at the door, here," she said, noting another spot on the map. "We might as well cripple Zarek's cause as much as possible while we're at it."

"The explosions should alert the guards on your side of the prison, to the problem," Striver commented. "Then you must convince them that they should run to lend aid. Hopefully, they'll look on it as a sign that you're on their side."

"And when the guards leave my side of the prison to help you, I'll get a chance to talk with my friends," Broden said.

"That's right."

"Are you sure about this?" He looked at each of his friends in turn.

"They'll never know we caused the trouble," Striver said. "We'll make sure of it."

Broden paced. "Is there any way you can use the distraction to escape? Take Yasmin and the others with you?"

Farida stepped up. "Striver, if the opportunity arises, you should go. But you can't take everyone. So you must take Clementine first."

Yasmin and Ghazala nodded their agreement.

"No," Broden said. "Tomorrow, Clementine goes with Mouse and me. I can't have her in the middle of all of this."

"Very well," Striver agreed.

"All right. One last time then: are you sure about this?" Broden asked.

"We can do it," Farida said.

Broden sat down and reached for Clementine. When she stood before him, he cupped her elbows. "I'm concerned for you," he said, looking into her eyes. "I pray nothing goes wrong tomorrow. I just want you to know how terrible I feel— putting you in the middle of all this."

The girl glanced at the others, then turned back. "It's all right, Broden," she said.

He rubbed the back of his neck, then put his hand on the drawing. "Fine then, we're agreed," he said. "Now, I won't need much time, but the more ruckus you cause, the more likely I'll get my chance to speak to my friends."

"Tomorrow then?" Striver asked.

"Yes. Tomorrow."

At that moment came a shuffling sound outside the door.

Striver grabbed his drawing and rushed to the fireplace. He dropped it over the flames just as the door opened.

A guard stood in the threshold. "Broden," he said, "Zarek awaits you."

Moaning, Lucy sat up.

"Are you all right?" Mara asked.

"Yes, I'm . . ." She rubbed her head. "Never mind me. How about you? How are you feeling?"

Mara briefly explained how she'd lost Mariella.

"Mariella?"

"Yes, 'Ella' for short."

"Ella! Oh, goodness."

"What is it?" Dixon asked.

"Oh, Mara, Dixon, Basha was telling me the other day that Felicity had been crying for one she called 'Ella,' for the longest time. No one knew who she was talking about." She swallowed hard. "I am so sorry for your loss."

"Thank you, Lucy," they responded in unison.

A quiet minute passed. Then Reigna spoke up. "You took quite a blow to the head."

Lucy groaned. "I'm going to kill him," she said.

"Who?"

"Percival." She seethed. "I don't know how he managed to get information to Zarek, but clearly, he did." She stood, unsteadily, then approached the bars of her cell. On sight of Vivacitas, she grabbed her weapon's handle and pulled.

"You won't be able to loosen it," Mara said, "so you can save your breath."

She tried, nevertheless.

"Why did you come here? I told you not to."

Still struggling with her blade, Lucy said, "I wanted to help."

"And now look where we are."

"Lucy, who was that with you?" Reigna asked.

She let go of Vivacitas. Then, pacing, she said, "That was Petrus."

"Who?" Dax called out.

"Petrus. You remember. You trained with him. Petrus Feoras. He's been assisting us in your stead."

"Ahhh, Lucy . . . I don't think so."

"What are you talking about?"

Dax was silent for long seconds. Then he said, "Lucy, tell me again about Petrus's charge."

The other Oathtakers and the twins all drew near the bars of their cells, curious as to what he was talking about.

"What's this all about?" Dixon asked.

"Tell me, Lucy," Dax said again.

She sighed. "I don't understand what all the fuss is about. Like I told you, Petrus had a charge. He swore to his safety shortly before I first met him—and that was—Oh goodness, it was decades ago. His charge's name was 'Tam.' He was just a child at the time."

Again, Dax went quiet for some time. Then finally, he said, "You told me when we were in the city, that you wanted to recruit Petrus. If I recall correctly, you also told me that his charge had only recently died of old age."

"That's right." Lucy huffed. "Honestly, Dax, what is the problem? They've taken Petrus away—likely for further questioning. He knows all about our plans and might be forced to give the information over. You know, Percival knew that Petrus would be with me. He must have informed Zarek of that fact!"

She paced. Then, she said, "Presumably, Percival also told him about our various powers. They must have concluded that Petrus would pose little risk to Zarek. That's why they captured him. Oh, great Ehyeh," she moaned, "what if they torture him for information? His attendant power that allows for him to withstand significant pain could prove helpful, but even it won't last forever. What if they hurt him?"

"I don't think that's our primary problem," Dax said.

Lucy stomped on a skittering roach. "What are you talking about?"

The sounds of Dax's pacing filled the air. Then, "Lucy," he said, "if it's true that Tam died only recently, then why is Petrus an old man?"

She pulled back. "An old man! An old man? He's as youthful as I am!"

"No, he is not."

"What are you saying?"

"I'm saying that if his charge died only recently, that he should, as you say, appear as young as you. But the man who was here, did not."

"I thought he looked young," Mara said.

"Trust me," Dax said, "he must be using some sort of glamour or something. Whatever magic it is, it worked on you all, but not on me. I saw through it."

"But what could that mean?"

"Dax, I'm sure you're mistaken," Lucy interrupted. "There wasn't much light in here. You just didn't see clearly."

"I saw clearly, Lucy. That man was *old*. As I think on it, I agree that it was Petrus—but an *old* Petrus. He must have lied to you about his charge. And Lucy— if he lied to you about that, what else do you suppose he might have lied to you about?"

Chapter Forty-Nine

His heels clicked on the floor as, guarded, he made his way to Zarek's room of mirrors. He'd never been inside it before and was confused as to the man's unusual request. Why ask to see him now? Had Striver or one of the women deceived him? Had someone told Zarek something of their plans? Surely, none of them would have betrayed him. *Would they?* But if not, whatever else could be going on?

As they neared, he noticed more guards coming down another hallway toward them. In their midst was Brother Pestifere, and at his side, a grut.

Involuntarily groaning at the discovery that the priest had returned, Broden cocked his head. The man looked different, somehow. He wasn't using his staff—and he walked without his usual limp.

"In," a guard said, his voice clipped.

Following his command, Broden stepped inside.

There, Zarek sat, surrounded by mirrors. "Sit," he ordered.

He sat.

Just then, Pestifere entered.

Broden's eyes narrowed upon sight of him. Yes, there was something different. He looked—refreshed.

"Welcome home," Zarek greeted the priest.

"It is good to be back."

"How'd my guards do?"

Pestifere cracked the closest thing to a grin that Broden had ever seen. "Excellently. She is in custody." He turned Broden's way, suddenly all business. "Now, about you—"

Broden got to his feet.

"I said, 'sit,'" Zarek ordered him. Once he'd complied, the emperor turned to Pestifere. "You know we can't force this."

The priest glared at Broden. "You are running out of time. Your . . . *father*," he stressed the word with a grimace, "needs to know where your loyalties lie. So . . . whose side are you on?"

Broden leaned back. At this stage, he contemplated just telling the truth. But if Zarek killed him, his friends would never know what really happened.

"I'm not ready to commit," he finally said.

"Daeva!" Pestifere called.

In the midst of one of the mirrors, a ghoulish countenance burst forth, surrounded by what appeared to be flames that, notwithstanding their heat, consumed nothing. Instantly, the temperature in the room rose, and with it came smoke in twisted tendrils, looking as though it climbed up a trellis.

Broden broke out in a sweat. The heat and smoke made breathing difficult.

"Meet Daeva, the chief underlord," Zarek said.

He looked at the spirit. He felt the evilness of the creature crawl over his skin. So this was what his mother had followed—what his father followed, even now. Did they know something he did not? What was the attraction?

"Sssssso, we finally meet," Daeva said.

Broden nodded.

"Brother Pesssstifere is right. You are nearly out of time, my young one. But you should know that the other sssside—that of Ehyeh and Hissss Select and Oathtakersssss—hassss failed. You want to be winner, do you not?"

He shrugged. "I suppose."

"Then sssswear your allegianccce to me before it issss too late."

For a moment he contemplated what it might be like if he did as they asked. It certainly would make things easier. But then, shaking his head, he said, "I'm not prepared to do so, as yet."

Pestifere stomped his foot. "What is keeping you?"

Broden turned his way. "All I've ever asked of you, is answers to my questions. Until I get them, I'm unable to make a decision."

"Take him away!" the priest growled.

At that moment, the door opened, a guard entered, and then, quite unceremoniously, he ushered Broden out.

When he arrived back at his suite, he found Carlie, safe and sound. She was seated at the table, a cup of rose petal and lemongrass tea before her, its sweet scent filling the air.

She jumped to her feat. "Broden!"

"Oh, thank Ehyeh!" he cried. He ran to her and wrapped his arms around her. "I'm so sorry, Mouse! I didn't want to leave you behind, but . . . there was nothing I could do."

"I'm fine," she assured him, patting his chest, "but all is not well."

"What happened?"

"Sit down." Once he'd done so, she told him about Lucy's arrival and capture.

"She had someone with her, you say?"

"Yes."

"Who?"

"I don't know. In all the confusion, I didn't get a good look."

Broden slumped. He rubbed the back of his neck. "Wait a minute?" he said, jerking back up.

Striver, listening in, approached. "What is it?"

Broden explained about his audience with Zarek, Pestifere, and the lord of the underworld.

Striver's eyes narrowed. "Brother Pestifere is back?"

"Yes." Broden tapped on the table. "And . . ."

"And what?

"And Pestifere told Zarek that 'she' was in custody. You know . . . I think Lucy brought him here."

"What?" Carlie cried.

"I think she brought him here. I do! Pestifere seemed very pleased with himself." He shook his head. "But how could she do that? I thought she—"

"Don't jump to conclusions," Striver cautioned him. "As to Pestifere telling Zarek that 'she' was in custody, even assuming he meant Lucy, it doesn't follow that Pestifere arrived here with her."

"No, Broden, I think you're right." Carlie put her cup down on a saucer to a *clink* sound. "I didn't recognize him in the prison because I didn't get much of a look, but even then I thought there was something . . . familiar about him. As you well know, he ordered me beaten some time ago. His voice is one I'm not likely to forget—ever. It was him! I'm sure of it!"

Broden's jaw clenched. Then, "Did anything else happen?" he asked her.

She explained how Zarek's guards had made her strip Lucy of her blade and other weaponry, as well as of the bag of crystals that generally hung from her belt.

Broden dropped into a chair. "When does this end?" He hung his head.

"There has to be something we can do," Carlie said.

Turning her way, Broden confirmed that the next day, they would set their plans into motion.

Carlie patted his knee. "Good. When Striver and the others cause their disturbance, you might at least get the opportunity to tell Lucy the truth. Maybe she'll be able to think of something that you—that we—can do to help them all."

"There's nothing else to be done," Striver agreed.

Sighing, Broden said, "I've missed Lucy so much. She's been like a mother to me. You know?"

He stood, made his way to a window and looked out. "I appreciate that a lot of people find her . . . difficult, but I owe my life to her. Without her intervention, Ehyeh only knows what might have happened to me."

Stepping up, Carlie patted his back in commiseration.

"I don't know why she would have brought Pestifere here," he said, "but— Well, things aren't always what they seem, I guess. In any case, without firm evidence that she intended any harm, I'd do anything to help her."

CHAPTER FIFTY

With both Mugger and Mother gone, Pestifere had been free to devote his time to Zarek. In truth, he doted on him. Meanwhile, the boy never failed to please. Indeed, he committed his own first murder shortly after Mother's death.

Yes, the boy was strong, bright—and best of all—without restraint.

He introduced the child soon after he met him—in his seventh year—to Daeva. Fortunately, the underlord approved. Seven years later, he re-introduced him. Now old enough, mature enough, aware enough, to make decisions and to appreciate the consequences of them, he asked Zarek if he wanted to swear his allegiance to the underlord.

He did.

I wanted to get rid of Lucy—but a simple murder wasn't good enough for her. No, that which she perceived as her first interest—the Select—should go down with her. So, I made my plans, while Daeva made his. Fortunately, they coincided.

About that time, the underlord discovered Lilith's hatred for her sister. When, in her childish anger and resentment, she'd vowed with the vigor that only a young one could, that she'd do anything to destroy Rowena, he visited her. It was a connection the two would maintain over the years.

Time passed. Finally, when Zarek's twenty-first year arrived, he once again, re-committed himself to the lords of the underworld. Meanwhile, Lilith reached the ripe age of fourteen. She hadn't given up on her hopes of destroying her sister. Thus, she confirmed with Daeva that she would follow him; she needed him.

Since Lilith was willing to do what it would take to bring Rowena down, Daeva agreed to help her. It was unlikely, after all, that her own Oathtaker—Marshall—would ever notice her change in allegiance. He'd sworn his oath for her protection when she was just an infant—back when she was fully innocent.

Daeva knew the Oathtaker's bond to her would be severed as a consequence of her actions, but doubted the man would ever notice. It was more likely that he'd blame himself for failing her in some regard. Who, after all, would ever expect that such a young one could turn so completely against her own kind? But she, like Zarek earlier, had been fully aware in her teen years of what it was that she was doing. And so, Daeva would use her.

It was then that their plans truly began to take shape.

Over the years, until Lucy took refuge at the compound where he was unable to locate her, Pestifere left Zarek from time to time to return to Oosa—to spy on Lucy. He recalled in detail, the day he'd discovered her connection to Rowena. He knew it would devastate Lucy to lose her. Thus, he contemplated a simple assassination. But upon informing the underlord of all he'd learned, Daeva urged him to exercise patience, as his goal was to destroy not only Rowena, but the Select as a whole—once and for all. Wouldn't that be better, the underlord reasoned? Wouldn't Lucy suffer all the more?

Yes, she would—and Lilith had offered the perfect opportunity to bring that suffering about.

Rowena continued with her mission to bring about a seventh born daughter of a seventh born daughter of the Select. As she concentrated on her interests, he helped Daeva with plans for Lilith and Zarek. He was devastated when those plans did not work. Then he and the underlords spent the next two decades coming up with a new scheme.

And finally, it was coming to fruition.

CHAPTER FIFTY-ONE

Mara got into position, her palms and tiptoes on the floor, her body parallel to it. Her exercises were helping her to build back her strength. Still, it always seemed that muscle was lost much more quickly, than gained. She dropped down, lifted herself back up, then repeated the procedure, over and over again, counting out.

When she reached fifty, she jumped to her feet. She bent over and touched the floor several times. Then she stood with her legs wide, one foot directed straight toward the bars, her knee bent. She pointed her other foot to the side and ground it to the floor. Then she held her arms out at her sides. She stretched toward her bent knee and the bars, then to the back of the cell, then toward the bars again. With her front knee still bent, she squared her hips toward it. Fisting her hands together, she bent at her waist, and stretched over her bent knee.

In short order, her front leg shook from the added weight. Slowly, she straightened it. Then she lifted her back foot off the floor until her leg was parallel to it. She balanced, arms still forward, her hands still fisted. When she could hold the position no longer, she repeated it on her other side.

"Are you all right, Mara?" Reigna asked.

"Fine," she muttered through gritted teeth. Fortunately, her stretching, power-building exercises didn't take much room to do, and they kept her busy. As an added bonus, they also cleared her mind.

"What do you make of the situation with Petrus?"

She released her position. Then she stood on her tiptoes, her hands high above her head, balancing. Dropping her arms down and returning firmly to the soles of her feet, she approached the bars.

"I don't know what to make of it," she said.

"I'm sure Dax is wrong," Lucy sounded out.

"I'm sure I'm not," he said.

"Well, I'm not sure of anything anymore," Eden said. "You know, I've maintained that Broden is innocent—and I think I'm right. Those guards made sure he was removed from here last night before you arrived, Lucy. There must have been a reason for that."

"I don't want to think badly of him," Reigna said, "but if Petrus could fool

Lucy, then maybe Broden could fool you, Eden."

Just then, Broden and Carlie arrived for the day, along with the guards.

Pursuant to his usual routine, Broden grabbed the buckets of gruel and water. He shuddered at the sight of the bugs that crawled in the food and at the scum that floated atop the water. Then he made his way down the hall, Carlie in his wake.

When he arrived at the twins' cell, he glanced in at Lucy in the one opposite. She looked awful. Her hair was in a mess and her eyes were black and blue. Quickly, he averted his gaze.

Eden approached the bars, then whispered, "I still believe in you, Broden."

Noting a guard coming near, he flinched.

"See, Eden?" Reigna muttered to her twin. "He can't even look at Lucy. And the idea that you still believe in him unsettles him. So maybe he still has a conscience after all—however seared."

The guard stopped in front of Broden. "Zarek will be stopping by for a visit today," he said.

"Oh?"

"Yes. It seems he'd like to welcome our newest . . . guest." Looking in at Lucy, he chuckled.

"I see." Broden's eyes flickered briefly her way. "Ahhh . . . when?" Would the emperor stop by when Striver and Yasmin intended to cause a disturbance? If so, that could ruin his chance of getting to talk to his friends.

"Any time now."

Broden breathed a sigh of relief. Striver wouldn't act until twilight.

From down the hall came the sounds of footsteps shuffling, and heels *click-clacking*. They grew louder by the second.

Moments later, Zarek appeared. He marched onward until he stood just outside Lucy's cell. Upon arrival, he said, his brow arched and with a wide smile, "So good of you to stop by."

She spat at him.

"Now, now," he mocked her.

"Where is he?" Lucy asked. "Where is Petrus? What have you done with him?"

At that moment another person entered. His feet shuffled, making a *swish-swishing* sound. He made his way down the row of cells until he stood at Zarek's side. There he stopped and looked in at her.

"Petrus!" she cried. "Are you all right?"

"That's not Petrus," Broden said.

"Like I'd believe you!" Lucy growled at him. "You . . . traitor!"

Zarek folded his arms. "Go on then, Broden, tell her," he said.

"It's Brother Pestifere."

She glared at him. "Who?"

He pursed his lips, then looked hard at Lucy. "It's Brother Pestifere. He is Zarek's spiritual mentor."

"Wh—" Lucy stepped back. "He— You—"

Pestifere drew nearer. "He is right. Like so many other things, I left the name 'Petrus' behind."

"How— Why—"

He closed his eyes and shook his head in disdain. "You are such a fool, Lucy." He sneered.

She struggled to find words. Finally, she cried, "I don't believe you! You're an Oathtaker!"

"I *was* an Oathtaker."

She turned away, paced. "How could you turn like that?"

"How could you turn from *me?*"

She stared at him. "That's what this is about? Because I was unwilling— Because I wouldn't allow you to break your oath for—"

"For what, Lucy?" Pestifere pursed his lips. "Let me just say that you made it clear to me that if I wanted anything to say about my future, I would have to find another way."

She rubbed her head. "I don't understand. You swore to uphold Ehyeh's way."

"Yes, and I changed my mind. I was not the first to do so, you know, and I am sure I will not be the last."

"But you could have renounced your vow. Sure, you might have been found guilty of treason, perhaps served some time . . . But this?"

"Yes, well, I made my choice—and it was a good one. How do you think I managed to create a mechanism from which you cannot break free?"

He ran his bony finger along the lock on her door and in which her blade was jammed. "You see this here?" he asked. "This metal was once my blade. When I turned to Daeva, he told me how to use Ehyeh's own weapon against Him. I fashioned this prison," he added with a wave of his hand to indicate their surroundings, "with locks on the cells made from other blades like my own." He leaned in closer. "That is, from the blades of Oathtakers who turned away—the blades of those who ended the lives of their former charges so as to free themselves from their oaths." His lips turned up into a near smile. "They create a direct link to Sinespe. So your Vivacitas, in contact with a blade like mine, is rendered . . . useless."

"You killed your charge? You killed Tam?"

He nodded.

"Dax says that in truth, you're an old man. So . . . you must have murdered Tam when he was still young."

"Shortly after we parted ways, years back, yes."

Her mouth moved as though she couldn't find words. Then she asked, "How is it that there was no hearing following his death?"

Pestifere scoffed. "By eliminating his parents as well, of course. Who else would have had reason to ask around about him? Then I moved here, to Chiran."

She stared at him. "No doubt you waited to 'join' our cause until after Dax left with Dixon. You knew Dax could see through to the truth. But . . . how is it that you still manage to look young to the rest of us?"

"Through the use of a hex . . . and with Daeva's assistance, of course."

She turned away, then quickly looked back. "You say there have been others?"

"Do you really find that thought so unbelievable? Of course there have been others."

"And you used their blades to make the other locks on the other cells here?"

"I did, indeed."

Lucy stood mute for long seconds. She rubbed her temples. Then, "You framed Percival," she said.

Pestifere stood, mute.

"You left that note—and those books and maps in his room!" Her eyes narrowed. "And it was you who hid in the closet and spied on my meeting with Jerrett and Velia. You must have gone to the conference room later to steal a good look at the map." She glared at him.

Still, he said nothing.

She pondered. "I take it you were responsible for Salus's disappearance?"

The corners of Pestifere's lips turned up into an actual smile.

"What did you do to him? And why? Did he find out something you didn't want disclosed?"

Pestifere grunted. "Suffice it to say, he served a purpose."

Her mouth hung open. "Lucky for you, the barkeep at The Swindler's Cup erred as I did, mistaking Percival for you."

"You believed what you wanted to believe about me, Lucy—and about him."

"You see, Broden?" Zarek said to him. "It's like I told you. With me, you're on the winning side. Her way," he pointed at Lucy, "will no longer be an option for anyone."

"What do you want, Petrus?" Lucy asked.

"From you? Nothing. Not anymore."

"Leave," she ordered through gritted teeth.

Zarek, watching on, laughed outright.

She glared at him. "How long do you intend to hold us here? What is it you want anyway?"

Leaning in, the chains about his neck rattling, the emperor whispered, "I want to see you die. Your demise will convince all Oosians—like Broden here, who knows the truth—that Ehyeh's battle is already lost." He grinned and then added, "I now hold all of Oosa's most trusted leaders, hostage. What pleasure Brother Pestifere and I will have witnessing your misery as you watch at least some of your friends go before you. All we need do now, is determine who of you will be first."

With that, he and the priest walked away.

CHAPTER FIFTY-TWO

Striver, Yasmin, Farida, and Ghazala, reported to duty at the women's prison, as usual. Throughout the morning, Yasmin and Farida selected women to fill two caravans for transport. Striver struggled to keep the guards' attentions from the fact that, whenever possible, they chose the oldest and weakest of the prisoners. Meanwhile, Ghazala, as the guards had long since ordered, sorted through the women's belongings for anything of value. Slowly, a pile of miscellaneous coins, along with the occasional valuable trinket, or jewel, grew. Zarek would use the riches to fund his venture.

The day dragged on. As usual, the air was filled with the women's crying, and with their pleas for help. Added to them came the ominous and grating howls of the grut, scattered about the prison grounds.

Striver hated turning his back on the captives, but there was nothing he could do for them, so he stayed on task.

Around noon, a group of succedunt warriors arrived. A woman—Tanith—accompanied them. Striver knew her from the dinner with Zarek, months hence, when he'd accompanied Broden. Since then she'd returned regularly to escort new prisoners to the camp that she supervised, in Darth. This time, she caused added friction when she took over Yasmin's job of sorting through the prisoners to choose those she would take back with her. She preferred younger women at her camp, she explained to them all.

Midday came and went, as wagons rambled in and out. All the while, Striver kept a close eye on the whereabouts of those women who would play such critical roles in events to come. Then afternoon settled in. Goodness, but it seemed to drag on and on.

Finally, Striver noted that the sun neared the western horizon. Within minutes would come the gloaming.

He approached Yasmin as she struggled to separate a mother from her young daughter. The child couldn't have been more than twelve years of age. The two clung to one another, weeping.

"Are you about through here?" he asked.

"These are the last two," Yasmin said, tears in her eyes. "I'm trying to keep the young one at camp here, but her mother won't part with her."

Tanith stepped up, unexpectedly. "That's enough," she said as she grabbed the child's arm and yanked her loose from her mother's grip. She pushed her toward the group of prisoners she'd selected earlier and then ordered the child's mother to step aside.

Striver couldn't help himself. He approached the mother, then muttered near her ear, "Keep an eye on your daughter. Be prepared to rush to her side. When the opportunity arises, take her and run. Run for all you're worth. Head west for Oosa. Do not look back."

She pulled back and looked up at him, her eyes narrowed.

He nodded at her before turning toward where Yasmin stood. When she acknowledged him with a raised finger, he looked over the crowd again, eventually catching Farida's eye. Then came Ghazala. Once sure each of the women had her attention on him, he nodded, almost imperceptibly.

Per their prearranged plan, Ghazala returned to the prison entrance. She stood at the door, waiting. When her cohorts saw that she'd arrived there safely, they set out with their plan.

Yasmin strolled to the back of the transport wagon she'd been emptying. From there, the building full of weapons was located several long strides away. Fortunately, the door to it was open. She collected a crystal from the pack about her waist, pulled her arm back, and then, with an underhand toss, threw it inside.

At the same time, Striver targeted a spot beneath a now-empty wagon, around which several guards had gathered.

Farida did the same.

The explosions came one right after the next. More followed, when Striver and the women threw additional crystals at added targets.

Pandemonium erupted. The air filled with smoke, shouting, and screaming, as prisoners dashed away from the center of activity. Meanwhile, nearby guards, some leading chained grut, ran toward the commotion.

Striver searched through the smoke-filled air struggling for a view of Ghazala. He spotted her just as Yasmin and Farida reached her side.

He dashed toward them all.

Upon arrival, he grabbed Ghazala's hand. "Did you unlock the cells in the women's prison?" he asked her.

"Yes! The moment the first explosion sounded out."

"Good." Then, pulling her along, he ran. Yasmin and Farida followed.

A moment later, he stumbled over a body. He got up on his haunches to take a closer look. It was Tanith. Apparently she'd been on the other side of the wagon that blew up when he threw the first of his crystals. Blood oozed down the side of her head. Debris from the explosion dusted her face and hair, melding in with the gray streak at her widow's peak.

He reached down and felt for a pulse. She was dead. *So, Ehyeh is real after all*, he thought, satisfied with the result.

"It couldn't have happened to a more deserving person," Yasmin muttered.

"Yes," he agreed. "Now, hurry! Run!"

With that, the four of them set out in the midst of the confusion.

Through the pandemonium, they made their way nearer to the city wall. He, quickly assessing the situation before them, motioned for the women to duck for cover with him, behind a wagon. Then he grabbed another crystal from his pocket. He had to cause another distraction if they were to make their way any farther.

"Right there," Yasmin suggested, peeking out from the side of the wagon with him. She pointed out a team of nearby succedunt guards who were rounding up some of the escaping women prisoners who'd managed to make their way this far.

"But—I could harm some of them—some of the women."

She grabbed his arm. When he turned to face her, she held his gaze. "Striver, they're dead if they're taken anyway. Now, do it! Or I will."

Nodding, he stood and peeked out from behind the wagon.

Just then, a guard prepared to release the grut at his side. As the beast howled, Striver threw his crystal. It landed next to the grut and in the midst of a pack of soldiers on horseback. With the resulting explosion, the beast went up in flames and disappeared. The smell of sulphur filled the air as two horses and their riders went down. Dust and smoke billowed, mingling with the screeches of the nearby women and of the downed equines.

Two more mounts reared, screaming, their front hooves battling invisible opponents. They dropped their riders, then brought their front hooves down hard on them. With their ears pulled back and their eyes wild, they blew out hard through their noses, as they rose up and dropped back down again, pummeling the men.

Striver and the women ran to, and then skirted around, the corner of the city wall. Then, quite suddenly, Striver came to a stop.

A guard stood before him, a knife in hand, and with a grin on his face.

Yasmin dove, slamming her full weight into his knees, taking him down. As he hit the ground, the wind was knocked out from him in one great gust of expelled air.

Striver pulled a knife from a sheath at the man's waist, then thrust it before he could regain his breath.

As blood gurgled up into his throat, Yasmin grabbed Striver's hand. "Let's go!" she ordered.

"Wait!" Farida cried. "Look!"

Off to their side, several horses were hitched to a line of posts.

"This way!" Striver called as he ran toward them.

At that moment, a grut rushed their way.

Quickly, each of Striver and the women loosed the ties of one of the mounts. Then they all saddled up.

As they set off into the night, the grut turned back toward the mayhem.

When the explosions sounded out, the guards in the section of the prison where Mara, the twins, and the other Oathtakers resided, all jumped to attention.

"Hurry!" Broden cried. "Find out what's happening!"

The man nearest him stared at him, as though measuring him.

"Hurry!" he repeated. "I'll keep watch here. These prisoners can't escape. Now, go. Go!"

The man hesitated for a moment, then nodded. Seconds later, he ran out with his fellow guards at his heels.

"Gracious Good One!" Mara cried as the last of them exited.

"What is it, Mara? Are you all right?" Dixon cried.

"Yes! The explosion— The rock wall here cracked and— And my chain broke free from it!"

"Is it still bound to your wrist?" Reigna called.

It rattled when she grabbed and shook it. "Unfortunately, yes."

Lucy stepped to the bars. She glared at Broden who stood nearby, Carlie and Clementine at his side. "How could you?" she asked. "After all I've done to see to you and your safety all these years? It seems in retrospect that I should have let your mother have her way with you!" she spat.

He hung his head.

Reigna and Eden drew to the bars on their cell, watching the exchange.

"Yes, Broden, how could you?" Reigna asked.

"I still believe in you," Eden whispered.

He looked up at them, then turned back to Lucy, tears pooled in his eyes.

"Tell them Broden!" Carlie cried as Clementine leaned into her and started to cry. "The guards could return any minute. Hurry! Tell them!"

"I didn't join him, Lucy," Broden said. "I swear it."

"I don't believe you," she seethed.

"Listen to him!" Carlie begged.

Lucy looked at her, than back at Broden.

"I swear!" he cried. "Zarek has been trying all this time to get me to turn his way—to get me to follow Daeva. But I haven't. I didn't!" He rubbed the back of his neck in frustration.

"Look at this," he said, holding his arm up to show her the band he wore. "Zarek's men put this on me when I was captured at the compound. With it, he can make me feel pain. Now, I don't know what will happen to me as a result of all of this," he added, waving his hand to indicate his surroundings, "but I feel certain Zarek will believe I'm behind it—somehow. Still, I had to let you know."

"Are you behind it?"

"Yes! I had my friends cause the commotion out there," he said, gesturing toward the barred windows.

"Your friends?"

"Striver, my 'tutor' in all things Chiranian, and some women that Zarek 'assigned' to me—Yasmin, Farida, and Ghazala. I wanted to have a minute with you."

"You trusted them?" Lucy asked.

"Yes! But even if I hadn't, I would have chanced it. I wanted to put your mind at ease." He hung his head. Then he muttered, "Zarek's quarters are situated not far from here. He's sure to arrive soon. Now I may be as good as dead already, but I had to let you know that you didn't fail with me, Lucy." He looked back at her.

She stared at him. Finally, she snapped, "I don't believe you."

"I swear, Lucy. I would do anything for you. I would do anything for any of you—for all of you."

He turned to face Reigna. "I never betrayed you, Reigna. Never! I—" He wiped an errant tear from his eye. "I swear, I would die for you, for Eden, and for Ehyeh's cause."

At that very moment, the earth shook violently.

The Oathtakers' blades, jammed into the locks on their cell doors, broke free and then dropped to the ground, each with a clang. Then the cell bars, rattling, fell open on squeaky hinges.

"Great Ehyeh!" Mara cried. "We're freed!"

She stepped out, stooped down, and grabbed Spira. Then, recollecting how she'd once used her blade to open a lock, she placed it between the band about her wrist that remained connected to the chain that previously had held her to the wall. She flicked it up—and the band broke free.

Meanwhile, Broden stood, staring at his arm. The band he'd worn had fallen off.

"Looks like we won't need your singing magic after all," Dax commented to Mara as he stepped out from his cell and grabbed his blade, Immunis.

At that moment, one regular guard, and two of Zarek's succedunt soldiers, came running in, their boots clacking loudly.

On sight of the first of them, Mara recognized the man. He was the one who'd heckled her when she held Mariella, dead, in her arms. Recollecting her vow to see the man dead, she let her blade fly.

As always, her weapon met its mark.

The man's eyes bolted wide open. He stared at Mara. With that, and a gasp, he sank to his knees, and then fell over.

Meanwhile, Lucy retrieved her blade, and then threw it at one of the succedunt, while Dax threw his at the other.

One by one, the men fell to the ground, each with a crash.

"Hurry!" Mara cried. "Everyone out! Now!" She rushed to the body of the man she'd downed, to retrieve Spira. "We must make good, our escape!"

The twins and Lucy stepped over the bodies of the other fallen men as Dixon and Aliza made their way out from their prison cells, then retrieved their blades.

"Broden, I'm so sorry," Reigna cried when she reached his side. "I'm—"

"Forget it," he said, as he kicked away the band he'd previously worn and that now rested on the floor at his feet. "I know what things looked like."

Quickly, they all gathered outside Mara's cell.

"Come on, girls," she cried as she reached for the twins, "let's go!"

"No," Reigna said, pulling back. "We can all get out of here, but only if you do as Eden and I say."

"She's right," Eden said. "Now listen up, everyone!"

"Girls—" Mara began.

"No, Mara, listen to us. Now!" Reigna caught the eye of each of the others, quickly, and in turn. "Dixon," she said, "you take Dax. Lucy, take Broden."

"Broden—you've done it," Lucy interrupted, crying. "You fulfilled prophecy!"

"What?" he asked.

"'*Before evil claims all, the seventh seventh and she who is but is not, may seek deliverance. Pray for faith, that the bowels of the earth may heave.*' I thought it related to when the twins earned Ehyeh's favor while in The Tearless—but maybe it was actually about what you just did here!" Her word came in a rush. "I should have guessed something unexpected could happen in light of the many references that we should be wary, since things are not always what they seem."

"What's that?" Broden asked her.

"Just more prophecy." She looked at him, then suddenly, leaned in and inhaled deeply. "You've earned Ehyeh's favor!" she exclaimed, smiling. "Your scent is lovely—of mandarin, bergamot, rosemary and amber."

She reached up and turned his head to the side. "Your birth sign has returned, as well! And you showed today what being a first amongst the Select is all about. Protecting life." She held his gaze. "Oh, Broden, I'm so sorry I didn't believe you— that I didn't believe *in* you!"

"It's all right, Lucy, really." He gazed at Clementine. "But listen," he added, "I'm not going without the child."

"We can't save everyone, Broden," Lucy argued.

"I'm not leaving without her," he insisted. "You take her. Take Clementine."

He put his hands on the child's shoulders and turned her Lucy's way.

She stared at him, tears pooled in her eyes

"Here, Broden," Reigna said as she removed from around her neck, a leather band with a grut tooth attached to it. "You may need this to protect you from the beasts." She offered it to her cousin.

"All right then, girls, you're going with me," Mara said.

"No," Eden said, "you're taking Carlie and Aliza."

"I am not! I'm taking you."

"You can't all stay here!" Lucy cried, looking first at Broden, then at the twins.

Eden reached out her hand. In it, she held Rowena's shawl. "Reigna and I will wear this," she said as she opened it, then draped it over their shoulders. Together, the twins pulled it up over the tops of their heads—and disappeared.

"Reigna!" Mara cried. "Eden!"

They took the covering down.

"Did you hear us talking under it?" Eden asked. "Or could you catch our scents?"

"No—neither. Did you say something?"

"Yes. So, that's good. No one can see, hear, or smell us when we're under it."

"I don't like this," Mara said.

"In those days when deliverance is sought, trust not illusion when I am born," Lucy muttered. She turned to Mara. "It's more prophecy. I think you should let them go."

She scowled at her.

"Remember what I told you before," Reigna said. "We'll follow the city gates out and then head straight back to the place where we first met Zarek. If there's still a boat tied there, and if you get stalled for any reason, we'll take it and then make our way to Aliza's old place. If there isn't one, we'll hike along the river toward the border."

"Girls—"

"No, Mara. Once you get the others to safety, then you can return for us."

"Please, no. Don't do this!"

"We must. Now, you all need to go!" Reigna ordered. With that, she and Eden pulled the shawl back over their heads and said no more.

Mara reached for them, but felt nothing. A cry caught in her throat.

"Hurry!" Dixon cried. "There's nothing more to be done here." With that, he grabbed Dax's elbow.

"Hold on," Dax said.

"What?"

"Your magic won't work on me."

"What?"

"Leave me. You take Broden."

"I can't leave you, Dax! There's got to be a way!"

He shook his head. "There is not. But don't worry about me. I'll find my way out."

"Here!" Lucy rushed toward the dead guards, then dropped to her haunches. "Change your clothing out for these," she ordered as she took weapons, the black face covering, and the clothing off one of them. "Hurry!" She threw the items his way.

Dax caught them, then started pulling the man's clothing on over his own. "You all need to go," he said. "I'll get to safety."

Lucy took up a leather cord she wore around her neck. "Take my grut tooth," she said.

"I don't need it. I'm immune to the gruts' poison—it's magic." With that, he proceeded to drag the body of the dead guard whose clothing he'd taken, into a cell, out of sight.

"I'm staying here with Dax," Broden said.

"Broden—" Lucy argued.

"No," he said. He crouched down, pulled clothing off of the remaining succedunt soldier, and then, back on his feet, quickly donned it. Like Dax, he put on the black face mask that the man had worn. Then he pulled the dead guard's body into one of the cells.

"Take Clementine," he said when he was through, as a ruckus of faraway footsteps, fast approaching, sounded out.

"Are you sure?" she asked him.

"I'm sure. Get her to safety."

"Fine. Dixon, you take Aliza then," Lucy said. "And you, Mara, just take Carlie. Get her to Nina."

"I've got her," she said. She grabbed the girl's hand. "Ready?"

"I'm sorry, Mara," Carlie said.

She shook her head. "Don't be. The twins were right. We can all get out of here safely." She turned to Dixon. "I'll get her home," she said, "and then head straight back for the twins. Under no circumstances are you—or any of the others of you," she said catching the eye of each of the others momentarily, and in turn, "to come after me or to go after them."

He held her gaze for a long second, then embraced her. "Fine," he finally agreed, stepping back. Then, "Is everyone ready?" he asked.

"Yes," Lucy said.

"Let's go, then!" Mara cried.

And with that, they all disappeared.

The twins edged their way along the wall, past their cohorts' former cells. When they arrived at the door leading out, they stopped and waited until Dax and Broden rushed out ahead of them, Dax shouting, "Hurry! Hurry!"

Seconds later, they heard footsteps coming their way.

"Reigna?"

"Yes?"

"Did you hear Broden?"

"Yes."

"Are you thinking what I'm thinking then?"

"I believe I am."

"Let's go."

They waited as several guards entered the prison. Then they slipped out the door and down the hall.

"He said we were close," Reigna said.

"We'll have to hurry."

"Here, pull back."

They scooted up against the wall as more guards hurried by them, toward the prison.

After they passed, Reigna pulled her twin along. "I'm guessing his quarters are down this way since that's where all the commotion is coming from."

"Agreed."

They kept on, dodging the occasional person. Soon, they approached the doors of a room from whence they'd seen a number of people exit.

"Now?" Eden asked.

"The next time it opens," Reigna said, "we'll make our way inside."

No sooner had she spoken, than four succedunt guards exited the room. Quickly, the twins stepped inside, allowing the door to slam closed behind them.

Before them, Zarek and Pestifere paced. Both fumed. Their breathing came in heavy, angry gasps.

"Stay along the wall," Reigna cautioned her twin.

"Yes. Then when we find an opening, we'll draw near—and I'll kill them," Eden said.

Just then, the door flew open again. Two succedunt guards, looking like all the others of their kind, each with a black cloth over his face, entered.

"The prisoners have escaped!" one of them shouted.

"It's Dax!" Reigna cried.

Zarek, accompanied by Pestifere, rushed to the door. "Keep an eye out here," the emperor ordered.

The moment they exited, Dax turned toward the twins. "I thought you girls were headed straight out—behind Broden and me. But when I turned back, you weren't there."

"You can see us?" Reigna asked.

"Of course. That magic," he motioned with his hand around his head to indicate their shawl, "doesn't work on me. I can see through it. Anyway, I told Broden we had to turn back to find you. Fortunately, I saw the two of you just as you entered here. What possessed you to come this way?"

"I'm going to kill Zarek," Eden said.

He looked at her, his eyes narrowed. "What?"

"With my attendant magic."

He shook his head. "Listen, I know about your powers—or at least what we believe are your powers. Lucy found it necessary to share the information with me—although she swore me to eternal secrecy. But . . . what if she's wrong? Or . . . what if you have to reveal yourself in order to touch him? Or what if he doesn't die instantly and he still has time to harm you? No, this is no time to test things. Now, please, both of you," he said, looking at them each in turn, "we've got to go."

"But—"

"No. We have to get out of here."

Broden rushed across the room toward a wall on which numerous weapons hung.

"Ahhh," he cried, "here you are! I'd almost forgotten about you!" He reached up, then removed the great sword from where it hung. "I'll get you to safety," he whispered, running his fingers over the design engraved on its grip.

The twins stepped up behind him.

"No, Broden," Reigna said, as she pulled their shawl off, "we'll take it from here."

He handed it over.

Reigna sheathed the weapon so it would be hidden with her and her twin, beneath their covering.

"Let's go then," Eden cried before wrapping the shawl back over her and her sister.

At that very moment, the sound of the door squeaking open, sounded out.

Broden dropped to the ground. The twins, confused, stepped to the side.

Zarek and Pestifere entered.

"Master!" Dax cried, rubbing his head, feigning that he was delirious. Then he pointed at the wall. "Someone attacked us—and the sword is missing!"

"Ahhhhhh!" Zarek cried. "Get them! Go! Hurry!"

Dax pulled Broden back to his feet and then, with him, approached the door. When he opened it, he stood there for a long moment, waiting for the twins to exit before them.

"Next time," Eden whispered to her sister. "I'll kill them the next time I get the chance."

The moment the twins cleared the threshold, Dax, with Broden's arm draped over his shoulder, as though for support, stepped out behind them.

"We'll get them, master, Zarek," he said just before the door slammed closed behind them.

"That was quick thinking, Broden," Dax said.

"Yes, on your part, as well. Now, this way," Broden ordered as he led the way down a hall.

Soon, they came to a door leading to the outdoors.

Broden looked out. "I don't see my friends anywhere," he said. "I sure hope they escaped."

"Let's go, then!" Dax cried.

"No, wait!" Broden exclaimed. "Follow me. We're taking Marielle's remains with us."

He scurried around the side of the building, dropped down to his knees, and then took a dagger that he'd confiscated from one of the fallen guards in the prison. With it, he started digging. A minute later, he retrieved a small, locked, silver box.

"All right then, let's go now!" Dax cried.

Eden peeked out from under the shawl. "Follow us!" she said.

"We're right behind you." Dax said, grabbing Broden's arm.

She looked around, then pointed. "Horses!" she cried. With that, she and Reigna, the men in their wake, ran to a row of them, all tied up.

Reigna loosed one for herself and her sister to ride together, while Dax and Broden also each untied one. They all saddled up.

Then, "Hurry!" Dax cried as they set off into the night.

Chapter Fifty-Three

As Dixon's feet landed in the midst of Marshall's camp, he let go of Aliza, even as Lucy appeared at their side, with Clementine.

Several people ran toward them all.

"Dixon!" Basha cried. "You're back!" She threw her arms around him. "Welcome home!" Pulling back, she greeted Lucy and Aliza.

"Thank you," he said. "It's good to be here."

"Yes!" Lucy agreed.

Basha's brow dropped. "Where is Mara? Where are the twins?"

Quickly, Dixon explained the situation.

She glanced at Trumble, now standing at her side, and then back. "Felicity has had us in prayer since early last night," she said. "As you know, she speaks in riddles, but Trumble felt certain there was a prison break in the making."

"What did she say?"

"She rattled on about how we were to pray for the truth to win out—for the earth to shake with it. What happened, anyway?"

He told her of how Broden had sworn an oath, causing the release of their blades and the prison doors to break open.

"Broden swore an oath?"

"He did."

"Do you remember, Lucy" she said, addressing her, "how we all worried that because he'd never sworn a life oath for the twins' benefit, that we couldn't count on him? And do you recall how everyone was angry with you for not having seen to that detail earlier on?"

"I do."

"Just think. If he'd done so all those years ago, then things wouldn't have happened as they did for you today."

"I suppose you're right."

"It's true then," Aliza piped up.

"What's true?" Trumble asked.

"Ehyeh really does take all things and use them for good."

Her fellow Oathtakers nodded their agreement.

"Mara should be here soon," Dixon said. "She was to take Carlie to the palace to Nina, and then return to Chiran for the twins. Dear Ehyeh," he added, almost as an afterthought, "I hope they made it out!"

"They did," Basha said. "I'm sure of it."

"How can you be?"

"Because Felicity is resting easy for the first time in days."

Upon landing in the vestibule of the palace, Mara released her hold on Carlie. Bending over, her hands on her knees, she struggled to catch her breath. Everything had happened so quickly. When she pulled back up, her knees buckled. She fought to remain upright.

"Nina!" she cried as she grabbed Carlie's arm for support. "Nina!"

Adele entered, her heels clicking on the hardwood floor. Bane, at her side, growled as he approached the visitors. He sniffed at their feet, and then upon recognizing them, broke into a great grin and wagged his tail.

"Oh, it's you, Mara!" Adele exclaimed. "You're back! And— Carlie. It *is* you!"

"Get Nina," Mara ordered, her chest heaving. "Please, hurry."

At that moment, someone headed down the staircase toward them, casting shadows on the walls through the flickering candlelight.

"Mara!" Nina called out. "Is that you I hear?" Then, "Carlie!" she cried on sight of her daughter. "Oh, Carlie!"

She rushed down the stairs. When she arrived at her side, she threw her arms around her. "Oh, Carlie!" she cried. "I thought we'd lost you!"

"No, Mama, I'm fine."

From a hallway on the right that led to the conference room that the palace security team used, Jules approached. "Is everything all right here?" he asked. Then, noticing his daughter, he ran to her. "Oh, thank Ehyeh, you're home!"

Nina pulled back, tears streaming down her cheeks. She held her daughter's face in her hands for a long moment. Finally, she released her, then reached for her old friend who stood, faltering, at her side.

"Mara," she clasped her hand, "I should have known you'd rescue her. I should never have doubted you." She threw her arms around her. "I'm so sorry. I'm so, so sorry! Oh, goodness, the terrible things I said!"

Once again, Mara's knees buckled. Leaning on Nina for support, she murmured, "It's . . . all . . . right."

"But I said such horrible things!" Nina held her even more tightly. "I said you couldn't understand. But of course you could."

"What did you say to her, Mama?" Carlie asked, her eyes narrowed.

"I'm ashamed of myself, but I was so worried for you! I told Mara that because she'd never had one of her own, she couldn't possibly understand my pain in losing you." Nina shook her head. "It was wrong of me," she said, releasing her friend and turning back to her daughter.

Without Nina's support, Mara's eyes rolled up and back, her energy gave way, and she started sinking to the floor.

Jules, quickly assessing the situation, steadied her from falling hard.

"Even more so since Mara has experienced exactly that pain, Mama," Carlie said.

Nina stared at her, then dropped to her friend's side. "What is she talking about, Mara? What happened?" Tears welled in her eyes.

"Never . . . mind," Mara whispered, struggling to get each word out.

"Are you all right?"

"I can't— I have . . . to get . . . back."

"You're not going anywhere like this," Jules said.

"I have to get . . . the twins." Her words sputtered out slowly and slurred.

"What's the matter with her?" Nina cried, clutching Jules's arm.

"I have no idea."

"She was fine when we left," Carlie offered. "But, of course, she's been mistreated and underfed for weeks. Goodness, Mama, look at her!"

Mara could hardly catch her breath, but was determined not to dwell on her pain. "We'll talk . . . later," she managed to sputter out. "But I have . . . to return for . . . the girls." With that, her head dropped to the side, and she lost consciousness.

Jules glanced at Nina. "Help me get her to the infirmary," he said.

The two of them, along with Carlie, brought her to the suite Lucy had set apart for healing purposes. Gently, they laid her on a cot.

Carlie took Mara's hand. "Mara? Can you talk to me? Wake up, Mara."

She groaned.

"I'll go get one of the healers," Jules said.

"But the twins are waiting for her! In Chiran!" Carlie cried.

"She's not going anywhere like this," Nina said. "Go, Jules. Hurry!" she cried. "Oh, goodness, I can't believe the things I said to her. Carlie, what happened?"

"Mama, don't worry about that. You'll have plenty of time to make amends. Now help me get her washed up and changed into some clean clothes. Then we can put a cool pack on her forehead."

⚔

The twins, Broden, and Dax, rode through the chaos. As soldiers madly dashed about, as women ran screaming and crying, seeking the means to get away, they dodged through the mayhem, past the city gates, and out into the countryside. They were left unmolested, as others, seeing Dax and Broden with the black masks over their faces, believed them to be members of the succedunt, while the twins were invisible to everyone.

Reigna and Eden removed the shawl from over their heads shortly after passing through the city walls.

Not long later, they slowed. A mist in the air surrounded them. Above, the scant light of a partially cloud covered half-moon, shone.

"We should be close now," Eden said.

Just then, an unexpected sound met their ears even as the nighttime animals and insects, having returned with spring, stilled.

They halted.

A palpable silence surrounded them.

A moment later, out from the quiet, came again the sound they'd heard earlier. It was the softest sigh.

The leather of the twins' saddle creaked, as Reigna leaned forward to peer into the darkness.

When an owl hooted, she, her twin, Dax, and Broden, all froze again.

Several long seconds passed before the crickets chirped as before, but almost immediately, they went still again.

"Someone's here," Reigna whispered.

"That was a horse sighing," Eden added, her voice low.

Dax and Broden put their black face coverings back on.

A horse's whicker, then the sound of crunching gravel, sounded out.

"We should be near the river," Reigna whispered.

"Maybe it's Mara," Broden suggested.

The twins dismounted.

Immediately, Reigna unsheathed the great sword. She held it, two-fisted, prepared for battle. Eden, at her side, armed herself with a dagger that Dax had given her earlier. It was one he'd taken from the guard he'd killed back at the prison.

Dax and Broden jumped down. Now, armed with swords that they'd retrieved at the prison, each stood to one side of the twins.

Reigna stepped out. In the wan light, through the surrounding brush, she pointed toward glistening water and two tall, cylindrical, rocks.

"I think you're right, Broden," she whispered over her shoulder. "It's likely Mara. This is where we told her we'd meet her. Be careful now."

Suddenly, out from the quiet, came the sound of a slap. Then a horse ran out from the brush.

"This way!" Dax ordered as he hurried off.

Water splashed. Gravel crunched.

"Stop right there!" he cried upon reaching the water's edge.

Just ahead, in a boat, sat three people, unrecognizable in the wan moonlight.

"We need that boat," Dax said. "Out!"

As Broden drew near it, then stooped down to grab the rope hanging from it, someone came rushing out at him from the nearby brush, slamming him to the ground. Water quickly rushed up and over his face, as a man straddled him.

"You'll not take us!" a woman screamed.

Broden grabbed his attacker's arms. He struggled to pull his head back up through the water, and when he did, he gulped in a quick breath of air. Almost immediately, his head was submerged again.

He fought even harder. Water splashed wildly about him and his attacker.

Just then, Dax charged Broden's captor, pushing him off.

Broden surfaced and sputtered, trying to catch his breath. "Yasmin," he managed to get out, "it's me!"

"Broden?"

"Stop!" he cried as Dax raised his blade over the man who'd attacked him, now on the ground beneath him.

Dax's arm came to a halt. He glanced Broden's way. "Who are these people?"

Broden pulled the black covering off from over his head. "It's all right," he said. "I know them."

"It *is* you, Broden!" exclaimed the man on the ground.

Satisfied, Dax stood and sheathed Immunis.

Reaching down, Broden offered his hand to the man on the ground. "This is Striver," he said to Dax and the twins.

At that moment, as the cloud that had been covering the moon moved away, the light increased, allowing for greater visibility.

Turning toward the women sitting in the boat, now able to identify them all, Broden said, "And that's Yasmin, Farida, and Ghazala." He gestured toward each of them in turn. "In truth, we owe these four our lives."

Quickly, he explained to Dax and the twins, the part his friends had played in their escape. Once done, he told Striver and the others how Carlie and Clementine had been rescued.

"We'd best get moving," Reigna said after she and her twin had expressed their appreciation. Then she looked at the boat in which the women sat, frowning, her brow lowered.

"There's another one," Striver said, noting the concerned look on her face. "Another boat, I mean."

"Oh?"

"We hid it when we heard you coming from some way off. We'd hoped to keep anyone from pursuing us. I'll get it now." With that, he headed back into the brush.

Seconds later came the sounds of a boat scraping the ground, followed by a splash when it hit the water's edge.

Broden stepped toward Dax. "Thank you. You, too, saved my life tonight."

He shrugged. "That goes both ways, son." He caught Broden's eye. "You know, you are Select. Even if I didn't owe you my life for all you did to free us earlier tonight, I'd do anything to protect yours. On my honor, on my life, I swear—I would die for you."

At that very moment, the earth shook. The rocks to which the boats were earlier roped, broke way and crashed to the ground. The water rose in rippling, white frothy waves.

Striver and the Chiranian women all cried out.

Within seconds, things returned to normal.

"Oh my!" Dax exclaimed.

Reigna and Eden approached their cousin. Both smiling, they patted his back.

"I never realized, Broden!" Dax cried. "No Oathtaker had previously sworn for your safety?"

He hung his head. "I'm sorry, Dax, no." He looked back up, his eyes misted over. "I guess you're stuck with me."

Dax put his hand on Broden's shoulder. "Stuck? No, son, I'm not 'stuck.' I am honored." With that, he put his arms around him. "I am honored," he repeated as Broden returned the embrace.

For long seconds, no one spoke.

"Would someone please explain what just happened?" Striver finally asked.

Reigna chuckled. "We will—while we're on our way—but we have to hurry. Come on now, you two," she motioned toward Dax and Broden. "Something must have held Mara up. So, we'll continue on toward Aliza's former camp." She paused, then added, "Maybe there's something good to eat there."

Eden laughed. "Yes," she said, "if you all are hungry, just follow Reigna. She's sure to nose out anything edible. Now, let's get out of here before we have any more surprises."

Chapter Fifty-Four

The earliest morning birds called and cooed as the sun's rays thrust out from the eastern horizon. They cast light through breaks in scant cirrostratus clouds, outlining them in glorious shades of pink and orange, on their way to peeking into the window.

As the light kissed her face, Mara sat up in a rush. Glancing about her, finding nothing familiar, she gasped. She looked down to discover that she wore a nightdress.

What happened? Where am I?

Sounds of footsteps came from outside the door.

She was hungry and thirsty, but felt she had to get moving. She bunched her bedding in a fist and threw it aside. Her head suddenly pounding to the beat of her heart, she stopped to rub her temples. When the throbbing lessened, she put her feet to the floor, and then leaned forward, thinking.

Oh, I remember now. I'm at the palace. They must have brought me here, to the infirmary. Oh, great Ehyeh, I have to be on my way!

She looked about. Spira sat on the nightstand at her side. Her clothing was nowhere to be found, but fortunately, there was an armoire against the back wall.

She struggled her way to it. Inside, she found stacks of standard Oathtakers' garb in various sizes. She grabbed some items, returned to the bed, and then dropped them. After stopping momentarily to rest, and just as she was about to pull her nightdress off, a knock came at the door.

"Oh, Mara!" Nina cried upon entering, a tray in her hands. "You should get back in bed."

"I can't, Nina. I have to go."

"Valentina will be here any—"

"Valentina?"

"She's one of the healers that stayed here at the palace. She's been helping me attend to you, but I sent her away last night so that she could get a few hours rest."

Mara grabbed the clothing. "I couldn't find my things," she said, "so I got these."

She stepped behind a nearby room divider, draped the items over the top, and then removed her nightdress.

"Yes, I know," Nina said. "Honestly, the clothes you'd been wearing were so filthy and parasite infested, we had them burned."

"You bathed and changed me then?"

"With Carlie's help."

"Thank you. But Nina, I have to go."

"What's the hurry? You arrived here three days ago. What difference could a few more minutes make?"

"Days!" she cried, peeking around the edge of the divider for a look at Nina.

"Yes. Fortunately, I was able to keep you hydrated—for the most part, anyway."

Mara shook her head. "Well, in any case, I have to be on my way now."

A quick rapping came at the door. Then it opened, and someone stepped inside.

"What's this I hear?" the newcomer asked.

Mara pulled on a pair of trousers, then peeked out the side of the divider again. "Who are you?" she asked.

"I'm Valentina."

After donning a standard Oathtaker tunic, Mara stepped out, fully clothed. "I have to go," she said.

"Not yet, you don't."

"Listen, the twins are waiting for me. I was supposed to go straight back for them."

Valentina stood before her. "No, Mara, you listen to me. I need to check your vitals. If all is well, you must eat something. Then you can go."

"I don't need your permission," she snapped.

"I understand. But you could use my expertise. Now, please, sit here." She motioned toward a nearby table.

Huffing, Mara followed her direction.

Valentina proceeded with her examination, checking Mara's pulse and gazing into her with her magic. Finally, she sighed.

"Mara," she said, "I admit that I'm one of the lesser healers. My powers are quite minimal. In fact, they're not of much help for anything more than simple cuts and bruises. But when you arrived—" She paused, swallowed hard. "Well, in truth, you looked near death. The only problem was that I couldn't locate any injury, or identify any illness."

"It doesn't matter. I'm fine now."

"Still, something isn't right. Your heart rate is . . . erratic—" Valentina held her gaze. "I'm afraid everyone has been terribly busy around here, but I've arranged for Kayson—our lead healer here—to stop in to see you before you go."

"Yes, I know Kayson," Mara said. Then she shook her head. "No, I've been too long already. The twins are waiting for me. I shouldn't have stopped at all."

"Oh, like you had any choice in the matter."

She glared at her.

"Fine." Valentina tapped a rhythm on the tabletop. "But at least get something to eat first. Surely, you've time for that."

Nina filled a cup with tea and handed it to her. "Please, Mara," she said.

As she took the cup, then tasted the tea, Nina lifted the cover from a plate of food. She pushed the offering of hot oatmeal with cinnamon, fresh glazed scones, a slice of cold ham, and fruit, her way.

"Please, eat," she implored her.

"I have to admit, it looks good—and honest to Ehyeh, I haven't had a decent meal since . . . I don't know when."

After filling a cup of tea for herself, Nina nodded Valentina's way. "I'll take it from here," she said.

"Very well." Valentina stood. Then, "Please promise me, Mara," she said, "that you'll have someone take a look—and soon."

She waved her hand at the healer. "Sure. Fine. I will."

After the door closed behind her, Nina leaned in. "Mara," she said, lowering her gaze, "I am so, so sorry."

"Nina, please, don't give any of it another thought."

"I said such hateful things—and to you, my oldest and dearest friend—my . . . savior, really. I owe everything to you. And now—"

Mara grinned at her, wanly. "Believe me, Nina, I understood then, and I understand now. There is no grief quite like that of losing a child—born to you, or loved by you as though it had been." She took another bite of her food.

"Thank you for your understanding."

"I'm glad Carlie's safe." Mara set her linen napkin down. "But I have to go now."

She retrieved Spira from the nightstand. "I've been far too long. The twins are waiting for me—and I suspect that by now, Dixon is beside himself with worry."

Even as her feet landed in the dew-laden grass, she reached back for her blade. She crouched into a fighting stance, then spun in each direction, looking for any signs of potential danger. Moments later, something fluttered at her shoulder.

"Merc!" she cried. "And Spec!"

They, along with Evan, had returned to Aliza's former camp after Dixon, Dax, and Aliza were taken prisoner and they'd reported to Lucy.

"You've returned," Merc said.

"Yes." She held her hand out for him and Spec to land on. "I assume the twins passed through here. Right?"

"The twins? No. Aren't they with you?"

"Ahhh . . . no. Listen, I have to go to find them." She waved her hand for the flits to fly away. "Which way is it to the river?"

Merc flew at her side. "That way there," he said with a nod.

She stepped out into the rustling grasses, but stopped again only seconds later to catch her breath, concerned that although she'd only just begun, she already felt winded. It was going to take some time to restore her health.

"The twins were to make their way here," she said. "Oh, I do hope they've not run into any problems."

"Evan headed upriver this morning." Spec said. Then, as he looked up, he exclaimed, "Oh, here he is now!"

Evan neared. "Mara!" he cried when he was within hearing range. "I found the twins and Dax! They're pulling their boats out of the water now. They should be here soon."

Seconds later, the twins, followed by Dax, Broden, and their fellow travelers, stepped out of the surrounding forest.

"Mara!" Reigna cried on sight of her. "We hoped you'd be here." She, along with her twin, ran to meet her.

Relieved, Mara threw her arms around them. "Thank Ehyeh you're all right!"

"You don't look good," Eden said when Mara released her.

"I'm fine—really."

"You need a healer to take a look," Reigna said.

"Sure. Of course I will—when I get time."

Just then, the others neared. When Broden approached, Mara turned his way. She put her arms around him and held him close. "I could never thank you enough," she said.

He shrugged. "Not necessary."

"Now, who have we here?" she asked as she glanced Striver's way, then at Yasmin, Farida, and Ghazala.

Broden introduced them all.

After welcoming them, Mara turned to Dax. "Thank you so much for all of your help." She tipped her head the twins' way and grinned. "Any Select would be blessed to have you as their Oathtaker."

"And so I am," Broden interrupted.

Her eyes flickered toward him. "What?"

He, along with his fellow travelers laughed. Then he explained how Dax had sworn an oath for his protection.

"Well, you're in good hands with Dax," she said. "And Broden, thank you again," she said, taking his hands in both of hers. "You deserve the best protection possible—and now, you've got it." Finally, she turned back to the twins. "All right then, Dixon must be crazy with worry by now. Are you ready?"

"Ready!" they exclaimed in unison.

"Good." She took a hand of each. Then, "We'll meet you all at Marshall camp," she said. "You know where it is, Dax." With that, she and her charges disappeared.

Light and color surrounded Mara and the twins as she spun her magic. But contrary to the norm, the light was low, and the colors muted.

She grew anxious. Almost instantly, she regretted having traveled magically with the girls—and so soon after taking Carlie to the palace—and she not in her best form. Perhaps they should have simply hiked back to Marshall's camp.

I think there is something wrong with me, after all.

Almost fearing where they'd land, she struggled to open her eyes when her feet hit the ground. As she looked up, Dixon, Jerrett and Velia, along with Basha, Therese, and Trumble, all smiling, rushed her way. Behind them, came Lucy and Aliza.

Overcome with exhaustion, she dropped her hold on the twins. Her knees buckled, and she fell to the ground.

"Mara!" Reigna cried. She squatted at her side. "Oh, my! What's wrong?"

Her eyes quivered, but she hadn't the strength to open them.

"Mara?" Dixon called when he reached her side.

She recognized his voice, but was unable to respond. She struggled for a breath.

"Hurry! Hurry!" Basha cried. "We need a healer here! Quickly!"

Then Mara heard no more.

Chapter Fifty-Five

Dixon and the twins sat in the infirmary, at Mara's bedside. The sound of rain falling on the canvas tent overhead, met their ears. It seemed to weep for them, as Mara had not regained consciousness since she'd arrived with the twins at Basha's camp, seven full days hence.

As he and the girls had done repeatedly, to keep her hydrated, Dixon once again dripped water into her mouth. He'd follow later with some broth. He vowed that nothing would draw him from her side.

Mara's breathing remained steady, but slow and shallow.

Overcome with exhaustion, Reigna's head bobbed as she fell asleep against her every effort not to do so. Jerking back awake, she looked at Eden who, once again weeping, held their Oathtaker's hand. Then she glanced up as the tent flap opened.

Basha, Velia, and Lucy, entered.

"Dixon," Lucy said as they approached, "may I have a word?"

He glanced her way. "Go on, then."

"I mean . . . alone," she said. "Basha and Velia can stay with the twins."

"No."

"Dixon—"

"No. Anything you have to say to me, you can say in front of them all."

She bit her lip. Then she asked, "Would you just step over there with me then?" She pointed to a corner.

"Fine."

He stood and then followed her as Basha took up his former position to drip water into Mara's mouth. Velia watched on.

"Dixon," Lucy whispered, "I'm very concerned. We've none of the best healers here at this camp, I'm sorry to say, and of those who are here, no one has been able to figure out Mara's problem. The nearest they can tell, she's suffering from some sort of magic overdose. I had Effie and Fleet send one of the flits, Diaphanous—Daphne, I guess they call her—to the palace. She just returned."

"And?"

"And it seems that Mara broke down after delivering Carlie there, too. She was out for three days. That explains why it took so long for her to return for the twins.

In any case, against the healer's recommendation, she then set out to get the girls, shortly after regaining consciousness."

"And?" he repeated.

"Dixon, she was already weak. I don't imagine that her current emotional state, having lost Mariella, helped either."

He stared at her.

"The truth is that I've never seen a situation quite like this before."

He let out his breath slowly, deliberately. "So?"

"So—" She choked back a cry. "Dixon, I love you all. I know at times I haven't shown it, but—"

"What do you want, Lucy?"

She swallowed hard. "These are dangerous times. I'm hearing some noise that it may become necessary to have Mara remov—"

"Absolutely not!" he cried. Then, between gritted teeth, he seethed, adding, "How dare you!"

"I'm sorry, Dixon, but it's not me this time. It is others who are making the recommendation."

He looked at her closely, his eyes narrowed. "You think— You think she could—" He couldn't bring himself to say the word.

"If this is a byproduct of her having used too much magic, I can tell you that I've only seen a situation this bad once before."

"And?"

She hung her head, then looked back up at him. A single tear rolled down her cheek. Wiping it away brusquely, she swallowed hard. "And that Oathtaker," she whispered, "did not make it."

"How many days was he unconscious before he . . ." His voice dropped to nothing.

"Four."

Dixon nodded.

"And Mara just ended her *seventh* day."

"But this has happened before, you know—that she's lost consciousness. In fact, it happened several times after she was injured."

"Yes, but each of those instances, just like her recent one at the palace, were all limited, Dixon, to three days each. None lasted this long." Lucy stopped to listen to the rain beating on the canvas above. "Was there anything about those times that was the same as now, do you think?"

Sighing, he hung his head. "I don't know. But Lucy, if we're going to—" He choked back a cry. "If we're going to . . . lose her . . . then it won't make any difference if we just wait to have her replaced."

"I agree—and that's what I've told those who've brought the issue to me. Have no fear. I'm with you on this. I just thought you should be prepared in the event you heard anything."

"Dixon. Dixon!" Reigna cried. "Her eyes are fluttering!"

"Mara?" Eden let loose a wail. "Please answer us. Please." She released her hold on her Oathtaker, then turned to her twin and wrapped her arms around her, weeping all the while.

Dixon rushed to Mara's side, then brusquely moved Basha aside.

At that moment, Mara inhaled her first fully deep breath in days.

"Mara!" he cried.

Her eyelashes fluttered.

"Please, wake up." He wondered, and not for the first time, why he had to keep re-living these situations with her.

Her eyes opened slowly, and then just as slowly, closed again.

"Wake up," he urged.

Once more, she inhaled deeply. Then she opened her eyes again. She tried to speak, but the words wouldn't come.

"Are you all right?" Reigna asked.

She stared at the twins. Slowly, the corners of her lips turned up into a wan smile.

"Oh, Mara!" Eden cried.

Turning to Dixon, she worked her mouth, as though loosening it.

"Are you all right? Are you in any pain?" he asked.

"Nnnn," she gurgled. "No."

He stroked her hair, then looked skyward. "Oh, thank you, Ehyeh!" he cried.

She cleared her throat.

"Here," Reigna said, "let me get you a drink."

When she was through assisting her with one, Mara grabbed her hand. "Thank you," she said. Then her eyes quickly scanned her surroundings. "Where am I?"

A collective sigh of relief made its way through her crowd of visitors.

"You're in the infirmary at Marshall's camp," Dixon said.

"What happened?"

"As near as we can tell, you overdosed on magic—again."

She grinned. "Goodness, Dixon, you just can't help being . . . charming, can you?"

He laughed with relief, then kissed her forehead. "We've been so worried about you!"

"I'm fine. Can you help me to sit up?"

"It's too soon."

"No, I'm fine. Really." She turned to Reigna. "More water, please?"

Once she was upright and had taken another drink, she looked out at her friends.

"Oh," she said upon sight of Basha and Velia, her fingertips to her mouth, "how I've missed you two!"

Dixon moved to make room for the two of them as they dropped down at her side.

A long quiet moment passed. Then, "I lost her, you know," she said, catching Velia's eye.

She nodded. "I know. I'm so sorry."

Tears rolled down Mara's cheeks. "Thank you. I know. I know you are."

The day after Mara regained consciousness, Broden stopped in to see her. Still resting in the infirmary, she smiled upon sight of him.

With Dixon at one side of her, he sat at her other. He leaned forward, then kissed her cheek. "You look good," he said, smiling.

"Doesn't she though?" Dixon stroked her hair.

She nodded. "Ha! Well, that's very generous of you, I'm sure. Of both of you!"

"No, its true!" Broden insisted.

She grinned. "I am feeling a bit better today, I guess."

"Good."

She drew her fingers together, then picked at one of her nails, her expression turned serious. "Were you . . ." she began, then paused, taking in a deep breath. "I never got to ask Carlie . . . Were the two of you able to give Mariella a proper burial?"

"That's why I stopped by."

Her eyes met his.

"Carlie and I, ahhh . . . We prepared Mariella's body for burial, then placed it in dry sand inside a solid silver box. Once done, we locked it. In the hopes of bringing her back home one day, I buried her in a shallow grave."

He glanced at Dixon before looking back her way. When she said nothing, he took a deep breath, then continued. "When Dax, the twins, and I, made our way out of the prison, I insisted we first retrieve her remains. They are here, now."

She held his gaze. "Thank you." Her eyes filled with tears.

"In truth—" He stopped short.

She put her hand on his. "I know it's hard, Broden, but it's all right. You can say what you need to say."

He brushed away tears that had pooled in his eyes. "We should get her in the ground as soon as possible—as soon as you're feeling up to it."

She looked Dixon's way. "She was so beautiful."

"Yes, she certainly was," he agreed. "Like Carlie said—she was beautiful like her mother."

She smiled wanly.

"I . . . ahhh—" Broden began.

"Yes?" Mara asked.

"I thought the two of you might take a quick trip to the palace. I hope you don't mind, but I spoke to the twins. They agreed that you should place Marcella's remains in the grounds there. After all, you've no connection to this camp here and . . ." His voiced trailed off.

Mara turned to Dixon. "What do you think?"

"I suppose, so long as just the two of us go, it would be fine. But, for now, I don't want you taking any chances traveling with anyone else."

She nodded. "Agreed."

"If I might suggest something more," Broden said.

"Yes?"

"Your family and friends are, quite understandably, at a bit of a loss as to how to handle this all. They want to be there for you—and to acknowledge your loss."

"What do you suggest?" Dixon asked.

"Actually, it was Basha and Velia's suggestion. They've planned a short ceremony—if that's all right with you."

"Sure. We'd like that," Mara said, as Dixon nodded in agreement with her. "Would tomorrow work?"

"Tomorrow it is," Broden said, as he stood. "Well, I'd best get back to things. I've been filling Lucy in on everything I can recall from my time in Chiran—in the event any of the information might come in handy."

He stepped away, then turned back, a grin on his face. "What's more, I'm only now becoming accustomed to having an Oathtaker to call my own. I suspect Dax is already wondering about my whereabouts."

Mara chuckled. "He's a good man."

"That he is. So . . . tomorrow then. Let's say . . . at daybreak?"

"Daybreak it is. Thank you, Broden—for everything."

The next morning dawned as spring birds hooted, and sang, and called.

All the camp residents stood at attention, awaiting the arrival of Mara, Dixon, and the twins. One of the company, who happened to have a fiddle, played a sweet, but melancholy, tune. The notes lifted in the air, then seemed to hang there, inviting listeners to contemplate.

Lucy and Dax stood in the center of the crowd with Broden, who held a solid silver box, at the center of which was depicted, a lone dove.

When Mara, Dixon, and the twins, arrived, the camp residents made room for them to pass through to the center of the crowd. Along the way, their friends offered their condolences.

As Mara neared where Broden stood, Basha stepped forward and then embraced her friend. Once done, Velia and Jerrett did the same. Mara thanked them for their kind words. Then she and Dixon met Broden, who held the silver box toward them. They each placed a hand on it.

Mara inhaled slowly, deeply. "Thank you all," she said as she looked out over the crowd. She paused, momentarily, before continuing. "I am reminded of a prayer I once heard from a woman who'd lost her only son as the result of a tragic event. I may not get her words exactly correct, but I'd like to share the spirit of them with you all."

She bowed her head and recited:

Taken from us too soon,
Your life was
Ephemeral,
A fleeting thing.
Yet with us you shall always be.

Henceforth, we will
Feel you with each breeze
That wafts across our shoulders,
See you in each glimmer
On freshly fallen snow,
Hear you in every dove's coo.

Yes, our darling Mariella,
You were taken from us too soon.
Yet with us,
You shall always be.

Mara blinked fast to keep her eyes from tearing up, then turned to the twins. After embracing them both, she faced Dixon.

He took the box from Broden. "Mara and I will journey to bury Mariella on the palace grounds, in Shimeron," he said to the crowd. "We . . . ahhh . . . Well, we expect to return before nightfall, but given our new appreciation for how quickly things can change, at this time we merely say, 'Farewell. We hope to see you soon.'" With that he turned back to Mara and took her hand.

A second later, the two disappeared.

Chapter Fifty-Six

After Mara and Dixon returned from their trip to the palace to bury Mariella, they met with the twins. They decided that going forward, considering Mara's recent troubles with traveling, they would institute some changes. Thus, after much deliberation, they determined that they'd discontinue the practice of keeping the identities of the Council members secret. They simply didn't have the luxury of continuing to do so. Once done, they called a meeting for the Council and all of the leaders to be held at Marshall's camp.

Shortly thereafter, Dixon and Lucy set out on a series of quick trips to bring the necessary personnel to the camp. In addition, at Vida's request, Dixon also delivered her and Clarimonde there, one at a time.

Finally, all was in order for their scheduled meeting. The sun at its zenith shone brightly as birds chirped merrily. The smells of open-grill cooking filled the air. The camp fairly buzzed with activity.

Marshall made his way around a corner, then stopped mid-stride upon sight of Chaya.

"Marshall," she said, tipping her head.

He smiled. "You're looking well. It's good to see you."

Her eyes narrowed. "Oh?"

"You know, you've gained quite a reputation around this place. It seems you've worked miracles with some of the children."

"Oh?" she repeated.

"In truth, you've become a favorite here—both given your expertise in helping with the little ones, and as a teacher."

"I'm doing all right, I guess." She swished her short ebony hair away from her bluebird colored eyes. Then, "I have to go," she said. "I told Clarimonde that I'd see to the children while she attends the meeting."

"I see."

She folded her arms. Then, shaking her head, she said, "You know, Marshall, you're a mystery to me. After weeks—months—in Darth together, planning our escape, we finally made it out. But no sooner did we leave the compound, than you . . . abandoned me."

"Abandoned you!"

Her eyes narrowed. "What else would you call it? You've avoided me every step of the way."

He shuffled his feet. "Chaya, I didn't mean to avoid you."

She scoffed. "Well, you had a funny way of showing it." With that, she stepped away.

He ran to catch up with her, and with a hand at her shoulder, brought her to a stop.

"Chaya, my intention wasn't to abandon you," he said as he shuffled his feet once more. He looked away, then turned back. "Do you remember when you were telling Nina that I shouldn't return to Chiran because, having killed Cark, it would be too dangerous for me there?"

"Yes."

"Then you told me that you couldn't do without me—" He stopped short.

"I remember. What about it?"

"Chaya, in truth, you scared me."

"What?"

He let his breath out slowly, audibly. "In that moment I knew that you had to spread your own wings—find your own way. I wanted you to know—"

She glared at him.

"I wanted to know—and I needed for you to know—that if you were with me, it was because you *chose* to be, and not because you felt there was no other way for you. And I needed you to know that I was with you because that was *my* choice—not because I felt emotionally blackmailed into it."

She pulled back, scowling. "What are you talking about?"

"Chaya, when I first brought you here, to Oosa, you didn't know anyone except for me. But you needed to learn that you are strong and capable in your own right—that you can stand on your own two feet. I wanted you to know that you didn't need me, or anyone else, to fill any of your needs—physical, spiritual, or otherwise."

He sighed. "Too many times, I've seen someone in your position make a life-changing decision only to discover his or her own strength later—and then have regrets. I don't want you with me because you think you need for me to do something for you that you are actually quite capable of seeing to yourself, or because you feel indebted to me once you discover your own abilities. I want you with me because, strong in your own right, and capable of meeting all your own needs, you *choose* to be with me. Otherwise, we'd be destined to fail in the future."

"In other words," she said, "you don't want me until I've learned that I can live without you."

He chuckled. "I suppose that's one way of putting it. In fact, it's what my mother always told my younger sisters: 'Don't bind yourself to a man until you know you can live without him,' she'd say."

She cocked her head. "So . . . you really thought I only wanted to be with you because I needed you?"

He shrugged. "I feared as much."

Looking down, she said, "Well, I hate to admit it, but I think you might have been right. I mean—you were right that I needed to learn that I'm capable of handling things on my own."

He smiled.

"Now," she said, standing firm, "I know my own strength—and I've learned to rely on it."

"You're not angry with me then?"

She bit her lip. "No, I guess not."

"In that case, do you think—" He stopped short.

"What?"

"That you might want to have dinner with me tonight?"

"Hmmmm . . . Well, I'm sorry, but . . . I've other plans."

"I see." He looked at the ground.

"Tomorrow might work though." She grinned.

Turing back up, gazing into her bluebird eyes—those eyes that made his heart beat faster—he smiled broadly. "Perfect."

A group of Oathtakers, on their way to the meeting, brushed past the two of them.

Marshall shuffled his feet. "Well, I guess I have somewhere I have to get to."

"I understand."

"Tomorrow then?"

Nodding, she said, "It's a date."

With that, he rushed off.

Given the size of the gathering, it was held out of doors, under a tarp. Among others, the entire Council, all the Oathtaker trainers, the twins, and Broden, attended. For ease of communication, they sat in three rows around a center oval table. Mara and the twins headed it, with the rest of the Council members making up the remainder of the first ring. Before them, Effie and Fleet, along with a number of additional flits, sat on the tabletop. Behind them came Dixon and some of Mara and the girls' closest friends and confidants. Finally, in the back row sat the arms-trainers and the healers.

Reigna glanced out after everyone was seated. "This meeting is called to order," she said. "In the interests of time, Eden and I, with Mara's input, have determined that we will hear a report from each Council member on the topic under his or her particular domain."

She looked down at the papers before her, rustled through a few of them, and then pulled one out. She put it on the top of the pile.

"So. . . Mildred Crane," she said as she reached for her quill, preparing to take notes, "as you are in charge of issues relating to health and healing, you're up first."

When Mildred bobbed her head in acknowledgement, Mara noted how much grayer her hair was than when she'd first met her. Back then, the woman sported a single silver streak at her temple. Now, little of her former ebony tresses remained.

"Actually, before I get started, I thought Lucy might like a moment to discuss the situation with Percival Ferreolo, as it currently stands."

Lucy cleared her throat then addressed the crowd. "I am delighted to report that Percival is with us today." She looked up, caught his eye, and smiled. "Before I brought him back here for this meeting, I expressed my deepest regrets and extended to him, my sincerest apologies. I am happy to say that he has been gracious enough to accept them." She looked his way again. "Thank you, Percival, and welcome back."

The group broke out into spontaneous applause.

"Have you anything to add to that?" Mildred asked him.

"Only that I believe Lucy did the right thing," he said. "In truth, we can't afford to overlook what seems obvious."

"Yes," Lucy said, "but neither can we be lackadaisical. As we were reminded recently, prophecy provides that things are not always what they seem."

"Even so, the facts did suggest that I was the leak. I suspect . . . Well, I'll let Lucy tell you all."

She nodded his way, then proceeded to fill in for any of the others who hadn't learned the true facts as yet, the part that Petrus Feoras—Brother Pestifere—had played.

"Keep in mind that he mentioned that there are others of these Oathtakers—or more accurately, Oath*breakers*," she finally said. Then she turned to the professor, Skylar Hadwin. "Can you think of any way we might identify those from amongst us who've turned to the dark side?" she asked him.

"In truth, I cannot," he said. "Their actions are like a black spot on the character of you all, but I'm sorry to say, I know of no way of identifying them."

"Do you think there are many of them?"

"I do not," he said. "An Oathtaker's training, and the final exams one takes, weed out most of the potential problems, but . . . Well, we can hardly expect perfection in an imperfect world."

Lucy nodded, then held up her finger. "You know," she said, "when I traveled with Petrus—Pestifere—I experienced something highly unusual." She caught Mara's eye, then Dixon's. "When I travel, I see colors and light. Do you?"

"Yes," Dixon said.

Mara nodded. "Yes, I do, too."

"Have you ever seen black streaks running through?"

Mara's eyes narrowed. "Never."

"No, I haven't either," Dixon agreed.

"Well, perhaps it had to do with Petrus's—Pestifere's—true character. You might want to be on the watch for that in the future." She turned back to the professor. "Anything more?"

"Only that we're still trying to decipher a prophecy that we reviewed earlier."

"Oh?" Mara asked.

He cleared his throat, then recited:

Shall the tree determine the circumstances of its seed? A miniature kernel, containing its own survival, in itself is neither good, nor evil. That from which it is derived determines not the kernel's end. Consider, rather, the ground in which it sprouts, the purity of the water sprinkled upon it. Even when germinated in darkness, yet in clear light, it may thrive. Even when cast in the ashes, when transplanted to nourishing soil, it may live. Even that which emerges, surrounded by acidic waters, may find new life at the base of a fresh spring well.

"That was like my dream!" Mara cried.

"What dream?" Lucy asked.

"Remember? The one about the seed that was planted in chaos? Later, it was removed and received fresh water and clean air—and after it grew, it offered refuge to others." Mara's brow dropped. "You know, Lucy," she continued, looking her way, "in truth, that was a good summary of Broden's parentage, of his life, and of Rowena's and your parts in it. And it was due to him that we all escaped from that prison." She smiled. "We should have caught on to the parallels earlier."

"Agreed," Lucy said.

"Actually, it also reminds me of another dream I had. In that one, a thorny bramble somehow created a seed that started the takeover of a land of desolation." She closed her eyes in thought. "As I think on it, it seems to have meant that Broden—the seed of Zarek—offered an opportunity for rescue."

"*Lose not faith when deliverance is sought. The despot inevitably offers the seed of his own destruction,*" Professor Hadwin offered.

Smiling, Reigna nodded at Mara, then turned back Mildred's way. "Have you anything else then?"

Patting her hair, the woman addressed the group. "The healers ranks are in good order, although in truth, they've been overextended for some time now. Percival and I will stay in steady contact and I'll keep you all informed. But for the time being, that's it."

"Very well then," Reigna said. She turned to Eden. "Who's next?"

"Eben Taft."

"Right. Eben, as the chief scientist, have you a report?"

"Just this," he said, peeking through his unruly brows. "We've been experimenting with the crystals to come up with some more effective weaponry. The early results look promising."

"Can you give us any examples?"

"Well," he said, "we've discovered that when we use them collectively, some strange phenomena occur. For example, if we use together, one that starts fires and one that causes a gust of wind, we can create a blaze that proves highly difficult to extinguish."

"Doesn't water work?" Lucy asked.

"Well . . . yes . . . But it takes more than usual."

"Interesting."

"Thank you, Eben," Eden said. "Please keep us informed."

"Certainly."

"Next is . . . Piers Hamilton."

Mara glanced his way. She noted that the man, despite his advanced years, still exuded power.

"Well," he said, then cleared his throat, "I must admit that things of an economic nature are not at their best these days in Oosa. The many children that have come over the border have presented some difficulties. Where possible, we've worked to find families for them. My particular concern, however, is with respect to the numerous young men who've made their way here. For the most part, they lack job skills, as a consequence of which, it seems a number of them have turned to lives of crime."

"Not to mention that it seems some were trained for such purposes," Lucy added.

"Any recommendations there?" Eden asked.

"Aside from disallowing any more to enter?" Piers asked.

Lucy sat up straighter. "Actually, where possible, we're already doing just that."

"Nothing more at this time then," he said.

"Thank you." Reigna glanced down at her papers. "Skylar Hadwin." She looked his way and smiled. "Your report, Professor?"

"Ahhh . . ." He looked at his notes, then back up. "We've a team in place to collect all works of prophecy we can lay our hands on," he said. Then turning to Lucy, he added, "Had we been able to decipher more text earlier, we might have avoided having so many of you taken prisoner."

"Agreed." She nodded at him.

Reigna scribbled some notes. "Thank you, Professor."

She turned to Heather Larkspur. "Have you a report with regards to any legal maters?"

"Nothing at this time."

"Very well. Thank you."

She turned to Lucy. "As the expert with regards to how Oosian society is governed, you're up next," she said.

"Well, actually," Lucy said, "with the changes we're making here today—disclosing the identities of the Council members—I can't rightly speak on the status of much of anything. I do, however, recommend that we encourage all local communities to identify those whom they'd like to have represent them before this Council. I suggest an official title for the person chosen in each area. Perhaps 'mayor,' would be appropriate."

"Will you be sending notices out to that effect?"

"Yes."

Once again, Reigna made some notes. Then she turned to the row just behind her. "Dax, as commander of our fighting forces, have you a report?"

He leaned in. "Yes. Well, actually, with Petrus—err, Pestifere—now aware of many of the plans we'd been forming, we'll need to start all over again."

A collective groan made its way through the crowd.

"Right. Now . . . when Aliza and I left for Chiran, those troops who remained in the City of Light, continued training. At this time we plan to assign the majority of the companies to various strategic points along the border." He turned to Aliza. "Have you anything to add?"

"Only that the healers will be divided up so as to accompany the troops to their various stations," she said.

As Eden turned to whisper something to her sister, Mara suddenly gasped, then doubled over. "Ohhh!" she cried. Then her fear-filled eyes flashed Dixon's direction.

"Move!" he cried. "Everyone! Out of the way!"

As the twins pulled aside, he put his hand behind Mara's neck, then slowly laid her back.

"What is it?" he asked. "What's happening?"

"I don't know," she said, grabbing at his vest and pulling him closer. "Something's wrong . . . Something is very, very wrong."

Velia and Basha approached and knelt next to her. Velia rubbed her arm. Then, with the familiarity that only a dear friend may extend without first asking permission, she placed her hand on Mara's middle. She reached for her magic that would allow her to take on her pain.

Seconds later, her eyes went wide. She looked up and stared at her friend. Her breath caught in her throat.

"Mara," she said, "tell me again what happened with Mariella."

"It's just like I told you— I— I lost her," she said, her eyes spilling great tears.

Slowly, Velia's head turned right, then left, as she muttered, "Mara, you didn't lose the baby."

Chapter Fifty-Seven

Mara pushed her hand away. "I most certainly did! I saw her—and so did Dixon! Carlie saw her, too—and Broden. He brought her body back with him." A cry escaped her. "For goodness sake, Velia, we just buried her!" She stared at her friend. "How could you be so cruel?"

"No, Mara, I mean, you didn't lose *the* baby. You lost *a* baby!" Hesitatingly, she felt Mara's abdomen once again. "I can feel your unborn, Mara," she said, holding her gaze. "I can feel what it's feeling—warm, safe, and secure. You are still pregnant."

Eyes went wide and mouths opened large, as the other attendees all watched on.

"What?" Dixon asked.

"She lost a baby, Dixon," Velia said, holding his gaze, "but she's still pregnant."

"Is that even possible?" Reigna asked Lucy.

Lucy looked about. "Percival?" she asked.

"It's possible," he said, "although in truth, it is quite, *quite* rare."

"Oh!" Mara gasped. "There it is again! What's happening?"

Velia sucked in a breath, then chuckled. "Oh, Mara, your body is just preparing for the day this little one makes his—or her—debut! It's still some time off, but nature is taking its course." She squeezed her shoulder. "There is nothing wrong with you, I promise."

"Here, Dixon," she said, taking his hand. She placed it on Mara's middle, then watched for his reaction. "There! Did you feel that?"

"Yes!"

"That's the baby, Dixon. And that explains everything! Mara, listen," she said looking deeply into her friend's eyes, "you can't travel with more than one person unless you travel with the twins, and then you can only travel with the two of them. When you came here, you were carrying *three* people—the two you usually can carry together without trouble—but also, your baby!"

"Oh, great Ehyeh!" Reigna cried.

"Come here, Reigna," Velia said, motioning for her, "Feel this." She put her hand on Mara's middle. "You too, Eden. Come on!" When Eden neared, she took her hand.

All were mesmerized as they felt the unborn child move.

"Oh, my— Oh!" Mara covered her mouth, as a sob escaped her. "Oh, Velia, thank you!" she cried.

"Don't thank me!" She pulled back and held her hand up. "Thank Dixon!" Laughing, she leaned in and kissed her friend's cheek. "I'm so sorry for your loss— and so happy for what you've kept. You are going to make an amazing mother."

"Mara," Lucy interrupted, now standing nearby, "have you any idea how far along you were when you lost Mariella?"

Mara shared that she'd estimated she was somewhere between her twenty-second and twenty-fifth weeks at the time.

"Well, think now. When Zarek's men captured the three of you. What do you remember of that?"

"I remember . . ." Mara thought back. "I remember the moment we landed, near Aliza's former camp, I felt very tired, out of sorts. I felt slow. It was strange because traveling doesn't usually have that effect on me—except for that time when I joined Dixon and the twins in the City of Light and slept for almost three days afterward."

"Do you think your being pregnant at the time could have played a part in what transpired there?"

Everyone turned Lucy's way. Several lowered their brows. A few pursed their lips.

"Oh, I'm not suggesting any fault!" she exclaimed. "It's just that you," she looked back at Mara, "were pregnant then, too, yet you didn't pass out from the traveling . . ."

Mara closed her eyes in thought, then looked back at Lucy. "Actually . . . I did. They knocked me out when they attacked me. Then . . . Well, I believed all this time that they'd drugged me after that, but . . . maybe they didn't. Or maybe it would've made no difference if they had."

"It's true," Eden said. "She was out for three days."

"So," Velia said, "you traveled only five times since you became pregnant. The first time, you met the twins in the City of Light and, as you said, you were very weak for three days after your arrival. Consider that you were carrying two people then—your twins. Later, when you went with Reigna and Eden to the border, you passed out for a few days. That time, you were carrying four people—your twins, and Reigna and Eden. Next, you brought Carlie to the palace and again, passed out for three days. That time, you were carrying two people—your one child, and Carlie."

She paused, in thought, rubbing her forehead. Then, after looking about for a moment, she turned back. "Yes, and when you traveled back for the twins—you carried just your one remaining unborn child. So it makes sense that nothing happened that time. But this last time, when you brought the twins from across the border to this camp while also carrying your remaining child, you were out for seven full days. Perhaps the differences each time had to do with how much more developed your baby was—or babies were—and on how many people you carried with each trip."

"Huh," Mara said. "It's all so amazing." She paused, contemplating it all. Then she added, "Now that I think on it, it seems my dreams were about this, as well." She proceeded to tell them all about her dreams of being chased while carrying twins.

"All along I thought those dreams were about you girls," she said, nodding at Reigna and Eden. "But in each, I lost, or it seemed I was about to lose—one of the two babes I carried. And so, it seems, I have." Then she went quiet.

"Well," Lucy said, "you know you have my sincerest condolences on your loss. Now I'd like to offer you my heartiest congratulations on this child. I am truly delighted for you!"

Mara watched her closely. She nodded, bit her lip, and then motioned for her to come nearer.

When Lucy bent over her, she whispered just loud enough for her, and those immediately around her, to hear. "And I'm sorry for your loss, Lucy."

Those nearest looked from her to Lucy, but no one spoke.

Then, after a long pause, Dixon finally asked, "What loss?"

"Never mind." She shook her head. "Lucy knows what I'm talking about."

Lucy's eyes filled with tears. "Thank you," she said, patting Mara's arm, "but you know? You were right all along. And—I'm fine. Really."

Turning Dixon's way, Mara smiled. "Can you believe it? About the baby, I mean?"

Grinning, he shook his head. "Hardly."

"Well . . . congratulations . . . Daddy," she whispered.

Keep watch for Volume Four of The Oathtaker Series.

THE CAST OF CHARACTERS

Adamina, Rowena's sixth-born daughter, Reigna and Eden's sister, mentioned in passing

Adele, former maid to Rowena and then Lilith, joined Mara when the twins were infants, now head of the compound kitchens

Aden, son of Jerrett and Velia, eight years old

Adli, former Chiranian, convert to Ehyeh's ways, forges documents for those seeking to infiltrate Chiran

Aliza (Kensey), Oathtaker, second-in-command of the Oathtaker troops, can take on the persona of another, her former charge was Kimber Calder, her blade is Gloriam

Akka, one of the three lords of Sinespe, the underworld, along with Daeva and Sij

Arvid, Percival's second charge, deceased

Asmeret, Rowena's second-born daughter, Reigna and Eden's sister, mentioned in passing

Bane, the dog—err, wolf—Jerrett adopts that is connected to him by attendant magic

Barbara Jo, helps Adele in the kitchens and with cleaning at the palace

Basha (Constant), Therese's Oathtaker, her blade is Honora

Bernard, long time doorman at the palace of the Select in Shimeron

Birdie, one of the four teens the Oathtakers meet on their way to the palace, seeks to become a succedunt bride

Blink, a flit

Broden, cousin to Reigna and Eden, son of Lilith and Zarek

Caden, son of Nina and Jules

Calandra, youngest daughter of Nina and Jules

Cark, former head of Camp Cark in Chiran, former husband to Chaya, deceased

Carlie, oldest child, and daughter, of Nina and Jules, nicknamed "Mouse"

Carlow, Jerrett and Velia's youngest son, about one year old

Caveman, one of Zarek's men

Celestine, a barmaid at The Clandest Inn, an Oathtaker, cousin to Dixon Townsend, married to Ezra

Chaya, a Chiranian refugee, former wife of Cark

Clarimonde, Oathtaker to Vida

Clementine, a child slave in Chiran

Creovita, also known as Ehyeh, and the Good One, the creator of all

Daeva, chief lord of Sinespe, the underworld, assisted by Akka and Sij

Dalton, Oathtaker to Declan

Dax, *Galen Dax*, Oathtaker, leader of the Oathtaker troops in the City of Light, immune to magic, his blade is Immunis

Declan, charge of Dalton

Dianna, second eldest sister to Rowena and Lilith, mentioned in passing, deceased

Diella, Rowena's third-born daughter, sister to Reigna and Eden, mentioned in passing

Dixon (Townsend), former Oathtaker to Rowena Vala (Reigna and Eden's mother), married to Mara, his blade is Verity

Drew, son of Jerrett and Velia, five years old

Eben Taft, a Council member, a scientist

Echo, one of the four teens the Oathtakers meet on their way to the palace, seeks to become a succedunt bride

Eden, 'she who is but is not,' of prophetic fame, born of Rowena's seventh pregnancy but is not her seventh-born child, Reigna's twin, Mara's charge

Edmond, Dixon's former friend who betrayed Mara, Dixon, and the twins, providing their whereabouts to Lilith when the twins were infants, mentioned in passing

Ehyeh, also known as the Good One, and Creovita, the creator of all

Ella, unknown party that Felicity cries for

Ellian, the charge of Farrell, a compound resident

Ephemeral, (Effie), queen of the flits

Erin, a Chiranian refugee, sister to Nina

Ethereal, (Ethel), a flit

Evanescent, (Evan), a flit

Eve, eldest sister to Rowena and Lilith, deceased, mentioned in passing

Ezra, Oathtaker, innkeeper at The Clandest Inn, a spymaster, husband of Celestine, a healer

Fabiana, Oathtaker, archer, arms-trainer

Farida, a slave woman in Chiran that Zarek gave to Broden

Farrell, Oathtaker to Ellian, resides at the compound

Felicity, Select, Trumble's charge, has visions of events as they occur

Fidel, one of the oldtimers who were among the first to recognize Reigna and Eden as fulfillment of prophecy, specializes in prophecy

Filip, Percival's first charge, deceased

Fleeting, (Fleet), king of the flits

Fugacious, (Fuggy), a flit

Galen Dax, *Dax*, leader of the Oathtaker troops in the City of Light, immune to magic, his blade is Immunis

Georgiana, Oathtaker, healer, stays at the compound in the event of Carlie's return

Ghazala, Farida's sister, one of Broden's slave women in Chiran

Gonen, Zarek's secretary

Good One, also known as Ehyeh, and Creovita, creator of all

Grant, husband of Rowena, father of Reigna and Eden, not born of the Select, deceased

Harper Larkspur, Council member, a legal expert

Hatchet, one of Zarek's men

Hazarik, Chiranians of particular descendant, whose ranks include the succedunt who are also known as "the descendants"

Idaleen, Oathtaker, makes arrests under the Council's authority

Jabari Creed, Jerrett's chosen name while in Chiran

Janine, Rowena and Lilith's sister, a fourth-born of the Select, resides in Chiran, a follower of Daeva

Jedrek, son of Jerrett and Velia, three years old

Jerrett, (Jabari Creed), Oathtaker, husband to Velia, father to four boys, his blade is Fortitudo

Joed, Select, sides with Percival

Jules, head of compound security, married to Nina, father to Carlie, Caden and Calandra

Kayson, an Oathtaker, a healer

Kiera, an Oathtaker, a healer

Kimber (Calder), a cousin of Rowena's, Aliza's former charge, deceased

Leala, one of the oldtimers who were among the first to recognize Reigna and Eden as fulfillment of prophecy, specializes in history

Liam, Oathtaker, goes with Rafal into Chiran to spy

Lilith, Rowena's sister, a sixth-born of the Select, tried to murder Reigna and Eden when they were infants, Broden's mother, Marshall's former charge, follower of Daeva, deceased

Lucy (Haven), Oathtaker to the last two seventh-born daughters of the Select before Rowena, her blade is Vivacitas

Macall, Oathtaker, stays at the compound in the event of Carlie's return

Mad Dog, one of Zarek's men

Mae, married Max, Rowena's mother, Reigna and Eden's grandmother, deceased

Mara (Townsend), (formerly Mara Richmond), Oathtaker to Reigna and Eden, married to Dixon Townsend, her blade is Spira

Mariella, unknown person

Marshall, Oathtaker, Lilith was his charge

Max, married Mae, Rowena's mother, Reigna and Eden's grandmother, deceased

Mercurial, (Merc), a flit

Mildred Crane, a Council member, in charge of health and healing

Mouse, Broden's nickname for Carlie

Mugger, chosen by Zarek's mother to be his teacher, a child molester, deceased

Nadine, a young woman captured to be sold into slavery in Chiran

Nancy, a barmaid at The Clandest Inn

Nina, married to Jules, mother of Carlie, Caden and Calandra

Odin, a child at Camp Cark, in Darth, Chiran

Ozel, Oathtaker, makes arrests under the Council's authority

Percival (Ferreolo), Oathtaker, healer

Pestifere (Brother), chief priest in Chiran, Zarek's closest advisor

Petrus Feoras, Oathtaker, Lucy's former love interest

Piers Hamilton, Council member, specializes in matters of business and finance

Pina, Rowena's fourth-born daughter, Reigna and Eden's sister, mentioned in passing

Pretty Boy, one of Zarek's men

Prismatic, (Prissy) a flit

Rafal, Oathtaker, goes with Liam into Chiran to spy

Raiden, Oathtaker, assists Trumble

Raman, Oathtaker, one of the training leaders

Reigna, (whose name is derived from the word *reign*), seventh-born daughter of Rowena, Eden's twin, Mara's charge

Saga, helps Lucy with her books at the compound

Sally, Rowena and Lilith's sister, a fifth-born of the Select, resides in Chiran with Zarek, a follower of Daeva

Salus, Oathtaker, healer, engaged to Willow, meets someone in need of his help at *The Swindler's Cup*

Samuel, cousin to Jules

Scarface, one of Zarek's men

Scintillation, (Cindy), a flit

Shadow, one of Zarek's men

Sheva, Rowena's first Oathtaker, deceased

Sij, one of the three lords of Sinespe, the underworld, along with Daeva and Aka

Skelly, gave Rowena a white cashmere cloak years ago, was thought to be mad

Skylar Hadwin, a professor, the most renounced historian in Oosa, studies prophecy, a member of the Council

Sola, an addict to bibulous nut, who Salus is asked to aid

Spectral, (Spec), a flit

Striver, tutor to Broden in Chiran

Succedunt, Chiranian soldiers who, like Zarek, are descendants of the Hazarik, dress all in black

Sugar, one of the four teens the Oathtakers meet on their way to the palace, seeks to become a succedunt bride

Tam, Petrus Feoras's former charge, deceased

Tanith, Chaya's mother, advisor to Zarek, runs the concentration camp for women prisoners in Darth, Chiran

Therese, Rowena's sister and aunt to Reigna and Eden, a third-born of the Select, Basha's charge

Tivona, Rowena's fifth-born daughter, Reigna and Eden's sister, mentioned in passing

Trixie, one of the four teens the Oathtakers meet on their way to the palace, seeks to become a succedunt bride

Trumble (Alexander), Oathtaker to Felicity, his blade is Amora

Valentina, Oathtaker, healer at the palace

Velia (Bettina), Oathtaker, wife to Jerrett, mother to four boys, her blade is Justise

Vida, Rowena's first-born, Reigna and Eden's sister, her Oathtaker is Clarimonde

Wade, a child residing with Vida and Clarimonde in Ethanward before they leave for Shimeron

Willow, an Oathtaker, arms-trainer, engaged to marry Salus

Yasmin, a slave in Chiran that Zarek gave to Broden

Zarek, leader of Chiran, Broden's father, a follower of Daeva

Synopsis – *Oathtaker*
The Oathtaker Series, Volume One

Mara, an Oathtaker, trained to protect Ehyeh's chosen, the *Select*, those designated to carry His ways of life and freedom through the ages, is drawn from her intended path. She discovers a wayfarer's hut. Thirteen grut, underworld beasts, surround it. As she kills each, it goes up in a flash of fire. Thereafter left with a single weapon—her Oathtaker's blade—a weapon infused with a magic that will live for so long as she does, Mara steps inside. There, she discovers Rowena, the current ranking member of the first family of the Select, in labor. Rowena bears twins, although no Select had ever before had twins. She names them Reigna (derived from the word "reign") and Eden, releases her power as leader of the Select to them, and then dies.

Though Mara knows of no Oathtaker with more than a single charge, she swears a life oath to protect both infants. In exchange for her vow, Ehyeh bestows upon her, "continued youth" for so long as her charges live, and attendant magic—powers that will make themselves known to her over time. Upon the death of her charges, Mara may begin her life anew, but in the meantime, she may not be unequally yoked—she may not bind herself to another. Ehyeh confirms Mara's vow with an earthshaking.

The hut door bursts open and a man, Dixon, enters. Upon finding Rowena, his former charge, now dead, he blames Mara. The two enter into a weak alliance to work together to usher the infants to safety. When they find grut teeth on the ground, they collect the trinkets, as the creatures cannot harm anyone who possesses one. Then, seeking to hide all evidence of Rowena, they set the hut, with Rowena's body inside, on fire.

The Oathtakers make their way to the home of an old couple, Drake and Maggie. From them, they learn of an Oathtaker-run mission home in Polesk for young women fleeing to Oosa from a neighboring empire, Chiran. As the women often arrive at the place pregnant, or with newborns, the Oathtakers plan to head there to find a wet nurse for the twins. Although tempted, Mara restrains herself from thinking on her past, which seeks to worry its way into her thoughts

Previously on Rowena and Dixon's trail, Gadon and his men, who had called up the grut, arrive at the home of the oldtimers who lead them to believe that Dixon and *Rowena* had visited them, and that Rowena had born her *child*. In fear, the oldtimers tell the men that the two left for Polesk. Gadon sends one of his crew ahead in search of them, then kills the couple.

When Gadon's man intercepts the Oathtakers, they learn that someone from the palace of the Select at Shimeron, home of the first family, enlisted Gadon's assistance. Mara and Dixon dispose of the man, then stop for the night. Mara, now weary of Dixon's surly behavior, tells him to leave her. He apologizes for having unfairly blamed her for Rowena's death, then swears he would die for the twins. To Mara and Dixon's amazement, Ehyeh confirms Dixon's vow with an earthshaking. Since Mara is already the twins' assigned Oathtaker, the two are troubled as to the meaning of the confirmation. They make peace, then Dixon suggests that his friend, Edmond, might be of help. The two grew up like brothers after Dixon's father led a successful prosecution against Edmond's father for treason against the Select. Enamored with Mara's strength of spirit, Dixon allows her to believe he had loved Rowena, as he thinks it will help to keep a distance between them.

The Oathtakers arrive at the mission home where they meet Nina, a young Chiranian. Grieving over the death of the child she bore while escaping Chiran, Nina swears to protect the twins with her life. The Oathtakers are shocked when Ehyeh also confirms her oath, with an earthshaking.

While in Polesk, meeting with Dixon's old friend and mentor, Ted, Mara is startled when a compact she carries that had belonged to Rowena, starts "buzzing." When she opens it, a woman's visage greets her. Dixon recognizes Rowena's friend, Lucy, who reveals that she has prepared a safe place for Rowena. Mara informs Lucy of Rowena's death, and of the twins' birth, then makes plans to join her.

The Oathtakers head for sanctuary. There, they discuss the significance of the first- through seventh-born children of the Select, and ponder over the difficulties that one who is a sixth-born—one most interested in pursuing his own desires— could cause. Mara comments on a dream she had the night before, in which a woman took the infant girls from her. She had not recognized the dream as the working of some attendant magic, bringing her a warning, but Dixon does. He insists she leave immediately. As she exits through a back door with Nina and the twins, Lilith a sixth-born of the Select, Rowena's next older sister, arrives.

Hearing of her sister's death, Lilith assumes Rowena's child also died, and that she, Lilith, is now the ranking member of the Select. She bands Dixon, cutting off all magic getting to or from him. He, now sure Lilith sent the assassins after Rowena, willingly accompanies her to the palace in Shimeron, so as to avoid raising her suspicions, although he grows fearful that she intends to make a scapegoat of him.

At the palace, Dixon finds his friend, Edmond, who insists he is friendly with Lilith so as to keep the peace. Dixon also discovers another friend and fellow Oathtaker there—Basha. Dixon meets Basha at the falls where her charge, Rowena's sister, Therese, was believed assassinated some years back. Her body was never found. After a rustling in the underbrush momentarily interrupts Dixon and Basha's conversation, the two speak freely. Basha believes Therese still lives, because she occasionally feels her bond to her charge. Further, she believes Lilith was behind the assassination attempt on Therese's life. Dixon reveals nothing of his suspicions about Lilith, or about Mara and the twins.

Mara and Nina check into an inn. They learn from the local fliers, that Lilith holds Dixon, and that he will be tried for treason. Then Mara discovers more attendant magic powers: she can taste and smell color. As a consequence, she believes a woman who watched her earlier that evening during dinner, is outside her door. Fearing for the infants, Mara arms herself, then opens the door. The woman standing just outside, introduces herself as Therese. Recollecting details from a dream, one in which she rustled through some brush, then felt as though she was physically present with Dixon and Basha at a falls, Mara tests the woman with information she had learned from her "dream." When Therese proves true, and discloses that she has been staying with Lucy, Mara reveals her true identity and that of the infants. Joyous over the children's survival, Therese swears a life oath to protect them. Once again, the earth shakes with Ehyeh's confirmation.

Later, while seeking rest, Mara "awakens" in a room where Dixon soon arrives. He informs her that Lilith captured him, took him to the palace, and will have him tried, but Mara disappears before he can think to have her remove the band Lilith put on him to block his magic powers. Back with Nina, Mara discovers she returned from her "dream" carrying Dixon's flint.

Lilith meets with her spirit guide, Daeva, lord of the underworld. He informs her that Rowena's *child* lives, and that Rowena released her power to her child before she died. As a consequence, Lilith is not the legitimate new ranking member of the Select. Then he assures Lilith that there is still a way for her to become the ranking member so that she may reign over Oosa, and he endows her with dark magic.

Lilith, furious to learn the true facts, questions Dixon. When he refuses to tell her of the *child's* whereabouts—as Lilith is unaware that Rowena bore twins—she tortures him with her dark magic.

Mara and Nina, with the infants, travel toward Lucy's with Therese and her bodyguards, Jules and Samuel. When the group stops to rest, Mara again finds herself magically transported to Dixon's side, although now he is in a cave of sorts, and unconscious from a severe beating. When Basha shows up there to see to Dixon, Mara recognizes the woman from her dream, when Basha spoke with Dixon at the falls. When a maid arrives to warn Basha that Lilith is on her way to see Dixon, Mara returns, magically, to her friends. Moments later, she discovers more magic—the power to heal. She longs to return to Dixon to heal him. Then, realizing that she magically traveled back from her first visit to him carrying his flint, Mara surmises that she might rescue him from Lilith's clutches. She ponders whether she wants him with her to assist her with the infants, or because of her growing interest in him. Later, Jules and Samuel swear to protect the twins with their lives. Each receives Ehyeh's confirmation of his vow, when the earth shakes.

When a storm erupts, the travelers find shelter in a barn built partially into the ground. There, Mara discovers a grut guarding a path that extends deep into the earth. As the grut tooth she wears protects her from the beast, Mara nears, then kills it. Then she finds, back in the cave, a shrine with an oracle—a book—that refers to a seventh seventh "and she who is but is not." Mara recollects something that Rowena had said when Eden was born—that the child was of a seventh pregnancy, but was not a seventh-born child.

Mara discovers that the book provides the identical message on every page: "Go." Thinking it means she is to go to rescue Dixon, she magically travels again, back to his side. Once again, she finds Basha with him. Although Mara tries to heal him, and to take him away, she is unable to do so. To test her powers, she urges Basha to travel with her. Upon Basha's agreement, the two instantly return to the barn. There, Basha and Therese are reunited. Basha then recollects that Dixon is banded. Therese informs Mara that as Oathtaker to the twins, who are the rightful ranking Select, she possesses the power to remove the band.

Mara magically returns to Dixon's side. She removes his band. Just then, the maid, Adele, arrives to warn Basha, who she knew had gone to see Dixon, that Lilith is on her way to see him. Moments later, Lilith enters. Adele grabs Mara and is caught up in the Oathtaker's magic. Back with her friends, grateful that Lilith did not also tag along for the magic ride, Mara heals Dixon and then, passes out. Later, he awakens her from her magic hangover.

Mara learns that a few years prior, Lilith had a son, and that when circumstances suggested the child was not safe with her, Rowena took him away. No one knows his father, but Therese informs the others that the child stays with Lucy. Both Basha and Adele swear life oaths to protect Rowena's infants. Each receives Ehyeh's confirmation of her vow.

Lilith meets with Daeva. He agrees to have the Chiranian leader, Zarek, who also serves the underlord, provide her with an army. When it arrives at the palace, Lilith tells the soldiers her plan: she will tell the people that someone is trying to pawn off a fraud as a new seventh seventh, then will encourage the people to give up the child she seeks. If they do not, she will kill all the infant girls. Her venture will begin in Polesk, but she will travel throughout Oosa to do the same elsewhere, as necessary, in her search for the child.

Erin, Nina's sister, and a slave to Zarek's soldiers, breaks free and runs to

Polesk. She meets a woman, Hattie, who rushes her to the mission home where they find Dixon's friend, Ted. They inform him of Lilith's plan. Ted relays that Lilith could cut off the twins' rightful line of rule if she kills them with a living Oathtaker's blade. Then, believing that sanctuary is the only safe place for the children of Polesk, Ted attempts to save them, but he is unsuccessful. Lilith's soldiers begin to follow through with her plan.

Wanting to dedicate the infant twins at a sanctuary, and to confirm that one of the three artifacts intended for the ranking member of the Select, the great crown, is still in the City of Light where Rowena left it, Mara leads her group to the city. They arrive at The Clandest Inn, owned by Dixon's friend, Ezra, a spymaster. Mara worries over the attention the barmaid, Celestine, pays to Dixon, though she reminds herself once again, that while he is now free of the oath he'd sworn to protect Rowena, she is still bound to her oath to protect the twins. For the first time since the girls' birth, Mara allows herself to think on a child she had abandoned in her past.

Mara and Dixon learn, along with Ezra, that Lilith travels with an army, that she seeks Dixon, and that she claims someone is trying to pawn off a fraud as a new seventh seventh. Mara tells Ezra about the twins. Delighted, he swears a life oath to protect them. Ezra receives Ehyeh's confirmation of his vow in the form of an earthshaking. Then the three make plans for Ezra's spies to spread false rumors of Dixon's whereabouts throughout Cosa, so as to lead Lilith astray.

When Mara takes the twins to sanctuary, two oldtimers, Leala and Fidel, intercept her. They recognize the twins as fulfillment of prophecy and swear life oaths to protect them. Ehyeh confirms the oldtimers' oaths, and they join Mara's entourage.

A guest arrives at Lilith's camp. He believes he can find Dixon, that Dixon will trust him, and that he can deliver the man to Lilith. She uses her dark magic on her guest, so that he cannot reveal his true intentions, and then sends him off in search of Dixon.

Meanwhile, seeking information about Lilith, Mara and Dixon travel magically to Polesk. There, they learn from Ted, of Lilith's venture, and of the deaths of many infants.

Lilith's soldiers capture Velia, an Oathtaker. Possessing the power to tell truth from falsehood, Velia learns of Lilith's plan to kill Rowena's seventh-born child. She agrees to accompany the woman, so as to gather evidence against her to take to the Council.

Mara confirms that the great crown is in the City of Light, and she knows Lucy has the second of the artifacts, the sword, with her. When the oracle once again tells Mara to "Go," she ponders whether it is telling her to go to Shimeron in search of the last of the artifacts, the scepter, where she believes it to be, or if it is telling her that she should go away from Dixon, whom she has come to love. She plans a trip to Shimeron and asks Basha, who was a palace regular, to accompany her there.

Concerned over Mara's state of mind, as she has been inseparable from the twins since returning with him from Polesk, Dixon encourages her to go walk with him. While out, she breaks down weeping. She tells Dixon that it pains her to leave the girls, as she left a child once before—one she'd sworn to care for. While comforting her, he confesses his love for her. Though she loves him in return, the two know they cannot act on their feelings, as Mara remains bound to her oath. Heavy hearted, they agree not to speak of such things again.

Mara and Basha travel magically to Shimeron. There, Mara discovers she can create crystals that make powerful weapons, and that allow her and Basha to communicate silently, by magic. They search Lilith's chambers. When Daeva shows up there in Lilith's looking glass, Mara casts him out with a crystal. Then she finds the scepter. She takes it, and also some books she finds at the palace, back to the inn.

Nina, to whom the ways of Oathtakers are largely unknown, asks Mara why she avoids Dixon when everyone knows they love one another. Mara tells her the truth: that subject to her oath, she is not free. Acting on her feelings would be an act of treason. At a minimum, it would mean losing the girls, and that is not a prospect she will consider.

Mara sends part of her group ahead to Lucy's with the scepter, for safekeeping, along with some books she wants to study later, including one that discusses an Oathtaker's oath, and its "rules and exclusions." As the group leaves, Dixon's old friend, Edmond, arrives. Learning of the twins, he tells Dixon when Lilith is due back in the City of Light, then insists that he must set off for urgent business, but that he will return shortly.

A guard escorts Velia to Lilith's wagon, where Lilith introduces Velia to Edmond who has brought to her, news of Dixon's whereabouts and of Rowena's twins. Lilith asks Velia to accompany her and Edmond on a trip. They, with a single guard, Jabari, set out. When Lilith becomes suspicious of Velia's intentions, Jabari reveals to Velia, his true identity. He, also, is an Oathtaker. He joined Lilith's solders earlier, in appearance only, to gather evidence against Lilith to take to the Council.

Lilith, Edmond, Velia, and Jabari, arrive in the City of Light. They check into an inn. Edmond messages Dixon, pleading for him and Mara to meet him at sanctuary the next day. There, he will share with them, news of Lilith. Although the Oathtakers had planned to leave the city the next day, at the oracle's urging to "Go," they agree to the meeting.

Hiding her true identity, Lilith checks in at The Clandest Inn, then watches out a window as Mara and Dixon leave to meet with Edmond. Lilith goes to Mara's suite. She stabs Erin, tortures Samuel with her evil magic, and then threatens Nina, demanding that she help her to get the twins to sanctuary. Meanwhile, Velia awakens at the inn, practically incoherent. Lilith had drugged her. Worse yet, Velia discovers, Lilith stole her Oathtaker's blade.

When Mara and Dixon meet with Edmond, Velia arrives at sanctuary. Distraught because she does not know where at sanctuary, Edmond's meeting with Mara and Dixon is to be held, Velia goes to the inner prayer room to seek Ehyeh's assistance. When an old woman asks her what is wrong, Velia tells her that she must warn two Oathtakers. When she reveals their names—Mara and Dixon—the old woman, Leala, rushes Velia to the meeting.

In the meeting room, Velia accuses Edmond of seeking revenge on Dixon, and of assisting Lilith. He denies her accusations, claiming that Velia cannot even prove she is an Oathtaker, as she has no Oathtaker's blade. Although Dixon finds Velia's accusation impossible to believe, Mara wonders. She asks Edmond to reassure her. Feigning outrage, he swears he would protect the infant twins with his very life. When the earth does not shake, Mara knows that Edmond betrayed them. She grabs Dixon and they magically transport back to the inn. There, they find Samuel, who is just able to relay to them that Lilith took the twins to sanctuary.

Returning immediately by magic, to sanctuary, Mara can smell and taste Lilith's ever-present red clothing. Though they make her ill, the smells and tastes draw her to the inner prayer room. After fighting off a pack of grut that bursts forth, Mara makes it to the door. Velia warns her that Lilith is inside, then recalls that the woman has her Oathtaker's blade. They all understand: Lilith can use it to cut off the girls' line of power.

Dixon and Velia enter the inner sanctuary through its front door. There, they find Lilith with Nina and the twins. Velia attacks Lilith, but Lilith spares the Oathtaker, as she needs her alive when she uses her blade to kill the twins on the altar, as Daeva has commanded her. Believing that the grut she had called up, attacked Mara, Lilith does not expect Mara to secretly enter the inner sanctuary through a back door.

Dixon distracts Lilith while Mara enters and then sends Nina and the twins out to safety. When he urges Lilith to turn back to Ehyeh, Lilith uses her dark magic on him. Mara announces her presence, but Lilith refuses to stop torturing Dixon. Mara throws her blade. It meets its mark, and Lilith goes up in flames.

Heavy hearted, as she has concluded she can no longer bear having Dixon so near, yet out of reach, Mara determines that they must part ways. But first, she calls a Council meeting to claim her rightful place as its leader, and to prove the twins' identity. When the meeting is to begin, Mara discovers that Lucy is a Council member, a fact Dixon had kept from her, as an oath bound him to secrecy.

Mara presents her witnesses. While testifying, Nina reveals that she recognized Lilith, whom she'd met in Chiran. There, Lilith acted as consort to Zarek, and went by a different name. Rumor had it that when Lilith left Chiran, she was pregnant. Mara and Dixon understand: Lilith bore Zarek's child, the one now living with Lucy.

As the hearing is closing, Lucy interrupts. There is an item of business remaining. Reports are that Mara and Dixon have fallen in love. Mara tells the Council that they need not worry, as Dixon will be leaving her. He, caught by surprise, is distraught.

Lucy laughs lightly, then composes herself. She questions Mara and Dixon about what it means to be unequally yoked. They assure her they understand. Lucy then pulls out a book that Mara had sent ahead with a part of her group, along with the scepter, to Lucy's. The book discusses the Oathtaker's oath, its "rules and exclusions." Lucy tells Mara and Dixon that, as they both swore a life oath to protect the same of the Select, and as Ehyeh confirmed the oath of each of them, they are not unequally yoked. In fact, they are free to be together.

SYNOPSIS – *SELECT*
THE OATHTAKER SERIES, VOLUME TWO

After moving to a compound for the safety of Rowena's seventh born, nearly two decades earlier, the Oathtakers used magic crystals to fortify its perimeter against incursions from outsiders. But a recent storm knocked down portions of those protections. Consequently, encroachments into the compound had become more frequent.

When Jules and Nina's eldest, sixteen-year old Carlie, goes missing, Mara, Dixon, and some Oathtaker friends, search of her. Finding intruders, they battle them. After vanquishing the enemy, Mara is missing. Dixon finds her at the bottom of a cliff, an arrow through her shoulder, and unconscious. Kayson, an Oathtaker-healer, heals her shoulder. Then Dixon carries her back to camp.

For three days, Mara remains unconscious. Dixon keeps her hydrated. Minutes after he goes to the compound sanctuary to pray, Therese informs him that Mara is awakening. He and the twins rush to her bedside. When she opens her eyes, he sends the twins for Lucy. After they leave, Mara asks him who they are. Subsequently, he discovers that she does not know him, or Basha, either. He encourages her to sleep, although she insists she must return home, to her mother's.

Dixon, Basha, and Therese, agree that if Lucy finds out about Mara's amnesia, she will try to have her removed as Oathtaker to the twins. To protect their secret, Dixon takes Mara from the compound. Once gone, those remaining discuss compound security. To Lucy's chagrin, the twins insist they be included. The group decides to send Marshall and Jerrett into Chiran, the obvious source of their troubles, for information. Meanwhile, Basha and Therese will check things at the palace, and then go to the City of Light where they will arrange for a census of the remaining Select and Oathtakers in Oosa. Later, the twins overhear Basha and Therese discussing Mara's condition. Feeling abandoned, they make secret plans to leave the compound to try to determine their callings.

As Mara and Dixon make their way through the countryside, Mara is angry that Dixon will not share details of her past with her. He fears that if he does, she might reject the information and never learn the truth. When a mountain lion attacks, Mara takes the beast down. Thereafter, she suffers a severe headache and passes out, remaining unconscious for another three days. When she awakens, she concludes that she is trained in weaponry.

While traveling to Chiran, Marshall reveals to Jerrett that Lilith, his former charge, abused her son, Broden, when he was an infant. Marshall rescued the child and then Rowena sent him to Lucy. After Lilith's death, Marshall moved to the compound and was reunited with him. He tells Jerrett that Zarek, the evil leader of Chiran, is Broden's father.

When the two arrive at The Clandest Inn, they meet with the innkeeper, Ezra. One of his spies tells the Oathtakers about a weapon used there—a "channel." Each soldier is assigned one to use it on himself rather than to give up any of Zarek's secrets. But using one's channel on another is forbidden. Magic would reveal the weapon's rightful owner, who would be put to death. Later, a former Chiranian forges documents for Marshall and Jerrett that will help them infiltrate the Chiranian troops.

Upon arriving at Camp Cark, Chiran, Marshall becomes Cark's new second-in-command. He meets his wife, Chaya. Because of the mass infanticide of girls in Chiran over the years, her parents had raised her, intending to sell her later, as a "wife." Cark purchased her, but he beats her. Chaya begs Marshall for a weapon so she can kill him and be freed from her torment.

The twins set out on their journey. Stopping at an inn, they hear traveling thugs planning to kidnap a set of twins for Zarek. Certain the men refer to them, they quickly move on.

With the oldtimers, Leala and Fidel, Lucy discusses crucial prophecy concerning the twins, and how the moons will act when Ehyeh tests them "through thirst, hunger and division." While she keeps it secret, the prophecy also predicts the end of her days.

The thugs invade the compound. When they take Nina's youngest, Calandra, captive, Broden arms himself with the nearest weapon and then approaches the men. He offers to take Calandra's place, and tells the men that he is Zarek's son— a fact Lucy was unaware he knew. The men take him away, along with the weapon he had carried, which was the great sword.

Basha and Therese visit the abandoned palace of the Select. They learn that Rowena's sisters, Sally and Janine, disappeared shortly after Lilith's death, and likely went to Chiran. Then they prepare the palace for the twins' possible return. Thereafter, they go to the City of Light where they find Lucy. She tells them of the twins' disappearance, the raid, and of Broden's kidnapping. In exchange, they inform her of Mara's amnesia.

Broden's captors take him to Chiran. Along the way, he recollects the day he learned his father's identity. Faced with the truth that both of his parents were evil people, he made a decision then about who he would serve in his future.

Broden is jailed. He meets Striver. Later, Zarek grants him an audience. His aunts—Sally and Janine—show up. They confirm his identity by a birthmark. Then one of Broden's captors presents Zarek with the weapon Broden had taken from the compound. Sally and Janine identify it as the great sword. Zarek, pleased, promises Broden a reward for it. Then he assigns to him, two young slave women, Yasmin and Farida. He also agrees to let Striver tutor him in the ways of Chiran. Just then, a group of new slave women arrives. Broden reminds his father of the reward promised him. He wants to choose one of the women. When Zarek grants his request, he chooses a girl he calls "Mouse."

Zarek and his chief spiritual advisor, Brother Pestifere, meet with the underlords of Sinespe. The underlords inform them that the great sword provides another means for taking down the Select, and ultimately, of ending Ehyeh's rule. Then Zarek and Pestifere inform the underlords of all they have done to infiltrate Oosa's various institutions—including the Oathtakers' ranks—over the years.

Back in Darth, Chaya discovers a secret place where Cark takes refuge, under their house. There, he keeps gold he has stolen from Zarek. When Cark leaves on business, he puts Marshall in charge. When Marshall vows he will help Chaya, she shows him Cark's secret place. The two go down into it and discover a tunnel leading away, beyond the camp.

The twins come upon a desert known as The Tearless, or Kiln. Once inside, a person cannot find his way out. They set up their camp nearby. While Eden keeps first watch, someone knocks her out. At dawn, Reigna finds her missing, then sees hoof prints leading into The Tearless. When she sets out to save her sister, a windstorm erases all sign of the way out.

Reigna finds Eden. Their canteens run dry. With nightfall, Eden suggests she would sell her soul for a swallow of water. From out of the darkness comes a man, Malefique. He offers the twins water if they will follow him for whatever purpose he might choose. They recognize his intent to trick them, and demand that he leave.

Nearer Mara's former home, she and Dixon camp at a place that seems familiar to her. When troubling dreams awaken her, she takes two canteens to the river, to fill. There, she finds the grut tooth she wears around her neck. Tired and confused, she travels magically, although she believes she is dreaming. She arrives in a desert where she finds the twins, nearly dying of thirst. She leaves the two filled canteens with them. Then, hearing Dixon call her, she returns, magically, to his side. Memories invade her thoughts and she passes out for another three days. When she awakens, Dixon confirms her suspicions—that she had been in the very place some time before. Although she is unaware, it is the place where Rowena bore Reigna and Eden, and where Mara had sworn her oath to protect them. When Mara recollects that someone had died there, Dixon confirms the person had been his charge. Then she shares with him, details of her "dream" of bringing water to the twins.

Back in Chiran, Zarek sets out to visit Camp Cark to view the new barracks that Cark is building to house women enslaved for the soldiers' use. Broden, Striver, Mouse, and others, accompany the emperor. Along the way, Zarek makes Broden study daily with Pestifere, text from *Serving Daeva*. Pestifere resents Broden's questions. When Pestifere calls for Mouse to visit him, Broden, accompanies her. He insinuates that the priest teaches about abstinence, while he seeks Mouse's favors. The priest throws them out. The next day, Broden finds Mouse severely beaten—at the priest's behest. Zarek warns Broden not to displease the priest again, then tells Pestifere that he likes Broden's spirit. Accordingly, from then on, Mouse is the one slave woman no one else may touch.

Back in The Tearless, the water Mara brought to the twins, saves them, but then, it starts to rain. The rain turns to snow. The twins discover an abandoned cabin. There, they intend to wait out the storm.

Mara and Dixon arrive at her childhood home to find her mother, Hedda, blind and unable to care for herself. She berates Mara and grows increasingly abusive. Then, just as Dixon suggests Mara accompany him to visit the local sanctuary one afternoon, her sister, Jo, arrives. Jo attaches herself to Dixon, making Mara, who has fallen for him, angry. Again, memories invade her consciousness—memories of Jack, a man for whom she once cared. When Jo taunts Mara, she mutters that she needs "to go shoot something." She takes off—on Dixon's horse.

Mara finds herself at The Meadow, a well-known hunting ground. She recalls events from days gone by: her interest in Jack; her discovery of Jo and Jack in Jo's bed; Jo's resulting pregnancy; Jo's leaving her newborn son, Seth, to Mara's care; and Jo's later return—again, pregnant. Mara had believed Jo would leave that child to her, as well. So, on the advice of Channer, who cared for the local sanctuary and who secretly loved Mara, she left Seth with a couple that wanted a child, and then left the area.

Back in The Tearless, the twins, now freezing, run out of food. They decide that, come morning, they will try to find their way out. They tear apart and then burn the shack to warm up. As the fire burns, Malefique shows up again. He promises them food aplenty, if they will follow him. The twins refuse and demand that he leave. Later, each spends time at watch. While doing so, each engages in an internal dialogue that eventually becomes a conversation with Ehyeh, himself. As a consequence, they discover their callings: Reigna is a warrior; Eden a peacemaker—although she knows warfare may prove necessary before peace may be known. The twins pass out in hunger.

At dawn, Mara, all cried out, still wants to "shoot something." She kills and then guts, a stag. Tired, she wraps an arm around its antlers as she searches for tools from Dixon's saddlebag. Instead, she finds a book—the oracle she had discovered when the twins were infants—although she does not recognize it. Each page reads: "Go." She travels magically, her arms still locked on the dead stag's antlers. She awakens in a blizzard. Seeing a fire nearby, she goes to it. There, she discovers the twins. She takes cuts from the stag and puts them over the fire. The smell of food awakens them.

Dixon meets Channer. He tells him about Mara's condition. He shares that before setting off, she said she wanted to "go shoot something." Channer thinks she went to The Meadow. The two arrive there just after dawn. They find entrails strewn on the ground. Dixon, thinking they are Mara's remains, shrieks in agony, but Channer recognizes them for what they are. Then Dixon shouts for Mara. She hears him from where she is with the twins and magically returns to his side. When she awakens in his arms, she tells him she is just where she belongs. Then she loses consciousness for another three days.

Jo argues with Dixon, telling him that she and Hedda know what is best for Mara. But Mara, upon awakening and recalling Jo's true nature, demands that she leave. Then Mara apologizes to Dixon for having suggested that in his arms was where she belonged. He is confused, as he had thought her memory restored. Then she shares her recollection of when the two of them first confessed their love for one another. Mara remembered their agreement never to speak again of their feelings. Since she knows Dixon's charge is dead, she surmises that he is married. Assuring him that she will abide by their former agreement, she falls into a depression. Later, Dixon convinces her that he should continue to accompany on her further, travels, for safety's sake.

Zarek and his entourage arrive in Chiran. Cark orders Jerrett to assist Zarek's people. Jerrett and Marshall see Broden and notice Zarek wielding the great sword. They conclude that Broden may have joined the man voluntarily, so they keep their presence secret from him. Later, while on duty, a dog, Bane, befriends Jerrett. When Jerrett witnesses Broden and a young woman leave a tent, he questions those remaining in it. He learns that Broden calls the woman "Mouse." Jerrett reports everything, magically, to Marshall, reminding him that "Mouse" was Broden's name for Carlie (Nina and Jules's daughter, missing from the compound).

Zarek hosts a dinner. Jerrett hides in a room below, listening. He hears of Zarek's plans for Oosa. Meanwhile, Marshall goes to Cark's to guard Chaya so that Cark may attend the dinner. He finds Cark beating her. Cark accuses Marshall of being a traitor and tries to kill him. In defense, Marshall uses his channel on Cark. Marshall and Chaya dump Carks's body into Cark's hiding place. Then Marshall informs Jerrett, magically, that he must leave Chiran. Jerrett and Bane make their way to Cark's home. When soldiers try to stop him, Jerrett discovers a magic connection to Bane—similar to one he had years ago, with his horse, Donagh. Jerrett and Bane kill the guards and then make their way to the secret tunnel. They meet up with Marshall and Chaya. The three set off for Oosa.

Basha and Therese engage the help of others to find all the remaining Select and Oathtakers in Oosa for a census, then do some looking themselves. Along their way, they meet Trumble, Oathtaker to a simple girl, Felicity, whom he had saved from Lilith, although she was left damaged. As a consequence, Felicity has visions of events as they occur elsewhere—but her ability to explain them is limited. Trumble tells Basha and Therese that Felicity has been praying for two young woman who have "the same face." Upon hearing Basha and Therese's story, he surmises that she means the twins. Consequently, he agrees to go with them to the City of Light. Along the way, he and Basha discover a strange new alignment of the three moons and are reminded of a prophecy about them.

Mara and Dixon arrive in the City of Light, after discovering that someone has been following them. They go to The Clandest Inn. Dixon informs Ezra of Mara's condition. Ezra assigns them the quarters they stayed in when the twins were infants. There, memories implode on Mara consciousness. Believing even more will come to her if she visits other places she has been in the past, she wants to go to Polesk.

The twins awaken after days seeking their way out of The Tearless, each now atop a tall narrow rock mountain. Two more similar ones stand in the distance. On one, is Malefique. He speaks to the twins. Although both can hear him, neither can hear the another. He tells them that their time for choosing nears.

Mara prepares to leave for Polesk. She discovers magic crystals in Dixon's pocket. They trigger yet another episode. She "awakens" atop a rocky spire. On each of two others are the twins. They cannot hear her. On the fourth, is Daeva. He tells her that the twins are running out of time to follow him. Hearing Dixon call for her, she magically transports back to his side. She looses consciousness—again, for three days. When she awakens, she insists they leave for Polesk, immediately.

The city is in an uproar with many Oathtakers and Select arriving for the census. Basha and Therese find Jerrett, Marshall, Chaya, and Lucy. At Felicity's demand that the girls "with the same face" need them, they all pray. Then, seeing the moons moving in an unusual manner, Lucy tells the others that the twins are undergoing a test.

A couple days out of the city, Mara and Dixon stop for a rest. Dixon heads to the river to clean up. When Mara looks out, she sees a man headed Dixon's way. Fearing for his safety, she empties her bag in search of a weapon, but finds nothing. Then she empties Dixon's bag on the ground. There, is a blade that she immediately recognizes as *her* blade. The second she touches it, all her memories come back: she knows who the twins are and that they are her charges; she knows about Rowena's death; and she knows that a magic exception allowed for her and Dixon to love one another and to marry. She wants to help him, but a memory of Lilith's voice, mocks her, asking: "Aren't you going to try to save him, Oathtaker?" So, since her first duty is to the twins, she travels magically back to where she last saw them.

Mara arrives back atop the spire-mountain. The twins refuse Daeva, telling him that they will follow Ehyeh's ways. With that, the three moons line up in the manner prophetically identified as showing that the twins chose the proper course. As they do, the earth shakes violently. Their friends, at sanctuary in the City of Light, experience the phenomenon.

Some time later, Reigna awakens. She hears a small voice. When she opens her eyes, she discovers two tiny creatures—Ephemeral and Fleeting—the king and queen of the flits. She also finds her sister, and Mara, nearby. The twins discover that they have found Ehyeh's favor, and that they have their birth signs and scents back.

The flits encourage the twins and Mara to head to the City of Light where many await them, but Mara wants to find Dixon, who was in danger when she last saw him. The flits send one of their own, Flutter, to look for him. Then Mara transports magically with the twins to the city. Later Flutter reports to Mara that he found Dixon's things, but not Dixon. Heavy hearted, Mara tells the twins they must get to business.

They call a Council meeting. Lucy tells Mara that she knows what happened, and that someone needs to answer for having left the twins in such danger. The twins bring the Council up-to-date. Then Lucy informs them that Mara had lost her memory, and that Dixon may have committed treason when he covered up that fact. Then she calls her own secret witness. Mara looks up to discover that it is Dixon, whom Lucy had sent a man after, to track down, band, and deliver to her. The Council members argue over who is at fault, but the twins demand that the discussion go no further. They all need one another now more than ever. They add that their leaving the compound was necessary so that they could determine their callings and find Ehyeh's favor. They order Dixon released. When he reaches Mara's side, she assures him that she remembers everything, and that she knows that in his arms is exactly where she belongs.

ABOUT THE AUTHOR

Patricia Reding leads a double life. By day, she practices law. By night, she reads, reviews a wide variety of works, and writes fantasy. She lives on an island on the Mississippi with her husband and youngest daughter (her son and oldest daughter having already flown the nest), and Flynn Rider, an English Cream Golden Retriever. From there, she seeks to create a world in which she can be in two places at once. She took up writing *Oathtaker* as a challenge and re-discovered along the way, the joy of storytelling.

Oathtaker is Volume One of *The Oathtaker Series*. *Select* is Volume Two of *The Oathtaker Series*. *Ephemeral and Fleeting* is Volume Three of *The Oathtaker Series*.

For more information, join the author at www.PatriciaReding.com. You may also like her at her Amazon page, and at www.Facebook.com/PatriciaRedingAuthor, fan and follow her on www.Goodreads.com, and follow her at www.PatriciaReding.BookLikes.com. For added insight into the writing of *The Oathtaker Series*, follow her on Bublish at www.bublish.com/author/view/6479.

AWARDS AND MORE

Oathtaker: The Oathtaker Series, Volume One, earned the Literary Classics Seal of Approval and was named a Gold Medal winner in the Literary Classics International Book Award Contest; earned the Readers Favorite Five-Star seal and was an Honorary Award winner in the Readers Favorite International Book Award Contest; and was named a Finalist in the Beverly Hills Book Awards Contest. WindDancer Films also selected *Oathtaker* for review for possible future film or television.

Select: The Oathtaker Series, Volume Two, earned the Literary Classics Seal of Approval and was named a Silver Medal winner in the Literary Classics International Book Award Contest; and earned the Readers Favorite Five-Star seal and was awarded a Finalist in the Readers Favorite International Book Award Contest.

NOTE FROM THE AUTHOR

Thank you for your kind attention to *The Oathtaker Series*. I would be delighted if you would take a minute to leave a review at (any or all of) Amazon, Barnes and Noble, Goodreads, Booklikes, Readers Favorite, Kobo, iBooks, or elsewhere. Also, please take a minute to add your name to my mailing list at www.PatriciaReding.com. Thank you. Thank you!